A Cozy Fantasy Novel

SOCIAL SORCERY

ALEX PEACHY

In Light Syrup LLC

Content Warnings

This novel includes a character dealing with and overcoming fat-shaming and low self-esteem. It is a minor point in the story with a positive resolution, but those triggered by such things should take care. While on an adventure, a lizard-like creature is killed, and a component is harvested from the corpse. This may be disturbing to some, but it is a brief portion of the adventure. During one scene, a cat sustains a minor injury, but I assure you, she turns out well. This novel describes the consumption of alcohol (whisky) for relaxation and, at one point, escapism. Finally, for those with arachnophobia, spiders play an essential role in the story, but they are quite friendly.

Acknowledgments

Before anyone else, I want to thank everyone who read my first novel, Distilled Magic, and gave me such wonderful feedback. The response gave me the encouragement to continue writing. You, my readers, are all amazing, and I thank you for reading my stories.

My wife has continued to support me both with marketing and order fulfillment. She offers a wonderful sounding board for my ideas and continues to be my primary alpha reader, helping me clean up my stories before anyone has to deal with the rough edges. Thank you, Rebecca, for all of your love and support.

I offer thanks to my editor, K.F., who has helped ensure my story makes sense and that my prose is worth reading. Hannah has given characters in Distilled Magic and Social Sorcery a visage, and I thank you for that.

While writing Social Sorcery, I continued to tread carefully into the LGBTQ+ community in an attempt to offer an inclusive story, keeping with the tone I set in Distilled Magic. I consider myself an ally and hope my stories normalize seeing characters of different backgrounds.

Chapter 1

That Blasted Creature

A small bundle of black fur raced between Zaq's legs when he opened the front door of his townhouse. His eyes barely caught the blur as it tore down the hallway, seeming to know exactly where it wanted to go.

"Sprung sprockets!" he exclaimed and shut the door, having made an impromptu and very annoying change to his mid-afternoon plans. He had been planning to zip over to the local Mystic Leaf & Toadstool for a cup of tea and perhaps something sweet to tide him over until dinner. However, the invasion from that unwanted demon threw those plans right out the window.

Despite his advanced years, Zaq could still move quickly when he desired. He didn't actually want to—move quickly, that is—but still, he raced down the hallway toward his workshop. He would deal with any aches and pains from the fallout later. Flinging open the door that he had inadvertently left open a crack, he arrived in the room to discover the creature sitting on the edge of his workbench, calmly licking a paw as if to suggest it belonged there and had been taking a bath for some time already.

The black cat looked up at him casually with pale yellow-green eyes, the pupils currently more vertical than round. It pulled its tongue in, closed its mouth, and gracefully set its paw down. If you looked closely, you might have noticed it had a few stray white hairs on that paw around the pads.

"Down!" Zaq demanded, thrusting a finger toward the floor.

The cat stared into Zaq's eyes with an unspoken refusal.

"Down!" he shouted again. "You are not supposed to be in this house, and should not be in my workshop, and most definitely do *not* belong on my workbench."

The cat stared some more until it appeared to get bored and smoothly jumped to the floor. The pressure from the animal leaning into his shins brought a scowl to Zaq's face. He glared at the cat as it wove around and between his legs.

Standing on its hind legs, the cat then stretched up its front paws. Despite being tall for a gnome, Zaq felt the feline pad lightly on his chest. A quivering tail rose straight up, making an acute angle with its back.

"Hrmph," Zaq grunted. "Only so I can deposit you back outside where you belong. You should be out there stalking mice or doing something else useful."

His hands slid under the front legs and wrapped around the cat's torso as he lifted it from the ground. Its back legs scrambled for purchase until Zaq cupped the paws in his left hand. Before he could get a proper hold of the beast, he sighed in annoyance as the cat snuggled into his arms, stretched out over his right arm, and leaned into his chest.

After a bit more shifting, the cat had apparently found the perfect position, and Zaq watched helplessly as it burrowed its head into the crook of his arm. The animal went limp and allowed its paw to dangle. A deep rumbling rose from the lump of fur, and vibrations flowed into his body.

"Figures. Now I have to hold this blasted cat."

Zaq stalked around the lower floor of the small house, going from room to room, making a point of checking on things and casting the occasional glare at the animal that had formed a lump in his arms. After several minutes, he decided it had been quite long enough—much longer than the cat deserved.

Carefully pawing open the front door with one hand while bracing the resting cat tighter against his body with the other, he managed to pop the latch. The door swung inward enough for his foot to slip into the crack and fling the door wide with a flick of his ankle. While backing out, Zaq grasped at the handle with the hand that was barely free of the cat and pulled the door closed with two fingers.

Just past the small stoop, Zaq released the animal, depositing it on the ground.

"There we go. This is where you belong. Stay out of my house."

"Mmrrrow," the cat shot back.

It sauntered over to the empty dish nestled in the grass under the cover of a bush full of periwinkle blue flowers. The cat sat down and made a point of alternating its stare between the bowl and the gnome.

"Go catch a mouse," Zaq instructed. "Prove you have some value around here. You don't live here. If I have a chance, maybe I'll put something in the dish later. I still need my tea."

"What's that?" a voice called from the stoop next door.

Much of the housing in Ryefeld was extremely close together, so it was unsurprising that his neighbor, Samantha, had heard him talking to the creature. Zaq lived on a street lined with tightly packed townhouses. The thin two-story dwellings were similar in style, but not identical. There were even a few with more than two floors. While the front side of the houses had small porches and yards, the back of the units opened into larger areas used for gardens and entertaining guests.

Zaq looked over at his neighbor.

"Nothing. Just telling this cat to go do something useful and stop acting like it lives here."

Samantha paused with the door halfway open.

"Ah, I was just getting home. Thought you were asking for tea. If you don't want that cat around, you shouldn't feed her. Have you given her a name yet?"

"Now, why would I name the blasted thing?" Zaq spat. "It's not my cat. It doesn't live here—just acts like it does. I only put some food out to make sure it doesn't starve. It seems to be keeping the mice and rats away. Maybe it doesn't need the food."

"Mmhmmm," Samantha nodded. "You would likely be a lot happier if you admitted you needed her."

"I don't need a cat," Zaq said, emphatically shaking his head. "No one *needs* a cat. I don't even need people, and they are infinitely more useful. I'm fine alone with my projects."

"You probably should admit you need others, too. But how is the latest project?" she asked. "What was it again? A pen that turns parchment into a temporary Mysti Message scroll?"

"Psshh," Zaq hissed air through his lips. "That was two projects ago. Had to give it up. Couldn't get it to interface with a standard scroll on the other end. Can't call what the pen made a Mysti scroll, either. That's trademarked. I'm retired from Mysti and definitely can't use that name. I'm working on a standalone temporary scroll now."

"I see," the human woman said, shaking her head lightly.

"Well, good luck. I won't keep you. I was just getting home and need to put these items away."

"Wait," Zaq called as curiosity continued to gnaw at him. "How do you know this horrible creature is a she?"

"I haven't given her a thorough inspection, if that's what you're asking," she answered. "But you can tell by the way she acts. She never really roams far from her home, and she's always asking you for attention. Even asks me for attention from time to time, but usually only when it looks like I might toss her a small treat."

"Never roams far from home?" Zaq asked incredulously. "What's that supposed to mean? This isn't its home. This is my home."

"Right," she agreed, nodding. "You keep telling yourself that. I've got to get this food put away. Have a good afternoon, Zaq."

Samantha pushed the door to her house the rest of the way open and carried her bags inside.

"Where does she get such ideas?" Zaq asked himself aloud.

A sudden gust of the crisp autumn air reminded him he should start moving if he wanted to warm his old bones with some tea. The walk to the teashop was short. Nothing he needed to get to on a regular basis was far from his home.

Ryefeld was a large, sprawling city-state comprised of several districts, which contained many of the essentials. Outside of the city proper, buildings gradually became more spread out, eventually fading into small farmsteads with extensive fields. The city had begun with little more than a handful of farms and a few fields of rye. Those original farms were long gone, but on the outskirts of the city, a few farms still grew rye— among a variety of other crops, as well.

Two rivers met in the middle of the sprawling city, mingling together to flow out into the Mirador Sea as a single larger river. These waterways created natural boundaries to the largest districts, each with several subdistricts.

As Zaq approached the Mystic Leaf & Toadstool outlet, the two dwarven owners were turning a winch with ropes attached to a tan tarp. As they turned the crank, the covering, held aloft by a metal frame, slipped over the patio seating area. The rainy season hadn't begun yet, but it would be here soon enough, and the couple was wise to put the tarp up sooner rather than later.

The Mystic outlet resembled many of the numerous other franchise outlets, which almost always had large patio seating areas with small storefronts housing an ordering counter and only a few tables inside. Many of them would also have a private upstairs space, which served as housing for the owners.

Zaq happened to know that this shop differed in that regard. It had an upstairs, but the stairs were publicly accessible. The area above was set up as office space, and the current occupant was a halfling accountant. Additionally, below the shop, accessible via a private stairwell, was an extensive underground system of rooms. It was there that the dwarven couple lived.

Dwarven home cities were always underground in massive cavern systems, usually burrowed deep into mountains. While some dwarves living in city-states like Ryefeld took residence in above-ground houses and apartments, many chose to go below, carving out areas which resembled their ancestral homes.

"Good afternoon, Zaq," Zhebtain called with a friendly wave. The dwarf with mahogany brown hair and a matching short-cropped beard was the more outgoing and social of the two. His quieter partner, Johmal, with sandy-blonde hair and a long beard, simply nodded and continued turning the winch.

Both Johmal's hair and beard were braided into several plaits tied off with leather thongs.

"Greetings and salutations. Zheb, Joh, good to see you," Zaq replied. "Must be slow today if you are both out here. No one's tending the counter?"

"True enough," Zheb agreed, looking at the sparsely populated seating area. "I can pop in and get you vatever you need."

"Good to hear," Zaq said. "I'd like an Elderberry Mist with a splash of that not-milk stuff you have and a half-spoon of sugar."

"Of course," the dwarf replied. "Anysing to nibble on? I have zis scrumptious simbleberry muffin. You must try it. It pairs vell vis zee elderberry tang."

"Sounds wonderful. Tea and a muffin, then," Zaq said and slid into a seat.

Zheb gave his husband an affectionate pat on the back before hustling to the kitchen.

The couple loved each other, and it always brought a smile to Zaq's face when he saw them interacting at the tea shop. It had been nearly a decade since they bought the franchise, and the neighborhood was all the better for it.

Joh finished securing the tarp into place, gave Zaq a nod, and left for the teashop proper. A few moments later, Zheb returned with a mug of steaming tea and a muffin three times the size of Zaq's fist. He set them down on the table.

"Anysing else today, Zaq?"

"No, this looks wonderful," he answered and handed Zheb some coins.

"Vell zen, I have a question for you," Zheb posed. "Do you sink you can look at our veazer shield? It vas having issues ven vee last used it."

"Oh, no. Sorry," Zaq said, shaking his head. "Much too busy. I can recommend some folks who might be able to."

"Vee vould pay you, of course," Zheb negotiated. "Or you can have tea and treats for a veek."

"Well, why didn't you say so?" Zaq quickly replied. "I'll look at it tomorrow."

"Sank you. Here, start vis zis."

Zheb handed the coins back to the gnome and returned to the shop.

Grinning at the thought of the free afternoon snacks, he allowed the steam from the tea to linger as he held the mug to his lips. After blowing gently, he took a small sip. Spicy ginger engaged with tangy elderberries in a battle for his tongue. The berries won, sending the ginger to linger in the back of his throat.

Small crumbs fell onto the plate as he tore off a hunk of the muffin top. The sweet, dense, cake-like texture was punctuated with pieces of thimbleberries—some as large as a whole berry. It was a strong pairing. Zheb always knew the perfect snack to pair with his tea.

With the weather changing, it might be time to switch to ordering more dragonroot tea. Thoughts of which spicy pastries would go well with the tea caused his stomach to remind him that he might want more than just that one small bite.

Before long, the enormous muffin was reduced to a few sparse crumbs on the plate, and Zaq sat back in the chair, sipping from the mug in a much calmer manner. The tea was creamy and delicious despite not containing any actual cream.

Dwarves tended to be highly lactose intolerant, and Zheb had decided not to use any dairy products in his Mystic franchise outlet. The two partners had experimented and found a way to blend oats with ackernuts. The fatty ackernuts mixed well with the oats when ground together and blended with water. Some people argued it was even better than cream itself.

Zaq was not one of them. Still, it was not bad, and with the right water ratio, it could be a strong substitute for cream.

Looking into his empty cup, Zaq realized it was time to return to his workshop. The break was over, and while he doubted he could solve the issues with the project today, he wouldn't know for sure unless he worked on it.

Chapter 2

Tinkering

At home, there was no sign of the cat anywhere. However, a gentle whine from the lower hinge on the door brought the creature bounding from who knew where. It flew past Zaq into the townhouse and once again disappeared into the workshop.

"Now, how am I supposed to get any work done?" Zaq hollered after the cat.

Entering his workshop, he found the cat staring at him from atop the bench. At least it wasn't batting his tools and parts around. The week before, the cat had knocked a partially finished prototype to the ground, where it promptly exploded into pieces, sending cogs and springs in every direction. Of course, it hadn't worked before the destruction, so aside from the mess, it hadn't mattered much.

The cat's entrance was enough to activate the motion-sensitive glow stones Zaq had installed throughout his house. They provided as much light, if not more, than candles and lanterns, and, after the initial cost, required no additional fuel. They could be manually controlled, but with his artificer know-how, he had set them up to automatically turn on and off based on his presence.

Zaq ignored the cat and looked over the work-in-progress on the bench. A larger set of parts and boxes, which were piled up against the back left wall, drew his eye. He knew he should focus on *that* project. It was destined to be the pinnacle of his life's work, after all—if he could ever get it to *work*, that is. Frustrations with it almost always sent him seeking refuge with easier projects, but those distraction projects often had their own issues and could be just as exasperating.

If Zaq was truly honest with himself, it had been quite some time since he made anything original that actually worked how he envisioned it. He had no trouble building magical items with known blueprints, and fixing something that had previously worked usually posed no issues. It was the pure invention of something new that taxed the gnomish artificer.

Shaking his head, Zaq decided his current work in progress was far enough along that it was worth more of his attention. He stepped up to the bench, pulled on his goggles, and laid out a fresh piece of parchment.

As he turned to grab the oversized pen, which was the bulk of the invention, the cat moved from her spot on the corner to walk on and sniff the parchment.

"No, no, no," Zaq admonished. "None of this is for cats."

He swept the cat to the floor with his arm, and it responded with an annoyed *hiss*.

Returning his focus to the pen, he carefully adjusted several screws, reorienting two crystals that pulsed in a chaotic rhythm. As the shards shifted their alignment under his guidance, they slowly adopted a gentle pulse in an alternating sequence opposite to one another. He continued to make minor tweaks until the pulse reached the frequency he was looking for.

Now, to prepare the parchment, he picked up a rune-etching quill and drew a series of intricate designs on the parchment with metallic ink. Runecraft required picking the right medium for creating the runes based on the substance to which they were applied. In this case, he needed something to store and deliver a message. The parchment fit perfectly, and a metallic ink allowed the magic and technology to blend together.

After finishing the last symbol, Zaq sprinkled crystalline finishing dust on the rune-covered sheet. The designs pulsed with a glow refracting in the dust, and when he blew the powder away, the runes had disappeared into the paper. Only a single activation port remained in the shape of a small circle located in the lower right-hand corner.

Zaq glanced at the clock. Over three hours had slipped by without him even noticing. Once focused, he could lose more time than he often expected, but artificery was a demanding discipline.

Holding the oversized pen to the activation port on the parchment, he flipped a small toggle on the pen and tapped it three times while chanting a simple incantation.

His eyebrow quirked up, and he waited for any sign that something might have worked. There was no visible acknowledgment of his binding, but that didn't mean what he had done hadn't worked.

"Only one way to know for sure, right?" he asked the cat, who was on the floor, looking up at him with eyes he knew were begging him to pick it up.

"Later. I need to test this."

The soft scratching of the pen as he wrote was the only sound. Zaq held his breath as he carefully formed each letter. If his adjustments worked, the message should fade away moments after he read the words. Once he finished scrawling the final word, he again tapped the port in the corner of the parchment, careful not to even glance at the message. This time, the metallic dot briefly glowed red, then vanished. Trading the pen for the parchment, he held the paper up and read the words aloud.

"This is a test of a temporary message."

Flames bit at his fingertips as a soft pop sent flashfire racing from the center of the parchment, radially outward.

"Ow! What happened to the gentle fading away?"

Zaq sucked a singed finger and scratched his head with his other hand. An unpleasant, acrid odor filled his nostrils. *What was that smell?* Then, frantically, he pulled his finger from his mouth and slapped at his goatee, extinguishing the smoldering flames that had leapt from the paper to his facial hair.

"I suppose it was a temporary message. Not how I meant it, but no one will be able to read that message again."

He felt the pressure from the cat as it pressed into his legs while weaving in between them.

"I'm fine," he assured it. "I suppose you need to be held again? Such a waste of time. But, I suppose it will let me ruminate on what I might do differently to avoid that explosive result."

Zaq pulled off his goggles and tossed them to the bench. As he looked down at the cat, it immediately noticed the attention and stopped weaving. It lifted on its hind legs and stretched its arms up at him like a small child asking to be picked up. Sighing, the gnome grabbed it up and let it nestle itself into his arms. He gently bounced the cat as he climbed the stairs to the second floor. He needed to see how much damage his beard had endured.

In the bathroom, he peered at his face, rotating it in different directions to take it in. The flames hadn't reached beyond his chin. His white goatee had been waxed to a point.

His slapping had smushed the hair, but most of the beard appeared intact. The hair on his head was also white, without even a trace of the vibrant blue it had been in his youth. His face did not yet appear too wizened, having only just retired from Mysti Messages, and he could likely look forward to many more years before the deep wrinkles set in. Gnomes tended to wear their age well.

The cat stared at Zaq, staring at himself. He noticed the yellowish eyes reflecting in the mirror, the pupils wide and round. Then the cat leaned its head back and looked at him upside down. *What goes through the head of a creature like this? And why am I indulging it?*

"I think it's time I fixed something to eat. Did you need something as well?"

The cat simply looked at him, then opened its mouth extremely wide, baring its sharp teeth as it yawned.

That wasn't a yes or a no—not that he had expected the cat to answer in any intelligible way. So, he walked downstairs, taking care of his footing since he was holding the blasted creature. It always needed much too much attention.

Zaq looked around his kitchen for something easy. He really didn't want to cook anything, but with only a meager pension coming in each month and a small percentage of royalties, he needed to use discretion with his spending so as not to dip too much into his savings. His eyes fell on half of a small loaf of bread that likely needed to be eaten soon before it became too stale, or, worse, moldy.

Tossing the cat to the ground, he rummaged in the KoldBox and found some sliced ham and a crock of soft, spreadable cheese.

The KoldBox was of gnomish design, though not his, of course. He had studied the design and built this unit himself. Zaq saw no point in paying someone else to do what he could easily do on his own. By the time he paid for and gathered the supplies, and factored in any reasonable value for his time, he had likely spent more building it than if he had just paid for a unit.

At the counter, he spread the yellow-orange cheese on two pieces of bread and laid several slices of the pork on before folding them together into a sandwich. Zaq cut one slice of ham into small pieces and took it and a container of milk outside, leaving his meal on the counter.

As he expected, the cat bounded after him, screeching its demands.

Zaq placed the strips of meat into its bowl and poured some milk into a shallow saucer next to it. The cat immediately began gnawing at a strip of ham, and he ducked back into the house, closing the door quickly behind him.

"At least now I can eat in peace," he announced to the empty room.

The cushions of the lounge chair, oversized for a gnome, gave way and folded up, wrapping his small form in their snug embrace. Not much could beat the feeling of being hugged by a chair.

Zaq propped the plate on his lap and took a bite of the simple sandwich. The sharp tang of the cheese melded with the smoky pork, and the slightly stale bread gave the bite an extra chewiness, which felt satisfying.

As he chewed, his mind wandered to the temporary message project. Technically, the message could only be read once. Perhaps the extra flare might even be appealing to some clandestine people using the scrolls to convey sensitive information.

He really ought to be working on the massive multi-user project. Just the thought of *massive* made him laugh, which in turn caused him to choke on a bite. He wasn't even sure if he could get it to support four connected scrolls. The runes didn't seem to be able to handle it, or they weren't efficient enough to pull enough ambient mana.

"What I really need is some parts that are much harder to come by than the ones I've been using," he muttered to himself. Over the years, he had started conversing with himself more and more, especially when working alone as much as he did.

"But you know you're too old to be adventuring about. You'll just have to try cheaper alternatives or save up for the parts that are too expensive."

The conversation continued in circles as the sandwich grew smaller and smaller. Eventually, he snapped out of it as he popped the last bite into his mouth. Yet again, he had been spiraling into the same unhelpful pattern.

"What I need is something to occupy my mind," he muttered as he poured a small glass of rye whisky.

Zaq pulled a book from his shelf and sat back down in the chair with his drink. The title embossed on the cover read, "Epic Tales of Tirgan the Adventurer." He had always dreamed of one day going on adventures, but instead, he settled for his work as an artificer at Mysti Messages. Books with exciting tales that could sweep him up and take him along with the hero were the next best thing.

Before opening the book, he took a small sip of the dark amber spirit. Black pepper, cloves, and cinnamon gently burned on his tongue. The spices gave way to a light molasses sweetness that lingered even after he swallowed, leaving mild, sweet heat in his throat. There were several distilleries in Ryefeld, and they made a number of different whiskies, but, not surprisingly, the city was best known for its rye whisky. This particular one was produced by Basil Estate Distillery, which was run by a halfling named Basil, who was a master distiller.

The rest of the evening drifted by as he sipped his whisky and followed the adventure page by page. When the glass was empty, he decided that was likely enough crusading for the night and closed the book.

Glancing briefly at the front door, he shook his head and climbed the stairs to his bedroom. Zaq quickly prepared himself for bed and slipped under the blankets.

"Tomorrow, I'll make some progress."

Chapter 3

Weather Proofing

A loud but deadened *crack* released the tension in Zaq's back. Straightening himself out of the twisted pose, he pulled on a uniformly green outfit and laced his work boots before descending to the first floor.

He saw no point in dealing with breakfast here at the house when complimentary tea and a pastry could be had at Mystic if he got to work on the repairs first thing. So, instead of the kitchen, he swung by his workshop to grab his goggles and a small box filled with various tools and parts.

Having no desire to deal with that damned cat this morning, he carefully opened the door, wedging his booted foot and most of his leg into the tight opening. The cat was, in fact, there, ready to bolt inside, but it stopped short when it saw how little egress Zaq and the door allowed. Its eyes, with extremely narrow slit pupils, watched him for any mistake. It was left to stare wistfully at the door as Zaq finished passing through the small crack and pulled the door firmly closed behind him.

The cat changed tactics and shifted its focus from the

house to Zaq himself. It released a soft meow and danced around, attempting to get his attention. However, Zaq was not about to fall into its trap this morning. He had work to do. The weather sealant system at Mystic wasn't going to fix itself, and even if he carried the cat there, it would just find its way back to the house. It was best just to leave it where it was if he had no means to rid himself of it.

Shivering in the cold morning air, Zaq realized he should have grabbed his coat or at least a hat. Despite the bright sun, which made him squint, there was no warmth to the day. There was nothing for it, though. He would not reopen the door and instead would just endure. Besides, if he did his job right, the patio at Mystic would be warm enough once he fixed the system. So, with that decided, he set a brisk pace, letting the burst of exercise help stave off the cold.

When he arrived at the Mystic teashop, he felt no difference between the air on the street and the air inside as he passed under the canvas tarp Joh had spread over the area the day before. He had no reason to doubt the dwarves, but personally verifying an issue existed was always much more satisfying than trusting a second-hand account.

"Zheb!" Zaq called as he wove around the mostly empty patio tables toward the crowded entrance of the shop.

Not surprisingly, no one had much interest in consuming their breakfast tea in the cold. He pushed ahead of the crowded line, accidentally bumping into a gruff-looking orc. The orc didn't seem to care and offered no response, so Zaq mumbled apologies and pushed deeper into the shop.

Once he could fix the weather seal, the people should disperse to their seats outside. Until then, it would be a tight fit in the shop as customers jockeyed for positions to either order, steal an open seat, or lean against a wall.

"Zaq! Mornin' to you," Zheb called. "You squeeze into a spot near zee end of zee counter. I vill have some tea and a fried cake for you momentarily."

Joh must have been in the kitchen baking because there was no sign of him in the small shop. Of the two dwarves, Joh was the better baker by far and tended to focus on those duties, which suited his personality just fine. He was not nearly as talkative as his partner. Zheb, on the other hand, loved to chat and mingle with the customers.

The counter featured sections of differing heights to suit the shop's diverse clientele. With the range of races typical in a city like Ryefeld, it was best to be accommodating when possible. The last section of the counter ended in a lower stretch, and Zaq squeezed in next to a halfling and a goblin, both of whom were still waiting for their orders.

Much to the annoyance of the two he squeezed in next to, Zheb set down a cup of white tea and a fried cake generously covered with pale yellow frosting in front of the gnome.

"Zer you are. You eat first, zen you help clear out zees customers by fixing zee shield."

"Thank you, Zheb," Zaq replied with a wide smile. "Don't you worry. I'll have it fixed up in no time. I appreciate you seeing to the rumble in my gut first."

He hadn't even finished his sentence before Zheb was moving on to fetch the orders for others. He served tea and pastries to everyone as soon as the Kwikbrew would allow, which was pretty fast.

The round cake in front of Zaq looked delicious. He took a bite, experiencing a delightful sensation on his tongue. Hidden in the pastry was a sweet blueberry jam filled with chunks of berry. The fruit, mixed with the tangy lemon frosting and gentle spices in the cake, created a flavor profile that had Zaq sighing in contentment.

Even though he knew everyone would appreciate him getting the shield system working as soon as possible, Zaq stood at the counter, enjoying each bite of the cake, occasionally washing it down with a sip of the tea. The time flew by faster than he would have liked, and before long, he had finished chewing the last bite and drained the last drop of his tea.

"I'll look at the weather shield system now," Zaq called as he wove and pressed his way through the tightly packed crowd.

Outside, the brisk air surprised him and covered his arms in gooseflesh. The difference in temperature between the crowded interior and the patio was astounding. Rubbing his hands together in an attempt to circulate his blood and warm himself, he looked around the area.

Short shrubs lined the building's exterior and continued around the patio, creating a natural barrier with occasional openings for customers to pass through. Embedded in a section of the shrubbery was a boulder with a somewhat unnatural shape.

Zaq approached the large rock and felt around the surface. An audible *click* sounded when his fingers found the spot, and the illusion fell away, revealing a metal box with pipework bent and twisted around it. A glass bulb at the end of a long tube was half-filled with red liquid.

Normally, the liquid in that bulb would be churning in constant movement as the artifact measured the ambient heat of the surrounding area and the output of the device. The fact that the liquid was as calm as a lake on a lazy summer day proved that something was definitely wrong with the unit.

Slipping his goggles on, Zaq could see the runic lines that traced pathways over the surface better. One area immediately caught his eye. The lines were much denser than they should be and didn't form any well-known runes. Occasionally, sparks of mana leapt from the tangle as the artifact continued to attempt its job.

Each time the sparks danced along the surface, a faint hint of berries tingled his nose. That was very odd, and closer inspection confirmed his suspicion. The extra lines appeared to have formed when a jam, compote, or other fruit mixture fell on the unit. This normally wouldn't have been enough to cause this kind of trouble, but unfortunately, it had landed on a sensitive section of runes. As the mana coursed through the jam, it etched new, random pathways, leaving the true runes convoluted.

Zaq used some elbow grease and vigorously rubbed the area with a cloth to no avail. The new additions to the runes were permanent. He could still see the difference between the original pathways and the new additions and made a mental note of how they should be in a functional system.

Removing a tool from his bag, he held it up to verify it would do the job. The instrument was a thick tube of bronze etched with runic pathways and embedded with chips of crystal. At one end, a blue crystal carved in an octagonal shape protruded from the handle. The other end held a smaller spindle of metal capped with a steel disc encrusted with rough specks of sparkling grit.

The device awoke as his finger depressed a button on the tube, causing the disc to spin at an incredible rate. With a firm hand, he applied the spinning disc to the marred section of runes on the generator. He used deliberate but delicate movements to buff out the area, removing the stains as well as the original pathways.

Once the area was completely smooth, he exchanged the tool for another. The new tool had a stick of silvery metal extending from one end, while the other end featured an extremely slender tube with an angled tip. Zaq activated the new tool and waited while a light pulsed yellow. When the light turned a steady red, he used the sharp tip to draw the missing section of runes. The stick of silver metal shrank as he worked, leaving behind silver lines on the machine wherever he drew.

After completing the last circuit, Zaq turned off the tool and laid it down to cool. He removed a pouch of finalizing dust and sprinkled a liberal amount over his work. Through the dust, he could see the lines pulsing as they fused with the existing network of pathways. Then, after a final large pulse, it went dark, and his breath scattered the remaining dust.

The red liquid inside the bulb began to churn. Soon, it was bubbling and sloshing in its glass container. It appeared he had successfully healed the pathways.

Zaq wiped the artifact clean, then flicked the switch to re-engage the illusion of the rock. He stood up and walked a complete circuit around the patio, examining the space between the edge of the overhead tarp and the shrubbery below. His goggles revealed a faint shimmering curtain, which he took as a good sign that the shield was back in place.

Gradually, the patio reached a pleasant temperature, and Zaq dusted his hands together in satisfaction—an easy fix for a somewhat silly problem.

"The patio should feel much more comfortable now," he hollered to the people in line at the shop.

Patrons began filing out and picking tables. Soon after, Zheb emerged, looking around until he spotted Zaq.

"Ah, zer you are. Excellent vork, Zaq. You sit down, and I vill bring you a little somesing."

Despite having the fried cake just a couple of hours prior, he would never turn down another of Joh's delightful treats. However, he knew he should be headed home.

"I suppose I can take a little something for the road," he

said with a wink. "I wouldn't want to miss out on something from Joh."

A few moments later, Zheb emerged with a paper-wrapped spiced apple turnover.

"Sank you again," the dwarf said. "Vee hoped it vould not be a tough fix. Be sure to come back soon."

Chapter 4

An Unwanted Proposal

Zaq managed to return to his workshop without the cat making an appearance. When he had arrived home, the cat was nowhere to be seen, and he entered his house without the uninvited guest.

After clearing space on his workbench, he sat on a stool, filling out the forms for filing his patent. At this point, he had more patents than he could count or remember, though that may have been a sign of his age rather than the vast number. Still, he had quite a few, but unfortunately, none had taken off with great success. Even Zaq's most successful endeavors gave him very little in terms of royalties.

His brows knitted, and deep wrinkles dug into his forehead. After a moment of sitting and allowing his mind to dwell on his unpleasant memories, he shook his head. There was no use getting sucked into that nonsense again when there was so much else to do.

Focusing on the paperwork in front of him, he filled it out thoroughly, describing the pen and the special scrolls designed to work with it. It occurred to him as he wrote that one benefit of the destruction of the scrolls is that, once used, the owners of the pen would need to purchase more scrolls. If use of these pens caught on, this invention could actually earn him more than some of the other devices he had patented.

After pulling out the schematic drawings he had made for the system during its construction, he diligently copied them onto fresh sheets of parchment and attached them to the forms. His eyes then landed on the empty spot in the form he had skipped before. The pen froze as he stared at the cobwebs in the ceiling corner.

"Ah ha!" he exclaimed and set pen to paper again, this time filling in the previously empty spot for the name of his newest invention. "Vanishing Secrets. That's perfect. As soon as the secret is shared, it vanishes."

Zaq signed the forms, gathered them up, and left for the nearest AARI office. Although it was farther from his home than the cafe, the office was still not a long walk. However, by the time he could read the sign for the Arcane and Alchemical Registry of Inventions, his right leg was sore. The exercise was good for it, but too much, and the pain would radiate from his lower back and travel down his leg.

Ignoring the gentle throbbing, he pulled open the door and found a human clerk he recognized behind the counter looking over a document.

"Welcome to AARI," the man said with only a brief glance up. "I'll be with you in just a momen—"

He stopped his automatic greeting when his eyes flashed recognition.

"Ah, Zaq! Welcome. Sorry, I was a bit distracted. Come in," he said in a friendlier tone. "Have something new for us today?"

"You know it, Henry," Zaq replied and set the envelope of paperwork on the counter. He then dug through his coin pouch. "It'll likely be of most use to folks with clandestine operations. So maybe something the government might pick up? Either way, I'm feeling good about this one. Ah, here's the fee."

He placed several coins on the counter next to the application. Henry swiped them into his palm and transferred them to a lock box before examining the papers in the envelope.

"Well, well. This all seems to be in order. Not that I would expect anything less from you. More people could stand to learn from your attention to detail. I'll get this reviewed and filed. In the meantime, you are free to sell and market the system to anyone you'd like. Based on what I see, you likely are right about the government."

"Thank you, Henry. Though I doubt anyone would want to learn from me, and I certainly don't want to teach anyone. I'm better off focusing on my inventions alone."

"If you say so," Henry acquiesced. "I look forward to seeing what you bring in next."

"See you next time," Zaq agreed and left the shop.

The sun was already low in the early autumn sky, and Zaq decided a supper out at a tavern was warranted. Maybe his latest invention wasn't as complete as it could have been, and maybe it wouldn't find commercial success, but he felt filing the paperwork declaring it done was a good enough reason to celebrate.

As it so happened, he was just down the street from the Inn Side Out, which had a reasonably large tavern. He knew the elven proprietor, Alaquine, well and enjoyed the food he served. Alaquine couldn't cook himself, but he was smart enough to hire one of the best halfling cooks. Glorya made the richest and most savory food. The elf, on the other hand, enjoyed tending the bar and talking with the patrons.

Zaq pushed open the door, and the dull roar of a multitude of conversations filled his ears. There were enough warm bodies in the tavern that it likely wasn't needed, but the large fire in the corner hearth was a welcome sight. The room was filled with vibrant green plants with gorgeous, brightly colored flowers. There were even vines crawling up the walls, wrapping themselves around the rafters. Many elves had a love of the outdoors, and Alaquine differed only in that he decided to bring the outdoors inside his Inn.

He spied an open table near the wall, not far from the hearth. At least for now, it also had a buffer of several other empty tables between it and the other patrons. Those tables would surely fill up as the evening progressed, but for the time being, Zaq would enjoy the extra privacy. An entertainer was in the process of setting up across the room, and if Zaq were lucky, people would be more interested in the songs and stories than in striking up a conversation with him.

Zaq eased himself into the chair with the wall behind him. The pressure in his back released with several pops, and he propped his right leg on the chair across from him. The relief was welcome as his muscles and the tension in his nerves relaxed, creeping up his leg to the small of his back. He hadn't realized how much the dull pain from walking so far had been building.

The table had a small, square top suitable for only two people. It was simple but well-polished, and the wood felt sturdy when he rested his arms on it. A plane-touched woman wearing an apron approached his table with a circular tray tucked under her arm. Zaq didn't recognize her, but he didn't come in here often enough to know all of the waitstaff.

"Evening. I'm Jess, and I'll be helping you," she said,

wearing a large smile on her face that showed off her long incisor fangs. Her teeth and the short, protruding horns above her temples were the only signs that gave her demonic ancestry away. While her skin had a faint red tint, it wasn't drastically different from that of many humans. The plane-touched had distant ancestors from the lower or upper planes, often demons or seraphim.

"Thank you, Jess. I'm Zaq," he replied. "I'll have a corn whisky—whatever Alaquine recommends—and tonight's special. I trust Glorya has something tasty cooking back in the kitchen."

"Of course. I'll bring that right out, Zaq," she said and walked away toward the bar.

Zaq watched the entertainer continue to set things up while he waited. Based on what he saw, it seemed the orc bard would be singing and playing an instrument or two. He hoped very much that the music would not be a lot of loud screaming and drumming, like many young folks often played. The fact that he hadn't seen any drums and instead only a stringed instrument and a tambourine was a good sign, but he wouldn't let his guard down until the music started.

The nice thing about ordering the special was that his food was served almost immediately. Jess approached his table and set down a plate and a glass of whisky.

"Here you go," she smiled. "Alaquine said to say hello and to let you know that the whisky is eight years old and aged for the last three years in port barrels."

He knew it was a good move to let the elf choose. The spirit sounded delightful.

"Thank you. That should be all I need for now," Zaq said as he turned his attention to the plate of food in front of him.

Two generous slices of meatloaf filled nearly half of the plate. The dense slices were stuffed with coarse herbs and spices. Despite the fact that the meatloaf did not seem at all dry, the halfling cook had included a sauceboat of brown gravy. The gravy smelled like it would also pair well with the roasted root vegetables that took up the rest of the plate. On a small side dish, Jess had left a dark rye roll with a ball of butter.

Zaq knew that Glorya often played it cautious when serving her food. She wanted the customers to decide how they would dress and eat the food. However, he also knew that if she included something like that tub of gravy, it would be a crime not to drown the food in it. With that, he picked up the container and poured the gravy, glistening with oil, all over the meatloaf as well as the roasted vegetables.

He picked up a fork and speared a chunk of potato. Zaq pushed it through the gravy, then popped it into his mouth. The salt hit his tongue and then gave way to earthy notes of mushrooms and mild spices. The potato itself was fluffy and broke apart easily in his mouth. He followed it up with a much denser bite of purple beet, the sweetness playing against the savory gravy nicely.

A voice interrupted his thoughts, and his eyes snapped open. Zaq hadn't even realized he had closed them while enjoying the meal.

"Excuse me. Are you Zaquocorin Flickerwhizzle?" asked an extremely young-looking gnome with bright pink hair pulled back in a ponytail.

She had a cute face despite the large circular depressions around her eyes and up on her forehead. Clearly, she often wore goggles. Freckles sprayed across her pale, chubby cheeks, which had an excited flush to them. Next to her stood a very tall human. So tall, in fact, that his waist was a fair bit higher than the top of the gnomish girl's head. His wavy black hair covered his ears and fell to the base of his neck. He kept his tanned face clean-shaven, which was common for many humans from the southern lands.

"What—er, I mean, who are you? Can't you see I'm enjoying my supper?"

The gnome wore a wide grin plastered across her face. "I'm Wyndi Crinklepot. But are you Zaquocorin Flickerwhizzle? You are, aren't you? I just know it."

Zaq shook his head, not in disagreement but in disappointment. Then he simply sighed and decided the best way to be rid of this intrusion was to play along and answer her.

"Yes. Yes, I am. But most folks just call me Zaq. What are you up to? Why do you care who I am? And who is that long bean of a fellow with you?"

"This here is Francis, but he likes it when people call him Frank, so I call him Legs," she replied and glanced up at her companion, her eyes tracking from the floor up to his face.

The tall human snorted. "Let's just go with Frank, please. Wyndi's the only one who can call me Legs."

"Let me do the talking," Wyndi said before turning back to Zaq.

"I knew it was you. You have to help us," she implored now that her attention was fully on Zaq. "We need a mentor. Everyone knows you are the best artificer in the city. We want you to teach us."

Just then, a small goblin at a nearby table shoved his chair back, causing a loud screech to cut through the air, grabbing everyone's attention. He looked sheepish but hopped up anyway and came running over to Zaq's table, leaving his goblin companions behind.

"Can I get in on this, too?" he asked, inserting himself right into the conversation. "That's why I came to Ryefeld. So I could find a mentor. I never even thought I might meet Flickerwhizzle. I'm Flek, by the way."

"Now, hold on," Wyndi said. "Legs and I were here first. We don't know how many apprentices he can take on. Besides, don't you goblins just make things that explode?"

Flek threw her an annoyed look and seemed about to make a retort.

"Zero," Zaq stated, and did his best to ignore the small group gathered in front of him. He deliberately took a bite of the meatloaf and chewed with determination.

"Zero what?" Wyndi asked, confusion written all over her face.

Zaq swallowed and calmly took a small sip of whisky. "You said you don't know how many apprentices I can take on. So, I did you a favor and enlightened you. The answer is zero."

"Zero? What do you mean, zero?" Wyndi asked. "But you're amazing. How can the best artificer in Ryefeld not take on apprentices? Or do you mean you already have enough?"

"If he just needs one, that can be me," Flek added helpfully.

"No, she's right," Zaq said. "I already have enough. I don't need any."

Wyndi's face fell, and Zaq noticed the grin her friend Frank had been wearing vanished.

"Oh. Well," she paused, taking a breath. "I should have expected that. Of course, you already have enough apprentices. How many do you have? Who are they? Maybe I know them."

"Zero," Zaq stated again and took another bite of his food.

"Well, that's ludicrous!" Wyndi bemoaned. "If you don't have any apprentices, you can't say you don't need any. We can help you a lot while we learn from you. Please, Mr. Flicker-whizzle. At least think about it."

"And while you're thinking about it, think about bringing me into the group, too," Flek added. "Or it could just be me if that's easier. I need to find a mentor before the others leave.

Otherwise, I'll have to go back to Chubug with them after the Serenya concert."

Wyndi shot ice daggers from her eyes at the goblin.

"I don't know who this goblin is. You don't need to factor him into the equation when you think about it," she explained.

"Fine!" he said, raising his voice more than he meant to. "I'll think about it if you'll all just leave and let me eat my meal in peace."

Dimples formed as Wyndi's smile filled her face. Glancing up, Zaq noticed Frank was wearing a happy-go-lucky grin again as well. Even the goblin looked happy.

"Wonderful!" Wyndi effused. "Thank you. I'm sure you'll decide to bring us on. We could help you so much. How much time do you need? Ten minutes? Thirty?"

"I'm not making a decision like this on a whim," Zaq said calmly, poorly hiding his agitation. "I'll return here once I've decided to bring on any students."

"Oh. Wow. Okay," Wyndi said, scrunching her face. "That's fine. We'll be here. Don't worry."

Speaking up, Frank said, "We'd better let Mr. Flicker-whizzle finish his dinner in peace if we want any chance of him taking us on."

Zaq made a mental note that at least one of them had some sense and went back to eating his dinner while the tall young man guided the interlopers away. While the food was still quite tasty, Zaq grumbled to himself under his breath about how much everything had cooled.

Chapter 5

Unwelcome Visitors

Zaq deposited the scraps of meat Alaquine had given to him into the dish tucked under the bush outside his house. Looking around, he scratched his head. *Where was that cat?*

"I guess the blasted thing isn't hungry. At least it won't be bothering me this evening."

As he opened the front door, the cat bolted around the corner of the house and under his legs. The cursed thing had ignored the offering of food and displayed cunning Zaq didn't think it capable of. Shaking his head, he hurried inside after it.

The lights in the hallway glowed as he briskly walked down the hallway to his workshop. He pushed open the door, noting the cat hadn't tripped the light. As he entered his favorite space, the lights slowly rose, illuminating the whole room. There was no sign of the cat. *Where had it gone?*

Thud.

That noise had come from the sitting room. Sure enough, the book he had been reading was now on the floor. The cat was rolling around, holding his bookmark between its front paws and biting at the tassel at the end of the braided string connected to the thin wooden placeholder.

"Give me that!" Zaq yelled at the cat, who froze, staring up at him, the tassel dripping out of its mouth and the string firmly wedged between its teeth.

With a yank, he pulled the bookmark away from the cat and placed it in the book as he picked it up from the floor. Zaq set the book back on the side table and sat down in his cozy armchair.

Before he could even settle, the cat leapt onto his lap and curled up on his thighs.

"Well, that's fine. I wanted to sit and think anyway."

A low rumble emanated from the lump of black fur.

"What do you think of those young kids?"

The soft fur slid across his palm, filling in the spaces between his fingers. The rumble increased in volume and intensity.

"The kids. The ones at the tavern. I suppose you wouldn't know of them."

Zaq thoughtfully nodded to himself.

"They clearly don't have enough experience. They'd be a bigger hindrance than help. Besides, what could I even teach them?"

Merrr?

"Well, of course, I know more than they do. There is plenty I could teach them—in theory. I more meant, 'would they be capable of learning?'"

The silky hair caressed his hand.

"And what about that goblin? He didn't seem to be with the others. The girl seemed annoyed. Goblin artificers tend to focus on explosive inventions, but that's not all they can do. She'll need to get over that hangup."

Merrr-ow.

"You're right, I'm just as bad with the explosives—the Vanishing Secrets scroll is rather combustible."

The rumbling resumed, perhaps louder than before.

"And that string bean fellow. How would he even work at my bench? Oh sure, there are human artificers. Not common, though. Are they? No. No, they are not."

The cat's head butted up against his hand, reminding him that he should keep stroking it.

"Wait a minute! I'm not supposed to be stroking the cat. In fact, it's time it went outside and had some of that meat I brought home. Can't have it spoiling out there."

Zaq scooped the bundle of fur up in his arms as he slid out from the cushions cocooning him in. He walked to the door and tossed the cat out.

Mmro-OW!

He slammed the door before the cat could slip back in.

"It's late. I should retire for the evening. Maybe my dreams will bring me inspiration for what to tell those kids."

After a nice breakfast of a soft-boiled egg and toast smothered in creamy butter, Zaq sat, sipping a cup of dragonroot tea. He opted for just a drip of honey and no cream. The spicy root tea danced playfully on his tongue. As it cooled, he let it linger longer and longer in his mouth, enjoying the flavor.

His mind had just started to wander back to the tavern and his meeting with the kids who had interrupted his dinner, when he heard a crisp knocking at his front door. He wasn't expecting anyone. *Was it Samantha?*

"Coming. Hold on."

Zaq opened the door and found the trio from the tavern. It

seemed the goblin had inserted himself into the group after all, but Zaq could still sense some tension between them all.

"What are you doing here?" Zaq questioned in a sharp tone.

"Mr. Flickerwhizzle? We were just wondering..." Wyndi trailed off. "Um, we were wondering if you had decided yet?"

"What? Decided what? About the apprenticeship? We just spoke last night."

"Right," Wyndi agreed. "But we just thought, maybe you said that because we were in public. Maybe, here, with just us, you could actually answer."

While everyone was distracted by the conversation, the cat raced through the door that had been left open during the discussion.

"Sprung sprockets!" Zaq exclaimed. "Now look what you did. Come in here and help me get it."

Leaving the door half-open, Zaq hurried down the hall toward his workshop. He paid little mind to the three hopeful youths who shuffled behind him. They were murmuring comments about their observations in the house, but none of what they were saying really registered.

In the workshop, the black cat sat upright on its haunches. It held its head high and blinked slowly at Zaq and the others from its perch on the workbench. Its ears stood at attention, focused forward, and its tail wrapped around, draping over its front paws.

"By the gods! She is too cute!" Wyndi exclaimed.

"It looks pretty proud of itself," Frank added.

"That's a nice cat you have," Flek remarked. "We don't have a lot of cats in the warren. Snixil has a raccoon that's wicked smart."

"Be quiet! All of you," Zaq said in exasperation. "It is not cute. It's a nuisance. And I'm sure it is proud—it keeps finding ways to do this. But this is not my cat. I don't have a cat and don't want one, either. It just keeps sticking around."

"Do you feed her?" Wyndi asked. "I only ask because I saw the bowl under the bush out front."

Zaq scratched his head and slid his hand down the side of his face to tug at his beard.

"Well, yes. I feed the cat scraps and whatnot. I can't have it starving. Then there would be a dead cat outside my house attracting all sorts of insects and vermin."

"Um. Mr. Flickerwhizzle? I'm pretty sure that's why she stays, and that pretty much makes her your cat since you take care of her feeding," Wyndi said, her face scrunching.

"Balderdash!" Zaq rebuked. "You sound like my nosy neighbor, Samantha. This cat is not mine, and it's definitely not welcome in my house."

"I can take it out for you," Frank offered, reaching for the cat.

The cat backed away and hissed. He continued forward confidently with his arms outstretched. Just when it looked like he might grab the cat, it leapt to the side and off the bench. Frank swiped his arms futilely, catching nothing but air.

The blur of black raced from the room and out the front door, which had been left ajar.

"I suppose that's one way to get it out," Zaq said. "But I'm not sure it showed any skill and only worked because you foolishly left the door open."

"Er, no, sir," Frank said, his cheeks flushing. "It wasn't clear if we were staying long or if you actually wanted us in your house. I should have shut it."

"You're right," Zaq said, nodding. "That may not have been clear. But I'll make it clear now. I do not want you in my house. Please leave and shut the door behind you."

"But, sir," Wyndi implored. "This workshop is amazing. Look at all this equipment, and your projects look brilliant."

"Stop looking at that!" Zaq snapped. "I don't want you stealing my ideas. Besides, this workbench is too short for your friend. You need to leave. I haven't made up my mind, but you aren't helping your case with talk of stealing my ideas."

"We weren't stealing your ideas," Flek interjected. "Or at least I wasn't. I don't know about Wyndi. You might want to just bring me on as an apprentice and not the others."

"Shut it, Flek," Wyndi barked. "When I said you could come, it wasn't so you could steal the spot for yourself."

Wyndi turned back to look at Zaq.

"Sir, I wasn't stealing anything. I was just admiring your work. Besides, you know as well as I do. If you draw up a standard apprenticeship agreement, we can't steal your work. It's enforced by the contract."

"I suppose that's true," Zaq admitted. "But there isn't one in place yet. So, you could steal the ideas. So, get out. I told you I'd come to the tavern if I wanted to bring anyone on."

"Did you hear that?" Flek quietly asked the others. "He said, 'yet.'"

"Yup, heard it," Frank said, nodding.

"Shut up," Wyndi said out of the side of her mouth.

She then addressed Zaq directly and said, "We'll wait for you at the inn. Sorry to have intruded here today. We'll show ourselves out and shut the door."

Before he could say anything else, the trio skittered toward the front door and closed it behind them.

"The presumption of those kids," Zaq said to the now-empty room. "Where do they get the nerve?"

"You know. I could really use a nice cup of tea and a sweet treat after that nonsense. I'll just pop over to Mystic and see what Joh has baked today."

The morning rush at the tea shop had passed by the time Zaq arrived. There were still a few patrons seated in the covered patio area, but numerous tables were empty, and a sole customer stood at the counter ordering.

Zaq waited patiently for the orc in front of him to order. The gentleman was wearing an impeccable full three-piece suit, and when he stepped toward the receiving end of the counter, Zaq approached, flashing a smile to Zheb.

"Greetings and salutations, Zheb. Does Joh have anything interesting coming out of the oven this morning?"

"Hey zer, Zaq. It just so happens he decided to make pumpkin loaves today. Zey are small loaves wiss a vanilla icing drizzled on top."

"That sounds divine," Zaq said, his grin widening. "I'll have a loaf, and what do you think? Dragonroot? Or keep it simple with a black tea? Maybe a Royal Mist?"

"Zose vould be good, yes," Zheb nodded. "But, I sink maybe you might like zis maple spice tea. It's a black one, but viss a nice mellow spice."

"Sold," Zaq said. "It sounds perfect. I'll just find a spot on the patio."

Zaq almost reached for some coins, but remembered this treat would taste even better since he had complimentary tea and snacks this week. Thanking the dwarf, he found an open seat at a table removed from the other guests.

It was always fun to observe the customers in a tea shop. He recognized a few of them by face, if not by name. However, there were several he didn't recall seeing before. The gnoll he spotted surprised him as they don't often appreciate tea, but she appeared to be with an orc, so perhaps it was his choice.

A halfling couple occupied one of the lower tables like his

own. The two women kept gazing into each other's eyes, and Zaq was sure their tea would cool before they could finish drinking it. One of the women hadn't even touched her pastry.

He was pulled from his observations when Zheb placed a mug of tea in front of him, followed by a small plate, which made the pumpkin loaf look even bigger than it was. Zaq knew he wouldn't even be able to eat the entire loaf, no matter how large or small it appeared.

"Thank you, Zheb."

"Of course, of course. Did zose apprentices of yours find your house? Zey seemed anxious, and I vas vorried zey vould be late."

"Oh, ho!" Zaq chuckled in bemusement. "So, it seems I have you to blame for those scamps knocking on my door this morning. They are no apprentices of mine. Not that it has stopped them from asking."

"Oh dear. Oh my," Zheb muttered, his cheeks reddening to a bright crimson. "Zey seemed so sure of zemselves. I vas sure you vould know of zeir coming."

"I'm sure of that," Zaq nodded. "They seem very eager for me to take them on. I'm sure the fault is with them and not you."

"Zey seemed polite, zough," Zheb said, wringing his hands. "Don't you sink you could use zeir help? Vhy not take zem on?"

"I work best alone," Zaq said flatly. "You know that. I already caught one of them looking with too much interest at one of my projects. I'm sure they'd take the ideas right from under my nose, and I'd have no one to blame but myself."

"Aren't zer protections you can employ?"

"Well, sure," Zaq admitted. "They even pointed that out. Shows they admit they couldn't likely get away with my ideas easily."

"And vat off your big project? Couldn't you use zeir help to get zee parts and ingredients you need?"

Zaq coughed, choking on some pumpkin bread crumbs. He calmed himself and took a sip of tea.

"Now, that could be a very good reason. It hadn't occurred to me. I can't get off on adventures anymore, and paying to hire a team or to purchase from a vendor who marks the price up even more is too much for my savings."

"Right, right. You see," Zheb said, patting Zaq on the back. "Take zem on as apprentices. Put a rider in zee contract."

"You know what?" Zaq said, clapping his hands on the table. "I'll do it. But maybe I should let them stew a bit longer. I'll think about it."

"Don't be cruel," Zheb admonished. "Zey seem like good kids."

Zaq merely nodded and continued eating the pumpkin loaf. Zheb had known him long enough to know their chat was over, so he returned to the counter to help the customer who had been waiting. The spiced bread had a delightfully dense crumb, but it was well-baked and not claggy, and the vanilla icing added a perfect counterpoint of sweetness. The dwarf had also been right about the tea. It was sweet but not overly so, and the spice blend didn't clash with the loaf.

As it turned out, Zaq was wrong. He had been able to eat the entire loaf. He washed the last bite down with the dregs of his tea and then set off down the street toward home.

Chapter 6

Wyndi's Crew

"Well, now. That didn't go as planned," Wyndi complained as they walked far enough away from the artificer's house to avoid being seen or heard.

"I told you we shouldn't have gone," Legs said. "It would have been better to just keep a lookout for him at the inn like he said."

"Clogged coggs!" Wyndi snapped. "You're only saying that because it didn't work out. If he had taken us on as apprentices when we showed up at the house, you'd be thanking me for taking the initiative."

She nodded so vigorously in agreement with her own point that her pink ponytail whipped forward and smacked her in the face. Brushing it back, she acted as if it were all part of styling her hair.

"Nah," Flek said, shaking his head. "Frank is right. I didn't think it was a good idea to go either."

Wyndi jumped and twirled one-eighty, landed, and continued to walk backward, glaring at the goblin.

"What?!" Wyndi screamed. "You were begging for me to let you come along. You can't tell me you didn't think it was a good idea."

"Yes, I can," Flek pushed back. "I just didn't want to miss out. But that doesn't mean I thought it was a good idea."

"Whatever. You're both wrong. It was the right move. You can't use confirmation bias as the basis of your argument."

"Okay. You're right, Wyndi," Legs acquiesced. "However, if he doesn't come and invite us on as apprentices, then that's pretty hard evidence that your plan messed things up."

"No, no, no," Wyndi moaned. "You're doing it again. He might not ever have said yes. If he doesn't offer us apprenticeships, you can't assume it's because I annoyed him by showing up at the house. What kind of artificer are you?"

"Well, I'm not," Legs said. "That's kind of the whole point, right? Like, why we're trying to get these apprenticeships."

"But you can still act like one," Flek pointed out. "Logic is logic whether you have full training or not."

"I hate to admit it, but the goblin is right on that point," Wyndi said, not even glancing behind her to see where she was walking. "But how's this for logic? If he does come to the tavern and take us on as apprentices, it proves my plan to visit him didn't ruin our chances."

"True," Flek agreed. "That checks out."

Legs sighed and mumbled something unintelligible under his breath.

"Your mouth is too far away up there, Legs," Wyndi jabbed. "I couldn't make out anything you just said. Either talk louder or stoop down closer."

If there was one good thing about the goblin, he was at least an appropriate size. She sometimes wondered how she ended up getting along so well with the extra-tall human, but they had been the best of friends for as long as she could remember.

Legs stayed silent. Wyndi sighed, as usual, he had failed to take the bait. It was hard to poke fun at Legs. He was never very bothered about her size jokes. *Maybe his sense of humor is stretched too thin in that long and lanky form.*

With the confrontation over, she turned back around to walk properly, paying at least some attention to where she was leading them.

"So, what do we do now?" Flek asked. "Just sit around and wait to see if he shows?"

"I don't know if *we* need to do anything," Wyndi pointed out. "Legs and I are going back to the tavern to wait and see if he shows up. I can't stop you from doing the same, but you can do whatever you like."

"Might as well stick with you until he shows," Flek said as he turned onto the next street, following Wyndi's lead. "Trinx and Quilka were going shopping today to find outfits for the concert tomorrow night. I'm sure Vex is following along to watch out for them."

"Like I said, I can't stop you," Wyndi said. "But I'm telling you. If he decides to take on an apprentice or two, Legs and I get first dibs. It was my idea in the first place."

"It's up to Flickerwhizzle," Flek retorted. "If he only wants one, he probably wants the best. So, you and Le—Frank will have to find someone else to learn from."

"Thanks for using my name. It's understandable if you slip, considering how often Wyndi tosses Legs around."

"At least you don't prefer Francis. I like Frank better." Flek grinned, flashing his fangs.

"He'll always be Legs to me," Wyndi said. "His legs are taller than we are!"

Legs looked bemused and rolled his eyes, but stayed quiet.

"Wait a minute," Wyndi said, stopping their walk abruptly.

"Don't think I didn't notice that. You just implied you'd make the better apprentice. That's ridiculous."

"It is ridiculous," Flek agreed. "I didn't imply I'd make the better apprentice."

Wyndi frowned. "Yes, you did. I heard it."

"No, I implied I was the best, which is true," Flek said smugly. "I have more experience as an artificer than either of you."

"More experience blowing things up," Wyndi winked and continued leading the way back to the inn.

"Just because the goblins I learned from focused on explosives doesn't mean the artificery wasn't good," Flek defended. "I learned a lot, but I want to learn some more constructive runes and techniques."

"It sounds like Flickerwhizzle destroys his fair share of things," Wyndi said. "When I asked that dwarf at the tea shop about him, he mentioned the latest invention had self-destructed."

"Yeah, but that was just part of it," Flek said. "The important part of the invention is that pen. I'm pretty sure, anyway."

"Hey," Legs interrupted. "I'm getting hungry. How about you two? Should we get some food?"

"I could eat," Flek said, licking his tongue over his fangs.

"Sure, fine," Wyndi reluctantly agreed. "I'm not that hungry, but maybe I'll have a bite of something."

Wyndi's thoughts drifted to her stomach and her rear, both of which she already viewed as too round. *Why do I have to be as stocky as a dwarf?* The others didn't seem to notice or care. Maybe it wasn't a big deal. But sometimes, she felt it was.

"We're almost to the tavern," Wyndi declared. "We can just get some food there."

"But that's all we've been eating lately," Flek moaned.

"That's fine by me," Legs said. "I like the food that halfling cook whips up. She knows how to cook, that's for sure. If I were a halfling, I'd probably have five meals a day like they do if she were cooking all of them."

"Fine," Flek mumbled. "But we should try some other places, too."

"They'll have to be close," Wyndi said. "We need to be around in case Flickerwhizzle comes by. If we miss him because we're eating some snack at another place, I won't forgive either of you."

Before long, Wyndi pulled open the door to the Inn Side Out and let the other two file in first. She watched as the boys found a table and fell into two of the chairs, leaving two for her to choose from. Wyndi chose the one facing the stage. It was really more of an area kept free of tables and patrons, but it did have a small rise to it. There was no one performing, but that could change at any time, and she wanted to be able to watch if it did.

A plump human who had a very feminine-looking face despite having a full, neatly trimmed beard approached the table. The server had a noticeably large chest and wide hips.

"Haven't seen you in here, so before you make any assumptions one way or the other, I've been feeling more masculine lately and prefer you use he/him pronouns when speaking of me. Lately, I've been trying out Cal, and it's been feeling good, so you can call me Cal. Can I get you anything?"

"Noted on the pronouns," Flek nodded. "I use the same ones. So does Frank, and Wyndi uses she/her. As for what you can get us, that depends. Are you serving lunch? I could use a sandwich and maybe a bowl of soup?"

"We can do that," Cal said. "How about you two?"

"I'm hungry," Legs announced, which didn't surprise Wyndi at all. "I'll take a sandwich, some soup, and do you have any potatoes? Or something equally filling?

"I'm pretty sure we have some roasted potatoes. We also have a new sandwich we've been trying out. A traveler gave Glorya the idea. It's a single sandwich, but it has three slices of bread. Between the first and second slices are layers of roast boar, mild cheese, and tangy mustard. Then, between the second and third slices are layers of turkey, smoked cheese, and a creamy garlic sauce."

"Never mind the two sandwiches," Legs hurriedly said. "I'll have one of those instead. It sounds large and very tasty."

"Hey, change mine to one of those, too," Flek instructed.

Cal smiled at their enthusiasm and turned to Wyndi, simply quirking an eyebrow.

"Oh, right. I'll just have a small bowl of soup. I'm not really that hungry."

"Got it," Cal said. "Just water? Or anything more interesting to drink?"

"Water's fine," Wyndi said, speaking for the group, and with that, Cal hurried back to the kitchen.

While they waited for their order, a trio of goblins entered the tavern—two women and a large hobgoblin man. One of the women had blue-black hair braided into two plaits, each with streaks of cyan and magenta woven through them. The other woman had maroon hair pulled back into a ponytail, while the taller hobgoblin had short-cropped chestnut-brown hair with a full, neatly trimmed beard.

"Hey, Flek," Wyndi poked him to get his attention. "Aren't those the goblins you're traveling with? You need to go join them?"

"What?" he asked, looking up and then scanning the room. "Oh, yeah. Those are my friends. Looks like they finished shopping, or at least took a break. But I don't need to join them. I'm good here with you two."

"Hmm. Okay," Wyndi said, wrinkling her nose. "That's fine."

The goblins sat at a table, and one of the women noticed Flek and waved at him with a wide grin. He waved back, then motioned at Wyndi and Legs, presumably to say he was staying here and not joining the other goblins.

Cal returned with a large tray, somehow balancing it on the flat of one palm. He lowered it to a nearby table and then began distributing the food.

"There you go. Anything else?"

"No, this is good," Flek said, his eyes locked on the enormous sandwich in front of him.

The sandwiches the guys had looked amazing. Wyndi imagined how they might taste. Then, with a shake of her head, she dipped a spoon into her soup. Despite her blowing on it, the hot soup still felt a bit too hot on her tongue.

She forgot about the intense heat as the taste amazed her. The broth was salty and rich with bits of carrot, celery, and chicken. She hadn't gotten any on her first spoonful, but as she stirred the soup to distribute the heat, she saw several pieces of short noodles.

With a soup this good, Wyndi didn't mind horribly skipping the giant sandwiches, but her eyes lingered on the roast potatoes on Leg's plate. They glistened with oil, and large flakes of salt clung to them.

"You want one?" Legs asked, snapping her out of her gaze. "Go ahead. This is more than enough."

"Oh, no," Wyndi refused. "I'm fine. I was just thinking how it's been a while since I had roasted potatoes."

It had been a while, and it would be a while longer. She knew if she had one, it wouldn't be long before she'd eat several. *No, I'll just stick to my soup. It really does taste amazing.*

Two musicians hauled some equipment to the stage a few hours after the trio had finished eating. They had stayed at the table, ordering drinks on occasion to pass the time while waiting to see if the artificer would return. One musician, a dwarf, began setting up a full set of drums. The other, an elf, set down a stool. He then took a seat, rested one of those newer guitars on his leg, and began strumming some test chords.

After the dwarf finished setting up his kit, he took a seat and played a basic rhythm. The elf matched him, altering the chord progression to fit the drum beat.

A hooded entertainer wearing a cloak joined them on the stage. Her voice was captivating as she started right in on a simple melody. Wyndi thought she might recognize the song, but couldn't place it.

"She's doing a Serenya cover!" exclaimed the goblin with the braids whom Flek knew. Wyndi was pretty sure she was the one he called Trinx.

"This is a great way to get ready for the concert tomorrow," the one who must be Quilka bubbled.

The whole tavern was captivated by the music. The woman really could sing. The notes danced in Wyndi's ears, lifting her spirits.

When the song finished, the singer said, "For this next one, I really need to project, so I'll be pulling down my hood. Try not to overreact."

As she began to sing a much more uplifting song, the drums picked up a more aggressive tempo. The singer lifted her hood and pulled it back, allowing it to fall around her shoulders. She was a gorgeous elf with extremely pale blue-tinged skin. All northern elves tended to have skin with a blue or green cast.

A shriek filled the tavern as Trinx leapt to her feet and

climbed up onto the seat of her chair. The chair threatened to topple over as the goblin jumped up and down, screaming, "It's her! It's her!"

"You're right! It is. She must be practicing for tomorrow night. I can't believe she's here at the same inn," Quilka effused.

Well, it could be, Wyndi thought to herself. *No reason it couldn't actually be Serenya Dawnwhisper*. The goblins were obviously enthusiastic fans. She just hoped all the commotion wouldn't keep Flickerwhizzle away.

Chapter 7

Conditions

The list of special equipment and rare ingredients Zaq would need to pull off the dream version of his project was daunting, even if he was going to have help from the young, would-be artificers. He had spent the afternoon revisiting all of his notes and making what amounted to an impossible wishlist. This would be the price, though, if those kids wanted to apprentice with him.

With a smirk, Zaq thought of the perfect way to deliver his list. He would use his latest invention. By this point, he had prepared several of the scrolls, and he spread one out on the workbench.

Zaq picked up the pen, keyed it to the blank scroll, and then laid out the message.

Would-be apprentices,

You must sign an apprenticeship agreement.

You must gather the following for my projects:
** Exquisite Mana Crystal, minimum one cubic rod*
** Mana Conduit Vein, mimic or similar*
** Grimbark core, 2 rods tall, 4 rods in diameter*

Sincerely,

Zaquocorin Flickerwhizzle

After he finished signing the note, he tapped the control pad in the lower right of the scroll to lock it in, he then folded it in thirds. Zaq decided to make it more impressive and melted some wax. The warm ooze dribbled onto the outer fold, and he pressed a seal with an elaborate F into the wax.

In addition to the note, Zaq gathered three copies of a standard apprenticeship agreement. It was well-written, and he had used a version of it many years before while at Mysti Messages. This version had been modified by a lawyer friend to lock all rights to himself rather than the company.

The primary purpose of all such agreements was to protect the mentor. They were not designed to protect the apprentices. In fact, they had to relinquish all rights to anything and everything they created or worked on to the mentor. This protection, including a non-compete clause, would last for two years after the end of the apprenticeship. The only reason apprentices would agree to this was that they would retain full rights to anything they did after the end of the apprenticeship. As one might expect, the apprentices were often guarded with their ideas and focused on assisting the mentor with their projects rather than divulging any of their own ideas during the apprenticeship.

"You know, I should have included dinner in the note. That's fine. I can still request it, even if it's not in the note. But, speaking of that, I should head over to the inn. I could use a little something-something."

Out his window, the clouds were heavy tonight. It wasn't actively raining, but at this time of year, it could easily start pouring later in the evening. He chose a thick cloak with a hood and let the comforting weight rest on his shoulders, leaving the hood down for now.

The dusky early evening air clung to him as he walked. It was definitely going to rain at some point. Maybe not before he returned home, but certainly by morning. The cloak had been a good idea.

It was clear that the harvest festival was approaching. Houses had gourds, haybales, and other decorations in the yards and on the small porches. In the sky, the two moons were visible, and Zaq was sure they would both be completely full at some point during the festival.

The cool breeze in the air nipped at his nose and his large, rounded ears, which were common among gnomes. Zaq picked up the pace, spending less time admiring the decorations and more focused on reaching the warm tavern. Despite the cold, he smiled as he thought of the quiet inn, good food, and the crackling fire Alaquine was sure to have burning in the hearth.

Zaq's mood flipped when he pulled open the door to the inn, and the music and cheering from the crowd assaulted his ears—so much for a quiet evening. *Perhaps this was a bad idea,* he thought as he stood holding the door open, frozen with indecision.

Scanning the room, he saw there wasn't a single table free.

While some patrons were seated around tables, many stood, some even on their chairs. The stage area had a full drum kit set up, and a dwarf with a long, full beard braided into five plaits ferociously attacked the drums with his sticks. One elf played a guitar, while another stood front and center, singing in a catchy melodic voice.

Zaq decided he was doing no one any good by standing in the doorway, and despite his better judgment, he finished entering the room, letting the door fall shut behind him. He heard the crowd chanting "Serenya," and his mind clicked. *That's right, I do recognize the singer. She's quite popular among the young folk.* Judging by the crowd, she was evidently popular among other generations as well.

It was strange for her to be performing in such a small venue. It must have been a surprise; otherwise, Zaq likely wouldn't have been able to reach the door, much less enter the tavern. Still, with no open tables, he was unsure whether he should stay or leave. Just as he decided to go, a group of frantically waving hands caught his attention. The would-be apprentices were here after all and clearly had still been waiting for him.

With some effort, Zaq maneuvered his way through the tables until he reached Wyndi and her crew.

"Greetings and salutations, young would-be-apprentices."

"See!" Wyndi said, giving Frank a jab with her elbow. "I told you he would come. We're going to be apprentices!"

"He might only pick me," Flek pointed out, thoroughly amusing Zaq.

"Or I could still pick none of you," Zaq said, joining right into the conversation.

"Please, sir," Wyndi rolled her eyes. "You came all this way. Clearly, you plan on taking at least some of us on."

"But how can we have any sort of reasonable discussion

with all this noise? Perhaps I'll go and come back on a calmer evening," Zaq mused.

"We don't have to talk here," Flek chimed in, raising his voice. "My friends and I have a room upstairs. We can use it to talk."

Zaq remembered the group of goblins Flek was motioning to earlier. An upstairs room would be a much more sensible spot to discuss things, but he was hungry.

"Have you all eaten? I was hoping to get a meal and perhaps a glass of whisky to sip."

"We haven't," Wyndi answered, then glanced at the others, making various motions with her hands. "I think we'd all be up for some dinner. We can order and have it brought upstairs. We'll even cover your meal if you stay."

"Make sure to include a glass of whisky, and I'll stay," Zaq said, his eyes glinting. "We can talk upstairs. Flek, lead the way while Wyndi orders our dinner."

"Of course," Flek said, almost knocking his chair over as he scrambled to his feet. "Right this way."

Zaq and Frank followed Flek and left the young gnome to put in their orders.

"I'll be up shortly," Wyndi said. "Don't do anything important without me!"

"Don't worry, Wyndi knows where we are going," Flek said as they climbed the stairs.

"I can't say I was worried," Zaq casually replied. "If she couldn't find us in an inn this size, I'm not sure she's equipped to be my apprentice."

"Excellent point," Flek agreed. "It's fine by me if you just take me on. You only need to bring on Frank and Wyndi if you think they can handle it."

Frank released a restrained chuckle, and Zaq wasn't sure if it was nervousness or amusement at the goblin's brazenness.

Flek pushed open a door midway down the right side of the hall and held it for the other two before entering himself. Zaq noticed he had left the door ajar.

The room was quite spacious. It did not have its own bathroom, but there would be a common one down the hall. It did, however, have a separate bedroom with a large bed. The room they were currently in also had a bed against one wall, and a bedroll was stretched out along another. In the center of the room was a square table and four chairs.

All three of them sat down at the table, and Zaq pulled a bundle of paperwork out from under his cloak, carefully arranging it on the table in front of him. He made three stacks and then laid the wax-sealed envelope on the center one.

"Are those contracts?" Flek asked, his eyes widening twice as large. "You really are going to take us on?"

Frank glared at the goblin but didn't comment.

"Not necessarily," Zaq stated, resting his hands on the table with his fingers intertwined. "An artificer should always be prepared, and these documents represent me being prepared. I still don't think this is a particularly good idea. However, I've come up with enough reasons why it might be that I'm willing to discuss the matter in more detail."

"Great," Flek said. "The number one reason—"

"No," Zaq interrupted. "That's enough of that. We wait for Wyndi, or I pack up and go."

He was sure he saw the goblin open his mouth to say something, but, likely thinking better of it, Flek simply licked his tongue across his fangs and closed his mouth again.

The three sat in a silence which seemed comfortable for only two of them. The goblin seemed unable to sit still, constantly fidgeting in his seat and glancing at the partially open door.

The mood finally broke when Wyndi shoved the door

open, strode confidently across the room, and flopped into the remaining chair with a broad smile on her face.

"Thanks for waiting for me. The food should be up soon. I ordered today's special for everyone to make it easy, and I asked Alaquine to send up a whisky he thought you would like. He seems to know you well enough."

"Wonderful!" Zaq clapped. "You've already passed your first test of competence. Maybe this won't be a horrible idea."

"That was a test?" she asked, her smile faltering. "I hope if you have any more, they are more challenging. My ability to order *and pay* for your food is not a test of an artificer."

"Quite right," Zaq nodded. "But it *was* a test of your ability as an apprentice, which doesn't necessarily always involve artificery. Now, why don't you tell me more about why you want a position like this? I'd like to hear from each of you. This isn't an all-or-nothing kind of deal."

"See, I told you he might only want me," Flek hissed at Wyndi, then turned to Zaq. "I'm new to this city. Just got here a couple of days ago, in fact. But I have experience learning from goblin artificers back home. I don't want to make the perfect bomb, though. I want to create something incredible that could change lives. Trinx taught everyone in TQ House that we can change the world if we put our minds to it. That's why she brought me along when she came to see the concert."

"Really?" Wyndi asked him somewhat rhetorically. "You really want to make something to change the world? That's actually pretty cool, I guess. Makes it sound like I'm just copying, but I'm not. I want to make a great invention. I don't know what it will be yet, but I want it to be amazing. Everyone knows that you're the best, Mr. Flickerwhizzle. I want to learn from the best to give me the best chance of making something astounding."

"The best?" Zaq asked, quirking a bushy eyebrow. "I'm not

sure everyone knows that. As far as I know, most people think Arti Flashcrank is the best. He runs Mysti Messages, after all."

"Well, maybe most people think he's the best," Wyndi admitted. "But among the artificers, we know the truth. Most think the rumors are true. A lot think you were the one who actually came up with the first Mysti Message scroll."

Zaq shook his head with a bemused expression on his face.

"I can neither confirm nor deny that, and if you are well enough versed in those rumors, you know that."

"Yeah. Come on, Wyndi," Frank said, finally speaking up. "You know that was settled a long time ago, and it's all sealed in court records. I'm sure Mr. Flickerwhizzle doesn't need you bringing up old history."

"Thank you, Frank," Zaq nodded. "You are quite right. Now, why don't you take your turn? Why are you here? Why do you want this?"

"Wyndi's like the smartest artificer I know, and she says you're the best to learn from. I'm already at a disadvantage. Everyone knows humans aren't as good at artificery as gnomes and goblins. I just want to give myself the best chance."

"Nonsense," Zaq laughed. "That's hogwash backed only by tradition and faulty common knowledge. The problem with common knowledge is that it is common and rarely covers the whole truth of anything. You may not be a great artificer, but I can guarantee it's not because you are human. It could simply be plain incompetence."

"Er. Thanks? I guess," Frank mumbled, scratching the back of his head with his right hand.

"You are quite welcome," Zaq grinned. "Those all seem like good reasons, actually, but you may all be lacking some critical pieces of information. I am not a good teacher. I could take you on as apprentices, but I can't guarantee you'll learn anything. In fact, I'd safely bet you won't."

"We'll take that risk!" Wyndi snatched at the almost-offer. "We think you're a better teacher than you think. Besides, just watching you build your inventions should teach a lot, even if you don't actively explain it."

Zaq shook his head slowly, not negatively, but more to clear the doubts still lingering.

"I'll be straight with you since I still have my doubts. I feel you need to know what you'll be getting into. I'm old, as you can clearly see. I still have grand ideas. One is perhaps even too grand, as it has eluded me most of my life. In order to have a chance of it ever working, I need materials I cannot afford, and I'm in no shape to venture out to collect them on my own. Your apprenticeships are contingent on your agreeing to assist me."

Zaq slid the wax-sealed scroll over to Wyndi.

"Read this, and if you all agree, we can move forward."

Chapter 8

Apprenticeships

Wyndi picked up the folded parchment that Mr. Flickerwhizzle slid over to her. It was unusually heavy, not by a lot, but noticeable enough that it couldn't all be explained by the wax seal. The seal had a filigreed F embossed into it, and she noticed a corner of the parchment had a silvery circle, apparently made of some form of metal. If there was metal embedded, that could explain the additional heft to the letter.

Flek was leaning over with his head practically blocking her view of the note, intruding into her space. She gave him a firm elbow.

"Ooff," he said overdramatically and backed off a small amount.

Legs seemed content just to watch, likely assuming she would read it aloud, which she did, in fact, intend to do. He had a certain calmness about him. He wasn't easily ruffled and tended to assume things would flow his way eventually. They probably would.

Wyndi broke the seal, unfolded the letter, and began to read aloud.

"'Would-be apprentices'—I like the sound of that; he's already considering us. 'You must sign an apprenticeship agreement'—of course. That's standard, right, guys? 'You must gather the following for my projects'—wait. What? We're a delivery service?"

"What does he want?" Flek asked, leaning over again to try to read. "Maybe it's nothing too difficult to get. I'd often have to fetch things for my mentor back in Chubug."

"Let her keep reading," Legs said. "We can't know anything until she shares it."

Wydi glared at Flek and flashed a smile to Legs for the support.

"Anyway. Here's the list," she said before continuing to read aloud.

"'Exquisite Mana Crystal, minimum one cubic rod'—that's huge! We can't afford to buy something like that. We'd have to steal it or mine one.

"'Mana Conduit Vein, mimic or similar'—A mimic? We're supposed to hunt down a mimic and kill it? It certainly wouldn't just give us the gland freely. It says or similar. Maybe we can find something else to enhance mana flow, but it will take some research.

"'Grimbark core, 2 rods tall, 4 rods in diameter'—okay, this one isn't that hard, but we'll still need to travel quite a ways to find a tree. We'd need a strong axe, too. Grimbark is extremely tough. 'Sincerely, Zaquocorin Flickerwhizzle.'"

As she finished reading his name, the parchment developed a flame in the center, which rapidly spread out in all directions, eating away the scroll. Wyndi released the parchment, but not before the fire licked at her fingertips, singeing them and leaving a black residue.

"Ow!" she exclaimed and jammed a finger in her mouth.

Mr. Flickerwhizzle clapped his hands, looking quite proud of himself and grinning maniacally.

"Was that one of your latest inventions we heard about?" Flek asked as he bounced in excitement with a smile wide enough to show off his fangs.

"It was! Isn't it wonderful?" the old gnome replied, still looking very smug.

"As interesting as that was," Wyndi said loudly, drawing attention to herself. "It didn't even make any sense. How are we supposed to remember what you wanted us to get? The list is gone!"

"The list was not that long, and you all heard it," Mr. Flickerwhizzle said matter-of-factly. "Besides, if you are worthy of being an apprentice, you surely have strong recollection skills."

"He's right, Wyndi," Legs said calmly. "I'm sure that was startling, but I think we can remember the items. Besides, I'm sure if we fail to get them, he won't hesitate to remind us we need to."

"I can remember it all," Flek said with too much confidence. "That's why I'll make the best apprentice. Are those the agreements? I'll agree. Give me one, and I'll sign it."

"Yes, yes," Mr. Flickerwhizzle said. "You can all sign them if you'll agree to the terms and would like to come on board. But you must take turns. I only have one enforcement pen with me."

He pulled out a pen that Wyndi recognized from other contracts she had signed. The pens could create a binding agreement when used to sign a document. The terms were then magically enforced. In many cases, you literally couldn't break them if you tried. If you did manage to break the terms, a mark would develop on all copies of the contract, and the ink would turn crimson.

Truth be told, the power of the pens always scared her. Wyndi didn't know how they worked, and understanding the unknowns of powerful devices like this was one of the reasons she desired this apprenticeship. She would read this agreement very carefully before signing.

Despite Flek's extreme eagerness to sign, she was impressed he was taking the time to read through his copy while she and Legs read theirs. Maybe he had more sense than she gave him credit for.

Then again, maybe not, she thought as she saw him finish reading first and sign his name without any questions.

"This part here," Wyndi said, pointing at a spot on the contract with her finger. "It says we agree to fetch, procure, or otherwise obtain any item or service you need as long as it will not put me in excessive danger."

"Yes?" Mr. Flickerwhizzle asked, quirking one of his bushy eyebrows. "What about it? It's fairly standard for apprentices."

"I just find it odd because the list you gave us was detailed, and this is very broad," Wyndi said, pausing to gather her thoughts and frame her questions in the best way. "Why give us the list and have it destroy itself if your contract requires what was on the list and possibly more?"

"Simple," he replied. "The list was to give you an idea of what might be required. If it was enough to dissuade you, then it did its job. If not, well, I hardly think it matters if I ask for a few more errands or not. And the self-destruction? Well, that was just fun, don't you think?"

Wyndi wrinkled her nose at his idea of fun.

"Fair point, I suppose. And what about the danger? Excessive is not a very comforting word. That implies there could still be quite a lot of danger."

"I cannot, and more accurately, will not, ask you to do

anything I think is too dangerous," Mr. Flickerwhizzle assured her. "But there is always some risk of danger in nearly everything we do. In fact, just building some of our artificer projects can be dangerous. There is often a chance they'll blow up, or worse."

"That makes sense," Legs interjected. "It was still a great question, Wyndi. I was wondering about some of that myself."

"What do you think, Legs? Some of this seems pretty one-sided in his favor, but I think that's pretty normal. I doubt we'd get an opportunity with someone as good with better terms than these."

"Agreed," the tall man said. "I'm ready to sign if you think this is a good idea. It looks like Flek is already in."

Wyndi rolled her eyes and stifled a laugh.

"Yeah, I think we can sign these. Besides, we can't have Flek running around telling everyone Flickerwhizzle chose him over us, even if it was our decision not to sign."

Without any more hesitation, she grabbed the binding pen. The tip of the instrument scratched lightly on the parchment, leaving her name, "Ailawyndi Crinklepot."

Wyndi handed the pen to Legs. He leaned over the table and brushed his hair back out of his face before signing his document, "Francis Zinzelxi."

Mr. Flickerwhizzle gathered all of the documents together and double-checked each one.

"I appreciate the formality of signing your full names, but since this is an artificer-made item, I'll let you in on a small part of how it works. The pen works on intention when forming the binding. You could write a nickname or even a random set of words, and the pen wouldn't care. The binding would be to your being."

"Thank you, Mr. Flickerwhizzle," Wyndi said. "I'd love to

know even more about the pens and many other devices. They are all so mysterious."

"We'll get to all that, I'm sure," he said as he counter-signed all three documents. "But now that you are all officially in my charge as apprentices, I'd like you to stop with this *mister* business. Everyone just calls me Zaq. You should, too."

"You got it, Zaq," Flek said, apparently completely comfortable with the more relaxed informality. It made sense. Goblins rarely have more than a single name, but often associate with their larger clan name when more formal situations present themselves.

"If that makes you comfortable, I'll adjust," Wyndi said, though she wondered if she could think of him as a companion rather than a more formal mentor.

"Thank you for taking us on, Zaq," Legs added.

"So, what happens now?" Wyndi asked.

"Hopefully, we'll eat," the old gnome said mischievously. "You did order us some food, didn't you?"

"She did," Cal said from the doorway. "I was just waiting for you to finish. It all seemed so important, and I didn't want to interrupt. We put some warming caps on the plate, so everything should still be hot."

"Wonderful," Zaq clapped. "Bring them in. We are all quite ready to eat and celebrate. You can formally meet my three new apprentices."

Cal entered carrying a tray and set down a covered plate in front of each person. He followed them with glasses of water and a fifth glass containing the whisky Wyndi had ordered for Zaq.

With a tap on the sensor atop each lid, the seals released with a soft hiss. He pulled each covering off, stacking them together, then waved before leaving the room.

Wyndi inhaled the spices caught in the steam that escaped when the seals broke. The oregano was most prevalent, and the other spices blended in a way she was unable to pick them out. She was sure that would change when she took a bite.

The entire plate was covered with a piece of flatbread. This, in turn, was covered in a rich tomato sauce cooked with ground meat and large chunks of vegetables. Finely grated, crumbly hard cheese dusted the top of the saucy mixture.

She picked up her knife and fork, then cut a small piece, making sure to get a large chunk of mushroom. When she popped it in her mouth, the rest of the spices in the sauce surfaced. Basil mixed with the oregano along with rashthistle, thyme, and spicy flakes of dried chili pepper. The sauce must have been simmering and reducing for a long time because the tomato was incredibly rich.

Looking up from her plate, her face took on a quizzical expression as she watched Flek. The goblin had taken his knife, and rather than cut a small piece as she had, he had cut across the entire flatbread four times, creating eight wedges. He slid his long green fingers under one of the wedges and lifted it. Both hands guided it up to his mouth, careful not to allow any of the topping to fall. Flek made short work of the slice, and with a wide grin, he reached down for another.

Wyndi noticed Legs and Zaq were eating their meal in the same way she was, but the old gnome seemed to watch Flek as if he were taking mental notes for the next time he was served a dish like this. She shook her head and continued eating, enjoying every bite. Each was delicious and different, depending on which of the many vegetables ended up on that piece.

After several bites and with their immediate hunger settled, Zaq lifted his glass of whisky.

"Welcome, young apprentices. Be sure to be at my house no later than mid-morning, but mind you aren't too early. I need time to get dressed and break my fast."

The old gnome then took a sip and sighed with a smile on his face.

That was it. They really were all officially apprentices.

Chapter 9

First Demo

The following day, the clothes hanging in the closet vexed Zaq. They refused to indicate which outfit would be best for the first day with his new apprentices. He usually gave little thought to what he would wear. If he were experimenting or fixing something, like he did the other day at the tea shop, he would simply wear utility trousers with numerous pockets and a tight-fitting tunic that wouldn't get caught in any gears or machinery.

Perhaps that was for the best. He'd be wearing something like that sooner or later, and it might as well be sooner. Still, he would not likely be doing any actual hands-on work today. It made much more sense to go over some of the plans so the kids would know what they were getting into.

"Maybe I should ask that darn cat—not that it ever answers. No. Wait. Don't be ridiculous. We certainly don't need the cat in here today. It'll be crowded enough with the apprentices. Well, there you have it, then. I just need to pick something, and then I'll still have time for a bite to eat."

Realizing he was talking to himself yet again, he shut his

mouth and forcibly decided on a utilitarian brown work outfit with a pair of work boots. He pulled it all on without ceremony and went downstairs to the kitchen.

Soon, two sausages sizzled, hissed, and crackled in a large frying pan. Next to them, two slices of wheat bread slathered heavily on both sides with butter sat, making much less noise. The spicy aroma filled the small kitchen, and Zaq's stomach rumbled loud enough that he could not just feel it, but hear it as well. Occasionally, he rolled the sausage links and flipped the slices of toast.

When both looked sufficiently browned, he transferred everything to a plate and spooned a generous amount of orange and lemon marmalade on each piece of toast. The tea had finished steeping, so he poured himself a cup and sat at his small table. He saw no point in taking his breakfast to the dining room. These days, he really only used it for formal gatherings, of which there had been very few.

Zaq alternated bites of sausage and sticky jam-covered toast. The sage and thyme paired well with the tangy-sweet marmalade. He was down to only a couple of bites left when he heard a knock at the front door.

With no time to waste, he stuffed the remaining food in his mouth, causing his cheeks to puff. He rinsed the plate and left it in the sink. The pan still sat on the stove with the fats congealing as it cooled.

"I'll clean that up later. I'm sure the kids won't mind a small mess in the kitchen."

Zaq opened the door to find all three apprentices standing on his small porch. The girl, Wyndi, was holding the blasted cat, and it seemed quite at home in her arms.

"Greetings and salutations. Welcome to my home. I can be a much more gracious host when you are expected. Come in, but leave the cat outside. Why are you even holding the wicked thing?"

"Your cat seemed to want to come in," Wyndi answered. "I noticed the bowl was empty and thought maybe it was hungry. She's so precious, I couldn't say no when she asked me to pick her up. Her cute little tail was quivering with so much excitement."

"That's not my cat. I told you that before. Make sure you put it down before you come in, and don't let it follow you in here."

Wyndi shrugged and put the cat down, making sure it remained outside before she entered behind the boys.

"Something smells really good in here, Mr. Flickerwhizzle," Frank said, craning his neck around to see what was in the kitchen.

"Yeah, it does," Flek agreed, licking his tongue across his fangs.

"Yes, it *was* good. I hope you all ate. I told you last night—call me Zaq."

Frank's smile flattened, and his forehead creased. Flek, the goblin, actually swiped a finger through the cooling grease in the pan and sucked it off in his mouth.

Zaq shook his head and waved them all to follow him back to the workshop.

Everyone filed into the room, which seemed awfully small now that it held four people. Zaq maneuvered a slab of slate he had mounted on casters into a spot where everyone could see it and picked up a thick piece of chalk.

"Chalk? I would think you'd have some fancy artificer device with runes and control points," Wyndi remarked.

"Gadgets are fun. That's why I practice this craft," Zaq admitted. "However, not everything needs magic to be useful.

For conveying ideas, a piece of chalk and a large slate work just fine."

"That makes sense," Flek said. "Obviously, Wyndi's gonna want to see something neat because she hasn't had much exposure to items made by artificers. But that takes resources, and what you have there should work fine."

Wyndi shot the goblin a glare, but Zaq ignored their competitive tension.

"Now, the first thing I'm going to do is show you a high-level view of my master project. I haven't ever shared this with anyone, but since you are all under those apprenticeship agreements as of last night, I don't see any reason why I shouldn't share. After all, it might be good to know what you are gathering those materials for."

"Yes, please," Wyndi implored. "I've been going over that list in my head since I saw it last night, and I'm having trouble imagining why you need those things."

Zaq began to draw diagrams on the slate and narrated while he scratched the chalk across the black surface.

"You all, of course, know of Mysti Messages scrolls. I know you do because you accused me of inventing them. But that's neither here nor there. The key issue is that they are always linked in pairs. They might be the basic one-way versions or more elaborate two-way versions with extra bells and whistles. Either way, though, there are always just two scrolls. But I ask you, what if we could link more than two scrolls? What if we could share messages between an entire group? Or subsets of the group? Or one-on-one, but you can choose who when you write the message."

"That's ridiculous!" Flek spit. "The scrolls would need to be huge to hold that much logic in the runes."

"It's clearly not ridiculous," Wyndi defended. "He

wouldn't be bringing it up if he didn't have an idea on how to solve it."

"Quite right. Quite right," Zaq said, continuing to scrawl on the board. "What you see me drawing now is a central device I call a distributor. Instead of linking one scroll to another scroll directly, the scrolls are linked to the distributor. Rules in the distributor then ensure messages written on one scroll appear on the proper scrolls."

"Wouldn't it—" Frank started to ask before Zaq cut him off.

"No, no. I've got this all worked out. I've been at this for a long time. You can't likely understand what I'm describing yet. Let me continue, and I'm sure it will all make sense to you."

Frank closed his mouth and stayed silent as Zaq continued drawing on the slate and talking faster.

"And so, you see, instead of scrolls, we will use robust devices with a surface similar to this slate I'm drawing on. But not with chalk. Oh, no. A pen or stylus, rather. And a tap on the control can erase the entire thing, optionally storing a copy for retrieval later."

"But this distributor," Wyndi interrupted, "how does it know where to send the message if multiple devices are connected?"

Zaq set his chalk down and excitedly clapped.

"That's the beauty of the system, isn't it? You tell it! Just write the name of the person, and it will distribute it to them. Or better yet! Write more than one name! They each will receive the message."

The old gnome began cackling in delight. Zaq had these ideas trapped in his head all to himself for so long that it felt good to get them out.

"The mana cost must be ridiculous," Flek ventured. "How can you power all of this?"

"That's one of your assignments, isn't it?" Zaq shot back. "I need that large mana crystal. It goes right here in the heart of the distributor. See? But also, each slate will require a small crystal. The small crystal should recharge from the user's natural mana or the ambient levels in the environment."

"What about the big one?" Frank ventured a question. This time, Zaq allowed him to get it out. "It seems to me that even a large one will burn out quickly with any significant number of users. That's why I was asking earlier if—"

"Right, and that's why I stopped you earlier," Zaq interrupted again. "You haven't fully taken in the sum of it. That's where the mana conduit vein comes in. We may need more than one. With the right runes, we should be able to increase the natural mana drawn from the environment greatly. We simply keep the area with the distributor steeped in mana."

Frank frowned but apparently decided against poking further.

"And all of this will be encased in the hollowed-out grim-bark cylinder," Zaq said as he drew a shape around the figures he had been drawing on the slate.

Frank had a pensive look on his face, apparently waffling on whether or not to speak, not that Zaq paid him that much attention. He was quite tall, after all, and craning one's neck up was never comfortable.

"How many of these slate devices can be connected to a distributor?"

"Oh, ho!" Zaq clapped excitedly. "Now, that's a question worth asking. According to my calculations, it should be almost limitless. It all comes down to how rich of an environment we can put the distributor in. But even then, it will be highly efficient. I imagine anyone who wants to purchase a slate will be able to connect to the distributor."

"We might need to make the crystals in the slate a little bigger, just to be safe," Wyndi offered.

"Details. Details. Yes, yes. I'm sure we will need to determine that through experimentation," Zaq said, waving his hand as if to bat away the silliness of making such low-level suggestions at this stage. "Speaking of which—how would you like to test it out?"

Zaq's face grew into a mischievous grin, and both of his bushy eyebrows danced like furry caterpillars on his forehead.

"What? Really?" Flek practically leapt forward. "How? I thought you needed us to get those supplies?"

"Why, it's a prototype, of course!" Zaq said, his giddiness still making him bounce. "It can only support a handful of slates, and the slates are much larger than they will be. Much more cumbersome to use as well. But never mind that. They do work. Let me just set things up."

Zaq rummaged in his project box in the corner of the room and emptied several items onto the workbench. Eventually, the bench held a miniature version of what he had been drawing on the board, as well as five bulky devices, each the size of an enormous book. The devices had wires and components protruding, and each had a receptacle with a mana crystal mounted. The surface looked like the black slate of the board he had been writing on, but it clearly wasn't plain slate, and they were adorned with several exposed gears, buttons, and lights.

Waving them over, he said, "Go ahead. Take one of the slates. There is a pen attached. You see? I'll get the distributor fired up. All of the slates have already been paired with the distributor; they should come alive in just a moment."

Each of the apprentices shuffled forward and picked up one of the devices while Zaq tapped on the small distributor, bringing it to life. The device lit up and emitted a low buzz that filled the room, forcing everyone to speak a little louder. Lights blinked and danced through the various gems and crystals embedded in the grimbark.

Wyndi and Flek stood close, watching every one of the old artificer's movements carefully, while Frank stood back, having a perfect view from above.

"Let me show you how this works," Zaq said as he grabbed up one of the devices. "I'll just use the pen to write each of your names. Now, I'll write a simple message. And finally, all I need to do is tap the send button."

As he spoke those final words, each of their devices beeped, and a green crystal pulsed a steady rhythm.

"First test message for my new apprentices," Wyndi read aloud as she watched the words appear on her device.

"That's what mine says, too!" Flek shouted and thrust it at Frank to show him.

Frank was busy looking at his own device and didn't notice until the goblin's device bumped into the tall human, unfortunately punching him in his groin. He doubled over and dropped his device. It landed on the floor and broke into several pieces, gears, wires, and crystals clattering across the hard floor.

"Ooofff," Frank moaned. "Now look what you made me do. I'm sorry, Mr. Flickerwhizzle. I didn't mean to."

"Spung sprockets!" Zaq shouted. "This! This is why I always thought it was a bad idea to bring on apprentices—they always wreck everything. It's much too crowded in here. If we had more room, that wouldn't have happened."

"I'm sorry," Flek mumbled. "To both of you. I didn't mean it. I'm not sure if more room would have helped my carelessness."

"Of course, it would help," Zaq spat. "It's downright cramped in here. But we can salvage this. You three can learn a thing or two as you put that device back together. You can use the working devices as a manual."

"Really?" Wyndi's eyes lit up. "That's amazing. I'm sure we can figure it out."

"Yes. Yes. You'll work the rest of the day on that project," Zaq said, shaking his head in frustration. "And then. Yes. Then, tomorrow, you have a new assignment. You must locate an alternative workshop with much more room. We can't be tripping over each other in here."

"How are we to do that, sir?" Frank asked, still hunched over and holding his hands defensively over his groin.

"I suppose that's part of the test now, isn't it?" Zaq shot back. "I'm sure you'll figure something out. We can move my equipment there once you've found a suitable place. Make sure it is at least twice as large as my workshop here, maybe even three times."

Chapter 10

Workshop Hunting

Wyndi led the trio down the street, Flek walking next to her and Legs following closely behind. He seemed to have recovered from the incident in the workshop the day before, but the goblin wasn't dropping it.

"I'm really sorry, Frank. I didn't mean to get you right there. Now that I know how that feels, it makes it all the worse."

"What do you mean?" Wyndi interjected. "Did someone hit you in the crotch recently?"

"Well, not recently, but it definitely happened since the area has been more susceptible to pain. I know it always hurts, and I'm sure you'd think it hurt if someone hit you there, but now I know it really does hurt guys more."

"I still don't get it," Wyndi asked, more confused now than before. "You are young—I guess. So, you're saying since you hit puberty?"

"Right," Flek said, nodding seemingly more to himself than her. "You wouldn't know. I forget sometimes because it's no longer obvious, and everyone back at TQ House knew. You could say it's been since the second puberty. Since I started taking this amazing potion, Trinx came up with."

"Oh!" Wyndi clapped. "I think I've heard of that. It's hard to come by because it's a designer potion, but you're friends with the alchemist? And you used to be—"

"No," Flek said, cutting her off. "I didn't use to be anything. I always was a boy and later a man. But it was only when I started taking the potion that my body fully reflected it. Thankfully, my uncle Pox donated the materials for the potion."

"Of course," Wyndi said, grimacing in embarrassment. "I didn't mean—or I guess. Never mind. It didn't come out how I meant. That's really cool, though. So, yeah, I guess you would know it from both sides."

"And that's why I feel so bad," Flek said, nodding. "I didn't mean to, and I know it must have been a shock to Frank. So, yeah. Frank, I'm really sorry."

"I told you, it's fine. Really. It felt awful, but I know you didn't mean it. Flickerwhizzle has a point, I think. It's pretty crowded in there. Plus, I'm not sure how well I'll do at a workbench that size if he ever lets us try any hands-on work beyond repairing that slate I broke."

"I wouldn't guess he'll do that anytime soon," Wyndi complained. "But, yeah. I can see how it was cramped in there. But that doesn't help us figure out a better place. How are we supposed to find a workshop?"

"Don't ask me," Flek said, waving his hands. "I just got into town. I don't know where anything is."

"I know my way around," Wyndi assured him. "What I don't know is where someone might have a space available we could use as a workshop. We don't have to find an actual workshop. We can turn just about any space large enough into one. Zaq said we could move his equipment."

"True," Legs agreed. "I can tell you one thing, though. My

bet is that whatever we find, better be close. He seems like the kind of guy to complain if it's too far away."

"Sometimes places that are available for sale or rent have signs out," Flek offered. "Don't know the area, but I can look for signs. Haven't seen any yet, but we could just walk up and down the streets looking."

"Honestly, that's probably the best idea," Wyndi admitted, even though it annoyed her to cede a point to the goblin. "At least it's not raining. It's a bit chilly, but no rain."

"Speaking of chili," Legs said, patting his stomach. "I could go for a nice warm bowl of spicy chili. Think we can find someplace come lunchtime?"

"You know that wasn't what I meant," Wyndi admonished him. "I meant it's cold. But I guess, with it being so cold, a bowl of chili wouldn't be bad—as long as it isn't too spicy. But let's hold off on food until we've looked around."

"Fine, fine," Legs reluctantly said, shaking his head. "We can look for a workshop first. I know a good place for lunch, though, that serves soups in hollowed-out loaves of sourdough bread. They might have some chili on the menu today."

"Really?" Flek bounced excitedly. "We're definitely going there. Too bad we can't go yet."

"All you two think of is food," Wyndi grumbled. "There's more to life than food."

She frowned, annoyed with herself that she couldn't find joy in the idea of a sourdough bread bowl full of steamy chili. A small bowl of chili would be fine, but in a bowl made of bread? She doubted she could evade the temptation to eat the entire bowl.

"Sure, there's more to life than food," Flek said. "But not much can make you a lot happier. What do you have against food? The gods only know it makes me happy."

"It's easy for you," she said, looking him up and down. "You must have the metabolism of a wild vornash. It seems the food I eat loves to collect in my thighs, belly, or rear."

"So?" Flek asked, somewhat rhetorically. "What does that matter? I never paid much attention until you pointed it out. But even now that you said it, it looks good on you."

The goblin's cheeks took on a lavender hue, and he averted his eyes.

"Whatever," Wyndi dismissed him. "What do you know? You're a guy. But let's drop it. I'll have some chili at lunch. Don't worry about it."

The mood seemed to have soured, and the trio fell into silence as they walked through the crisp autumn air, scanning the buildings for signs indicating they might be available. While she didn't see any signs, Wyndi did appreciate the trees which looked stunning with their multi-colored leaves full of rich reds, oranges, and yellows.

After walking for some time without a word, Legs was the first to spot something.

"Hey, look over there. Do you see the sign in the upper window? It looks like the space on the fourth floor is available."

"It is! You're right," Wyndi said, squinting while looking where he pointed.

"Let's go ask them," Flek said as he took off jogging toward the building. "You think the owner is on the first floor?"

As it turned out, the first-floor space belonged to a tailor, or rather, he rented it.

"Interested in the fourth-floor spot, are you?" he asked. "It is available for rent, but I'm not the owner. He did give me leave to show it off to interested parties. I'll take you up."

"Thanks!" Wyndi smiled hopefully. "If you wouldn't mind, that would be wonderful."

"No trouble at all," the elven tailor, whose name turned out to be Tanisian, said. "As you can see, I don't have a single customer at the moment. I've just been working on hemming several pairs of pants someone recently dropped off. Or wait. You wouldn't happen to need tailor services, would you?"

"Not really?" Legs answered with half a question. "We really just need a new workshop."

Tanisian's face fell, but he quickly recovered. He likely hadn't thought there was much of a chance, but it was clear he was, first and foremost, a businessman looking for leads anywhere he could find them.

"That's fine. Expected as much. Follow me."

The elf led them outside and then up a switchback set of stairs to the fourth floor. On the way, Wyndi wondered how they would manage to move all of the equipment up all of these stairs. That was definitely one knock against this place, and they hadn't even seen the room.

Why did the space have to be on such a high floor?, Wyndi thought as they emptied out of the staircase onto the fourth-floor walkway. Tanisian led them to the door and fished in a pocket for longer than she thought necessary before pulling out a key and opening it.

Inside was spacious, with quite a lot of light coming in from the windows. That could be good or bad for a workshop. It would be nice to have the extra light to see by during the day, but on days with a lot of sun, they would likely have to put up heavy drapes. Otherwise, they would risk the sunlight interfering too much with their projects. She knew enough from her limited training that before an item was complete, external stimuli of any sort could impact the components significantly.

Several large tables broke up the space. Only a few were fixtures that were built-in and attached to the flooring. The rest could be moved around if needed. Only one was at an acceptable height for a gnome, and that could prove troublesome. Legs likely wouldn't care and actually might even be happy that the rest of them were better suited for his size. Most of them were nearly as high as his waist.

"I'm not sure," Wyndi said as her eyes scanned the room in an appraising manner. "It's enough space, which is good. That's what we need. More space."

"Yeah, but get a load of these tables," Flek blurted. "Some of them, I can barely see the surface even if I stand on my toes."

"We don't have to use them," she pointed out. "I'm sure we can move most of them out of the way. Only a few are attached to the floor."

"I don't see a problem," Legs added, not so helpfully. "Makes it a lot easier to work on projects, actually."

"I figured you'd say that," Wyndi said, rolling her eyes. "You're outnumbered. It's three to one. We need to reverse the ratio of smaller tables to larger ones."

"Fine," Legs said, pouting. She suspected he was just pretending to pout. He knew the limitations of most of the group when it came to the height of the tables. "Like you said, I'm sure we can move most of them out and replace them with shorter versions."

"So, how much is it?" Wyndi asked.

"Oh. Well. Right," the elf hedged. "I knew that question would be coming. Mind you, I'm not the owner. I didn't set the price."

"It can't be that high," Flek laughed.

"Ahem. I don't like to speak of things I don't have any control over," Tanisian said, wringing his hands together. "I'll just give you the standard note I've been instructed to share with prospective renters."

The elf pulled a small piece of parchment from his pocket and handed it to Wyndi. She unfolded it and scanned it silently.

"You've got to be kidding me!" she practically screamed. "Is this a joke? Who in their right mind would pay this? Or wait. Maybe I misunderstood. Is this per year? Yes. It must be per year. I had been thinking of the monthly rent. I can just mentally divide."

"No. No," Tanisian said, waving his hands to get her attention. "Don't divide. That's the monthly price. I first signed on several years ago, and my rent is significantly lower. It's gone up in small increments over the years, but it's nowhere near what he wants to charge new tenants. I'm sorry, but that's the monthly rent."

"Ludicrous," Wyndi announced. "Flickerwhizzle would never pay that much. He didn't give us a budget, but I can tell he would consider this insulting."

Tanisian sighed.

"Did you really think we'd agree to that?" Legs asked, looking the elf in the eye.

"Honestly? No. I didn't. But you wanted to see the space, and I've promised the owner I would show anyone interested."

"You could have led with the price and saved us all a lot of time," Wyndi pointed out. "This has been a waste. But I suppose it isn't entirely your fault. Let's go find some lunch. Legs, take us to that spot with the soup."

"If you're sure?" the elf questioned, trying to stop them and potentially salvage a deal.

"Quite sure," Flek said. "It's time for lunch. The tables in here were too tall anyway."

Legs led the way to lunch, which turned out to be at a place called Joy Filled Bowls of Bread.

A server sat them at a round table inside the cozy restaurant. It wasn't big, holding only six tables, but the snug space was full of warmth both from the fire in the hearth and the knick-knacky decorations adorning the wall. Someone crafty was partnered up with the soup cook.

"I recognize one of you," the server said, nodding toward Legs, "but not the rest. Do you need to hear the menu? Or would you prefer to read it?"

"Not necessary," Legs answered. "All three of us will have a sourdough bowl full of chili if there is any on the fire today."

"There is," the half-orc server answered. "I'll bring three bowls out shortly."

"You two are going to love this," Legs told them, rubbing his hands together in anticipation.

"From what you described before, it sounds amazing," Flek said, licking his tongue over his fangs yet again. Wyndi wasn't at all sure if she found it endearing or annoying. That was the thing about this goblin. There was a lot she wasn't sure of about him, making her uneasy and awkward around him.

"So, that place," Wyndi said, pulling her mind away from places it didn't belong. "I'd say that's a no, right? There's no way Zaq would shell out that much. Right?"

"Your assessment seems sound," Legs nodded.

Wyndi felt somewhat bad for him. They had been seated at a lower table, and he was compensating by sitting cross-legged on a pillow on the floor rather than in a chair. His torso was so tall. His head was pretty much at head level for her and Flek.

"He definitely seems tight with money," Flek agreed. "I'm glad I have some saved up. I noticed our contracts don't account for any pay. I knew apprentices don't usually get much, but I was hoping for something to help with the expenses here in the city. Stuff costs more here than back home. Or maybe there's just more stuff I want to buy? I don't know."

Before anyone could comment, the server returned and set down three plates. Each held a round loaf of sourdough bread. A slice had been cut off the top, and it balanced at an angle. The loaf had been hollowed out and filled with a thick, rich chili full of bits of meat, beans, onions, peppers, and a thick tomato base. Raw onions and shreds of yellow cheese decorated the top. The cheese was already melting, disappearing into the chili.

"I'm not surprised there was no pay," Wyndi said, picking up the top slice of bread and tearing it in half. "It's rare to get paid for apprenticeships, especially from someone with a lot of renown. The pay is basically them teaching you. Some do offer a small something or even a place to live and food to eat."

Wyndi thrust the crusty slice of bread into the chili and brought it back out, dripping with steamy goodness. Bits of meat and peppers clung to it, and before they could fall, she brought it to her mouth and took a bite. *Damn. This was good.* The chili was definitely worth breaking her eating habits for. Besides, what had Flek said? *It looks good on you.* What does a goblin know, anyway? She put him out of her thoughts and took another bite.

"Depending on what kind of workshop we find, some, maybe even all of us, could stay at the workshop if you need a place," Legs said after swallowing a large spoonful of chili.

"I might just do that," Flek said. "If there's room, I mean. Once the others head back to Chubug, it's either that or find someplace affordable to rent."

"We'll keep that in mind while looking," Wyndi agreed. "I'm pretty sure we could all stand to save some money, so crashing at the workshop would be ideal."

"Of course," Legs interjected, waving his thankfully empty spoon at them. "We may not need a place to stay if he sends us out right away to get those materials. We don't have the coin to purchase them, so that means leaving town. If anything, we may need some camping gear."

Chapter 11

Gardening

Although the townhouse was narrow, the lot was twice as long as the house. The backyard was fenced off from his neighbors by natural-looking growth Zaq had planted around the entire perimeter. He had chosen a variety of shrubs, tall bushes, and trees. In some sections, he had installed posts with latticework trellises mounted on them, covered with flowering vines.

During the warmer months, Zaq spent time out in the yard, either relaxing with a good book in one of the lawn chairs or tending to his vegetable garden and the living fence around the yard. There was something about a garden that made gnomes feel at home, and Zaq was no different, even if he was an artificer at heart.

With the youngsters out hunting for a suitable workshop, he found he had time on his hands. The days and nights were getting colder, and seeing the decorations on the houses on his walk to the Inn Side Out reminded Zaq that he should collect most, if not all, of the remaining crops from his garden.

A large pumpkin, over half as tall as the gnome, instilled a sense of pride in Zaq. He had been holding off cutting it from the vine, but now was as good a time as any. He planned to use it as the centerpiece of his front yard harvest scene. In addition, he had several other nice-looking gourds that he felt would complement the pumpkin if he arranged them well.

Using a gardening knife, Zaq cut the pumpkin from the vine and did the same with the multicolored gourds he had selected. He decided to roll the pumpkin to the front yard, so he lifted it onto its side and then got behind it. Putting his shoulder into it, he shoved back, digging his feet into the ground. The thing was an absolute beast, but once it began to roll, he found it was round enough; he just needed to keep his hands on it and take purposeful steps to keep the momentum going.

If you were looking at the back of the house, on the left side, a path wound from the garden, under an archway covered in vines, and out into the front yard. Zaq rolled the pumpkin along this path, and thankfully, it just fit through the arch, but the stem caught on a piece of vine, pulling it off. It was regrettable, but it would grow back.

Zaq gave one last shove and stood back to look.

"Yes, that looks like a wonderful spot."

Just as he was about to push the pumpkin over onto its base, the blasted black fiend appeared and sat directly in the way.

"What are you doing?" Zaq practically screamed at the cat.

"You could have gotten squished if I hadn't noticed. It would serve you right. Maybe that wouldn't be the worst thing."

Zaq nodded but failed to convince himself that it was actually reasonable to topple the pumpkin onto the cat. Of course, it would likely move. Yes, it would definitely move.

"Last warning, move, or you might be squished. I'm going to push this over now."

The cat stared at him with haunting yellow eyes.

"Fine. Be that way."

Zaq walked behind the pumpkin to the stem and unwound the piece of vine that had been snagged. He tossed it aside, and while shoving his shoulder into the pumpkin, he tumbled it over onto the base.

As the enormous winter squash fell forward, a streak of black raced from under it to Samantha's yard. A screeching *merr-OW* cut through the previously quiet autumn day. It seemed it did have some self-preservation instincts, after all. The pumpkin continued falling, landing with a muted *thud*.

Zaq dusted his hands and noticed the cat glaring at him from the neighboring yard. Much of the hair along its back was puffed out, and its tail stood straight up, about three times the diameter it usually was. He merely shook his head and returned to the backyard. On the way back, he grabbed an empty basket from its place, leaning against the house, which he filled with the gourds he had selected.

A guffaw escaped him when he rounded the corner and found the cat staring him in the eye from its new perch on top of the giant pumpkin.

"I suppose you can't get into trouble if you are up there. You might even make a nice addition to my autumn tableau."

Zaq arranged the gourds around the base of the pumpkin, filling in small nooks and empty spots with a collection of dried, colored leaves.

Standing back with his hands on his hips, he nodded in satisfaction.

"That looks lovely, and that darn cat does actually improve it. Oh! Wait. That's a great idea."

After quickly hustling into the house, Zaq returned a few moments later with a brown wool blanket covered in fibrous pills, which showed its age and history of use. He shook it out, then refolded it into a pad he judged to be the right size. The cat seemed to realize what was happening and happily hopped onto the blanket as he slid it into place on top of the pumpkin.

A rumbling purr got louder as the creature rubbed its head into Zaq's hand, and then it danced about on the blanket for a few moments before curling up into a ball in the center.

"Of course, that may not be nearly so comfy the next time it rains. I'll have to keep an eye on the weather."

With the harvest scene complete, Zaq grabbed the basket and returned to the garden. He gathered almost all of the remaining vegetables and brought them inside the house.

"You know, I bet those new apprentices of mine would enjoy a meal tonight. And what about a treat? We could all use one, especially if they manage to find a workshop we can use."

Zaq split the gathered crops into piles. One pile he put in the KoldBox he had spelled to a cool temperature, but not freezing, unlike the other similar one he had painted an icy shade of blue, indicating its subzero temperatures. He put a pile of root vegetables in a wooden crate in the pantry. The rest he left out for his cooking and even added to the collection of items he didn't grow in his garden.

The gnome was practical and methodical in his cooking process. He had determined he wanted to make a large pot of vegetable soup and a pumpkin pie. After setting out the cast-iron pot, he diced an onion and sliced a full head of garlic. Next, he peeled several golden potatoes and two large sweet potatoes, then cut them into rough chunks.

Zaq followed this up by peeling and chopping three carrots. This year, he had planted an assorted set of seeds. He chose an orange, a yellow, and a purple.

While he had harvested several smaller sugar pumpkins from the garden, they would not do for the pie. He had some pumpkin puree in the KoldBox he had made a few days earlier that could be used instead. However, one of the sugar pumpkins would make a nice addition to the soup he was putting together, so he cut it open, scooped out the seeds, and cubed it into chunks similar in size to the potatoes.

With everything now prepped for the soup, it was time to make his crust for the pie so it would have time to chill. Zaq opted for a simple crust dough made of flour, salt, water, and, of course, butter, which he cut into it, gently mixing it all together. He formed it into a rough, thick disc and put it in the KoldBox to chill.

"Back to the soup, I should think. The flavors will develop better if it simmers for most of the afternoon. Once I have it going, I can switch back to the pie with plenty of time to get it in the oven."

Zaq poured a generous amount of oil into the cast-iron pot he had set out on the stove, then lit the burner. Once the oil seemed hot enough, he added the diced onion. The oil hissed and sizzled as he stirred the onion. He dumped a mound of salt into his palm until it looked about right and poured it over the glistening onion. After a good stir, he let that simmer.

Once the onion was starting to become clear, he added the sliced garlic. Zaq continued stirring occasionally until both looked translucent and were beginning to brown.

"Now for some spices."

Zaq scraped the onion and garlic out of the center of the pot and tossed in spoonfuls of turmeric, thyme, coarse-ground black pepper, cinnamon, coriander, and nutmeg into the oily center, along with some spicy dried pepper flakes and a pinch of very hot powdered chili. He stirred the spices on the hot surface, toasting them slightly. The aroma filled his nostrils, letting him know they were ready.

After quickly combining the spices with the onion and garlic, he tossed in all of the other ingredients he had chopped earlier, stirring them all together with his wooden spoon. He poured in enough water to thoroughly cover everything and topped it off with a cup of cream. After mixing, he left it to simmer while he focused on the pie filling.

He combined his pumpkin puree from the other day with eggs, heavy cream, salt, sugar, cinnamon, cloves, ginger, and nutmeg in a bowl and whisked it together. Zaq then took his crust back out of the KoldBox and rolled it out until it was thin enough to fill his pie plate.

After laying the crust on the pie plate, he trimmed off the excess dough and set it aside, then pinched the crust to make a nice pattern around the edge. Finally, he poured his pumpkin custard in, filling the crust to the point where he had made his pinched ruffles.

Realizing he still had the leftover dough scraps, he had wadded them into a ball. He rolled the ball out flat, brushed it with butter, and sprinkled cinnamon and sugar in a light dusting over the crust. He smiled as he put it on a flat baking sheet. The leftover crust would make a delightful snack with some tea later that afternoon.

Zaq slid the pie and the extra baking sheet of crust into the oven, feeling quite satisfied with what he had accomplished.

"I hope those kids come back hungry. Now, I just have to clean up this mess."

Chapter 12

Cause and Effect

"There has to be someplace suitable," Wyndi declared, once again trying to convince herself, if not the other two apprentices, that they would not fail their quest.

After lunch, the trio had been through three different possible workshops. One had been much too small. It was barely bigger than the current workshop at Zaq's house. Another was on the top floor of an eight-story building. The room had been big enough and the view of the Mirador Sea was wonderful, but climbing that many stairs, especially with equipment for a workshop, would be awful. While less per month than the first place they had seen, the lovely view pushed the price up higher than she thought the old gnome would be comfortable with. A nice view wasn't really necessary to craft artificer inventions.

The third space looked quite promising, but the catkin owner had warned Wyndi he already had someone else interested. Sure enough, while they had been looking at the potential space, a drake with shimmering purple scales had poked his head in the doorway.

"Excuse me, am I interrupting? I've verified with my partners. We'll take the space."

"Of course. Of course," the catkin had said, sweeping a hand over his head to smooth his already perfect burnt-orange hair. He at least had the grace to give Wyndi a look with an apology in his eyes. "I'm so sorry, but unless you can agree right now to a higher price, I'm afraid the room is no longer available."

And that had been that. They were back to square one with no leads.

"I agree," Legs said. "I'm not giving up. The city is large enough; there has to be a good spot. We likely have to spread out farther. Flickerwhizzle won't love it, but if it's a good space, I'm sure it will work out."

"We aren't too far from that Mystic shop run by the dwarves," Flek tossed in. "We could always strategize the next best places to look over some tea. I could use a break."

"I doubt there's much to strategize about, but I wouldn't mind sitting and re-energizing with something warm to drink," Wyndi agreed. "The chill in the air gets to you after a while, even with all the walking we've done."

Flek was right. They weren't that far from the teashop, so Wyndi led them down the street they were on, then cut through a narrow alley, and from there, it was only a bit further down the road.

At mid-afternoon, it seemed several people had a similar idea. The outdoor seating area was over half-full, but there were still plenty of tables to choose from. Wyndi chose one and waved for the others to sit down.

"I'm going to get some dragonroot. I think it fits the day. Do you two want something different? Or should I order a full pot for the table?"

"I'm good with dragonroot," Flek said. "I wouldn't mind a muffin or a slice of sweet bread. In fact, we can all have a snack, my treat, since you're getting the tea. Here's some coin."

"Thanks, Flek," Legs flashed his bright white teeth in a jovial smile down at the goblin. "I'll have dragonroot as well, then, so Wyndi can get the pot for the table. Next time's on me."

Well, today was already shot as far as her diet. Wyndi was sure the other two apprentices were not going to be a good influence when it came to eating. Still, it was more fun this way and more sociable.

She entered the small teashop and waited while an ashen-skinned half-elf ordered in front of her. He asked for green tea blended with mint, which was more of a summery drink. Zheb took the man's coin and told him to wait at the end of the counter if he wasn't staying on the patio.

The half-elf nodded and walked to the end of the counter, and the dwarf turned to Wyndi.

"Ah, you're vizz zee group of would-be apprentices, aren't you?"

"Yes, sir, but not so would-be anymore."

"Oh, really? Vell, I'm sure you'll be a big help to Zaq, likely in more vays zen he's aware of."

"What do you mean by that? He's got all types of ridiculous quests lined up for us. It seems he is quite aware of our help."

"I'm sure zat's true enough," Zheb nodded. "But zat old gnome needs to open up and trust ossers more. I have a feeling you sree will be a good influence. But enough gossiping about Zaq. I'm sure he vouldn't sink kindly of me talking behind his back. Just cut him a bit of slack if he gets too short viz you or doesn't share enough. Now, vat vas it you vanted to order?"

"We'd like a pot of dragonroot tea for the table, and please bring some sugar and cream with it. I'm not sure how the guys like theirs. We'd also like a baked treat. Maybe a muffin? Some sweet bread? I'd even be up for some cookies."

"Joh's been baking all day, so vee have all sree of zose options," Zheb smiled proudly. Wyndi could tell he admired his partner's skill in the kitchen. "However, he just pulled a tray out of zee oven full of oatmeal cookies viz dried tingleberries. If zat helps sway you one vay or anosser."

The thought of warm, freshly baked oatmeal cookies brought a smile to the young gnome's face. The dried berries were sure to be gooey. Pulling herself out of her thoughts, she realized she still needed to answer the dwarf.

"Sorry, I got lost in my head, or rather my tummy, just thinking of those cookies. Please send three of those out with the tea. We're sitting out on the patio."

Zheb chucked at her daydreaming and gave her the total. Wyndi stacked the coins and slid them over to him.

"Sank you. I vill bring it out shortly."

Wyndi returned to the table, where Legs and Flek were deep in conversation.

"What did I miss?"

"Oh, it's probably nothing," Legs said, absently scratching his head.

"It might be something, but I think he doesn't know enough yet to know if you get what I'm saying," Flek offered somewhat helpfully.

"I was just telling Flek that I'm worried about that project Flickerwhizzle is working on. He didn't seem too interested in letting me add any comments or questions, though."

"What are you worried about?" Wyndi asked, but kept going without letting him answer. "It seems pretty interesting. Imagine being able to send a message out to multiple people or even just one person without having to give them a connected scroll."

"I'm just not sure about the power," Legs said, tossing the hair back out of his face with a well-practiced shake of his head. "It seems like it will take a lot of mana. He seems to think he's got it covered, and I probably just don't have all the context, but are there enough protections against it burning out? It's fine. I should just watch and learn. That's why we got him to bring us on as apprentices."

"One hundred percent that," Wyndi nodded. "I'm pretty sure he's been thinking about this problem a lot longer than—well, probably longer than you've been alive."

"Yeah, he seems to know his stuff," Flek added. "The way he explained everything while drawing on that slate was great. I felt like I was learning already. I just wish he had given more details. I couldn't even begin to understand how any of it would work. He kept it too high level."

"I'm sure he'll share more," Wyndi defended the old gnome, thinking about what Zheb had just said inside. "We've only had one session with him. Of course, that's likely all we'll get if we don't find a workshop."

"Vat is zat about a vorkshop?" Zheb asked as he approached with a cart. "I sought Zaq had a nice vorkshop already? He's mentioned it before."

"It's a very nice workshop, especially if there is only a single gnome or maybe two working in it," Wyndi explained. "Unfortunately, with two gnomes, a goblin, and a human, it gets pretty crowded. We already had one incident yesterday with a minor injury."

"It wasn't an injury," Legs rebuked. "You make it sound like a bigger deal than it was."

Wyndi rolled her eyes. She didn't really want to get into the details of what happened with the owner of the teashop.

"Anyway, what happened doesn't matter. The issue at hand is that we have been out all day trying to find a larger space for a workshop. We haven't had any luck so far."

"Hmmm," Zheb mused as he stroked his beard. "Did you know zat Joh and I have carved out a home under zee tea shop? Currently, vee live in rooms under the shop building and zis large patio. However, it vas more economical to purchase below-surface rights to a larger area and have zee crew carve a much larger space."

Zheb paused and looked back over his shoulder at the tea shop.

"I vould have to talk to Joh, but vee already have an entrance in zee alley behind zee shop and vee almost never use it. Vee could lock up the door into our home from zat entrance and zen you could use zee rest zat spans zee area under zee building behind zee shop."

"Really?" Wyndi's eyes lit up. "That sounds like it could work and would be super close to Zaq's place, which I know he'd appreciate. Can we see the space? Or, I guess you said you need to talk to Joh first."

"Yes, yes. I vill show you zee space, but first I talk to Joh. You enjoy your tea and cookies."

The dwarf left them, walking back toward the shop.

"How amazing would that be if this works out?" Wyndi asked the others.

Legs picked up the teapot and poured each of them a cupful.

"I'd say we got pretty lucky if it does. Of course, we didn't even talk price. I doubt Flickerwhizzle will lay out too much, even if it is close."

Flek grabbed a cookie and poured a splash of cream into his tea.

"I knew I had a good idea stopping for tea. Not only are we having a nice break, but I just found us a workshop."

"You didn't find anything," Wyndi said, creasing her brow. "I'm the one who told him we were looking for a space."

"It's all cause and effect," Flek said, chewing a bite of his cookie. "If it all stems from my idea to stop for tea, the details of who said what don't really matter."

"That's not at all how cause and effect works," Wyndi said and took a sip of tea to calm herself. She had a feeling he was purposefully trying to get under her skin.

"If you say so," Flek grinned. "But it may all depend on who tells Zaq."

"Honestly," Wyndi sighed. "Not everything has to be a competition."

"Sounds like you don't care who tells him, then. I'll take on that burden," Flek said before sticking a bite that was a little too large into his mouth.

Ignoring the bait, Wyndi broke off a small piece of her own cookie. It still felt very warm between her fingers. The sweet cinnamon playing off the nutty oats hit her tongue first, but as she chewed, the tang from the tingleberries combined in a delightful way that made her forget Flek and put a smile on her face.

"These cookies are unreal," Legs said with his mouth still full of a bite. He swallowed and took a sip of tea. "Sorry. I should have swallowed first, but I honestly couldn't help it. Truly amazing. I suppose we might have a lot more wonderful treats in store for us if we can use the space for a workshop. It will be easy to take tea breaks."

Flek laughed, which caused him to choke. He calmed himself, but still snorted before he could comment.

"Maybe they won't charge too much for the space and

figure they can make up for it with increased sales from our frequent visits to the tea shop."

Chapter 13

This Smells Wonderful

The knock at the front door caught Zaq just as he was pulling the pie out of the oven. He started, and his hands wobbled, but there were no tragedies, and the pie made it safely to the counter. Dusting his hands on his pants, he scurried to the front door.

"We found the perfect spot," Flek announced when Zaq opened the door. No one was holding the cat this time, and sure enough, it took the opportunity to race in and hide. Zaq figured he would just have to track it down later.

"Come in, come in. You can tell me all about it. Make your way to the dining room. The soup should be done, so I'll dish you each a bowl. There's pie for dessert as well. I spent time harvesting the last of my garden while you were out."

"I saw your harvest scene out front," Wyndi commented. "It looks quite nice. Did you grow all of it in your garden?"

"I did indeed," Zaq beamed. "I thought it looked good, but that's easy to think when you make a thing. Thank you for confirming it."

"It was a nice touch putting that blanket on top so your cat has a bed," Frank added.

"It's not my cat," Zaq sighed. "But it did like the idea of using it as a perch, and adding an old blanket doesn't really hurt anyone, does it? Speaking of that cat, though, I may need your help after dinner to find it since you let it in."

"I'm sure we can get the cat out, Mr. Flickerwhizzle," Wyndi said, volunteering the group. "But we should tell you about the potential workshop first."

"I can tell him all about the workshop I found," Flek spoke up. "But I think he mentioned dinner, and I wouldn't want it to get cold. Let's go to the dining room."

"Hold up," Wyndi said. "We should stop by the kitchen and get a bowl. If anything, we should be serving him a bowl rather than him serving us. Go sit, Mr. Flickerwhizzle. Flek'll bring you a bowl, and Legs and I can get our own."

"That's kind of you," Zaq said. "There's a ladle in a utensil jar on the counter."

Zaq walked to the dining room instead of the kitchen and sat at the table. A few moments later, the apprentices filed in, each with a bowl of soup, except for Flek, who held two, one of which he placed in front of him.

The apprentices each took a seat at the table, with Wyndi across from Flek, and Frank taking a seat on a low stool next to the goblin.

"This smells wonderful," Flek said, running his tongue over his fangs. "But I'll try it in a moment. You need to hear about the space. It's under the building behind the Mystic Leaf & Toadstool that is run by that dwarven couple. They aren't using the space and plan to just keep the back door to their home locked. The price seemed reasonable, but you can likely hammer out an exact amount you are happy with when you talk to Zheb and Joh."

"It's a great size," Wyndi added, looking to Zaq like she was stopping the goblin from scooping all of the credit. "Plenty of room for a workshop, another smaller room that one or more of us could stay in if we needed a place to sleep, and a simple room with a toilet and sink."

Frank didn't have much to add and instead was focused on eating his soup. Zaq thought the human talked less than the other two by at least half.

"I had no idea those dwarves had so much underground space," Zaq said, setting down his spoon. "That would definitely be a convenient spot. Not far to walk, plus easy access to tea and tasty treats."

"That's what I thought!" Flek exclaimed. "I like a break in the afternoon, and the teashop right upstairs makes that easy."

Zaq's large spoon caught some potato and carrot in a shallow pool of spicy broth. He blew on it slightly, more out of instinct than actual necessity. The potato fell apart in his mouth, and he chewed gently on the carrot. The creamy broth burst with flavor, and he wondered if he had perhaps been too heavy-handed with the spices. They played nicely against the garlic, though, and personally, he liked a lot of flavor in his soup. No one seemed to be complaining, so that was a good sign.

"So, when is the space available? Can we move equipment from my workshop here to over there soon?"

"Zheb said we could start using it as soon as we were ready, as long as you were okay with the rent," Wyndi explained.

"Honestly, I'm not sure how much I should expect rent to be," Zaq admitted. "I'll chat with him and make sure I'm getting the best deal. I do have to watch my expenses now that I'm retired."

"Should we show up here ready to move your equipment tomorrow?" Frank asked.

"Yes. Yes. I think that would be good," Zaq said. "I'll get over there first thing in the morning and seal the deal. I should have everything set with them by the time you come over. We can spend tomorrow moving everything and getting it set up. Then the next day, you three can leave."

"Leave?" Flek asked, quickly swallowing the spoonful of soup he had just stuck in his mouth.

"Of course," Zaq nodded. "You need to fetch the materials I need for the project. No point kicking that down the road."

"Yes, we agreed to get your materials," Wyndi said. "But—but I think we were all just hoping we'd have a chance to learn a bit more beforehand. The explanation you started to give us was good, but it was quite high-level. We'd like some more practical learning."

"I'll get to that," Zaq said, spreading his arms out. "We'll cover that and a lot more. I just need those materials first. There is one thing more important than learning or gathering materials."

"There is?" Flek asked.

"Yes," Zaq nodded sagely. "We need to have some pie. It looks like everyone has finished their soup. Should I cut up the pie?"

"Yes!" Flek answered before anyone else could say anything.

The other two apprentices nodded their agreement and helped to stack the used bowls together. Zaq took the stack into the kitchen, leaving them to talk amongst themselves, but they continued to speak to him, just raising their voices louder.

"Assuming we can get everything moved quickly, could you take the time to show us some practical artificery?" Wyndi called. He heard a great deal of hope in her question.

"If there is time, I'll go over one or two things," Zaq yelled back after setting the bowls in the sink.

He started cutting the pie when he heard Frank's voice boom.

"That list of items will take several trips, and we can't be expected to turn around immediately and leave after retrieving each one. It seems you could do a bit more teaching during our brief rest between outings."

"I'm not entirely sure you can't just collect them all in one foray out into the world," Zaq called back, frowning. "But, you may be right. Now that I think through where you might have to look for the items, they could be in different directions."

"You know, there really wasn't much point in finding a bigger workshop if you were just going to send us away," Flek said from the doorway. "Need any help carrying the pie to the other room?"

"What?" Zaq asked absently, looking back toward where the goblin stood. "Oh, yes. Wonderful. Here, you take two plates, and I'll take two."

Flek walked over and grabbed a couple of plates holding thick slices of pumpkin pie, balancing a fork on each one. Zaq grabbed the other two and followed him out to the other room.

Zaq set a plate in front of Frank, and Flek gave one to Wyndi, then sat with his plate, ready to dive in.

The pie was impressive-looking with a crust that was flaky and golden brown. Its dark amber filling looked well set and full of spice flecks. Zaq wished he had made some whipped cream, but he used the last of his heavy cream in the soup. He would need to get some more from the market.

"Well, dig in," Zaq said. "I'm sure going to."

He forked a bite of the pie into his mouth, and the creamy custard melted on his tongue. The rich pumpkin flavor spiked heavily with cinnamon and ginger caused him to sigh contentedly. He took a moment to savor it before composing himself.

"I think there was a point, Flek, even if it isn't clear to you,"

Zaq answered the question the goblin had asked in the kitchen as if there had been no pause in the conversation. "I don't know how long it will take you to gather everything, but I wanted to be ready as soon as you had obtained all we needed. A good lesson for this evening is that preparedness and good planning are crucial to proper engineering."

"I've heard people calling artificers engineers," Wyndi commented. "Where does that come from? We aren't engineering anything, are we?"

"Of course we are," Zaq chuckled. "Artificers engineer solutions and items by melding technology and magic using runes. It's perfectly reasonable to call what we do engineering, and you can certainly call me an engineer. I'd be proud of it."

"Almost no one uses the term artificer in the warren," Flek added. "Anyone practicing artificery is just called an engineer."

"I suppose it may be somewhat regional as well," Zaq nodded. "A good point. Ryefeld has so many folks from all over; it makes sense that a combination of words is used for similar names and concepts."

Frank swallowed the last bite of his pie and wiped his mouth with a napkin.

"I can't believe you cooked all of this food today. The soup was superb, and that pie—well, let's just say I find myself having to hold back from marching into the kitchen for whatever is left."

"Thank you," Zaq said, beaming. "I find a lot of overlap between cooking and artificery. I treat both in a very exacting manner. Plus, it's an amazing feeling when you put in the effort and get to consume the fruits of your labor."

"I agree," Wyndi added. "I've always loved cooking, but I rarely have the time. My mother taught me how to bake. I think when I was younger, I got a little too carried away with how many baked goods I ate."

"Nonsense," Zaq rebuked. "One can never have too many baked goods. A happy gnome has a large, happy belly."

Wyndi simply shrugged, but whatever she was thinking didn't stop her from continuing to eat the pie.

The three continued to pepper Zaq with questions while they ate their dessert. When they had finished, Frank stood up and started gathering the plates.

"You can just put those in the sink," Zaq instructed. "I'll get it all cleaned up later."

"I'm sorry. I can't do that, sir," Frank said, walking the pile of dishes to the kitchen. "After all of that cooking, I must insist on cleaning this up for you."

"I'll dry," Wyndi volunteered.

"And I'll stay here and keep Mr. Flickerwhizzle company," Flek grinned. "Should I pour us an after-dinner drink? Do you have any spirits?"

"I can tell you may be the smartest of my apprentices," Zaq said, smiling widely. "I do have some whisky, but I'll get everyone a glass. You and I can get started sipping while the other two clean up."

At that, he walked to the sitting room, poured four glasses of hay-colored single malt, and returned in short order with the glasses.

"A toast to a successful hunt for a workshop," Zaq said, holding up a glass to Flek. "Thank you for finding it, Flek."

Flek grabbed a glass and raised it to clink against Zaq's.

A shout from the kitchen broke their celebratory moment. Wyndi's voice was infused with frustration.

"He did not find it! It was a joint effort, and Zheb offered it as a suggestion after I told him what we were looking for."

Chapter 14

Efficient Artificery

Zheb waved at the approaching trio as Wyndi led them down the street toward the cafe. He was out on the covered patio helping a human couple at one of the two-person tables. By the time they reached the patio and passed through the weather shielding into the warmth, he had finished and came over to speak with them.

"Good morning! Zaq and I have made a deal. All is set. You remember the vay down, off course. Do you need somesing to eat or drink?"

"No thanks, we had breakfast at the inn when we picked up Flek," Wyndi declined politely. "So, Mr. Flickerwhizzle is downstairs already?"

"Yes, yes. I sink he is planning out zee vorkshop space."

"Great, we'll head on down then," she said, flashing him a friendly smile. "I'm sure we'll need a break at some point and will come up to see what you have to snack on today."

"I am sure you vill find somesing to your liking. Good luck today."

Flek took off toward the back alley stairs, Wyndi and Legs

following up quickly behind him. The stairs down were narrow, and they formed up with Flek in front, then Wyndi, and Legs bringing up the rear of the group. The goblin ran into the open doorway on the right side of the small hallway as soon as he bounded from the second to the last stair.

When Wyndi entered the soon-to-be workshop, she saw Flek had stopped not far into the room, and he was watching Zaq intently. The old gnome held a wand-like device in his hand and was using it to take measurements around the room.

He would tap the wand on a wall, floor, or ceiling, then tap another spot some distance away. Each time he completed a second tap, the wand emitted a mechanical-sounding voice.

"Twenty-five point five zero zero two rods."

"Fifteen point zero zero three one rods."

After each, Zaq scribbled some notes on a small pad of paper.

Wyndi had learned of rods in her initial artificer studies, but other than in a few small personal projects, she had never tried using measurements with them. Supposedly, in the ancient gnomish kingdom of Coggsdeep, the high artificers had a vault sealed from all of the elements, including time. There was only one item in the vault: a metal rod made of adamantium. The rod's length was a single standardized unit of distance measurement. While its weight was a single unit of mass. The gnomes created their primary unit of time as the rod's age at the time they sealed the vault.

In a move that confused everyone except the gnomes, the rod was the unit used for all three measurements. This meant you could often only tell what it actually referred to by context. If someone said something was three rods, you had to understand from what they were referring to if they meant the length, the weight, or the span of time.

However, as a fundamental unit of measurement, the rod

was extremely useful. The rod measurement system was a base-ten system. A decarod was ten rods, a centarod was ten decarods, a kilorod was ten centarods, and so on. It also worked for smaller measurements. A decirod was one-tenth of a rod, a centirod was one-tenth of a decirod, a milirod was one-tenth of a centirod, and so on.

"Oh! Greetings and salutations, my apprentices," Zaq said, looking up from his scribbling and noticing the group for the first time. "I've been taking measurements to determine the best configuration for the space. I believe I know where everything should go, so now, we just need the things so they may be put in their proper places."

"Right, and did you want us to start hauling stuff over now?" Wyndi asked. "Do you have a cart or something similar we can use? It's going to take a long time if we have to carry it all in our arms."

"I'm not carrying anything all the way from his place," Flek protested. "There better be a cart."

"I have a cart, don't you worry," Zaq assured them. "There is a large shed behind the house. Inside, you'll find a cart. You can load as much as you can in there and haul the cart here. Of course, you'll need to bring it downstairs yourselves."

"You know," Flek said, scratching his bearded chin. "If you first taught us a bit more artificery, we could build an automaton. Then, we could have it carry everything. We could even make more than one."

"No," Zaq shook his head firmly. "You are much too inexperienced to control an automaton. It is safer for everyone if you just carry everything. So, get to it. The house is unlocked. Just be careful of the cat. I never did find it last night."

"Not a problem, Mr. Flickerwhizzle," Legs said. "We'll be back soon with the first cartload."

On the way to the artificer's house, Flek pestered Legs.

"You give in to him much too easily. If we pressed him, we not only could have learned something, but we wouldn't have to hurt ourselves carrying his heavy equipment."

"I seriously doubt he would let you build an automaton," Wyndi huffed. "But, Legs did give in a bit too quickly. I'm sure we could have gotten some more help."

"The sooner we get everything moved, the sooner he'll actually teach us something," Legs explained. "You heard him at dinner last night. He wants to send us out right away. If we take too long moving everything, we won't get any instructions before we need to leave."

"That's a fair point," Wyndi sighed. "Fine. Maybe it wasn't so bad giving in so quickly. He was never going to agree to the idea of an automaton in any case."

"Maybe not an automaton," Flek retorted. "But what if he had some sort of hovering platform or some tool? Anything that might help make it easier."

"It does seem like he doesn't use as many artificery items as I might expect," Wyndi said. "Maybe we can find some useful things in his workshop. We have to move it all anyway. Why not check to see how it works before moving it?"

The house wasn't that far from the Mystic tea shop, and after only a few minutes, Legs pulled open the door on the shed in the backyard. The inside of the shed was quite neat. Zaq seemed more like the fastidious inventor type than the zany scientist type of artificer. He had arranged a collection of yard and garden tools along one wall, along with stacks of baskets and sacks. A large cart occupied most of the space.

Well, it was large to Wyndi, Flek, and Zaq. Legs seemed to have no problem grabbing two handles that jutted out from the front of the frame and wheeling it out of the shed. Even fully loaded, the three of them should have no trouble getting the cart to the workshop.

The tall human wheeled the cart out in front of the house and backed it up just in front of the door. Wyndi opened the door for them, and a black blur of fur raced out. Then, the cat practically did a backflip as she realized something was different.

Mee-ow.

The cat sat staring at Wyndi with her iridescent yellow eyes. The pupils were large and circular, but rapidly shrinking and becoming vertical slits as the sunlight was clearly much brighter than the house must have been.

"You should stay out of the way," Wyndi said to the cat. "We're going to be moving a lot of items out of here. We don't want to trample you."

As if it understood, the cat leapt onto the cart and sat with her back straight and her tail wrapped around across her front paws.

Wyndi shrugged and entered the house with the boys following after. The lights in the hallway sprang to life as they walked, leading her to believe they must have size-related sensory input because the cat hadn't tripped them. Small, convenient touches like this light system were one of the many reasons Wyndi wanted to be an artificer.

The workshop was tidy, even more so than the shed had been. Wyndi noticed fewer things in the workshop than she thought she remembered from before. To be fair, though, they had made a substantial mess while attempting to fix the broken tablet after the incident. After Zaq sent them away to find a new place, she guessed he had tidied up and put everything away. When it was out, it must have looked like more.

"Well, I think we may be able to get all of this in one cartload," Wyndi said, her hands on her hips as she looked around the room appraisingly. "That is, if you think you could haul a cart that full, Legs."

"Shouldn't be a problem. The cart itself isn't that heavy, and the wheels on the axle turned smoothly. If you two can manage the rear to make sure the load stays on, we can do it."

"We should put the bigger items like his slate board and those boxes there in first," Flek said. "It will make it easier to get the smaller stuff in wherever we have gaps."

"That's a good point," Wyndi agreed, scrunching her face. Why did it bother her when he gave good advice or made valid comments? She shook her head. "Let's get the board in first. I think we can lay it down flat, then everything else can go on top. It might stick out the back some, but that should be fine."

Wyndi grabbed one end while Flek took the other. They walked it through the house with Flek walking backward, glancing over his shoulder from time to time. Once they reached the cart, Legs helped lift it up and orient it so it would lie flat. It fit the width nearly perfectly, with just a small space on either side.

However, even with the board flush against the cart's front wall, the end of the slate stuck out. If they stacked the rest strategically, Wyndi thought they might be able to put a few lightweight things on the portion that jutted out, as long as they secured them with a rope or something. The back flap of the cart would need to stay down.

The three filed back into the house and then formed a procession, carrying out boxes, tools, and various other items from the workshop. As they loaded the items into the cart, they strode back through the house and repeated the process. The work went smoothly with no major hiccups.

The only minor issue, and it was small, was that the silly cat was determined to sit on the cart or perch on the contents in one way or another. She had a knack for hopping out of the way at the last moment and finding a new spot higher up on the pile as they loaded items.

After they had loaded the last of it, Wyndi closed the front door and ran around to the backyard to double-check that they had shut the shed. At least one of them had closed up earlier, so they set off for the new workshop. Legs took the front, gripping the handles and pulling up as he walked. Wyndi and Flek followed behind the cart on the watch for anything that might be unstable or falling out, occasionally bracing items and pushing from behind when a rut in the road made it too difficult to pull.

The cat had decided it would join them and stared back at the two apprentices walking behind the cart. Wyndi knew Zaq wasn't likely to be happy about that, but she imagined it might not be too bad since the cat wouldn't be at his house anymore.

Unloading the equipment and supplies proved to be more difficult than loading had been. Everything needed to be carried down a flight of stairs. It's always awkward balancing weight well when descending or ascending stairs. More care is required, making the entire process that much longer and stressful.

In addition to the stairs, it also took longer to set everything up in the workshop itself. Zaq had very specific thoughts on where he felt everything should go. While they had been gathering the workshop contents, the old gnome had been measuring and marking out areas with chalk. He directed them to each item's proper place.

"We got everything in one trip," Wyndi announced after all four of them guided the large slate board down the stairs.

"Excellent work," Zaq clapped. "I appreciate efficiency in an artificer."

"But we weren't performing artificery," Flek bemoaned.

"That was just hard labor. Are you ready to teach us some artificery?"

"You must need a pick-me-up after all that work," Zaq said, dodging the request. "Let's go upstairs to the tea shop and get something to drink and a snack."

"Fine," Flek grumped. "But then, let's get some teaching."

Wyndi could tell the goblin was swayed by the idea of an afternoon treat more than he was letting on. Truth be told, she was, too. That had been a lot of work, and the pastries upstairs were delicious. She squashed down the nagging feeling she shouldn't be snacking.

Chapter 15

Assignments Over Tea and Cake

At the top of the stairs, Zaq spotted the cart at the alley entrance. Most of the cart was draped in midday shadows, except for a small section of the bed where the sunlight formed a trapezoid. Sitting in the middle of the sunlit spot was the cat, repeatedly licking its paw and wiping it on its face to smooth and clean it.

"Sprung sprockets!" Zaq snapped. "You were not supposed to move the cat. We don't need that infernal beast here in the new workshop. It will just get in the way."

"We didn't move it," Flek rebuked. "At least not on purpose. It just hopped up and came along for the ride."

"If anything, she slowed us down while loading," Wyndi confirmed. "She continuously danced out of the way, but I thought for sure we might squish her when loading some heavier items."

"It's possible that would have been a better outcome," Zaq harumphed.

"Don't say that," Wyndi pleaded. "I can tell you like her

more than you let on. I don't think it would be good for you if something happened to her."

"It does help me think sometimes when it forces me to carry it around," Zaq slowly admitted. "But I don't know. Well, nothing to be done about it for now. Let's get ourselves some tea and a sweet treat."

It was a bit too early in the afternoon for most folks to be taking a break for tea. Too close to lunch, though neither Zaq nor his apprentices had had a lunch break yet. In either case, the patio seating area at the Mystic shop was devoid of customers. Both dwarves, Zheb and Joh, sat at a table together, sipping tea.

"Greetings and salutations, my good dwarven friends," Zaq called as he led the group under the patio covering. The day was not overly chilly, just a slight nip in the air, but the cozy, environmentally shielded area was a welcome comfort.

"Ah, Zaq and his apprentices, velcome. Do you desire tea? Somesing to eat?"

"Both would be lovely," Zaq nodded with a smile. "But it seems we're interrupting your break. We can go elsewhere."

"Nonsense. You vill do no such sing," Zheb said, standing up. "I'll fetch vat you need and resume my tea with Joh. Have a seat. Joh, I'll be back shortly."

Zaq realized as soon as the dwarf had left that he hadn't actually taken their order. It likely didn't matter. He had yet to taste something at the shop that he disliked.

"I suppose he'll bring us something good as a surprise," Zaq commented to Joh.

Joh nodded; the metal disks and jeweled bobbles in his braided beard clacked lightly together.

"My bet is he returns with carrot cake. I baked it fresh and just iced it with whipped ackernut frosting right before we came out here. Likely dragonroot or Count Knob," Joh said, speaking more words than Zaq usually heard from him. He had a much lighter accent than Zheb, but Zaq could still pick up traces of dwarven sounds in his speech.

"That sounds wonderful," Flek cried, bouncing on his toes. "I hope you're right. I just realized how hungry I am."

"You always seem hungry," Wyndi said, shooting him a glance.

"Let's just take a seat," Frank said, pulling some high-seated chairs over to a table set at a more comfortable height for humans. He sat in a low-seated chair, much better suited for him.

Zaq frowned at the choice of table but figured it was only fair for the human to get to sit comfortably every once in a while. He and the other smaller-stature people climbed into the higher chairs.

A moment later, Zheb stepped out of the shop, wheeling a cart. Zaq saw that Joh's guess had been right on the nose. As a dwarf, being somewhere in the middle heightwise, he had no trouble setting everything on the table. The chattier dwarf transferred everything from the cart, narrating as he did so.

"Here is some vonderful carrot cake viz ackernut frosting. Zee frosting has some lemon for an extra zing. I sought you vould like some Count Knob viz it. Zee citrus should complement zee cake and frosting. Zer is sugar and ackercreme for zee tea."

"Thank you," Zaq smiled. "This should do wonderfully. Now, get back to Joh before more customers come and force your break to end completely."

Zaq turned his attention to the spread and his three apprentices, who had taken no time at all to sample what the dwarf had brought them. The goblin already had a large bite of cake in his mouth and was happily chewing while Frank sipped his tea. Wyndi also focused on the cake but with a more reserved approach, scraping some of the frosting onto her fork before tasting it. The frosting brought a smile to her face, and Zaq turned his attention to his own slice.

He slid his fork through the frosting and then into dense cake, putting the bite, roughly half the size of what Flek had shoved in his mouth, into his own. The cake, riddled with bits of dried fruit, was sweet and moist, offset by the tangy, creamy frosting. Zaq felt he could inhale the cake and still not satisfy the craving the flavor ignited in him. Restraining himself, he alternated sips of tea with bites of the delicious cake and bouts of conversation.

"So, you all want to learn about artificery?" Zaq asked, feigning his obliviousness.

"*Yes!*" Wyndi emphatically nodded. "That's why we signed your contracts and agreed to your terms. We want to learn."

"Let's talk about why. It will help me understand how best to approach teaching," Zaq said. "Let's start with you since you seem to be leading this motley group of would-be artificers."

"Why?" Wyndi started, seemingly caught off guard by the question. "What do you mean, why? I want to learn because I want to be an artificer."

Zaq shook his head with a rueful smile, then calmly took a sip of tea.

"No, that's more of an effect. You learn, and then, if successful, you become an artificer. I want to understand why that is your path. Why do you want to be an artificer, and how does studying with me help?"

The young gnome paused for a moment, a bite of cake clinging to the fork she held. Finally, she answered him.

"I've always enjoyed making things. When I was younger, I used to watch my father and my grandfather fix magical appliances. They were both minor artificers, capable of fixing them, but without the spark for creating new things. I wanted to make wondrous devices, but my father felt I should join him in his repair business, insisting that creating new items was foolish."

Zaq nodded, listening to her story, allowing her to get it all out.

"I want to prove him wrong, but—but more importantly, I don't want to prove him right. That's why I want to learn from the great Zaquocorin Flickerwhizzle. If I learn from you, I know I can prove him wrong."

"Thank you," Zaq nodded appreciatively. "That helps provide valuable context. This afternoon and evening, if necessary, I'd like you to work on fixing a broken glow lamp. It was among the things you brought over. I'll get it out, and I want to see what you can do with it."

"What?" Wyndi cried, likely speaking louder than she had meant. "I just told you I didn't want to be in the repair business. What was the point of me telling you if you were just going to ignore it?"

"I didn't ignore you, I promise you that," Zaq said calmly. "I think that's your best first lesson. Now, moving on. Tell me, Flek, what has brought a young goblin so far from home? Why do you want to learn?"

The goblin had clearly learned from Zaq's questioning of Wyndi and had planned his answer already. Of course, that likely meant he hadn't paid much attention to Wyndi's answer, but one thing at a time. There was clearly something between the two of them, but Zaq wasn't quite sure what it was—some kind of rivalry, but with nuanced undertones.

"That's easy! I came to Ryefeld to find a teacher. It wasn't necessarily you, but when I saw the opportunity, I reached for it. Back home, I studied artificery. I even had some great teachers. But they all had one thing in common. They found new and brilliant ways of destroying things. I want to build something. I don't want to just blow things up."

"A noble pursuit," Zaq agreed. "Being so far from home, I'd like you to get the most out of the knowledge you are looking for. I have a project I put aside some time ago. This afternoon, I'd like you to work on it. It's in the very early stages of what I like to consider early prototyping. Given a reservoir of fuel, I'd like you to create a series of controlled explosions capable of causing a weighted rod to rise and fall. I have some sketches and equipment you can use."

"No way!" Flek shot back. "You just did the same thing to me that you did to Wyndi. I just told you I don't want to make things explode."

So, the goblin had been listening to the exchange Zaq had with the younger gnome. Zaq decided it would be wise not to underestimate that one.

"I did not do the same thing to you. I didn't ask you to fix anything. I asked you to build something," Zaq said, purposefully dodging the accusation. "I would think you would know the difference between fixing and building. Now, finally, how about you, Frank? What is your purpose? I've known a few human artificers, but they are much more rare than gnomes and goblins. Tell me your why."

Frank swallowed a bite of the carrot cake. He had been eating it slower than anyone else and still had some left. He took a sip of tea, and Zaq appreciated his deliberateness. The human seemed much more measured than the other two. When he was ready, he answered with a broad smile on his face, showing off his white teeth.

"My mother was a mage, and she encouraged me to study magic when she noticed I had an interest in the mystical arts. I enjoyed the magic in the world around us and tried hard to study the books she let me borrow. I found it challenging. I consider myself fairly quick-witted and at least as smart as the next fellow, but the spells and incantations never fit easily in my head. I could perform a few simple tricks, but remembering much beyond those was difficult. Then, my mother died, and without her encouragement as a teacher, I looked for other ways to create magic."

Zaq gave him a sympathetic nod and was about to give him an assignment when the young man continued.

"I believe in the gods, just like everyone else, but I've never devoted myself to any, so deity-granted magic was not really in the cards for me. I've known Wyndi for quite some time, and she's told me about all the wonderful things an artificer can create by blending magic and technology. I think that's the kind of magic for me: building things rather than memorizing spells."

"Well, then, I think it's clear what your first assignment should be," Zaq said, leaning forward toward Frank across the table. "I'd like you to spend the rest of the afternoon studying the beginner's rune book. This evening, I'll have you inscribe as many runes as you can remember on a piece of parchment. I'll let you use proper ink for the runes, but we won't finalize them with dust, so we shouldn't have to worry about odd effects from the collection of runes on the parchment."

To his credit, Frank didn't shoot back a complaint like the others, despite Zaq having done the same thing to the human as he had to the other two apprentices. The young man merely nodded, trading his smile for a frown with heavy creases on his forehead.

"Assuming you can all complete your assignments today, I'd like you to think about the results when you leave on your adventure tomorrow," Zaq said. "Have you considered what you'll be going after first?"

Wyndi and Flek shook their heads, and the young gnome looked like she was going to respond, but Frank beat her to it, surprising both gnomes.

"My father is a woodworker, and I told him I would be leaving on a quest for grimbark soon. He told me that it is extremely durable when alive and even more so after it dies. We'll need something strong to cut down a tree of the appropriate size. Lucky for us, he lent me an axe that he claims should be able to cut the wood."

"That is lucky," Zaq agreed. "I thought that challenge might end up being too much for you. Your father is right about how sturdy the wood is."

"Are you really sending us off so quickly?" Flek asked, wrinkling his nose as if the idea smelled bad.

"I think it's for the best," Zaq nodded. "You all can think about your lessons, and we'll have one of the materials all that much faster. Take the cart. It will help with supplies and carrying the grimbark back. I'll send a portable KoldBox with food you can eat along the way."

"I'm done with my tea and cake," Wyndi announced as she stood up. "Thank you for the afternoon treat, Zaq. I still don't understand why you want me to fix a stupid lamp, but I'm going to work on it."

With similar disgruntled comments, the other two apprentices got up and followed Wyndi to the workshop.

Chapter 16

Project Work

Wyndi found the broken glow lamp in a box in the workshop. She remembered carrying that particular box to and from the cart. Maybe she would have been better off leaving it back at Zaq's house. No, then she'd likely just have to walk there and back.

The glow lamp was crafted in the form of a candle set in an elaborate candlestick holder. It was, of course, all one piece, and the "candle" wasn't removable. At the top of the faux candle was a pale yellow mana crystal, and she imagined if the lamp were working, the crystal would glow, emitting light similar in luminescence to a lit flame.

However, it was most definitely not working, and it wasn't clear why. There was no visible damage. No obvious switch, button, or other mechanism to turn it off.

"This is stupid. It doesn't even make sense why this isn't working. How am I supposed to fix it?"

"Did you try turning it off and on again?" Flek smirked, then frowned as he looked at the metal box he had found in a crate along with a canister of fuel and some scribbled notes and diagrams.

"Very funny," Wyndi said dryly. "Did turning your bombs back home on and off solve any of your problems?"

"Okay, okay. Fair point. It was just a bit of artificer humor," Flek said, waving off her return jab.

Wyndi noticed the goblin had the side of the box open and was pushing a metal rod up and down through the top of the container. The rod flared out on both ends with a small lip, so it couldn't fall completely through the hole, regardless of which orientation Flek held the box.

"How's that coming?" Wyndi asked. "Any ideas on crafting something to do what he said? Are the notes any good? Wanna trade assignments?"

"No way! No tradesies," Flek said, shaking his head vehemently. "Everyone knows it's better to make something than to fix it. But if you need help, I am pretty good at fixing things. I fixed a detonator back in Chubug that was giving a demolition engineer in the mines a lot of trouble."

"I'm sure I can get it," Wyndi assured him. "We can each focus on our own projects for now."

"At least you two have projects," Legs moaned, pulling his head up from a book he was studying. "I didn't whine about it to Flickerwhizzle like you two did, but this is a horrible assignment. Memorizing runes? I could have just stayed home and continued working on memorizing the spells in my mother's book."

"I'm pretty sure we'll all have to know those runes," Wyndi offered with a reassuring smile. "I did, of course, assume I'd always just be able to look up whatever runes were needed."

She dropped the conversation and went back to examining the glow lamp. Pulling her goggles down over her eyes, she focused on the artifact. Softly glowing runes took shape. They should be pulsing if everything was working as it should be. These had a faint glow, but it was static.

"The problem is, I don't know what half of these runes mean," Wyndi said. "When you think you can take a break with the book, let me look at it. I need to find some of these."

"Maybe in a little while. I really want to lock these in," Legs said, tapping his right temple. "Even though this is an awful assignment, I still want to show him I can remember a lot of them."

Deep creases formed on Wyndi's forehead, and her teeth ground together. Just as she was about to say something she'd likely regret, a thought struck her.

"You know, one of the best ways to memorize anything is to write it down. You could write down the runes you are trying to lock into your head, and then I can use the runes you write as a reference. Here's some parchment."

"Oh yeah, I've heard of that," Legs said as a smile drew across his face. "It should only take me a few minutes to get one set down. You can have them, and I'll work on another set, or maybe I should draw them on the slate board, then I can just erase them and start over."

"Perfect," Wyndi clapped. "Put your first set on the parchment, then switch to the slate. I don't want you erasing them when I'm trying to reference them."

"That's what I meant. Just give me a few minutes, and you'll have your reference sheets."

Not wanting to waste time, Wyndi got her own sheet out and copied the runes she could identify on the lamp. She could then reference these to the runes on the sheets that Legs was working on. There were a few she really wasn't sure about. It was possible they overlapped, which made it hard to distinguish the individual runes.

There were stories of advanced goggles that were artificer-made devices. They could zoom in on small objects or bring distant objects into view. Some reportedly had built-in identification functions that could highlight runes on an object and display the potential functions. Wyndi's goggles could do none of these things. She was lucky the runes glowed with the help of her goggles.

Her thoughts of advanced goggles came to an abrupt stop as the rune she was copying was ruined when a loud yelp filled the room. Wyndi whipped her head around to see that Flek had a hose running from the fuel canister to a port on the box. The rod was sticking straight up from the box, and a flame burned brightly around it.

"I'm pretty sure it's supposed to be a *controlled* explosion, Flek," Legs commented as he calmly looked up from the parchments. He had beaten her to the punch by offering the snide comment.

Wyndi tried to stifle a laugh, which only forced it to come out in a snort, sending both Legs and her into hysterics. Flek soon gave in and showed he could see the humor as well by joining in the giggling.

"That definitely seems to be the key issue," Flek said, scratching his head with one hand while sucking a singed finger on the other. "It's easy to make things explode. I don't have a clue how to make them do it with less enthusiasm."

"This might help," Legs said after composing his laughter. "I'll make another copy for Wyndi in a minute, but take this parchment—it has both a control rune and a flow rune. You also might think about sequencing. You'll want to cut off the fuel before the explosion, I would think. Maybe if you could cause quick bursts of fuel with an ignition after each release?"

"That might actually be a good idea," Flek said, almost giving Legs a full compliment. "I should have thought of that."

Wyndi watched Flek study the parchment Legs had given

him, then glanced back over at the human, who had decided to sit on the floor with his back against the wall. She just needed to be a bit more patient. Nodding to herself, she returned to transcribing the runes she could identify.

Before long, Legs had finished the parchments for Wyndi. He handed them to her as he walked over to the large slate and picked up a piece of chalk.

"Thanks, Legs," Wyndi said with a genuine smile. "I'm hoping this will help fill in the gaps."

She looked over the runes inscribed on the parchment, each one accompanied by its name, general purpose, and most common applications. By comparing these notes to both the runes she had transcribed as well as the remainder of the markings on the lamp, she identified all the runes except one.

"That doesn't even make sense," Wyndi complained. "All of these make sense, and I can even see why someone would link them together as part of the design for this lamp. But this rune here isn't anywhere on these parchments, and I can't figure out what purpose it could have in relation to the other runes. No wonder this lamp doesn't work."

"Let me see," Flek said, bumping her as he shouldered his way in to look at both the lamp and the parchments.

"It's right there," Wyndi pointed. "I have no idea what that is. It looks familiar and similar to some runes in the notes Legs made, but it definitely isn't one of them."

Flek stood, stroking his dark beard and peering at the runes both where she indicated and on the parchments. It lasted long enough that Wyndi wondered if he was still thinking or just wasting time.

"That's it!" he finally exclaimed. "Look at this spot that is free of runes altogether."

"Right, I've looked at that a few times," Wyndi nodded along. "I've suspected it might be the control spot for turning the lamp on and off, but it doesn't do anything, and it wouldn't make sense with the rune surrounding it. I don't recognize that rune at all."

"That's because it's not a rune," Flek said somewhat smugly.

"It is too a rune," Wyndi snapped back. "It glows a lot fainter than the other runes, but I suspect that's part of the problem."

"Nope, not *a* rune," Flek said, grinning and pausing for effect. "It's two. And I bet that spot there is the control pad—or at least it was at one point."

"What are you talking about?" Wyndi snapped. "Oh! Wait! You mean there and then that one there?"

"Yup." Flek nodded. "You see it now. The control pad has worn off. The two runes used to be more distinct, but a portion of each rubbed off along with the main activation pad."

"This must be ancient, then," Wyndi said. "Either that or someone had a nervous habit of turning it on and off."

"Could be either one," Flek agreed. "But I think you see the issue now. I'm pretty sure you can fix it. I think I'm getting close on the controlled explosions thanks to the advice from Frank."

"I'm going to do better than fix it," Wyndi declared. "This design is horrible. By putting the control pad there, the design was just asking for trouble if the surrounding runes got damaged. Which is exactly what has happened here."

Wyndi got to work fixing the flawed runes, but then drew some additional runes and conduits. She continued working on it until Flek interrupted her work yet again.

Barroooom. Put. Clap. Put. Clap. Put. Clap.

The goblin stood back from the box. The rod was shooting up to its full extent with each gentle explosion, creating a *put* sound. It then immediately fell, smacking the small lip on its head flush with the box and emitting a *clap*.

"Huzzah!" Flek shouted. "It really is possible to control an explosion."

"Nice work!" Wyndi said, holding out a hand. Instead of shaking it, the goblin gave her hand a smack, which was odd and also fun.

Legs came over to watch the rod moving up and down and gave the goblin an encouraging pat on the head.

"I think I've almost got mine, too," Wyndi said. "I'm adding in an aural pickup rune keyed to a specific sound. There we go. This should work."

She sprinkled finalizing powder on her fresh rune etchings, then took a step back. After a deep breath, she snapped her fingers twice.

Snap. Snap.

The crystal on top of the fake candle came to life, glowing brightly.

Snap. Snap.

Just as quickly, the glow extinguished.

"Perfect, it's fixed and better than before," Wyndi declared.

"Better, you say? I don't recall asking you to make it better. I asked you to fix it."

Chapter 17

Project Review

Zaq carefully walked down the stairs from the alley entrance. The pads felt rough but warm as the cat's back legs pressed into his left palm. His right arm formed a cradle supporting the bulk of its weight. The cat had demanded to be picked up and was burrowing its face into the crook of his right arm, apparently trying to meld with him.

As he reached the bottom of the stairs, he heard the voices of his apprentices through the open door.

"Perfect, it's fixed—*better* than before," Wyndi proclaimed to the others.

So, she had managed to fix the lamp, and she had clearly identified the design flaw and altered it to prevent future issues. Perhaps the others had finished their projects as well.

"*Better*, you say?" Zaq asked, smirking. "I don't recall asking you to make it better. I asked you to fix it."

"Oh! You're here," Wyndi said, looking flustered. "But why are you carrying your cat? I thought you didn't like her."

"The darned cat insisted I pick it up," Zaq fussed. "What else was I to do? I wanted to come check on you, but the cat was standing at the top of the stairs trying to climb me. I figured it would be safer to carry it, rather than to risk tripping over the beast."

"I think she really likes you," Flek commented. "Look at her nuzzle. I can hear her purring from over here."

"Whatever. It doesn't matter. Enough about the cat," Zaq said, trying to redirect the conversation back to more important topics. "Tell me more about making the lamp better, Ms. Crinklepot."

"Right, of course," Wyndi said, straightening herself. "For a while, I had no idea what was wrong. I didn't understand many of the runes. By the time I figured them all out, I thought I could just make a brand-new lamp. But you wanted this one fixed. I could have just fixed it, but then it would likely break again."

"Really? You're sure about that?" Zaq questioned.

"Yes, sir," the young gnome affirmed, standing her ground. "The issue was the mechanism to turn it on and off. It was touch-activated, you see. That much-repeated touching on the activation plate rubbed away the surrounding runes, which broke the runic circuit."

Flek made an overly exaggerated throat-clearing noise, and Zaq saw him shoot her a look with a quirked eyebrow. The gnome glared back at him, staring hard, as if to bore a hole through his head. She broke and sighed.

"Fine. I didn't actually identify the problem. I figured out all the runes except for the ones that were partially rubbed away. I noticed the bare spot and figured it was an activation spot, but I couldn't identify the rune surrounding it. Flek realized there were actually two runes, not one, and I hadn't recognized them because part of each was missing."

"I see. I see," Zaq said, rocking gently and bouncing softly.

The cat seemed to like the motion. "And how did you go about improving the issue while fixing it?"

"I figured that out all on my own. I removed the worn runes and replaced them with a different set with an aural capacitor rune," Wyndi said, beaming with pride. "Watch this!"

Snap. Snap.

The lamp flared to life, the crystal at the top of the stick glowing strongly, just as the cat leapt from Zaq's arms, digging its sharp claws into him as it tried to find leverage.

"Ow! What did you do that for, you blasted creature?" Zaq fumed at the cat. "Sorry. I think the snapping startled the foolish thing. That was quite impressive, though. Excellent choice for activation. Alternatively, you could have used a motion detection circuit like the lamps I used in my home."

Zaq left out the fact that his lamps had all started with the touch design, and he had had to rework the runes on all of them. He had never gotten around to fixing this one yet. The aural activation might make it useful as a bedside lamp. Snap on. Snap off. He nodded to himself absently until Flek's voice interrupted his thoughts.

"You should see this, too! I figured out how to control the explosions. That wasn't easy. Exploding things like to explode and keep exploding!"

"That they do," Zaq nodded, noticing the cat slinking around under one of the tables. He shook his head to clear the distraction. "But I see. Yes. Look at that piston rise and fall, with a regular rhythm even. Nicely done. I knew we could redirect that goblin training."

"What's it good for, though?" Flek asked, scratching his head. "I understand how to control the explosions now. Frank showed me some useful runes for control and flow. With them, I was able to create these tiny micro explosions. But is it really *that* useful to make a rod jump up and down?"

"It could be quite useful, yes," Zaq assured him. "Imagine if we had more than one rod and we attached them to other movable parts? What you've made there is a simple version of an arcane engine. It's a new technology that a number of artificers have been experimenting with. Some even say we'll be able to craft vehicles and automatons."

"Wow, I want to make a vehicle," Flek said excitedly. "Is that the next project?"

"No, no," Zaq shook his head. "You won't be making a vehicle any time soon. Someday perhaps. You know your next project is harvesting materials for my distributor. But let's see about Frank. Have you memorized the runes?"

"Yes, sir," the lanky human said, looking down at Zaq. "I think so, anyway. Wyndi gave me a good idea to practice writing them, and I was able to help her and Flek. So, I think I know them. Pretty well, anyway."

"We'll see about that," Zaq said. "I mentioned before I was going to have you write them on parchment, but I see you've been doing some drawing on the slate. Flek, wipe that slate clean, please."

The goblin grabbed a rag and thoroughly dusted away all of the chalk markings. He didn't even stop to ask if anyone needed them first. Flek might need some training in caution.

"Thank you," Zaq said, smiling at the goblin, then turned to Frank. "Now, grab some chalk. I'd like you to write each rune you can remember, one at a time. Write them large. After I see each one, wipe the slate clean and write the next one."

"Do I have a time limit?" Frank asked. It was good to see him asking questions. A skilled artificer always asks enough questions.

"No," Zaq shook his head. "There is no time limit. Although I'm sure your fellow apprentices would like to be able to have dinner at some point. I thought we could eat at the Inn

Side Out this evening. It will be a few days before you'll have a good meal indoors if you are going to harvest grimbark."

"Fair enough," Frank said, but Zaq could tell the mention of the trip caused some distress—or maybe he was just nervous about showing his runes off.

The tanned human grabbed a piece of chalk and drew his first rune on the board. Zaq's mind wandered, and he wondered if the boy's family had been transplanted here from the southern lands. The sun shone more intensely and for longer periods there, causing most in that area to develop deep tans, regardless of race.

"There's the first one," Frank said, snapping Zaq's attention back to the slate.

"Wonderful, that's right. Keep going," Zaq encouraged.

And that's exactly what Frank did. One after another, he drew a rune, then wiped it away. He worked at a steady clip until he apparently exhausted his memory. After wiping the board, he stood there staring at it. Zaq could tell the boy felt he should remember more, but he couldn't seem to pull any more out of his head.

"That's a good showing!" Zaq clapped. Excellent work. "I believe you only left out three from the book I gave you. That's a much better attempt than I thought you'd have."

"Thank you?" Frank said, raising his voice into a question. "I guess that's pretty good."

"It is. It is," Zaq assured him. He really needed to watch how he complimented them. It was always easier to see how a compliment might not have landed how he intended *after* he had said it. "Really. Well done."

The boy should have picked up enough to be capable of going head-to-head with the other two. They clearly had more practical experience, but Zaq guessed they both likely had to look up most of the runes. Frank probably was ahead of them now when it came to sheer knowledge of the possible runes. Of course, a skilled artificer not only knows the runes but, more importantly, understands the myriad of potential uses for them.

"I know there were some doubts about my assignments, but did you each feel you learned something today?"

All three apprentices exchanged glances. This was good. The gnome and the human already seemed a good team, but now it felt like the goblin was a full member of their group, making them a solid trio, rather than a pair plus one. Wyndi finally broke the silent conversation, proving further to Zaq that she was the true leader of the group.

"I think we all did, but I definitely learned more than I thought I would. I learned so much fixing that lamp, I could make one from scratch if I wanted to. But now—now I want to build something new."

Zaq could tell it took a lot out of the young gnome to admit his assignment hadn't been as bad as she thought. She had put up such a fuss over tea.

"I learned a lot, too," Flek stepped forward. "I wanted to leave the explosives behind, but I see how they can be a part of building things, not just destroying them. I'm going to build a vehicle!"

Frank nodded along with both Wyndi's and Flek's admissions but stayed silent for a few moments more. Eventually, he nodded more to himself than to anything happening around him.

"As much as I didn't want to do more studying, I realized it doesn't matter what profession you choose; studying will always be part of it. I think I'm better equipped to build now that I know about some of these runes."

"Wonderful, you all worked so well together and came out all the stronger for it," Zaq beamed at them all. "I know you are all anxious for more lessons and to build more artifacts, but tomorrow you must leave to start gathering the materials we need for my project."

"We could help you test more and maybe go over the design, looking for issues," Wyndi offered, her face lighting up with hope. "The materials will still be there in a few days."

"No, no," Zaq shook his head. "You'll go tomorrow. I'll put together some supplies for you, and you are welcome to take my cart. We can also take this opportunity to field-test my prototype. You'll each take a slate with you. The distributor can handle a handful of slates. You can keep in touch with me, as well as each other if you get separated."

"I guess trying out a new gadget will be fun," Flek admitted. "I'm surprised others haven't made something like that distributor."

"Mysti Messages has always focused entirely on point-to-point scroll-based communication," Zaq said. "They never seemed interested in branching out from there, so I never told them. That way, I could keep full rights to the idea. They're the biggest company involved in messaging, so if anyone were going to do it, I would think they would."

"Did you say something about dinner at the Inn Side Out?" Flek asked.

Wyndi elbowed the goblin, but Zaq simply smiled and nodded, waving them to follow him upstairs. He glanced back at the cat who was curled up on the floor under a workbench. It would be fine there for now.

Chapter 18

The Quest Begins

Wyndi arrived at Zaq's house alone the next morning. Frank had told her the previous evening that he would meet her at the house, as he was picking up the axe and some other supplies from his parents. When she stopped at the Inn Side Out, Flek was running late and said he'd catch up.

Zaq had the cart out in front of the house; he must have dragged it back from the new workshop either the night before or sometime that morning. In either case, he was busy loading it with things he must have thought would be helpful. He looked up when he saw her approach.

"Greetings and salutations! I hope the others will be along soon. I imagine it will take at least a couple of days to travel to the forests where you can find a suitable grimbark tree. My best guess would be to look in the foothills of the Haverston Mountains. You should be able to follow the Frey River out of town."

"Good morning," Wyndi called. "Flek is just being lazy, but Legs should be here soon with the axe and possibly more equipment. I filled my pack with some clothes and other basics. Do you need help loading anything else in the cart?"

Zaq looked over the cart, perhaps performing a mental inventory of what he had added so far, and then nodded.

"Looks like that should be everything I planned to send. I put a travel-size KoldBox in there with some perishable food items. There's also another crate with some pantry items. You all should be fine as far as food goes. I also sent along some blankets. You might need them to supplement your bedrolls. It's been quite chilly at night."

"That all should help quite a bit," Wyndi said, peering into the cart.

She was so focused on the cart's contents that she jumped when she heard Flek's voice from behind her.

"What's that smaller box there?"

"Oh, right," Zaq said, patting the small metal box. "These are the slates. I told you I'd send them with you. You can leave them in the box for now, but if you separate, be sure to take one with you."

"That didn't take as long as I thought it would for you to get ready," Wyndi told the goblin. "You can't have been that far behind me on the walk here."

"Yeah, I figured I'd just grab my pack and skip getting something to eat," Flek said. "I've got some snacks in my bag that I can eat along the way."

"You both should load your packs into the cart. No point in carrying them on your back," Zaq said, motioning at the open space.

"We haven't figured out the cart situation yet," Wyndi said. "I don't want to overload it. When we moved the workshop supplies, Legs just pulled it, but I don't want him to pull the cart the whole journey, especially if we load it down with our packs. We could maybe alternate. Legs can pull it at times, then Flek and I can work together to pull it."

"You may not have to," Zaq said, looking past the two apprentices at something further down the street behind them.

"Why's that?" Wyndi asked, turning to look at whatever had caught the old gnome's attention. He was so easily distracted by things.

Legs was walking down the street toward them with an enormous beaver beside him. Across the animal's back, it wore a set of bags that were strapped around its belly. The giant beast lumbered down the road, definitely not fast, but it looked strong. *Where had Legs acquired that thing?*

The tall man noticed they had seen him and waved, wearing a big, goofy grin on his face. The hand that wasn't waving held a large axe resting on his shoulder. Flek laughed, evidently finding the idea of Legs bringing a giant rodent along quite amusing. He wasn't wrong. It was pretty funny, but the beaver looked useful. There had to be some tale explaining how and why Legs had picked it up.

"Look at what my father lent us!" Legs called as soon as he was close enough to be heard. "He uses a variety of pack animals when out harvesting wood. Doodles is kind of slow, but he can haul a lot. Plus, he can help gather wood and pretty much anything else."

"Doodles?" Wyndi grinned. "That's a wonderful name. He's so cute. Is he soft and furry? Can I pet him?"

Legs was much closer now and could speak without yelling.

"You're welcome to pet him, but I wouldn't necessarily call his fur soft—at least not the top layer. Underneath is more fuzzy, but also kind of oily. He does appreciate some good scritches, though, so feel free to give him some pets."

Wyndi reached out and scritched him around his neck. The fur was somewhat oily but not overly greasy. The stiff fur felt extremely smooth as she ran her hand down his back. She had to stand on her toes to reach all the way to the top of him, so instead, she reached as high as she could, splaying her fingers apart to form a comb as she walked toward his rear.

Right before the fur gave way to his scaly tail, Wyndi scratched into the beaver's fur. She knew cats enjoyed being scratched here, and it seemed the beaver did as well. The tail began to beat the ground in an excited rhythm while she worked her fingers through the incredibly thick fur. He made cute vocalizations that reminded Wyndi of a small child.

"I figured Doodles would make hauling our cart a lot easier," Legs said, absently petting the beaver's head. "I sure didn't relish the idea of dragging it up the foothills. Dad said we'd likely need to head into the base of the mountains to find any grimbark."

"That's what Zaq recommended before you two got here," Wyndi agreed. "He suggested we follow the Frey River out of town and up into the foothills of the Haverstons."

"Makes sense," Flek added. "Good thing he put some extra blankets in the cart. It's probably colder up there."

"Excellent work bringing along that animal, Frank," Zaq commended. "Everything should be packed if you all want to toss in your personal bags. You can hitch up the animal to the cart and still have plenty of time to travel today."

Legs did just that, tossing his small pack in the back and attaching a harness to Doodles. Wyndi and Flek put their packs in the cart as well. Even though it wasn't too heavy, it felt nice not having the weight on her shoulders.

"Be safe on your journey," Zaq said as he waved them off. "Remember to use the slate to send messages if you run into trouble or even just to check in or ask questions."

"We will," Wyndi said, waving goodbye.

The Frey River ran right through the city. There were

bridges at regular intervals, but two wide thoroughfares ran alongside the river. The trio walked, guiding the giant beaver along Burnside Road with the water to their left.

Outside the city, beyond the smaller suburban areas and the outlying farms, the road along the river was well-traveled. Wyndi felt the journey finally becoming more real. They were actually leaving on a quest of sorts. Maybe it was not nearly as exciting as the quests she knew adventurers went out on, but it was something.

That was fine by her. She did *not* need any more excitement on this trip than there already was. If things went well, they would simply travel for a few days, find a tree, chop it down, and haul a chunk of it back to Ryefeld. Maybe Doodles could even help with the tree once the enchanted axe cut through the outer layer of grimbark.

The only problem with Doodles was the pace. It was hard to blame him. He was pulling a heavy cart, after all, which was a lot more than any of them were doing. Flek was clearly too impatient, with much too much energy. He kept zipping ahead, then circling back. Wyndi was sure he would run out of steam before they were ready to set up camp for the night.

Legs passed the time by whistling. The melody was nice, and he could clearly hold a tune. The notes carried across the open plains to the right, but the sound of the rushing river on their left engulfed the music.

"Do you think we should stop for lunch?" Wyndi asked. "Or should we just munch on some snacks while we walk? I have some granola with oat clusters, nuts, and dried fruit in my pack."

"Doodles has such a slow pace. I'd rather keep walking

unless people need a rest," Legs said, giving the beaver a friendly pat. We probably don't even have to stop to get the snacks out. I can just lift you up, and you can get what you need from your pack while he keeps walking."

Wyndi snorted. He was probably right about the pace, but she did not want him picking her up. Even if he didn't say anything, she knew how heavy she was.

"That's okay. I can climb up while he's walking. It'll be quick. I'll pull out my bag of snacks, and then we can eat while we walk."

"Suit yourself," Legs shrugged. "You have enough to share? Or should I dig out a snack of my own?"

"It's a big bag," she said, already standing in the cart, fishing through her pack. "Plenty for all of us to share. Even Flek, if he stops jogging back and forth."

Wyndi handed the sack of granola down to Legs, then scampered down from the cart. None of it seemed to bother Doodles, who trudged along, following the road.

Legs carried the sack for both of them and, every so often, he'd hold it low enough for her to scoop out a handful. Wyndi liked the sweet honey mixed with the crunchy oats. The clusters were her favorite part. The nuts and fruit were nice, too, but couldn't really compare to the sweet oats. However, when she chewed some almonds together with dried cranberries, the tangy, sour fruit offered a perfect counterbalance to the honeyed oats.

Occasionally, Flek would run back and claw a handful for himself before running off again. Really, what was the point of wasting all of that extra energy?

After eating her fill of the granola, she cut over to the riverbank and lay down on her stomach in the grass, right at the edge where it formed a sheer embankment. Her hand scooped cold river water up to her mouth. The refreshing gulps cooled her throat and rinsed away the gritty bits of nuts and oats that had been left behind.

When Wyndi returned to the cart, Legs traded with her, taking his turn to drink from the river while she guided Doodles down the road. The beaver didn't need much guiding, but occasionally, he seemed to want to jump into the river, and that wouldn't do while he was strapped to the cart. Wyndi decided they would remove everything from the animal that evening and let him spend some time in the water.

After walking for a few hours more, Legs broke the silence.

"So, what do you think of this distributor and slate system that Flickerwhizzle is working on?"

"It's pretty impressive, is what I think," Wyndi replied, looking up at him, trying to discern what he was actually asking. "Why? You don't think so? You saw how it worked. It's better than any Misti scroll I've ever used."

"Oh yeah," Legs agreed, nodding along, his head bobbing in full agreement. "The actual messages on the slates are really neat. And it's impressive how the same message is relayed to all of them. But I'm a little worried that design might not hold up for many people using it at once."

"How many friends do you have?" Wyndi asked, eyebrows raising at his concern. "He didn't go into it, but I figured most groups would have a distributor with each group member sending and receiving messages through it. It might be an issue with companies, I suppose, if they want to send messages to all of their employees. But that's why we need these materials."

"Hmm, I suppose," Legs said, not sounding completely convinced. "It just sounded like he was thinking bigger than that, but I guess we'll just have to see how many people can connect to the large distributor he wants to build."

"It would probably help if he told us more about the project plans," Wyndi said, tossing a stone she picked up into the river.

"He does seem kind of guarded, even though we signed all of the contracts," Legs agreed. "It's not like we could do anything with the information, even if we wanted to."

Flek ran up.

"I found a nice spot with a small copse of trees, only a few more minutes up the road. We should stop there for the evening. It's getting dusky, and we don't want to set up camp in the dark."

Wyndi put a hand to her forehead and thought she saw the area ahead of them.

"Sounds good. My legs are getting tired anyway. I can't remember the last time I walked this long. I'm sure it's good for me. I don't think I get enough exercise."

Chapter 19

Camping for the Night

The trio arrived at the spot Flek had found and immediately began unloading the camping supplies they would need, laying out bedrolls to claim their spots. Legs unhooked Doodles from the harness, and to everyone's surprise, he did not rush to the river immediately. Instead, he looked at Legs, as if asking permission.

"I know you want to swim, but could you help us out first? Help me gather some sticks and branches for a fire."

Legs went on to pantomime, gathering branches and pointing at the nearby trees. To his credit, Doodles apparently was a fairly smart beaver, or Legs's father had trained him remarkably well. The beaver approached the trees and began pulling loose sticks and branches into a pile. There weren't many, so he stood on his hind legs and gnawed through a few of the lower branches of a young maple tree.

Doodles continued to impress everyone when he gathered up the loose branches he had piled into his arms and, walking on his hind legs, carried them to the camp. Legs pet him and gushed praise, causing his flat tail to pound against the ground.

He dropped to all fours to allow the human to easily reach his neck, chin, and head.

"That was wonderful! You're such a good boy. Dad must have taught you well. You can have fun now. Free time for the rest of the evening."

Legs gave the beaver a final pat, and Doodles trundled toward the river. When he reached the bank, he launched himself into the water with his powerful hind legs, slipping smoothly under the surface.

"I just hope he dries off a bit before he comes back and gets everything soaked," Wyndi said, grinning despite her words.

"I'll build a fire," Flek offered as he organized the sticks and branches by size. "A few of these are too large. Frank? Can you chop these big ones into smaller pieces?"

"What? Oh, yeah. Sure thing," the human answered as he transitioned from watching the swimming beaver to what was happening in the camp around him. He grabbed the axe and made quick work of the large pieces of wood.

Wyndi opened up the KoldBox and the crate of dry goods. Zaq had sent enough food along that they could stay out for several days, if necessary. He had even chopped up many of the ingredients and portioned them out into ready-to-cook meals. The KoldBox worked just like one would at home, and every-thing was just as fresh as she might expect.

"What would you two think about some sausage and peppers stuffed into wheat rolls?"

"That sounds great," Flek said as he fed the small flame eating away at his pile of straw and twigs.

"Agreed. If it's not too much trouble, that sounds wonder-ful," Legs added. "Do you need any help?"

"Not really," Wyndi laughed. "It's hardly any work at all. That old gnome did everything for us. We just have to dump this packet into a hot pan. I suppose you could cut the rolls open and put them on plates."

"Sure thing," Legs said, walking over to the cart to stow the axe and find bread and dishes. "I wouldn't think he had the time, but I appreciate that he did."

Once Flek had the fire roaring nicely, Wyndi dumped the ready-made meal into a cast-iron pan. The onions, peppers, and sausage pieces were already coated in oil and started sizzling as soon as they hit the hot skillet. Zaq had included a smaller packet of grated cheese with a note to add it when everything was mostly cooked through.

As the meal cooked, the onions and peppers softened and shrank while the sausage browned. Wyndi stirred it gently with a set of tongs.

"Get those rolls ready, Legs. I'm adding the cheese now. It won't take long to melt. Then we can transfer it to the bread."

One at a time, Legs held out a plate with a roll he'd sliced open. Wyndi transferred a healthy pinch of filling with the tongs. Legs handed the first plate to Flek, then held the other two until Wyndi finished dishing it all up. Wyndi set the pan face down in the fire to let the remains burn off and sat down, accepting a plate from Legs.

The hot cheese scorched the top of Wyndi's mouth as she took a bite. Despite that discomfort, she relished the taste of the greasy vegetables and spicy sausage. The roll was chewy and soaked up some of the oil, infusing it with flavor. After swallowing the first bite, she blew on the sandwich in an attempt to cool it. She saw the others were doing the same, likely having blistered their mouths as well.

Flek released a loud belch after swallowing the last bite. Despite the crassness, Wyndi found she admired the completely free spirit he possessed. She often wished she were that free from concern about what others might think. She found herself drawn to his carefree attitude. *No. Stop it. We are not entertaining thoughts about the goblin.*

"So, we have a plan for the grimbark," Wyndi said, forcing her thoughts onto more productive topics. "Assuming we find some of it where we are headed, does anyone have any idea where we can get the other items?"

"Mana crystals can often be found in caves," Flek offered. "Seems random to just go spelunking in caves until we find one, but there may be some spots in the mountains. We might be able to knock out both items on this one journey."

"That would be lucky if that were the case, but you know what else is found in random mountain caves?" Wyndi asked, then answered before either of them had the chance. "Monsters. That's what. And I don't want to find any of those. We aren't exactly equipped as hardened adventurers. Even if we had weapons, we don't know how to use them."

"Very true. I wouldn't call it luck if we find the third item while looking for a crystal," Legs said, shivering. "I don't want to run into a mimic, but I'm also not sure where we can find a mana conduit. We might have to send Zaq a message requesting some guidance on that."

"I think we should focus on the tree first," Wyndi said. "We at least know generally where we can find that. But, I guess keep your eyes open for any caves."

"We could always send Flek in to make sure the cave is safe," Legs pointed out. "His clan lives in a huge cavern, right? So, he should be right at home in a cave."

"It's not exactly the same thing," Flek protested. "Uninhabited caves can be quite dangerous, but I can at least see a good distance in the dark or low light, so that should help."

"I don't think uninhabited caves are overly dangerous," Legs countered.

"You don't? Wyndi and Flek both asked at the same time.

"No. They should be safe enough. It's the inhabited ones that you have to worry about."

"Very funny," Wyndi grumbled as she threw a small stone at him, hitting him in the chest.

"Watch it! You could hurt someone," Legs admonished her, but couldn't keep his stern expression and broke into laughter.

Doodles took that moment to lumber into the camp, dripping wet. Legs pointed at him.

"Don't you dare shake off the water. If you want to shake, go over there first. But you can lie down by the fire to warm up and dry off."

The beaver took a few steps towards where Legs had pointed and violently shook. Despite stepping away, he was still close enough that water droplets showered everyone.

"Hey! Some got in my mouth!" Flek complained. "Wet beaver does *not* taste good."

Wyndi and Legs laughed at the goblin's antics, though inside, Wyndi was extremely glad she had her mouth shut and merely got some water in her hair.

Doodles grabbed a branch from the woodpile. He carried it with his paws and teeth to a spot near the fire, collapsed, and started gnawing on the wood.

"We should probably all turn in early and get some rest," Wyndi suggested. "Do you think we need to take turns keeping watch?"

"It wouldn't be a bad idea," Legs said. "We aren't far from the road, and the Ryefeld soldiers keep the main roads in and out of the city fairly safe, but the farther we are from town, the more likely someone or something might catch us unaware."

"I'm not tired," Flek declared. "I'll take first watch."

"Fine by me," Wyndi said. "Wake one of us up when you get tired and need to sleep."

She and Legs grabbed an extra blanket each and bedded

down for the night. Wyndi lay awake, staring at the clear autumn sky. Knowing she should be sleeping and actually being able to turn off her brain to do so were two totally different issues.

The stars formed the familiar shapes every child learned early on. Most can't do much other than navigate their land or sea with the constellations, but some know how to harness the power they hold. Most diviners and druids use the positioning of the stars for their predictions, omens, and rituals.

Wyndi had learned the constellations, but not the magic they held. Sure, she knew what it likely meant if you were born under the watch of certain star groupings and understood how that could even be used for simple, everyday predictions of luck and happenstance. Still, she knew nothing of the art of reading the stars or the seasonal rituals performed by the druids and diviners.

She was told that, having been born under Kitkunist, the spellbook of the elven mage, Wyndi was supposedly destined to find success in pursuits leveraging intelligence and the mind. Whether it was the stars guiding her or her following the stars, she felt studying to be an artificer fit that well.

Eventually, the stars blurred together, her eyes closed, and her mind drifted into the land of dreams.

Right in the middle of one such dream, which involved crafting glow lamps on a never-ending assembly line, she was yanked from the world of dreams and opened her eyes to find Legs shaking her.

"Wake up. It's your turn for watch," he hissed in a quiet whisper.

"I'm up. I'm up. Just give me a minute," Wyndi whispered back, waving him away.

Wyndi slowly sat up, rubbing the sleep out of her eyes. That was definitely not enough sleep. At least she had gotten a nice contiguous chunk. Poor Legs had a nap, then watch, and now he had to try and get a few more hours of sleep.

Once he seemed sure that she was awake, Legs crawled under the blankets of his bedroll and fell into slumber immediately. Wyndi decided to move from her own bedding to ensure she didn't accidentally fall back asleep. She grabbed a chunk of wood from the pile, added it to the fire, and sat crisscrossed near the stone circle surrounding the shallow fire pit.

The fire warmed the palms of her hands, and she alternated rubbing them together and holding them out toward the fire. The early morning darkness was cold and just this side of freezing. Another couple of weeks, and there might be frost, or worse, snow on the ground.

Wyndi gazed up at the stars again, finding comfort in the patterns. Both the cold and the constellations in the sky made her think of the harvest festival that would start soon. Except for the food and drink vendors, the city shut down during the festival, allowing the citizens to celebrate and show thanks. The food and drink vendors could take the time to celebrate as well, but most of them preferred to take advantage of the people looking to buy refreshments for their merriment.

Visions of spiced apple pies, cider, cakes, and indulgent feasts filled her mind. Wyndi always succumbed to the temptation to overindulge during festivals. Those celebrations were a good portion of the reason she felt she carried too much extra in her rear and thighs. What had Flek said again? *It looks good on you.* Did he really mean that? Was she reading too much into it?

As annoying as the goblin was, she did find him attractive. Wyndi wondered if he thought about her nearly as much as she found herself thinking of him. *Don't be daft,* she chided herself. He most certainly did not. That's obviously why he was always so annoying.

Crack!

What was that? Wyndi was suddenly very awake. *Why did something have to happen on her watch?*

That had sounded like a large stick or small branch snapping in two. Her eyes darted around the darkness, but she couldn't see very far by the light of the campfire. She pulled out a dagger and held it in front of her, not at all sure what use it would be against whatever had made that noise.

Rustling and grinding noises sent shivers down her spine. There was definitely something lurking. Scraping and scratching sounds followed, causing her head to whip from side to side. She couldn't pinpoint where it was coming from.

Just as she was about to yell to wake up the boys, Doodles rolled over with a large branch held firmly in his front paws. His webbed feet were kicking at it, and his enormous teeth scraped against the wood, peeling chunks off that he chewed with apparent glee.

The silly animal was having an early morning snack. That had nearly given her a heart attack.

Thankfully, the rest of her watch was uneventful, and the boys woke up as the sun broke over the horizon. They opted to keep breakfast light, having some fruit and granola that they could eat while they walked.

Wyndi saw no point in telling them about her scare and opted for other topics.

"So, Legs, based on what your dad said, do you think we can make it to the grimbark trees today?"

"I'm pretty sure. He wasn't exactly sure where we could find them, but based on the general area, there's a pretty good chance we won't even need to travel a full day."

"The foothills don't look that far off," Flek said, pointing into the distance. "See how the trees begin getting thicker and the river narrows?"

Both Wyndi and Legs nodded.

"Assuming it's not that far up the hills, we can easily get there in a few hours," Wyndi said.

"Unfortunately, Doodles isn't the fastest, but I'm pretty sure we'd be even slower if we were hauling the cart," Legs laughed.

Chapter 20

Field Test Help Request

Buzz. *Buzz. Buzz.*

The prototype slate tablet vibrated on the workbench, shimmying across the surface. Zaq dropped the pen he had been using to draw updated schematics, letting it roll across the desk.

"What was I thinking? I should have had the audible alerts on. It's a good thing I was close and noticed it."

Hopping off his stool, he dusted his hands on his pants and walked to the workbench, watching the dancing tablet as he hurried over.

"What could they need? It's only the second day. I hope there has been no major trouble."

He picked up the tablet, reading over the script that had appeared on it.

> Wyndi: We found a grove of grimbark trees, but there's a small issue.

> Flek: No, it's a pretty big issue.

Wyndi: Let me tell him. You're ruining it.

Wyndi: Fine, it's bigger than small, and we need some advice.

Flek: Just tell him about the forest walkers.

Zaq: Forest walkers? Be careful. Do not make them angry. Are they threatening you?

Wyndi: No. It's fine. They aren't doing anything to us. But, they are making it so we can't get to the grimbark trees.

Flek: They're guardians. They spread their branches and blocked the way.

Zaq: Could you scout for another grove?

Frank: I don't think so. I have a feeling if they knew that's what we were doing, some of them would just follow us and blockade the next grove as well.

Flek: These tablets work really well. It's amazing we can share the conversation.

Frank: But why are we all writing on our pads? We're standing right next to each other.

Flek: Zaq isn't.

Frank: Yeah, but we aren't even talking to Zaq right now.

Flek: Oh, right.

Wyndi: Sheesh. Please, you two. Zaq, what can we do about the forest walkers?

Zaq: I'm not sure. I'm not an expert on their kind. If they aren't telling you, then they likely expect you to know. They are quite intelligent and wise, but slow to converse unless it benefits them. That much, I know.

Wyndi: I guess we didn't actually ask them anything. When we tried to enter the grove, they spread their branches and blocked us.

Zaq: And what did they say when you asked for entry?

Wyndi: Nothing. That's what I meant. We didn't think to actually talk with them. Will they talk with us?

Zaq rolled his eyes and tugged at his beard.

"Oh my. This was a mistake. They didn't even try to deal with the situation before asking for help," he said to the tablet.

Zaq: I suggest you talk with them and find out what they want in exchange for entry into the grove.

Wyndi: I doubt they will just let us in if they know we want to chop down a tree.

Zaq: Make your request explicit. Tell them what you need and ask what they would like in return. I told you, these are intelligent treefolk. They can be reasonable. Talk to them. Negotiate.

Flek: I'll do it.

Wyndi: YOU WILL NOT! STOP IT!

Flek: Fine, you do it. But I'll jump in if it seems they don't like you.

Zaq: Just let me know if they won't assist you.

Wyndi: Wait. Before you go. There's something else.

Frank: Oh, right. Good point, Wyndi. Ask him about the crystal.

Wyndi: Why didn't you just ask him? You almost did.

Frank: Right. Zaq, do you know where we can find a mana crystal? We think we might be able to find one in the foothills or mountains. Maybe in a cave? But before we run all over, if you know, that would help.

Zaq: I don't know. However, I would have hoped you would have looked into that before leaving. What's done is done. No point in coming back just to turn around and go out again. I'll inquire at the guilds and markets today.

Wyndi: We'll let you know once we have the grimbark. Then you can tell us where we might find a crystal.

Zaq: If I can find out, I'll share what I can with you. Good luck with the forest walkers. Be careful.

Wyndi: How do we let you know we're done sending messages?

Zaq: Just stop sending messages. I'll get the idea you are done if they stop coming.

He stared at the slate for several minutes, but it no longer buzzed, and the message chain stopped.

"I guess they were done. Well, back to it. No, strike that. I should go and ask around about mana crystal veins and mines. I should take the slate in case they run into more trouble."

He already had the slate in his hand, but paused.

"These devices need an easy way to carry them. Some kind of holster? Something that could attach to a belt? Or should I use a clip?"

Zaq spent the next hour trying various options with leather, cloth, cord, metal clips, and many other materials. Eventually, he crafted a canvas pouch attached to a carabiner clip with the heavy-gauge cord. The clip fastened to his belt loop, and the slate hung along the side of his leg.

"That should work," he said to himself with a satisfied smile. "Perhaps I should pop upstairs for some tea. It's quite possible the dwarves might know where to find a crystal. Worth a try anyway, and some afternoon tea would be lovely."

As he was about to leave the workshop, the cat appeared at his feet. Evidently, it had been napping somewhere, likely under a bench or in some box. Either way, it was now demanding attention. It wove tight circles around his legs, making small squeaking noises. Then, it rose up on its hind legs, stretching high with its forearms. The tail was quivering so much it seemed it might vibrate right off. *Was it actually that excited?*

He reached down, and the tail looked like it might detach— it was vibrating so much. The cat practically climbed into his arms and snuggled down, burying its face in the crook of his right arm.

"I guess you can come up for tea as well, but I'm not buying you any. Better than leaving you unattended in the workshop. That's for sure."

So, carrying the cat, which he still most assuredly felt was not his cat, he climbed the stairs to the back alley and then walked around to the tea shop patio.

"Good afternoon, Zaq," Zheb called cheerily as he found a seat.

"Greetings and Salutations," Zaq replied, then looked around, unsure of what exactly he should do with the cat in his arms. Without any better ideas, he simply sat in the chair, and the cat promptly let out a *meer-row*, leaping out of his arms. He quickly lost sight of it and turned to find the dwarven proprietor.

"Joh has some freshly baked cranberry scones. Perhaps you vould like one viss a cup of Ginger Tiger tea?"

"That sounds lovely."

Zaq pulled out his slate and reviewed the conversation, not for its content but more to marvel at how well it was working. He had performed some basic tests on his own, sending messages between multiple slates, but this was a live field test. The trio of apprentices was miles away, yet the messages came through without issue. And all of them were sending messages —not that they had to, as they had been right next to each other.

He couldn't blame them, though. Like him, they likely found the technology novel and interesting.

"Vat is zat?" Zheb asked as he set down a plate with a scone on the table, followed by a mug of tea. The steam from the tea rose from the cup, dancing through the air despite the warmth of the patio.

"Ah, this?" Zaq asked. "It's the project those new apprentices of mine are helping me with. They are off on an adventure, gathering supplies for the full version. This is merely connected to a prototype."

"And zey are messages?"

"Yes, it's a multi-party messaging system. The prototype can't connect more than a handful of tablets. The materials they are gathering will allow for a much larger version. Say, you wouldn't happen to know someone who might know of a mana crystal cave? I don't know of such a person, and you know how I hate striking up conversations with random people."

Zheb cupped his chin in an L formed from his index finger and thumb. He lightly tapped his finger against his closely cropped beard.

"Zer is a dvahrfen mining operation. Vat vas zer name. Ah, yes. Ore-ange and Lapiz Extraction. Zey are punny dvahrfs. You can find zem in the trade and commerce sector on Rose Street."

"Thank you, Zheb. I'm sure I can trust a dwarf to know the best spots for mining. I'll just have this delicious-smelling scone and tea, then head over there."

"You can ask for Troshkin and tell him Zheb sent you. Zat should loosen his tongue on zee best places."

With that, the dwarf left to check on the other customers, and Zaq broke off a piece of the scone, popping it in his mouth. The crumbly morsel was sweet and buttery until he bit into a tart cranberry that added surprising depth to the tender biscuit. He washed the bite down with a spicy sip of tea. The ginger had notes of orange zest, and it balanced against the scone perfectly. Joh was a master at these creations, and his husband Zheb always seemed to know the right tea to pair with his bakes.

After finishing the last of his tea, Zaq admitted to himself he had procrastinated enough. Those kids were counting on him to help guide them, and after all, they were the ones out there adventuring around in the wilderness at his behest.

The materials that those three were gathering were critically important. If he had any chance to turn this invention into something he could actually release to the world, he needed a distributor capable of handling a large number of connections. He could sell distributors to large companies, government agencies, and even large families. There really wasn't anything more important than building a production-grade version of the distributor. Once he sold one, he could easily line up pre-orders for others and afford to buy the materials from that point forward.

Of course, if it worked well enough, he might even be able to use the one distributor and license its use to anyone who wanted to use it. But he was getting away from himself. Selling distributors to organizations was a safer approach. By his calculations, a distributor of the size he was making should be able to handle enough users for even a large-scale company.

"But what was I doing?" Zaq asked himself, more to stop his daydreaming than to actually ask himself the question. He stood up and left to track down the mining company on Rose Street.

The sign above the guild house was painted in bright orange and blue, reading "Ore-ange & Lapiz." This was the place. He pulled open the door and approached what was clearly the reception desk, behind which stood a dwarf with red-brown hair and a long beard braided in elaborate knots.

"Greetings and salutations. Is there someone by the name of Troshkin working here today? My favorite tea shop owner, Zheb, sent me."

"A friend of Zheb's, are yeh? Troshkin is here. I'll go fetch him."

The dwarf, whose name he had failed to obtain, left through a door, only to return several minutes later, followed by a slightly taller dwarf with dark hair peppered with strands of grey. His beard was full but not overly long, lacking any braiding or ornamentation.

"Zheb sent you, did he?"

"Yes. Troshkin, I presume? I had some questions on where I might do some resource gathering."

"Vell, you can ask, but I may not answer. Vee don't give up our mining spots, at least not vithout compensation."

"I don't mean to start a mining operation," Zaq assured him. "I merely need a single large mana crystal. I've sent my apprentices out to get one, but they aren't at all sure where to look. They are in the foothills of the Haverston Mountains currently. I was hoping you might know of a spot where they might find a larger crystal."

"Ah, vell, yes. That is different. If you are just looking for one, I can tell you of a cave since you are a friend of Zheb."

"Thank you. I swear we won't abuse your mining spot."

"No. No, you von't. Vee'll see to that. I'll need you to register the crystal here so vee know vat you took. Vee'll check against our records ven next in the mine."

"Of course. Of course. I'll have them bring it here before they bring it to me. We'll keep it all on the up and up."

Troshkin then told Zaq where he could find the cave mouth and even drew him a simple map of the foothills.

Chapter 21

A Bargain

Wyndi stowed away her slate and looked at the cluster of imposing trees before her. Between the trees, she could see the deep purple of the grimbark trees farther in. The thick branches of the trees guarding the way were intertwined with each other. If she didn't know better, she would have thought it was merely a dense portion of the forest.

When they had first approached, the trees looked like any others and were spaced farther apart. Legs had been the first to see the grimbark and pointed it out. Flek took it upon himself to make a dash for it, despite having no axe or other means of doing anything with it—he just wanted to get there first.

Before the goblin had made it halfway there, the forest walkers moved closer to one another. The ground had writhed and rippled as roots literally waded through the soil. Each of the supposedly sapient trees had positioned itself roughly ten rods apart, which normally would be plenty to still walk through. However, the forest walkers then spread their branches, stretching them down as well as toward each other, twisting them together, to form a barricade. It was clear to everyone that they would move again, as necessary, should any of the apprentices try to get through.

Flek moved toward the grove, and Wyndi cleared her throat, motioning him back.

"Pssst, I said I would talk to them. Get back here."

With Flek in check, she turned to address the trees properly.

"Um. Hello? Can you understand me? I've been led to believe that you are sapient and capable of conversation."

The trees shook, leaves rustling, in what could only be interpreted as some form of laughter. A portion of the central tree's trunk split, forming a jagged, toothless mouth.

"The child questions a guardian. The youngest among the guardians has lived hundreds of the child's lifespan. The guardians understand the common tongue. The guardians understand many languages used by descendants of the first people to walk the land. Does the child have a question that is not pointless?"

The voice of the forest walker was raspy, like the sound of wading through piles of fallen leaves. Feeling somewhat ashamed of her opening address, Wyndi tried again.

"I apologize, guardian. We need to harvest a grimbark tree. We need a piece from a trunk that is two rods in diameter and one rod tall. That is all we require. However, if we could have more than one, so as not to waste the tree, we would take it. May we offer you something in exchange?"

"The guardians of the forest need nothing material that the child may offer. The child asks a great boon of the forest. The child asks for the death of a noble tree. The child asks for sacrifice. The child is one of three. Which of the three shall be presented as sacrifice in trade?"

"You—you want to trade one of our lives for the life of a tree? You can't be serious."

"The child's request is serious. The terms provided by the guardian are serious. Balance is achieved."

Wyndi paused for a moment to think. This was not at all going as she had hoped. She glanced at Legs and then Flek. There was no way the goblin was going to do any better. He'd likely just make them angry. She filled herself with resolve.

"Are the grimbark trees thinking trees like the guardian forest walkers?"

"The grimbark trees lack the spark. The grimbark trees still live."

"But new trees can be grown. If they have no spark, no intelligence, then can't they be replaced? A guardian walker like yourself cannot be replaced, and neither can one of us."

A soft rustle of leaves settled across the grove as the forest sighed as one. Moments passed before the speaker for the forest walkers replied.

"The child has a valid point. The guardians agree that the life of a child is not equal to that of a simple tree. The child will perform a task of recompense. The child states that grimbark trees can be grown. The child will plant ten grimbark saplings. The child will return annually to nurture the grimbark saplings. The child will return until the grimbark trees count twenty years of life."

Wyndi looked to the others, who both shrugged with questions written all over their faces. She waved them closer, and they huddled their heads together, whispering to each other.

"What do you think?" Wyndi hissed. "Planting trees is easy enough, but coming back every year for twenty years?"

"What do you think they'd do if we don't come back?" Flek asked, grinning mischievously.

"Be careful what you say," Legs said, smacking Flek lightly

on the back of the head. "We have no idea if they can hear what we're discussing."

"Something tells me we don't want to find out what happens if we don't come back," Wyndi said, creasing her brow heavily. "If we agree to their terms, we need to be ready to follow through. The question at hand is whether or not it's worth it."

"The cost could be a lot higher," Legs pointed out. "They honestly aren't asking that much. We only traveled two days to get here. We could even ask them if we could plant the trees closer, so we don't have to travel so far."

"That's a good idea," Flek nodded. "Let's ask them about planting them just outside of town. We could even turn it into a park."

"I like that idea, Flek," Wyndi said, smiling at him. "Thanks for thinking outside the lines."

"So, is that it then?" Flek asked, blushing a light purple at the compliment. "Frank? You good with this?"

"Yeah," Legs nodded. "If they let us make a park outside of the city, then their request is not unfair at all."

Wyndi patted them both on the back, and they all broke the huddle. She turned her attention to the forest walkers, taking a step forward.

"We have discussed it, and I believe we can agree to your trade, but we have a request."

"The guardians agree. The saplings may be planted near Ryefeld. The child will ensure no harm comes to the trees in close proximity to the city. The trees will be tended for twenty years. All ten trees will see that twentieth year unharmed. The child may fell a single grimbark tree in the grove today."

Wyndi gulped. Flek was lucky that they didn't take his initial hypothetical to cheat them as an insult.

"We agree. We will choose one, and only one, tree to

harvest. We'll plant ten trees in recompense, forming a safe-guarded preserve in the outskirts of Ryefeld and care for them for twenty years."

"The guardians agree. The children agree. A bargain is struck."

The branches of the forest walkers untangled and resumed a more natural formation. Waves and ripples formed again as roots writhed through the ground, carrying the forest walkers farther apart and clearing a path toward the grimbark grove.

There were several attractive trees among those in the grimbark grove. The sunlight danced across the iridescent purple bark, causing it to shimmer. Wyndi approached one, running her hand across the rough bark.

"Spread out. We need to find the best one. It needs a large enough diameter through enough of the trunk so we can get a few segments. We should harvest everything from the tree, if we can, so as not to waste it."

"Do you really think we can carry a whole tree back with us? Even if we chop it up?" Flek asked.

It was frustrating when he made a good point. She should have thought of that. They were a team, though, so could she really be upset when he was helping the group? It was a much better situation than early on, when he was focused on himself so much that he didn't seem to care if there even was a group.

"Well. Yes. That is a good point. We can take what we can, and I suppose we can leave the rest. That nurtures the forest, right? I think that's the case anyway."

"I'm pretty sure that's right," Legs agreed. "So maybe we shouldn't take a lot of it with us? Maybe the best cylinder and one or two backups, just in case?"

Right about then, Doodles bumped his head into the back of Legs's, well, legs.

"Hey, what's the big idea?" he chastised the enormous beaver.

"Maybe he wants us to make sure he gets a branch or two?" Flek offered.

Doodles thumped his tail excitedly against the ground at the suggestion. Legs burst out in laughter, followed quickly by the others as their mirth drove the beaver into a more excited state.

"We'll be sure to bring along a branch or two for you to eat, but you need to leave the trunk pieces alone. Flickerwhizzle needs those intact," Legs told the animal, who nuzzled his hand until he began petting him.

"What do you all think of this one?" Wyndi asked, running her hand over the bark before pulling out a measuring tape to ensure it was the right size.

"It looks big enough, and the bark looks uniform. There aren't any weird spots on it," Flek said, joining her in feeling the tree.

"Yeah, if that one is big enough, I'll get the axe," Legs said, already heading to the cart.

"I just measured it three times, and each time I measured a larger diameter than we need, so this one should suit our needs."

Legs pulled the enchanted axe from the cart and strode over to the tree with the axe slung over his shoulder, looking not at all like a burly woodsman. He may not have been the best suited for the job, but he was by far the best among the trio of would-be artificers. The axe handle was longer than either the gnome or the goblin was tall.

"Stand back, I don't want to hurt anyone. I don't exactly

have a lot of experience with this, despite my father's desires to the contrary."

Legs gripped the axe handle with both hands and held it poised over his shoulder. The axe head sliced through the air as he brought it down, stretching out his arms and holding the axe horizontal to the ground. The blade dug into the tree, slicing through the magically strengthened bark. It chipped through the bark and into the wood, but only barely.

The tall man pulled the axe back up and repeated the process several more times, each time chipping away a larger portion of the tree. The chopping was slow going, but he made steady progress.

"My father made this sound like this would be a lot easier with this axe. If that's true, I don't even want to imagine what it might have been like with a regular axe or saw. I think I'll focus on getting through the tree with the axe, then I'll maybe chop one large piece that could be cut into smaller cylinders back home."

"That should be fine," Wyndi said from her position several paces back from where Legs worked. "It should fit in the cart well enough, and we don't need you exhausting yourself chopping wood."

"Don't forget to lop off some branches for Doodles once you have it down," Flek added.

"I won't forget. I'm pretty sure he wouldn't let me forget even if I wanted to."

With his brief rest over, he continued chopping into the divot, which was over halfway through the trunk. Legs took a step back after several more swings and rested the axe head on the ground with his hands resting on the base of the handle. Strands of his long hair, damp with sweat, clung to his face and neck.

"That should do it, much more, and I won't have any control over it. We should all get on the other side for safety and push it over. I believe I lined things up so it should fall without hurting any other trees."

The group moved to the other side of the tree and pushed as one unit. After shoving as hard as they could, putting all of their weight into it, they resigned themselves to the fact that Legs would have to chop a while longer, but the giant beaver trundled over, making a chuffing sound. He gnawed at the tree opposite the large divot Legs had made, then stood on his hind legs. Leaning over, he pushed his paws into the tree, giving a large shove with his tremendous weight.

Craa-aaack!

That was enough. The weakened section of the tree broke, and it crashed to the ground, sending up leaves, dirt, and small undergrowth plants into the air. Several of the tree's branches snapped when it hit.

"It worked!" Wyndi exclaimed. "We didn't even hurt any other trees. Nice job, Legs—and Doodles!"

Flek walked up to the fallen tree and measured out a long stretch from the jagged edges to a spot long enough they should get at least two, if not three, pieces that would suit Zaq's needs.

"Once you've caught your breath, I think you should chop here. That should give us a good size to bring back to the artificer."

"Agreed," Legs nodded and walked forward to the prone tree. "Just step back, I'll need to chop all the way through this spot."

Either not understanding or not caring, the beaver walked over to one of the branches that had snapped off. Doodles was a safe enough distance, and Legs diligently chopped through the remaining trunk. While his human worked, the beaver had a branch gripped between his paws and gnawed on it with his huge teeth. Evidently, the beaver's teeth could get through the bark. Wyndi wondered whether the animal could really understand everything, or if it was just happy to have some wood to gnaw through.

Chapter 22

A Little Extra

By the end of the afternoon, the portion of the tree that the apprentices were not taking with them lay across the grove. They had stripped the branches from it and stacked them up in what they hoped would become a mulch pile, after saving a few choice pieces for Doodles, of course. The trunk piece they planned to take back to Zaq was loaded into the cart and secured with a rope. It should yield three cylinders as big as the one the old artificer was looking for.

"It's pretty late in the day," Wyndi commented, squinting up into the late afternoon sky. The sun was bright in the crisp, clear autumn sky, but it had already begun its descent toward the horizon.

"You thinking we should set up camp here for the evening?" Flek asked. "If so, I'd vote yes. I don't think we can get far before dark, and this clearing in the grove is pretty nice. Plus, the portion of the tree trunk we didn't use could be used as a seat or just to lean back against."

"I like your thinking," Legs said, looking around the area as if to appraise its suitability.

"That's what I was thinking, yeah," Wyndi agreed. "I thought we could set up camp, have some dinner, and send a message to Zaq letting him know we got the grimbark. I'm hoping he might have had luck with a location on the crystal."

"I'm pretty sure the crystal won't be that hard to get," Flek said confidently despite the uneasy vibe she felt from him. "We have a pickaxe in the supplies Frank's father sent along with Doddles."

"I don't think anyone thought harvesting the crystal would be hard. It's more the finding it that is the hard part."

"Beyond the crystal, there is that last item we need," Wyndi said through pursed lips.

"Right," Flek nodded. "The mana conduit. Zaq said we could harvest one from a mimic, as if we just run into mimics all the time."

"Never mind the fact that mimics are notoriously dangerous, especially if they surprise you," Legs added.

"Mana conduits are present in a lot of magical creatures," Flek continued. "I wonder why he called out mimics. I'm sure we can find another suitable monster that is less dangerous."

"It could be the size," Wyndi offered. "Zaq didn't specify a size, but maybe he had in mind the size of conduit we might get from a mimic."

"Maybe," Legs nodded slowly. "The other items all had specific measurements, though. If it mattered, you'd think he would have said."

"Well, I say we just get the first mana conduit we can from the easiest creature we come across," Flek announced with his hands on his hips. "We aren't really set up to battle any creatures, so the easier they are, the better."

"Agreed," Wyndi said, and gave Flek a reassuring pat on the back.

Did she really just touch him? He didn't seem to mind.

Maybe there will be other opportunities to naturally give him a pat. Gah, was she really thinking about him like that? Did she even have a chance that he might think of her that way?

"I'll write Zaq about the grimbark," Flek offered, crashing her thoughts of him as he proved interested in trying to grab more credit again.

Not wanting to miss the conversation, Wyndi pulled out her slate as well.

> Flek: Mr. Flickerwizzle? We have the grimbark.

> Zaq: Excellent. Did everything go well with the forest walkers? No major issues?

> Flek: Wyndi struck a deal with the forest walkers. We all agreed to plant ten grimbark trees in a park near Ryefeld. We need to take care of them for quite a few years.

> Zaq: Wonderful. Very resourceful thinking. I think you got the better end of that deal if they are guardians of that grove. Well done. And the axe? It worked well enough on the tree?

> Flek: Frank chopped it down. The axe worked well enough, but Doodles had to help push it over.

> Zaq: As long as you felled it, that's the important part.

Wyndi was impressed—Flek didn't take all of the credit. He really was just being helpful, reporting on their success. She realized she should ask about the crystal.

> Wyndi: Did you find out about the mana crystals? Any leads on where we can find some?

Zaq: I did indeed have some luck. A friend of Zheb's actually shared some information. I need you all to promise that you'll only gather the one crystal. The cave has quite a few, but the mine is already staked, so letting us take a crystal is a favor.

Wyndi: That shouldn't be a problem. We got more grimbark than we needed, but we had to chop down a tree either way, so we took what we could. We'll limit the crystal gathering to just the one.

Zaq: You'll need to bring it to Ore-ange & Lapiz mining before taking it to the workshop. They want to log what we harvested.

Flek: So, where is it?

Wyndi: Yeah, where is this cave or mine?

Zaq: I did some experimenting with two other tablets here. With a minor adjustment to the runes on the distributor, I can show you where they are. Look at this!

Under their messages, a drawing slowly emerged, filling the surface of the tablet. It was a basic map of the surrounding foothills, and somehow, their current location was shown by three dots on the map. If Wyndi understood the scale of the map correctly, the marked cave was only a couple of hours from where they were.

Flek: I can't believe you can send images! This is great.

Wyndi: Yes, and the cave looks like it's not far. We'll still rest here tonight and head out in the morning.

Zaq: That's a good plan, yes. Don't rush to the cave tonight. Get some rest, and let me know once you have the crystal.

Wyndi: Will do. Thank you, Zaq.

Still not used to proper etiquette on these tablets, she considered writing more, but finally managed to convince herself to just stop sending messages like Zaq had suggested before. Sure enough, he didn't send through any more either, indicating the conversation was indeed done.

"Should we have some dinner?" Wyndi asked. "Legs, you should rest. You did the majority of the work today. Flek can help me put something together. It looks like Doodles started dinner already."

The oversized beaver was happily gnawing on a branch of grimbark. It wasn't at all clear how his teeth could get through the incredibly tough wood. Perhaps being a semi-magical creature gave his teeth the extra sharpness and power they needed to get through.

"Look at him go!" Flek barked as he started laughing. His laughter warmed Wyndi in a way that surprised her. He calmed himself soon after and stifled the remaining giggles. "But anyway. Yeah, sure. I can help. You want me to put a fire together? Or make the food?"

"Zaq did a nice job setting up ready-to-cook meals like the one we had last night. I'll find something for tonight if you put together the fire. Do you think we should use the grimbark? I'm not sure what happens when it burns."

"It would probably be fine?" Flek said, then added, "But maybe not worth the risk. I'll collect some wood from the trees that aren't enchanted."

"Just don't harvest anything from the forest walkers," Wyndi grinned.

"Something tells me they wouldn't let me even get close enough to try," Flek called as he wandered off, staring at the ground as he hunted for kindling and fuel for the fire.

Wyndi dug through the KoldBox and dry goods crate until she found a combination of things she felt would make for a hearty meal. The prepared packet she found contained peppers and onions, like the previous one, but instead of sausage, she found shredded pork, black beans, and mushrooms. Everything was marinated in oil with generous spices, including chili powder and cumin. Zaq had included another portion of grated cheese, along with a note suggesting that it be stirred into the rest or sprinkled on top.

In the crate, Wyndi found a bag containing large flat tortillas, and she thought that she could use them to wrap the portions of the meal once it was heated. Whether that had been Zaq's intention or not, she wasn't sure, but having hand-held meals sure made dinner easier, and clean up would be a breeze again.

Once Flek had the fire going strong enough, she used the cast-iron pan to heat that evening's mixture. Legs and Flek voted for adding the cheese right into the food while it was in the pan, so it would get melty and gooey. When everything seemed thoroughly heated, she spooned it out on the tortillas, stuffing them full when rolled and folded.

"These look great," Legs announced. "Thanks for putting it together, and thanks for the fire, Flek. I feel like a bum having just sat here."

"You swung that axe all afternoon," Flek reminded him. Wyndi was pretty sure Legs was putting on a polite protest, but it was good to see Flek appreciated the contribution.

"I suppose I did," Legs chuckled. "That's probably why my arms are so sore. Did you know that grimbark is so tough it sends reverberations back up the handle of the axe on each strike?"

"I can take first watch tonight," Wyndi offered. "That way, you can get some sleep to recover."

"Good idea," Flek nodded. "I'll take second, that will give Frank a nice chunk of uninterrupted sleep."

Having learned her lesson from the previous night's meal, Wyndi cautiously bit into her wrap. The conversation had allowed it to cool enough, and she avoided burning her mouth. The warm filling felt very good. While the temperature was fine, the spice mix Zaq used was perhaps a bit heavier-handed than she would have been.

The spice clung in the back of her throat, but it wasn't overly unpleasant. Flek didn't seem to mind at all, but if she recalled, goblins tended to like their food especially spicy. Legs had beads of sweat on his forehead as he chewed bites of his handheld meal. Clearly, the spice affected him even more than her.

"Too much heat for you?" Flek smirked at Legs. "We need to train you on a goblin diet. Brizla makes a bunnycorn stew that has a pretty serious kick."

"Who's Brizla?" Legs asked after washing down his last bite with a large amount of water.

"She's the cook at the Arsonist's Tender," Flek answered. "That's a tavern where Quilka works. Quilka was one of the three folks I came to Ryefeld with. I think you saw her at the tavern."

"Ah, right," Legs nodded. "I remember now. You were telling us about them and the others back home the other day. I may be up for trying that stew sometime, but maybe I'll let my stomach rest some from this dinner first."

Flek laughed some more, and Wyndi couldn't help but join in. She found his laughter infectious.

"I don't think we'll be visiting Flek's home in the warren anytime soon," Wyndi said. "So, your stomach should get plenty of rest. The harvest festival is starting soon, and the food served during the festival doesn't usually have that kind of heat. The spices in the festival always remind me of sweetbreads, cookies, and pies my grandma used to make."

"Speaking of the festival," Legs said. "I hope Zaq can get the production-grade version of his invention finished by then. It would be a great place to show it off."

"Is the festival a large affair in Ryefeld?" Flek asked. "I get the feeling it is from the vibes in town and the way you two talk. We celebrated in the warren, but it was never that big a deal there. Probably because we don't do a lot of farming. We buy or *cou*-steal-*gh* most of our crops."

He strategically coughed over one of his words, but Wyndi was pretty sure he admitted to his clan stealing. She didn't know a lot about warren life out in the rural areas. Studying goblin inventions and artificery? Sure, she did plenty of that, but she had never paid that much attention to goblin culture. She decided she should learn more about it. Flek was in Ryefeld now, and she could tell him what to expect if she understood more about his background.

"Harvest festival is *huge* in Ryefeld. It's a really big city and considered pretty metropolitan, but its roots go *way* back. The entire city started as a small collection of farms, primarily growing rye. You're in for a treat. I can show you around the festival once it starts."

"Sure, I'd like that," Flek said, then took a bite of his wrap. He probably didn't notice her blush since he was focused on his food.

"Oh yeah," Legs sounded excited. "We can make sure you experience the full festival."

Wyndi shot Legs a glare, but he seemed completely oblivious. Not *everything* needed to involve all three of them.

"You should probably get to sleep, Legs. You must be tired after all that work today."

"Good point," he replied while stifling a yawn. "The axe work today, and making it through that spicy dinner, took a lot out of me. Wake me for last shift, Flek."

"Sure thing," Flek said. "I should get to sleep, too, so I can wake up for second shift. Not really tired yet, though. I wish Zaq had packed us some sweet goodies. I miss hanging out at that Mystic with the dwarves and their tasty treats."

"That would be nice," Wyndi agreed. "But, it's probably better for me out here in the wilderness without extra treats to further my padding. The exercise has been good for me, too. Maybe if I just had more exercise, I could have some more goodies."

"You shouldn't focus so much on that," Flek said, a surprising warmth in his voice. "Back at TQ House, we make sure everyone is happy about who they are, whether that's shape, size, gender, anything. Trinx is very insistent on that."

"I don't know about that. I mean, I'm fine with everyone else and how they are, but how can I be okay with myself when I know people probably think I'm too big? Especially for a gnome."

"If you're unhappy with what you look like, then sure, that makes sense. There are things you can do about that. But it sounds like you're more worried about what other people think. The good people in your life won't care if you are thin or if you have a little extra. I think you look good. I think you'd look even better if you believed you looked good."

"That's nice of you to say, but how can I believe others think that too? I've seen some of the looks I get sometimes."

"*Whatever.* If people give you looks, those people don't matter. Stick with folks who don't do that. What makes you happier? Having a tasty treat? Or thinking some person you don't even know thinks of you a certain way?"

"The treats are pretty good," Wyndi sighed. "I just can't help it sometimes worrying what other people are thinking about me."

"We get a few people at TQ House who wrestle with the same thing, not necessarily about weight, but whatever their thing is. They want to fit the perfect image of what other people have of them, even though they don't even know those people. It's not healthy.

"I happen to like a little extra on people. I spent a lot of time on the street when I was younger and was forced into being thin. Same with some others I knew. Seeing someone with extra—well, it just makes me think they are doing pretty well. I like it."

Wyndi couldn't believe the conversation she was having. Clearly, Flek had no problem with her size. Maybe she shouldn't be that worried about what others think. Zaq never even seemed to notice, and Legs had never said anything. Even though she tended to project thoughts on others she didn't know, for some reason, she felt he never entertained those kinds of thoughts.

Flek not having a problem with her size was one thing, but he probably didn't actually think of her the way she was starting to think of him. Maybe he'd like to get a treat together, just the two of them, at the harvest festival. She found herself smiling, and then Flek's voice broke her out of her thoughts.

"Looks like maybe you're having a change of heart? I see a smile. I'm going to get to sleep now. Wake me up when it's my turn."

"Oh, right," Wyndi said, shaking her head. "I do think I feel better. Thanks for the talk. It didn't solve everything about how I feel, but it helped. Get some sleep. I'll wake you up in a few hours."

Chapter 23

Spelunking

When Wyndi woke the next morning, Flek was still sleeping under the blankets of his bedroll. Legs had tidied up the camp and had everything she and Flek weren't actively using packed into the cart. He was currently playing a dangerous game of tug-of-war with Doodles using a grimbark branch.

On the long log that was all that remained of the grimbark tree they felled, lay two cloths, each with a packet of granola and an apple. Wyndi assumed this was breakfast for herself and Flek. She drew the corners of one cloth up so that all four met and formed a pouch, then sat on the log near the fire. Legs had kept the fire stoked and fed. Warmth radiated from it, cutting through the morning chill.

Wyndi debated waking Flek, but he'd likely wake on his own soon enough. Instead, she sat thoughtfully, popping honeyed oat clusters and nuts into her mouth as she reflected on the conversation last night. She had thought about it a lot while looking at the stars during her watch. To both her frustration and admiration, the goblin had made a lot of sense.

When she had first met him, he seemed so full of himself. That had been annoying, but also, that self-confidence was attractive. He knew who he was and what he wanted. She knew what she wanted, but had nowhere near the same self-confidence. But she could have that if she let herself. If she just accepted who she was and stopped worrying about what others thought. It was something to work on, anyway. Flek's voice broke through her thoughts again. How did she keep getting so lost in her mind that she failed to notice him?

"Is that for me?" He was pointing at the other cloth.

"Oh? Sorry. Yeah. I think so, anyway. This one was next to it, there on the log. I figured Legs set them out for us. He's been busy with the beaver, so I can't know for sure. For all I know, he was planning on eating all this himself." She snorted, then took a bite of her apple.

"I'm sure it was for us," Flek said, scooping up his breakfast. "Seems like the kind of thing he'd do. We should probably get going if you're ready. I can eat while we walk. It looks like he has everything else prepared."

"Good point," Wyndi nodded. "It would be good to have time to explore the cave today. It looked to be only a couple hours away, but the sooner we get there, the sooner we can find a crystal."

"Hey, Frank!" Flek shouted. "I think we'll be good to go in a moment once we toss our bedrolls in the cart. Get the harness on Doodles as soon as you're done playing."

"Oh! You're both up," Legs called. "I'll be right there. I didn't notice."

At least the tall, gangly human had been having fun while on watch. He clearly wasn't paying much attention to the camp since he didn't notice they had gotten out of bed. It was quite possible the forest walkers had kept them safe in the grove. That hadn't been part of the bargain, but Wyndi also didn't think they would have let some unruly monster attack their camp. Maybe they all could have gotten a full night's sleep.

It didn't take long for Wyndi and Flek to pack up their rolls and stow them in the cart. By the time they finished, Legs had Doodles harnessed to the cart, and they were ready to head out.

Legs got out his tablet and used the map Zaq had sent to guide the beaver toward the cave. Wyndi and Flek followed behind and ate the rest of their breakfast while they walked. All three of them made small talk and commented on the lovely fall foliage.

The forest was ablaze with reds, oranges, and yellows. Wildlife in the woods all appeared to be preparing for the coming winter. Wyndi saw three squirrels collecting and stowing nuts. One kept stealing some of the nuts that the others had packed when they weren't looking. He was smart, though. He never took them all, just one or two extra to ensure he had the most.

At one point in the walk, Flek climbed up into the moving cart.

"I totally forgot. Being out here in the wilderness threw off my regular routines. I was due to take my potion yesterday. It's okay, though. I always leave myself plenty of buffer."

"Oh! You mean that potion you mentioned the other day?" Wyndi asked carefully. "The one...the one that changes you?"

Flek laughed. "Yep, that's the one. Don't be shy about asking. It's not a big deal. It's like I was telling you last night, we are who we are. I guess it maybe sounds hypocritical since I'm taking a potion to change my appearance. But I'm not changing it for other people. I don't care what they think. I take it for me. I like how I look when I take it. It makes me feel more...me."

"That makes sense, I suppose," Wyndi said. "I'm glad you remembered to take it. Does it make you look a lot different?"

"Maybe not a lot," Flek said, then cleared his throat. "Or,

well. I mean, it changes quite a bit under my clothes. And I don't need to take a separate potion for my beard, but I do anyway because I like it to be fuller. As far as my other features, though? Not a lot different. It takes away some of the softness, my ears change a bit, and my neck and shoulders have more bulk. Overall, it's a lot of small things that add up to make me feel right."

"Whatever it does, I think it looks pretty good," Wyndi said. Flek's cheeks took on a faint purple cast. She had heard goblins, orcs, and trolls tended to blush purple on their green skin. Was he blushing?

After drinking two potions—one for his overall change and evidently one for filling out his beard—he hopped back down from the cart and resumed walking. It was only a few minutes later when Flek pointed at a dark spot at the base of a hill to the northeast.

"Is that it?" he asked.

"Lemme see," Legs answered, peering at his tablet and scanning the surrounding area. "Yeah, I'm pretty sure that's it. You've got good eyes."

"I've spent a lot of my life in and around caves. You get an eye for them."

Wyndi looked at the cave opening, the cart, and then the cave opening once again before stating the obvious for the third time.

"I don't think there is any way we can fit the cart in the cave and still be sure we can get it back out again."

"We *know*," Flek said, folding his arms across his chest. "I'm pretty sure saying it again won't change it. At least the cave is tall enough that Frank doesn't have to duck, but we don't know if this entry tunnel will widen or not. We can't risk getting the cart wedged in there."

"I'm sure it will be fine," Legs said firmly with his hands on his hips. "We can take Doodles with us, and I highly doubt anything will mess with our cart while we are in there."

"Fine," Wyndi said, shaking her head. "I just wish we had someone to watch it. One of us could stay, but I'm more afraid we'll all be needed inside—especially if there is anything dangerous."

"Dangerous?" Legs's voice quivered. "You mean like... *spiders?*"

"There might be spiders—it's a cave after all," Wyndi said. "But I was thinking something bigger."

"Spiders can get big!" Legs defended. "I've heard some giant varieties can get as large as a gnome or goblin."

"I doubt there will be giant spiders in there," Wyndi said in a placating tone. "There might not even be small ones. But if we see any, I'm sure Flek or I can handle them if you are that worried."

"Wait! I just realized something," Flek announced, thrusting a finger in the air. "I've got something in my pack. I've been using it as backup during watch. I'll just need to change the settings."

The goblin hopped into the cart and rummaged through his pack. He soon triumphantly held up a small metal dome with an antenna sticking up from the center.

"What's that?" Legs asked before Wyndi could.

"It's a proximity alarm. It has dials. You can adjust the sensitivity and range it senses things. I can set this up and put it on top of our stuff in the cart. If anything comes near, I'll have it scream an alarm."

"Wait. What?" Wyndi looked at him, flabbergasted. "You've had that the whole time and didn't tell us until now?

And you've been using it on your watch? You could have let us use it too, or better yet, we could have just set it up and let everyone sleep."

"I wasn't sure if we wanted to fully trust it," Flek explained. "And I used it for backup on my watch because I was always worried I'd let you two down and fall asleep."

Wyndi let out a deep sigh.

"Well, I guess we can't change the past, but it should be very helpful while we are inside. Let's get some equipment together. Legs, load up some stuff in Doodle's saddlebags."

"Yeah, we probably can't," Legs said, musing as he gathered things into the saddlebags. "But I agree that the sensor will be useful."

"Probably can't what?" Wyndi asked.

"Change the past," Legs said flatly. "You made a pretty big assertion, and I was just agreeing...mostly. I think there's still a lot of research on the subject."

"Legs," Wyndi said, then pressed her lips tightly. "It was a figure of speech, not a declaration of what actually is and is not possible with regard to magic and artificery."

"Oh, right," Legs nodded. "Got it. I pretty much have Doddles packed up. I have the pickaxe in case we find a crystal, and I brought the enchanted axe in case we find something more dangerous than a crystal. You two have any weapons?"

"I have a dagger," Wyndi said. "It's not much, but it should help against smaller threats."

"I have one too," Flek offered. "Plus, I have some flashbangs and three shredders."

"Are those explosives?" Wyndi asked. "I thought you were trying to distance yourself from goblin artificery."

"I want to get away from *just* making them," Flek said. "That doesn't mean they aren't useful, and I'll still make some from time to time."

"Zaq gave us glow rods," Wyndi said, holding one up. "You each have one handy? I was playing with it. By default, it produces a diffuse light that fills a small area, or you can change the mode to a beam that is tighter and directional, which goes much farther."

"Yeah, I noticed that, too," Legs said. "Whoever is in front should use the directional setting so we can see what's up ahead better. The rest of us can use the other mode to light up the area immediately around us."

"Sounds like a good plan," Flek agreed. "You can lead with the directional beam, and the two of us will follow with Doodles."

Wyndi snorted and grinned at the goblin.

"That's an excellent plan."

Legs shook his head in bemusement, then pulled his hair back, holding it in place with a cord. He slung his axe over his shoulder, holding it with his right hand, while pointing the glow rod out in front of him, letting the bright beam of light break up the darkness of the cave entrance.

"Well, come on then. Follow me."

The lights cast away most of the immediate darkness. The same narrow tunnel that caused Wyndi's consternation with the cart proved to be a blessing when it came to seeing what was around them. The floor of the tunnel was fairly even, while the walls and ceiling looked rough. There had likely been enough traffic in and out of the cave to wear the ground smooth. The only question, of course, was what kind of traffic.

Small offshoots from the main tunnel occasionally opened on the left or right, usually with tens of rods between them. Each time they encountered one, Legs directed his light down the side passage. Most appeared to end in a dead end. They may have been exploratory branches someone made while looking for minerals. At the entrances of the few that continued beyond what they could see, Wyndi marked the wall with some chalk.

Thankfully, they had quite a lot of light, and Wyndi could keep her nerves in check. She had never been fond of dark, enclosed spaces. *How in the world did goblins live in places like this?*

As if to answer her thoughts, Flek commented on the cave system.

"This is not at all like the warren. In the warren, we have lights throughout, mounted on walls, buildings, or even in the upper reaches of the large caverns. It's also a lot less cramped. But overall, this is not a bad cave system. It's clear it was created or at least expanded by miners."

"Zaq did say he found out about the cave from a dwarven mining company," Wyndi said.

"Yeah. It makes sense that the place would show signs of purpose-built tunnels," Legs agreed. "I'm surprised this main tunnel hasn't opened up into a larger area yet. Or wait—I spoke too soon. Hold up."

Wyndi and Flek stopped, as did Doodles shortly after.

"You see something?" Wyndi asked, craning her neck around him and peering down the tunnel.

"Yeah, not too much farther; I see the walls stop being visible when I aim my light at the sides. It's got to be a wider part of the cave."

Chapter 24

Vulin

"Back!" Legs yelled as he walked backward, running into the group that wasn't far behind him.

"What is it?" Wyndi asked, a lump of fear wedging itself into her throat, making it hard to get the words out.

"Just move! Quickly. And put out the lights. We know what was behind us. We don't need them right now."

Everyone flicked off their glow rods, plunging the tunnel into complete darkness. Scuffing sounds like something heavy being dragged across the floor came from the cavern ahead. Wyndi turned and tried to run, but ran into the oily fur of the giant beaver. She pushed on him, and he got the idea without further prodding.

Soon, Doodles was leading them all back down the tunnel the way they had come with Legs bringing up the rear. He explained in hushed whispers while they stumbled through the darkness.

"I'm fairly certain it's a vulin. They can sense mana and

will head to the largest source near them. We need to keep the glow rods off, and maybe it won't follow us."

"Was there just the one?" Flek asked.

"Probably? I don't know," Legs admitted. "I didn't fully assess the cavern. I saw the thing shuffling toward me, and we ran. Luckily, they don't move fast and more drag their bodies than actually walk or crawl."

"If there's just one, we could probably use one of the side tunnels," Flek said. "Lure it to us with the glow rods. Then we can attack it."

"Attack it?" Legs gasped. "Are you nuts? I don't want to fight anything, especially not a magic-eating monster."

Scales grating against stone like the sound of rustling autumn leaves gone horribly wrong reverberated down the tunnel.

"They eat magic?" Wyndi's voice cracked as she glanced back over her shoulder despite the darkness surrounding her.

"Among other things," Legs said. "I can't attack it with the enchanted axe. My dad would kill me if I brought it home drained of its power."

"I'm pretty sure I know what you're talking about," Flek said. "They are pretty common in cave systems. They're more pests than anything else. In fact, my uncle often has to clear out small ones from time to time. We don't ever let them get very big in the warren."

"What counts as small? How big was that thing? I couldn't see it," Wyndi hissed.

"I guess it wasn't huge," Legs said. "It surprised me more than anything. It was low to the ground, but long, dragging the rear half of its body. If it had hind legs, they weren't very useful. It was pulling itself along with its front claws."

"Doesn't sound like it was even as big as me," Flek said, sounding much more sure of himself.

"Probably not, no," Legs agreed.

"This'll be easy, then," Flek said, flicking his glow rod back on.

"What are you doing?!" Wyndi yelled in a harsh whisper. "Legs said they follow the mana."

"Right. And I need to see this thing," Flek said, pushing forward. "Let me in front, Frank."

Flek's light illuminated the tunnel, and Wyndi could see a shape far down the shaft at the opening of the cavern. It really wasn't all that big. It would likely only come up to her waist, but it was long, just like Legs had said.

The vulin's head snapped up and pointed at them. It had no eyes, as far as Wyndi could tell. The head looked triangular and scaly. The rounded front of the head ended in a round mouth with teeth lining the entire circular opening. She remembered seeing a lamprey once in a jar at an alchemist's shop. That fish had had a mouth much like the one she was looking at now.

The creature put one leg in front of the other and dragged itself toward the group, clearly attracted by Flek's light. It definitely was slow. They probably hadn't needed to run down the tunnel in the dark. Fortunately, no one had tripped or gotten hurt.

Thick, rough scales covered the body, and now that it was more visible, it was clear that it had no hind legs. The only claws it had were at the end of stubby limbs that it used to drag the long torso, which tapered into a tail. The mouth stayed focused on the rod Flek held, despite the distance.

"Do you have some kind of plan?" Wyndi asked Flek, her voice rising in pitch.

"Mostly? I guess it's more just an idea," he said, and she could see the grin on his face in the light from the rod he held. "The main danger is that they drain mana. But we don't have that much mana—mainly just these rods. It likely lives here because there are supposed to be mana crystals in these caves."

"Those teeth look like they can drain more than mana," Wyndi whined. "Seems like blood could be drained pretty easily with those teeth."

"They aren't fast," Flek rebuked. "We can just dodge the mouth. Or better yet, I'm thinking we just toss it a small crystal. I've got a few in my pack, maybe you can fish one out for me."

"You want this thing as a pet?" Legs asked. "I'm not sure that's such a great idea."

"No, not a pet," Flek growled. "It's just a distraction. While it's eating, we can attack it. I'm just working on figuring out the best attack. I don't want to use a shredder. It would take it out, but it would ruin it completely. There wouldn't be much left."

"I'm pretty sure that would be fine by me," Wyndi assured him. "I'm not looking for a trophy. If the shredder will kill it, go for it."

"Oh, did you still want to fight a mimic?" Flek shot back.

"What are you talking about?" Wyndi asked in exasperation. "I don't want to fight anything. What does a mimic have to do with anything? Thankfully, we haven't seen one. Have we? I know they disguise themselves."

"No, I haven't seen a mimic. I don't even know where to find one."

"Oh! That's right. You do know what you're talking about," Legs told the goblin with a goofy grin on his face. "Vulen have mana conduits. Pretty large conduits if I remember right."

"Exactly!" Flek said, pumping his fist in the air in excitement. "If we kill and harvest this vulin, we will have the other material Zaq wanted."

Meanwhile, the vulin was still dragging itself toward the group and had nearly closed the gap by half. Its laborious movements were slow but steady, never wavering from the prize it sensed in Flek's hand.

"Um, guys," Wyndi said, staring at the lizard-like creature shuffling toward her. "We should probably think of some way to kill it or get moving again."

"What about Doodles?" Legs asked.

"What about him? He's fine," Wyndi said.

"No, his tail packs a pretty big wallop," Legs explained. "If Flek distracts it with a crystal, Doodles can pound it with his tail. Even if it doesn't kill it, it would likely knock it out. Then we just slice it open with our daggers."

"Urg," Wyndi retched. "I'm not slicing it with my dagger, that sounds gross."

"The whole point of having the dagger is to poke or slice something," Flek pointed out. "But it's fine, I don't mind slicing it to extract the conduit if the beaver can knock it out."

"It's all yours," Wyndi said, grimacing.

"Can you get that crystal out of my pack?" Flek asked. "You do that, and Doodles and I can take care of the rest. Frank can be my backup."

Wyndi searched through the pack strapped to his back until she found a handful of small, rough mana crystals. She took just one and dropped the rest back into the bag. Reaching out until she felt his hand, she placed it in his palm, letting her finger brush his as he closed a fist around the crystal. *Stop it. Now is most definitely not the time*, she admonished herself in her mind.

Flek led Doodles forward, gripping the glow rod in one hand and the crystal in the other. He tossed the dark blue mana crystal at the monster, and it caught it with its mouth. The mouth closed like an iris, the teeth overlapping each other.

The vulin sat motionless in the hallway, apparently sucking

on the treat Flek had just tossed it. A wet squelch rose and fell with the undulating pattern of the creature's bobbing head.

Legs ordered Doddles to move forward and attack. Surprisingly, the beaver took the command without issue, as if this were a completely natural occurrence. The large, flat, leathery tail rose and fell rapidly on the creature with several loud *thwacks.*

Before falling back, Doddles swiped a front claw across the vulin's throat, splitting it wide open. Dark blue ooze ran from the gash, which seemed to be enough to remove the stun effect from the tail. However, the brackish blood was flowing freely, and the creature soon bled out.

"Nice work, Doddles!" Legs called.

"Guess, I don't need to finish it off," Flek mumbled. "The beaver took it out himself."

"We still need that mana conduit," Wyndi said, frowning at the light-blue scaled monster bleeding out in the middle of the tunnel. "So, you can harvest that since you don't mind using your dagger."

"Good point," Flek said and moved to do just that.

He flipped the lizard over and worked the dagger down the middle, from the gash in the neck to the end of the torso, where it formed a tail. The underbelly scales were not nearly as tough as the ones on its head and back. They parted easily, and he spread the torso open.

Wyndi didn't want to look, but for some reason she found herself oddly fascinated by the scene. Inside the vulin, a pulsing blue tube ran the length of its body. Flek cut away the connective tissue holding it in place and carefully removed the entire mana conduit.

The organ was surprisingly flexible. Flek coiled it like a length of rope, wrapped it in cloth, and stuffed it into an empty sack he had pulled from his bag.

"Will that—will it dry out?" Wyndi asked. "Do we have to do something to preserve it?"

"That's a good point," Flek grimaced, looking at the partially gutted corpse. "I'll stuff the bag with some of this wetter offal. We might even want to put it in the KoldBox once we get back to the cart."

"You are not putting that anywhere near my food," Legs rebuked, waving his hands.

"Relax, the KoldBox has compartments and drawers," Flek gently shook his head with a grin. "I'll make sure it doesn't touch any food."

It was actually amazing that Flek had done that. Wyndi was not at all confident she could have forced herself to gut the lizard. There were many reasons she studied artificery and not alchemy. Not touching gross things was just one of them.

"Hey, Flek," she casually asked for his attention.

"Yeah?"

"Thanks. Thanks for taking on the messy work there. And thanks for using your knowledge of the pests to keep calm. This is all new to me, and you—well, you just handled it better than I think I could have. So, thanks."

"Hey, we're a team," Flek said, his cheeks flushing with magenta. "I don't love doing that kind of stuff, but I spent a lot of time with my uncle growing up. He gave me odd jobs to help him out with his exterminating. I guess I got used to killing pests."

"Still, thanks. He probably didn't have you gutting them," Wyndi grinned.

"You'd be surprised," Flek shrugged. "There are a few pests, these included, that have useful parts. A lot of folks don't know, but exterminators do pretty well as a business. People hire them for the work of getting rid of pests, but there's also money coming in on the back end as well."

"That's smart," Legs said. "But speaking of smart, you two think we should go back to the cavern at the end of this tunnel?"

"If there are any more vulen, at least we can be ready for them," Flek nodded, looking down at the remains of the lizard. "Doodles seemed to do pretty well, too. I'm glad he's on our side."

"Hopefully, that's all that is in here," Wyndi added, sounding less nervous despite her statement. "It might be worth reporting in with Zaq. We can tell him we found a mana conduit."

Chapter 25

Zaq Receives an Update

Z aq clumsily fished the vibrating tablet out of the makeshift holster he now wore on his belt. He had wondered when he would next hear from his apprentices and had debated reaching out to check on them. Hopefully, they had run into no issues while searching the cave for the crystal. The dwarves at the mining company would have mentioned any dangers in the cave. *Wouldn't they?*

Flek: We did it!

> Zaq: You did? Wonderful. So, you found a crystal with no major issues?

Wyndi: I told you that you needed to tell him what we did.

Flek: I was getting to it.

> Zaq: Wait. Does that mean you haven't found a crystal? What did you do then? The map led to the cave, didn't it?

Frank: Yeah, the map was great. I followed it easily enough, and Flek spotted the cave. We had to leave the cart outside. Hopefully it's fine out there.

Zaq: Hopefully? You didn't leave anyone to watch it?

Frank: Don't worry. Flek set up a sensor.

Flek: Yeah, I took care of it. My sensor will let out a large, wailing alarm if anything comes near.

Zaq: That sounds like a smart device. I'd like to see that when you return.

Flek: Sure, I can show it to you. I got it in the warren. The goblin mining teams often use them in the mines to alert if anything tries to enter while they are inside.

Zaq: That sounds wonderful. I'd definitely like to—wait a minute. Stop distracting me. What did you do if you didn't find a crystal?

Flek: We came across a vulin. Doodles and I killed it. Okay, Doodles killed it. But I gutted it. Got a nice long mana conduit.

Zaq: Wonderful! Vulen are much safer adversaries than mimics. Mimics are more common, so I thought you'd have an easier time finding one.

Flek: Hopefully, the vulin was alone and didn't get too many of the crystals. We're going back to exploring the cave. Wyndi said we should let you know about the conduit.

Zaq: Good for her. I appreciate being kept abreast of the latest news.

"That was unnecessary. I wish they would realize I was ending the conversation. Good luck seems like a valid ending."

Zaq stared at the tablet, deciding the best course of action was to just stop responding. The apprentices did not seem to catch on until he stopped responding. Perhaps it was a show of respect since he was their mentor?

Not responding did the trick. There were no further messages from the team.

A nearby clock struck the hour, emitting a lovely chime and drawing his attention.

"Three in the afternoon? How did it get so late? I could use a little pick-me-up."

The workshop table was littered with various parts he had been toying with to see if they might yield an interesting effect. Nothing dangerous seemed to be lying about, so he left it all as it lay.

Zaq climbed the stairs and emerged in the alley behind the Mystic Leaf & Toadstool.

"I do like this location—much less of a walk for a treat than from my house. Of course, I'll have to watch this," he said to himself while patting his stomach.

"Or not," he chuckled at himself. "I'm just an old fuddy-duddy gnome. I certainly don't mind a little extra in spots. Of course, my back sometimes minds, I think."

Shrugging his shoulders, he put the thoughts behind him

and rounded the corner to the tea shop. Zheb wasn't anywhere to be seen, and the afternoon crowd filled the patio with a line of people snaking out of the door. Sighing, Zaq got in line, knowing the reason he didn't see the dwarf was certainly because he was busy taking orders and doing his best to stay on top of the rush.

With this many people, it seemed like Joh might need to extract himself from the kitchen and help manage the customers. Zaq knew that wasn't his favorite activity, and he much preferred one-on-one dealings with people, or at most a small group.

Zaq glanced around the patio while he waited. He loved the variety of people that could be found in Ryefeld. This afternoon, the patrons at the tables included halflings, dwarves, elves, nagas, various beastkin, goblins, orcs, and a couple of gnolls. It was a packed house. He couldn't see inside the shop. In front of him stood an extremely large troll who Zaq guessed was ordering for both himself and the troll sitting alone at one of the tables.

Eventually, Zaq made his way to the front of the line, finding Zheb, as he expected, behind the counter.

"Greetings and salutations, my fine dwarven friend."

"Hello to you, Zaq. Vat vill it be today?"

"I'm in the mood for dragonroot this afternoon with a splash of that not-milk stuff. I also feel like I've earned a treat, so I'll have whatever is freshest out of the oven."

"One dragonroot tea and a cinnamon bun viss ackernut frosting. It vill be ready shortly. Step to zee end of zee counter."

"That sounds wonderful. I can't wait," Zaq said, sliding a few coins across the counter and walking farther into the shop to wait for his order.

It was always nicer when he could just relax outside on the patio, but Zaq knew that when it got busy, the dwarves simply didn't have the staff to handle the counter and the patio at the same time. While a Mystic Leaf & Toadstool was a good franchise to own, he also knew that in a city like Ryefeld, where you could find one on practically every block, it could be hard to find success. It was unlikely the dwarves could afford to hire anyone, especially when, outside of the rush hours, they handled it just fine on their own.

Mystics in general were designed for efficiency, from their Kwikbrew spouts to the pastry cases with stasis enchantments to ensure freshness; it didn't take long at all to fill the customers' orders. Case in point, only a few minutes had passed before Zheb slid toward him a hot mug of creamy dragonroot and a plate which only barely contained the enormous cinnamon roll with thick white frosting coating the top and melting down the sides, forming a gooey puddle of sugar around the base of the bun.

Taking the mug in one hand and the plate in the other, Zaq made his way out to the patio. He scanned the tables, but not a single one was open.

"Another benefit to a workshop right underneath," he muttered to himself as he shook his head at the crowd.

Several friendly people offered him a chance to join them as he passed through the patio. Zaq did not want to spend his afternoon break listening to strangers talk about whatever frivolous things strangers chatted about. The peace and quiet of his workshop would be fine. Besides, there was a whole table he had devoted to non-project work. He had set up some stools around it, intending it to be a social area when people weren't hard at work.

Zaq carefully carried his precious cargo down the stairs. He thankfully noticed the cat sitting in the way on the second-to-last stair. He kicked lightly at it to prod it out of the way, then continued into the workshop.

The sleek black cat stalked into the room behind him, pacing circles around his legs as he walked. *Was it trying to kill him? Or wreck his afternoon treat?*

Thankfully, he made it all the way to the table in the workshop he had reserved for rest and relaxation. It was devoid of clutter, making it the perfect spot to gather, eat, and drink. Of course, the other people who might share the space were off killing monsters in caves, so he had the table to himself.

"What stupendous luck they found a vulin. Come to think of it, I don't know a lot about them. I hope they aren't horribly dangerous. The kids seem to be doing fine. I'm sure everything is in hand."

He arranged his tea and plate, then grabbed a fork from a basket in the center of the table. The frosting on his roll had become even softer, and the puddle of sugary fat had grown. He pried off a bite, and it almost slipped right off the fork. Bending over the plate so as to bring himself to the bite, rather than the bite come to him and risk being lost, he quickly pushed the dripping piece of sweet bread into his mouth.

There was enough sugar in that one bite to last most people an entire day. At first, there was only sweetness, but that gave way to a deep blend of cinnamon, cloves, and nutmeg. The bread itself was nearly lost in all the flavor, but it held firm enough to offer Zaq something to chew. It was soft and pillowy, and the entire experience brought a smile of ecstasy.

After a sip of the tea, he mentally patted himself on the back for only having ackermilk added, and no sugar. The spices in the dragonroot played nicely with the roll, and the sugary residue in his mouth was plenty to take the edge off the bitterness of the hot drink.

Zaq noticed the two glowing yellow eyes of the cat staring up at him from beneath the table. It was watching his every move.

"None of this is for cats. You wouldn't like it. Too much sugar will do bad things to you. Have you caught any mice lately? I know I've been putting food out so you don't starve, but you should help fill your belly as well."

As if the cat understood, it stood up and stretched itself out as if it had been sitting way too long, despite the fact that it had been there just as long as he had, and then trotted across the room. Moments later, it came out from under a workbench, batting something with its paws.

"What in the world is that? Did someone drop a tool under the bench? Be careful with the tools."

The cat did not have a tool. It alternated smacking the dead mouse with each of its paws, working it across the room toward Zaq, who froze once he realized what the creature was doing.

"What?! If you find and kill a rodent, you need to eat it or take it away. Don't play with the thing like some kind of toy."

Oddly enough, the cat seemed to understand him yet again. It snatched the dead rodent up in its mouth and trotted up the stairs. Zaq watched it leave, ensuring the dead animal was removed from the workshop.

"I don't know why I put up with that beast."

Shaking his head, Zaq returned to eating his treat and drinking his tea. While the tea was lovely and he finished the entire cup, he only made it halfway through the sweet roll. It proved to have too much sugar, and he feared he might develop a stomachache if he continued.

"Too bad I can't send this off to the kids. I neglected to send them any treats. Some cookies would have been nice. If they need to go back out, I'll make sure to send cookies next time. I could have easily split this roll between the four of us."

Zaq gathered the dishes and took them back up to the cafe before heading home. Originally, he had planned to work more in the shop after his break, but his stomach, while not aching, still wasn't feeling one-hundred percent after eating so much of the pastry. Tonight, he would make himself some dinner with food that had more to it, not sugary confections, and relax with a whisky. A nice high-proof rye would be good. *That should settle my stomach.*

<h1 style="text-align:center">Chapter 26</h1>

<h2 style="text-align:center">Mana Crystal</h2>

Wyndi put her tablet away and watched Flek and Legs do the same with theirs. She could tell Flek had appreciated being able to report to Zaq about the vulin. He earned it after making sure it was dead and harvesting the organ. She appreciated him for it and was glad she hadn't been the one to do the deed. However, now they needed to continue the quest for the crystal.

"Is everyone up for continuing? We should check out that cavern and find ourselves a mana crystal large enough for the project."

"You bet I'm ready," Flek answered enthusiastically. "That's the only thing left on the list. Once we have that, we can head back to the city."

"One-hundred percent with the goblin on that one," Legs nodded vigorously. "I appreciate a good camping trip, but I appreciate my bed even more."

"Wonderful. Lights on. Let's go."

The trip back down the tunnel went faster than before, as they had already checked the various side passageways.

When they reached the end and the hall gave way to a small cavern roughly thirty rods deep and twenty rods wide, they painted their light beams over the floor, ceiling, and walls of the space.

Wyndi didn't spot any movement; however, her heart sank as their lights danced through several crystals jutting up from the floor. Instead of the vibrant blue she would expect to see, the crystals ranged from dark black to clear, with various shades of translucent grey in between.

The vulin must have been here for some time. No wonder it had been so large. It must have fed on every crystal in the room. The clear ones might still have some mana in them, but it wouldn't be enough. They needed a large, deep blue mana crystal, full of concentrated magic.

"These aren't going to work," Flek said, stating what was on her mind.

"There are other tunnels," Legs pointed out, shining his beam at three separate exits from the cavern. "We can hope it was on its way in and not on its way out."

Wyndi sighed in frustration, looking around at the crystals again in the hope that she could change their state by observing them again.

"That's at least a possibility. That tunnel across the way is roughly in line with this one. Let's take it and see where it leads us."

The trio crossed the room, casting long shadows as the glow lights illuminated various portions of the space. Wyndi slid a hand over a crystal as they passed. It was smooth, but had no pulse. No energy left within.

Light danced down the dark tunnel, the beam running over the ground, walls, and ceiling. The tunnel itself seemed uninteresting, and it was long enough that the light faded before hitting anything.

"Doesn't look much different than the one we came in," Wyndi said.

"It's a good choice to go down this one, then," Flek said. "It's possible these tunnels were made by a mining crew. It makes sense that they would go straight before branching off."

"But wait," Legs said, scratching his head. "There are tunnels that go out to the left and right. If you are right, and they go straight before branching, doesn't that mean we're less likely to find more crystals straight ahead?"

"Possibly," Flek said slowly, drawing out the word. "There were still quite a few crystals in here before the vulin got them. But I'm fine if you want to try a side tunnel."

"No, let's stick with straight," Wyndi said with authority. "Barring any more vulen, we should find at least some crystals down this path. I'd rather keep our route as straight as possible. That way, we can easily make our way back out."

"Good point," Flek said, "Let's continue then."

The trio pressed forward through the tunnel with Doodles trailing behind. The path continued for at least a hundred rods before opening into another cavern.

Their lights shone through brilliant blue crystals, proving the vulin had not made it this far into the cave system. Unfortunately, they were all fairly small. None met the measurement requirements that Zaq had provided.

"I knew we should have used a side tunnel," Legs muttered so quietly Wyndi almost didn't hear him, but the acoustics of the cave system brought the sound to her ears.

"What was that?" she asked, despite knowing the answer.

"Nothing," Legs said louder. "Should we try one of the other routes?"

"I think we have to," Flek said, shining his light on every wall. "This room has no exits."

Feeling somewhat discouraged, Wyndi backtracked to the

cavern of dead crystals, then took a right, which would have been on their left when they came through the original tunnel.

"If you're going to turn, you should turn left first," she said. "But we should use the left from our original entry, not our current left."

"I agree. Left is the right choice," Flek grinned. "Right is the wrong choice, except when it's this right, which was our left."

Wyndi rolled her eyes and led the group, navigating them down the dark tunnel with her glow rod.

The corridor stretched on much longer than the others had, with no offshoots. Wyndi hoped that meant something good, rather than an eventual dead end. As she walked, her mind wandered to Flek. How could someone so annoying be so interesting? His nonsense about the directions was just silly, but at the same time, kind of cute.

Yet again, Wyndi wished she had some kind of manual for understanding people, like the ones she had for her various tools and appliances. Trial and error with feelings and people had much greater consequences than experimenting with runes and machinery. What if she said the wrong thing to Flek or made the wrong move? Would she be stuck working with someone who hated her?

"How long do you think this tunnel is?" Flek asked, ripping her mind back to the present. "I can see a fair bit farther than the light illuminates thanks to my goblin eyes, but I haven't seen anything yet."

"I envy your eyes," Legs said, stealing a thought from Wyndi's mind. "I can barely see what the glow rods illuminate, much less anything beyond them."

"They're great until it's a bright sunny day in the middle of summer. A lot of goblins won't even go outside when the sun is high at that time of year. Having eyes capable of seeing in very low-light situations is great if that's where you are, but it makes the opposite painful sometimes."

"I never really thought about that side of it," Wyndi added. "It makes sense now that you mention it. Of course, what I'd love is a better pair of goggles. There are goggles that can do all sorts of things. Low-light vision enhancements, shade and polarization from bright lights or the sun, and zoom features for things far away or super close."

"Have you seen the pair Zaq has?" Flek asked. "I'd love to try them out. I'm pretty sure they can do all of what you said, maybe even more."

"I know, right?" Wyndi nodded excitedly. "I couldn't tell all of their features without trying them out, but based on the dials, lights, and lens, my guess is all of that and more."

"Do you think he made them? Or bought them?" Legs asked.

"I bet he made them," Flek said confidently. "He seems like the kind of guy who won't spend money unless he has to, and he has the know-how to do it. I'm pretty sure he made the custom KoldBox he sent with us."

"I think you're right," Wyndi agreed. "Both about the KoldBox and his bias toward making instead of buying."

"That's why he hired us on as apprentices, isn't it?" Legs said. "I mean, he doesn't have to pay us more than with knowledge and some food, and he has us running around the countryside collecting items for his project."

Everyone burst into laughter at the truth in his words. Zaq most definitely only brought them on because he saw it was advantageous economically—a means to an end for creating his project.

"What do you all think about the communication system?" Wyndi asked. "So far, it's been amazing on our trip. The ability to send and receive messages from him any time we want! Plus, the way the map and other drawings can be shared! I want to see this spread."

"Oh yeah. I'm glad we get to try it out," Flek agreed. "I just hope we can keep using them after the trip."

"They are pretty fascinating," Legs mused. "I still wonder how well they can actually work. This crystal should help, and the conduit as well, but I'm not sure it will scale. I think we are pushing the limit of the distributor we are using now. With better equipment, I'm sure he can handle twenty or twenty-five tablets. You know what would be amazing? Hundreds. Thousands. More! What if everyone could communicate with each other?"

Wyndi barked a laugh.

"That's quite the dream. I think we need to focus on something realistic. You'd need a crystal the size of a mountain to power something that could distribute messages to the world."

"You're probably right," Legs said, scratching his head. "I think too big sometimes. That's always been my problem with the things I try, like my mom's magic. I always wanted it to do more than it could, and so it never worked at all for me."

"It's not bad to dream big," Wyndi assured him. "I shouldn't have laughed. Without big dreams, a lot of artificery projects would never be built."

"I think that's true of a lot of things," Flek added. "Not just artificery, but a lot of creative projects. The most promising alchemist I know dreamed big, and it got her almost everything she ever dreamed of."

"Exactly!" Wyndi clapped, almost fumbling her glow rod. "That's what I mean. How would we have stories without the authors who imagine them and capture the tales in books? Or beautiful paintings and sculptures? They had to start as someone's dream."

"We should do it then," Legs said. "We should build a

massive system. Maybe Zaq is thinking too small with this crystal."

"I don't think we can get anything larger," Wyndi cautioned. "Zaq made it clear. The dwarves who pointed out this place said we could take one crystal that met the requirements for the current distributor plans. The distributor might not be able to handle the world, but Zaq seems to think it can handle a lot. If it's not enough, we can figure out getting a bigger one."

"Good point," Flek said, then jumped excitedly. He was always so excitable. Sometimes it was contagious. "Look! The tunnel is ending."

"There you go, rubbing in your awesome vision again," Legs chuckled. "I'll take your word for it. I can't see anything."

Several paces later, Wyndi got excited, too.

"Oh! He's right, I see it. Look how the sides of the tunnel fade off. Let's hurry."

The team picked up the pace, even Doodles, who was by far the slowest member of the team. The lights from the glow rods bobbed and danced across the tunnel walls as they jogged.

When they reached the end of the tunnel, Wyndi directed her light over the whole cavern from left to right. There were no offshoot tunnels from this cavern, just the single entrance where they stood. Deep blue crystals of all shapes and sizes thrust up from the floor in irregular patterns. Some were small, like in the previous room, but others were quite large.

Flek ran toward one in the right half of the room. His eyes clearly let him see nearly perfectly in this light.

"I'm pretty sure this one fits the bill."

"We should measure it to be sure," Wyndi said, walking toward it. "But I think you're right. It looks large, but not too large."

She pulled out a measuring rod and used it to measure out the width, depth, and height.

"Yes, this will work. We just need to be careful harvesting it. It won't do us any good if it is damaged."

Legs pulled out the pickaxe from the bags Doodles had been carrying.

"I'll be careful. I'll start by chipping away the rock around the crystal. Once we've exposed it and cut away the rock, it might just come free. If not, I can carefully chip through the crystal."

"Let's try to expose the whole thing if we can," Flek added. "These crystals are more effective if you can harvest the entire thing, rather than breaking off a piece."

With a nod, Legs began chipping at the surrounding stone, sending bits of rock spraying to the sides. As he removed chunks of the stone floor, the sides of the crystal tapered in. That was a good sign, and he continued working at the stone rather than attacking the crystal itself.

"Hold it steady. I think I'm getting close to freeing it."

Both Wyndi and Flek took hold of either side while Legs worked his way around the base of the crystal, breaking up more and more of the rock. Eventually, he broke through a piece of rock that was clearly the main remaining support because the dark blue crystal felt extremely heavy all of a sudden.

Seeing them straining, Legs dropped his pickaxe and helped stabilize the load.

"This is pretty heavy. It's really too bad the cart didn't fit."

"We'll just have to work together to carry it out," Wyndi said, shaking her head. "Flek and I can brace it. Pack up the pickaxe, then you can help us carry it out."

Legs did just that, but as he was putting the tool away, he spied a ball of netting his father had packed.

"Hey, Doodles," he said, patting his side. "Would you mind if we strapped this gem to your tail? We have some netting, and your tail is reminiscent of a sled."

The beaver chittered cheerfully. Wyndi wasn't sure if he was actually on board with the plan, but it was hard to tell how much the beaver understood. He was clearly more intelligent than the average animal, but perhaps not fully sapient.

The three of them carefully transferred the gem to the middle of the beaver's tail. Legs used the netting to wrap around both the crystal and the tail, securing the cargo as best he could.

Chapter 27

Surprise Welcome

The trip out of the mine was uneventful. The group took the long, dark tunnel back to the room with the drained crystals, then turned right so they could leave via the original tunnel they had entered. Wyndi was quite happy the cave system was not more labyrinthian, but Flek assured her several times that he could have navigated them through, no matter how complex the layout was.

For all she knew, he probably could. Goblins from a warren like his spent most of their lives underground. She knew dwarves had an uncanny knack for navigating below the surface; there was no reason to think it wouldn't be the same for goblins. Before long, they came across the remains of the vulin.

"Should we do something about this corpse?" she asked, hoping the answer was *no*.

"It would be the right thing to do. I don't think we need to drag it out, but perhaps we could take it down one of the dead-end tunnels that shoot off from this main one?" Legs suggested.

"I'll help you," Flek said, already moving to grab the rear

portion where the torso met the tail. There's a dead-end tunnel just ahead on the left. You grab the front half under the arms."

Legs nodded and did just that while Wyndi guided them with a glow rod. She directed the beam down the tunnel Flek had mentioned. Sure enough, it ran about twenty rods in and ended in a pile of rubble.

"Flek was right. This should work. There is even a pile of rubble you could use to bury it, so it isn't left exposed."

"Good idea," Legs said and swung into the tunnel, dragging the vulin. It didn't look that heavy to Wyndi, just awkward due to its length and shape, and gross since its guts were sliced open.

Flek followed into the tunnel carrying his portion. Wyndi was happy to stay where she was and helpfully shine the light down the passage. Doodles waited next to her and didn't seem to care much about the whole ordeal.

When the two men reached the end, they dropped the lizard and used the loose rubble to cover it as best they could. Once it was covered, they jogged back to the main tunnel to meet up with Wyndi. She adjusted the light as they approached to illuminate the path without blinding them.

"I think that counts as my good deed for the day," Flek said, dusting his hands. "That was over and above what anyone would expect."

"It was very nice of you, Flek," Wyndi agreed. She felt a little bad that her first thought had been just to leave it in the middle of the tunnel. But seriously? She was not going to drag around a dead lizard. "Thank you both for taking care of it."

The rest of the walk out was reasonably straightforward. Wyndi ignored the side tunnels since they had already achieved their goal. However, as she approached the mouth of the cave and could see the dusky light of late afternoon, she froze.

High-pitched voices drifted down the tunnel along with several muffled clashes of equipment, laughter that sounded like bells, and the crackle of a fire.

"Hold!" she hissed out in a whisper while holding her hand up.

"Do you hear that, too?" Legs whispered back.

"Yes," she said, drawing out the word. "Why else would I say to stop?"

"I was just making sure," Legs said, sounding slightly hurt.

"Sorry, I didn't mean to sound harsh," she apologized. "It just caught me off guard. There are clearly people out there."

"Just because there are people, doesn't mean they are mean-spirited or bad," Flek pointed out. "Let's just go see who's there."

"I think that's a good idea," Wyndi agreed. "I didn't think we should stay in here. I just wanted us to be careful. Hopefully, they are friendly, but we need to be cautious."

Carefully, Wyndi led the group the rest of the way out of the cave. As she exited, she saw what had been making the noises.

Three fairies had raided the supplies in their cart and were actively cooking something over a fire that smelled absolutely delicious. The diminutive people stood only as tall as Wyndi's waist, which was not very tall at all. Looking at the cart, it appeared they had only gotten into the KoldBox and dry goods crates, and from the smells, they had brought their own spices and ingredients. Of course, fairies were also known to have household magics and could have summoned the missing things they needed.

As Wyndi stood taking in the scene, one of the fairies noticed the group and called out in a high-pitched voice that sounded like a bird chirping excitedly.

"There you are! See Gilly? I told you that someone had left this cart here."

"I never said they didn't," the one apparently named Gilly said. "Of course, someone left the cart here. The question, Milly, was whether they went into that cave or not."

"Don't forget the important question of whether they would come back out," called the third fairy, who was actively attending to whatever was cooking over the fire.

"Well, yes. I didn't forget that, Tilly. But that wouldn't matter unless we knew if they went in there or not."

"Shut it both of you," Milly said in a stern but not at all mean way. She was clearly accustomed to bringing them back on track from potential tangents. "Those were both good questions. My point had been that they didn't matter. Wherever they went, they would likely be coming back. No one would leave a perfectly good cart full of supplies out here."

"Excuse me," Wyndi said, trying to grab their attention. "Milly, is it? We did, in fact, leave the cart here when we entered the cave. Now we're back, and I'm somewhat worried you've taken our belongings."

"Oh no!" Milly said, and bell-like laughter chimed from all three fairies. "We haven't taken your belongings. We've been watching them as proper guardians. We used a few of your supplies, but only because we wanted to prepare something delicious for you. I knew you would be back soon, no matter where you had gone."

"That does smell amazing," Flek said with a grin splitting his face, ear-to-ear. "Is it almost done? I'm starving."

"It is!" called Tilly. "In fact, Gilly, bring me some plates. I'll dish up food for everyone."

The fairy named Gilly manifested a stack of plates from nowhere and brought them to Tilly. One at a time, she held one up, and the cook spooned a heaping pile of vegetables smothered in a dark-brown sauce onto the dish. She followed that up with a warm roll made with rye and a slice of apple pie.

After each plate was laden with delicious-looking food, Gilly sped it to one of the three apprentices, who each found a comfortable spot to sit. She looked at the giant beaver and made a *tsk-tsk* noise to herself.

"We were not expecting the beaver. Though, to be fair, something had to have been pulling this cart. We should have thought of that. Do you mind if I serve him one of the branches you have in the cart? I'm sure he'd love grimbark."

"Oh, he does," Legs assured her. "That's fine. That's what they are for, actually. We collected some extra branches to give him treats on the way back home."

"Wonderful!" Gilly chirped and hauled a branch three times her size over to Doodles. Wyndi could tell he wanted to thump his tail, but he couldn't do so with the large crystal strapped to it. He didn't seem to mind and happily began gnawing on the branch.

Once everyone, including the beaver, had food to eat, the fairies served themselves and sat down in a circle with the apprentices.

"What were you doing in the cave?" Milly asked.

"They were mining crystals," Gilly admonished. "Isn't it obvious?"

"Of course it's obvious," Milly said. "However, it's polite to ask. Give them a chance to tell the tale."

"Yeah," Tilly agreed. "You can't go ruining their story before it even starts. How are we supposed to get a story as payment for the food if we tell it before they can?"

Gilly seemed to accept the chastising and focused on eating, but looked expectantly at the apprentices.

Wyndi and Flek both had their mouths full, so Legs took it upon himself to answer.

"Yes, we were mining for a mana crystal. We needed a large one of a specific size for Mr. Flickerwhizzle. We're building an amazing—"

Legs cut off when Wyndi shot him a glare.

"Right, I guess I shouldn't say exactly what we are doing with the crystal. We have non-disclosure agreements in place. Buttoned up tight. Legally sound."

"Be careful with contracts of binding law," Milly cautioned. "Laws are as strong as the world interprets them and sometimes even stronger than that. Contracts bind powerful spells of ancient magics."

"Then you understand," Legs nodded. "I shouldn't go into more detail. But we did need to get that crystal over there. Luckily, we ran into the vulin before it drained all of the crystals in the cave."

Wyndi let Legs and the fairies continue their discussion about the vulin and the findings inside the cave, focusing instead on her food. These fairies knew how to cook, but that wasn't surprising. Fairies were renowned for their cooking and baking throughout the land. They rarely set up permanent shops in any of the cities or settlements. There are exceptions. Ryefeld, for example, has at least one bakeshop run by a fairy that she was aware of.

The brown sauce coating the vegetables was rich and thick, adding a deep umami flavor to the carrots, potatoes, onions, and parsnips. It was salty and earthy and reminded Wyndi of wild mushrooms with hints of thyme, coriander, and a touch of cumin.

When she finished the vegetables, she dredged her roll through the sauce left on her plate. The bread was dense and chewy—whatever fats made up the sauce clung to the roll and seeped in, giving it the perfect amount of moisture.

She had saved the pie for last, despite the constant temptation it offered her while she ate. She had no idea how hungry she had been. Flek must have been as well, since he was as focused on his meal as she was on hers. How did the fairies even make a pie? It's not like you can easily cook one over a campfire. Then again, why question fairies? There was magic in almost everything they did.

The first bite of pie delighted her mouth. The apples were firm but gave way under gentle pressure. Wyndi had never been a fan of baked apples that were too soft. The fruit was glazed in a sugary syrup infused with cinnamon and cloves. But the crust—the crust was to die for. It was flaky, buttery, and dusted lightly with sugar. It was quite possible she would need to see about a second slice if there was any left.

She re-entered the conversation to find Flek describing the burial of the vulin.

"Thankfully, it was more awkward than heavy. It shouldn't attract anything beyond bugs and small vermin with all that stone on top."

"Excuse me," Wyndi interrupted. "You don't happen to have any more pie, do you?"

The bell-like laughter tinkled from all three of the beautiful fairies.

"We cut the pie into six pieces and each had one," Tilly said. "But do not fear, we will leave a fresh pie for you when we go."

"Speaking of leaving," Milly transitioned. "We should be off so they may bunk down for the night before heading home. They earned our hospitality with their lovely tale."

"Thank you so much," Wyndi said. "I'm sorry I didn't offer

much to the story. I was so hungry, and your food was better than anything I've had in quite some time."

"Remove the worry from your head," Milly giggled. "Your companions told us all about your spelunking adventure. Good luck in your endeavors bound to secrecy with your contracts."

"Good night," all three of the apprentices wished the fairies almost in complete unison.

Chapter 28

Heading Home

As the night drew to a close and dawn gently shooed away the darkness, Wyndi sat, tending the fire. Autumn dawns always came softly, unlike in the summer when the rising sun would burn away the darkness. Of course, this time of year, foreboding rainclouds often threatened in the sky, and you never knew if they would bring a lazy drizzle or a torrential downpour. On those days, the sun was rarely even seen, and the black of night would simply fade to gray.

Thankfully, there had been no rain on their trip. Surely the gods looked favorably on their mission and Zaq's project. The early morning was cold enough that Wyndi wore a warm coat throughout her shift, and she stayed by the fire and the heat it radiated.

All three of the apprentices decided to take turns keeping watch, despite the fact that Flek had a sensor to detect intruders. Neither Wyndi nor Legs fully believed that it worked as well as he had claimed. When they pointed out that the fairies had not tripped the alarm, he had waved away their concerns with excuses that fairy magic was strong and they meant no harm. She could still hear his voice in her head.

The fairies have old magic, old enough to get by the sensor since they were not hostile. Most everything else would surely set off the alarm.

Once again, Wyndi stole a glance over at the sleeping goblin. Her gaze lingered, and she watched his chest rise and fall. She was almost positive at this point that she felt something beyond the bounds of coworkers and friends. But she wouldn't act on it—not without more of a sign from him. At times, she caught him looking at her, and she felt there were other minor signs he was interested, but nothing definitive. She would not put herself out there and look like a fool if she were wrong.

There was something about Flek. For all that he could drive her up the wall with his attitude and competitive behavior, she felt he was genuine. He was someone sure of himself—sometimes he was a little too sure, but sure of himself, nonetheless. Flek reminded her a lot of her father and how sure he was of his view of the world. Her father's view was closed, though, and not something she admired. While Flek had confidence and accepted everyone he met as they were.

The thought tripped in her mind, and Wyndi broke the silence of the early morning with a giggle. Flek may think he was a better artificer than her, but he appeared to have no doubt she had the skills for invention as well. If only her father could see that potential instead of insisting she could only succeed by performing repairs like he did. And, of course, there was the constant criticism of her weight that her father practiced continuously.

Flek, on the other hand, saw her for who she was and didn't even mind that she carried a little extra. He made her so comfortable. She hadn't even paused to think last night before not only eating her pie, but asking for more. The Wyndi from a few weeks ago would never have allowed herself to do that. But maybe he was right. Maybe a little extra did look good on her. She still smiled when she thought back to the first time he had said that.

That was just it, though, wasn't it? Perhaps Flek was just too nice. He was competitive and often tried to put himself first, but he was also accepting and made her feel at ease. She saw that in the way he interacted with others, too, and how he talked of his friends from back home. That's why she couldn't move first. She needed a clearer sign that he actually felt something back beyond his general acceptance.

Wyndi snapped out of her thoughts as Flek and Legs increased their rustling as they woke. She purposefully looked down at the fire, poking it with a stick, intent on being sure not to let the goblin know she had just been staring at him while he slept.

"Ah, good, you two are waking up. I'm hoping we can make it back to the city tomorrow if we get a solid day of travel in today."

"That seems possible," Legs said through a yawn as he sat up. "We already loaded the mana crystal in the cart last night. I'm good to leave as soon as I pack up my things."

Flek was slower to respond, but when he did, he hopped up, having cast away his sleepiness in an instant.

"I'll be ready in just a moment," he declared as he gathered up his belongings.

"I found some sandwiches in the KoldBox: almond butter and raspberry jam," Wyndi said, pointing to a stack wrapped in paper she had set out on the back of the cart. "I figure we can eat while we walk."

Only a few minutes passed before everything was packed into the cart, Doodles was harnessed securely, and each of the apprentices held a sandwich, ready to head toward home. They walked down the hill toward the river that they planned to follow back to town.

"I sent Zaq a message, letting him know we have everything on the list and should return to Ryefeld soon," Wyndi said between bites of her food while they walked.

"Wasn't it too early?" Legs asked. "I doubt he appreciates his tablet getting his attention before he's even made it out of bed."

"I doubt he keeps it near him while sleeping," Wyndi justified, feeling defensive. "Besides, he didn't reply, so it probably didn't wake him. When he does get up, he'll have the news."

"Makes sense," Flek nodded. "I've been thinking about these tablets. There's a chance they could really change how we think about communicating."

"Maybe," Legs mused. "I'm still not sure how many people we can link to a distributor, even if it's a large one. Zaq seems sure. I'm probably still missing something."

"Don't completely dismiss your gut," Wyndi cautioned. "I think a lot of artificery is trusting those feelings if you aren't sure about something. The sure-fire way to find out is to experiment."

"That's very true. Well said," Flek agreed, offering her a compliment she hadn't been expecting.

Wyndi smiled to herself and finished her sandwich. A few minutes later, her tablet buzzed. She had it stowed in the cart, and it took her a moment to realize what the noise was. Hopping into the moving cart, she fished out the slate and looked at it.

> Zaq: Thank you for the update. Safe travels home. I'll prepare for the materials.

A thought of sending a brief reply made its case in her

head, but she tossed it aside. The old artificer had gone a long time before responding. He had likely been asleep and was then putting together his morning meal. None of that mattered, though—the message she had sent just stayed there waiting for his attention. Legs was right, this non-immediate style of communication was strange, but powerful. Maybe they could change the world.

"Looks like Zaq got my message. He wished us safe travels."

"That was weird," Flek said.

"What's weird about him wishing us safe travels?" Wyndi quirked an eyebrow. "That's a common enough thing to do, and he has always seemed proper and polite, even if he can be a bit of a grump."

"Not that part," Flek shook his head. "The weird part was that only your slate buzzed. All of our slates have been buzzing when we get a message from him."

"Why didn't I notice that?" Legs asked, giving Flek a pat on the back. "Good eye for detail there."

"Oh! Well, yeah," Wyndi said, trying to think of a good answer. "I guess that is weird. Let me look at that again."

She fished the tablet back out from where she had just repacked it. A few minutes slipped by as she lost herself tapping on various controls.

"Got it!" Wyndi exclaimed, turning the device so everyone could see. "Zaq sent the message directly to me in response to my message instead of to the entire group. I hadn't even realized that was possible, but there are a lot of options on here. He hasn't explained even a third of them."

"That just increased the usefulness even more!" Flek said, jumping up and down while he walked. "Not everyone on the same distributor needs to share their message with everyone else. This is huge. The tablets allow for group communication, but that ingenious old gnome made it possible for smaller groups to communicate privately without sharing everything with everyone on a distributor."

Wyndi hopped down from the wagon, and all three apprentices continued to talk about the possibilities this distributor system held while they walked alongside the river.

Doodles pulled the cart between two maple trees while Legs directed him. Wyndi had pushed the group to go as far as they could to keep the next day's travel short, but her determination lost out as dusk gave way to night.

That evening, she put together a fire while Flek found some food to cook. He found a packet in the KoldBox containing tiny cubes of carrot, celery, onion, and pre-cooked chicken. Like the previous packets, the contents were doused in oil and spices. Holding up a note in one hand and thrusting out a pot, he called to Legs.

"Can you fill this pot with water? We're having chicken and rice soup tonight."

"Sure thing," Legs said, jogging over to grab the pot Flek held out.

The goblin climbed down from the cart with the meal packet and a loaf of crusty white bread. He waited until Legs returned from the river with a pot full of water, then dumped the ingredients from the KoldBox into the pot along with a cup of rice. Flek cooked the soup over the fire Wyndi had built, and she found some bowls.

Before long, the soup was bubbling, and the rice had puffed up. Flek gave it a few final stirs, then ladled it into the bowls.

"This should be good. Soup's ready!" he called.

As Wyndi sat down to eat her meal, small droplets of water hit her face. Larger drops splashed in her bowl. The rain stayed just a sprinkle while they ate, which they now did with hurried gusto, trying to finish eating before the rain fell harder.

"Almost made it home," Legs said wistfully. "This won't be a fun night."

"I say we skip watch tonight," Flek said, holding his bowl up to his mouth to take a large gulp, finishing it off. "It'll be unlikely anyone or anything will come around to bother us. We can all sleep under the cart. It'll be tight under there, but more of us should be covered than not."

"That's a good idea," Wyndi said. "We need to keep as dry as we can. Huddling together should keep us warmer as well."

They left the rain to put out the fire and grabbed some blankets from deeper in the cart that hadn't yet gotten wet. Legs pulled a tarp out that must have been in the saddlebags Doodles had brought. He covered the contents of the cart as best he could and let the heavy, oil-treated canvas hang over the sides.

It was definitely tight under the cart, but they squeezed in together. This was not precisely the way Wyndi thought a night of cuddling up to Flek might be. The cold and the rain drove any thoughts she might have harbored about the situation from her head, and she forced herself to get some rest for the final leg of their journey the next day.

When they woke, Wyndi was surprised to find Doodles had been industrious overnight. He hadn't been bothered by the rain and had taken it upon himself to improve their shelter. The beaver had stacked branches and rocks all around the base of the cart.

"That was certainly helpful?" she said with a question in her voice.

"I'm sure he thought so," Legs chuckled.

All three of them kicked away the debris and extracted themselves from under the cart. Doodles was happily gnawing on a maple branch, stripping it of leaves. He must have thought his good deed had earned him a tasty breakfast.

"Let's get this cleared away so we can get back on the road," she said, grabbing two larger branches and pulling them away from the cart.

"This won't take long," Flek declared with his usual confidence.

He was right. Working diligently, they made short work of the cleanup project. The rain had stopped at some point during the night. All that remained to remind them of it was the muddy ground.

"You never know if it might start raining again," Legs commented as he rubbed oil that faintly smelled of cedar and citrus into his face, neck, and arms. He slipped the bottle back into his pack, then tucked the tarp into the cart, leaving everything covered.

"Don't do that!" Flek cried. "You never invite the bad, especially by preparing for it."

"That's just superstition," Wyndi shook her head, grinning. "It might rain, it might not, but based on the sky currently, I'm guessing we'll make it home before it starts up again."

"Still, let's just stop taunting the gods," he said. "Everyone good with granola and fruit while we walk?"

"Yeah, that's fine by me," Legs agreed. "I don't want to waste time with unpacking and repacking and a fire and everything else that will push out getting to Ryefeld even more."

The rest of the day passed quickly with Doodles dictating the pace. By mid-afternoon, Flek pointed out the central city buildings, which were the tallest in Ryefeld.

"Shouldn't be that much farther now. Do you think we should go straight to the mining company?"

"That's a good idea," Wyndi said. "They'll want to take a look at the mana crystal we took."

"We should tell them about the vulin," Legs pointed out.

"Right," Flek nodded. "We don't want them to think we did something to all those crystals."

"That's not exactly what I meant," Legs shook his head, grinning. "I doubt they'll blame us. I hope not anyway. I just meant they should know who *was* responsible and maybe do more to guard it."

"Either way, I agree we should let them know about the drained crystals and the lizard creature," Wyndi said.

Legs directed Doodles through town until they came to the sign marking, "Ore-ange & Lapiz."

"I'll ask someone to come out," Flek said, already halfway into the building.

A few moments later, he returned, accompanied by a dwarf with dark hair and a full beard, both of which had streaks of grey betraying his age. The dwarf approached the cart.

"You three are the apprentices, then?"

"Yes," Wyndi said. "Zaq said we should bring the crystal here first for you to record."

"Thank you. I'm Troshkin. I appreciate you coming. It proves vee vere right to trust Mr. Flickerwhizzle."

Legs pulled the tarp up to expose the large mana crystal and waved over the dwarf to look.

"This is all we took from the cavern."

"But you should know about something we found," Wyndi said. "Your group might want to post a guard out there if you want to keep things secure."

"Yeah, we found a vulin!" Flek jumped in excitedly. "Doodles and I took care of it, but we found it had drained almost all the mana crystals in the first large cavern."

Troshkin's face paled, and he shook his head in dismay.

"I knew this might happen, but they vouldn't listen. Thank you for the report. I'm glad the creature didn't hurt you. You're free to take this crystal to Zaq."

"Thank you, Troshkin," Wyndi said. "Good luck with the mine."

Chapter 29

Success

Zaq sat at a table in the Mystic Leaf & Toadstool patio area, sipping a cup of Elderberry Mist. He set the mug down and jumped to his feet, regretting it immediately as the movement sent a spike of pain down his right sciatic nerve. He pushed the discomfort aside and shuffled out to the street to meet the intrepid team of apprentices and their beaver pulling the tarp-covered cart to the alley entrance.

"Greetings and salutations. Welcome back. Thank you for your hard work. I guarantee it will have been worth it. Now let me see! Let me see what you brought."

The three were all grins, clearly happy to be back in the city. The tall, lanky human, Frank, pulled back the tarp, exposing several large sections of grimbark tree and a mana crystal even bigger than he had hoped for. Seeing the crystal, Zaq realized he should have been clear that the measurement was a minimum, but this gem looked like it would suit the project.

"Wonderful! Wonderful! And you brought more wood than needed. That will save a trip in the future. I'm sure once we prove this works and start selling, we'll need more grimbark. And what about...what about the conduit? You said you ran into a vulin?"

"It's right here," Flek said as he hopped into the cart and found the sack he was looking for in the KoldBox. The goblin reached in and pulled out a long, coiled mana conduit, sticky and dripping with offal. Zaq supposed that was one way to keep it fresh.

"Right," Zaq winced. "Well, thank you. Yes. You can return it to the sack."

"Should we bring all this downstairs?" Frank asked, motioning at the cartload of materials.

"Oh, yes. Please do. We can get started right away!"

"Hey, Doodles. You want to help? Like before? With the crystal in the cave?" Frank talked to the beaver as if it had complete comprehension. Zaq realized he wasn't entirely sure it didn't. He wasn't an expert on the giant forms of animals.

Frank and Flek removed the harness from the animal and pulled some netting from the back of the cart. They glanced at each other, the crystal, then back at each other and nodded. Wyndi saw what they were doing and lent her help as well. All three of them carefully put the crystal on the flat tail and secured it with the netting.

Doodles, the beaver, carefully trundled down the stairs and turned into the workshop, following after Frank. Zaq couldn't help his curiosity and followed the group. He directed them to put the crystal on a free workbench, and then they returned upstairs with the beaver.

Zaq stayed down in the workshop, admiring the crystal and running his hand over the smooth, deep blue surface. *Yes. Yes. This will do nicely.*

He turned when he heard the beaver brush his way into the room again, this time carrying a large log of grimbark on his tail.

Frank and Wyndi undid the net and moved the log to an empty spot on the floor. They would need to saw off a piece of an appropriate size and hollow it out.

A moist bag that smelled of rotten meat swung into view in front of Zaq's eyes, startling him out of his thoughts. He did what any reasonable gnome would do and let out an *eep* while taking a step back.

"That's quite all right, Flek. Why don't you find a spot for that in the KoldBox on that far wall?"

"Sure thing!" Flek said, grinning, and took his bag across the room.

"I know you all had a long journey and are most likely tired, but I'm so excited to get started!" Zaq said, clasping his hands together tightly. "I can control myself, though. We should all have a celebratory dinner for your triumphant return. Let's walk to the Inn Side Out. Will your beaver behave here in the workshop? Or is there someplace else he should be?"

"I've got it. He'll be good," Frank said and turned to the animal. "Stay here and don't get into any of the equipment. You can chew a branch of grimbark, or better yet, you can cut this log into segments for us, here and here. Don't eat the log, only the branches."

Zaq was amazed as it seemed the animal really did comprehend at least some of what the human had told it. He turned to leave when he heard Frank give one last instruction.

"Leave the cat to herself. She'll leave you alone if you leave her alone."

Looking across the room and under a workbench where he had seen Frank point, Zaq saw the black fiend of a cat crouched, staring intently, seemingly unsure what to do about the massive creature. He was sure that if it were truly uncomfortable, the cat would run out and find somewhere else to be.

"That's that then," Zaq said. "Thank you for addressing the animal. Shall we head to dinner?"

"I am more than ready," Flek said, running his tongue over his fangs. "I have to say, though. The food you sent along was wonderful."

"Yes! Thank you for that," Wyndi agreed. "I loved how easy you made the cooking with your preparations, and it tasted amazing."

"It was even better when the fairies got their hands on it," Frank said. "But I suspect they may have supplemented with their own ingredients."

"Fairies? What fairies?" Zaq asked, raising an eyebrow as he looked up at the human.

"We'll tell you about it over dinner," Frank laughed. "We had quite the adventure. There will be plenty of time to tell the tales while we eat. Let's get going before Flek joins Doodles in gnawing on the grimbark."

The plane-touched woman, Jess, if he remembered correctly, came to the table to take their orders.

"Good evening. We have a wonderful special tonight with deep-fried curry dumplings served alongside bunnycorn masala with garlic flatbread. Or, if you'd like, I can give you a menu."

"Really? You have a bunnycorn dish tonight?" Flek asked, smiling so wide he exposed all his fangs. "I'll have that, and you all should, too. I'm sure it will be amazing."

Wyndi and Frank laughed at the goblin but agreed that they would have the same.

"Oh, twist my arm, I suppose," Zaq said. "I'll have the special as well. It does sound good. Please have Alaquine pick

out a nice whisky for the meal—a glass for everyone. We're cele-
brating."

"I'll be back soon with your food and drink," Jess said with
a warm smile before turning to go put in their order.

"It rained here last night," Zaq said. Weather topics were
always a good way to break the ice, right? He appreciated all
the apprentices had done, but really wasn't sure how best to
converse with them. "Did it catch you?"

"Unfortunately, yes," Wyndi answered for the group.

She seemed to have improved the group dynamic during
the trip. Frank, whom she still called Legs, seemed to defer to
her as a good friend. Flek, the goblin, was interesting. Zaq
suspected there was more between him and the young gnome.
He caught the goblin stealing glances at Wyndi on a regular
basis. He hoped there wouldn't be issues down the road.

"We managed well enough using the cart for cover," she
continued, breaking him out of his thoughts about the group.

"Doodles even walled us in while we slept," Flek said,
laughing and giving a sidelong glance at Wyndi.

"He was just being helpful," Frank said. "I'm going to miss
him. I'll need to return him to my father tomorrow since we
finished our journey. I can always go and visit him, but it was
nice having him on the trip."

Jess returned, pushing a tray full of food. She placed a plate
in front of each of them, followed by four glasses of dark amber
whisky.

"Alaquine said you'd enjoy this one and that it was good for
a celebration. It's a single malt, aged in Fallowden port wine
barrels."

"Thank you, Jess, that sounds wonderful," Zaq said, giving
her a slight nod in appreciation.

He picked up the tulip-shaped glass in front of him and
waved for the others to do the same.

"To a successful mission!"

The four of them clinked their glasses together before sipping the strong whisky.

Over the next hour, the trio spent the meal retelling their tale, filling Zaq in on all of the details they hadn't sent via the tablets. They ate their fill of the spicy food, and Zaq found the goblin had been right. The gamey bunnycorn was delicious in the creamy sauce. Each bite left a pleasant heat lingering in his throat.

At the end of the meal, Zaq called for cherry pie, and Jess brought out four large slices, oozing dark red filling and topped with a melting scoop of vanilla ice cream. The pie was the perfect ending to a wonderful dinner. Everyone ate with gusto, and Zaq noticed the gnome girl didn't say anything about the food, not even once. Something had changed there. Perhaps the time outside of the city had done her some good.

Zheb and Joh were closing the teashop when Zaq led his apprentices back to the workshop. He called out before the dwarves could finish.

"Hold up, please. I can see you are retiring for the evening, but our evening is about to begin. We need something strong so we can work late into the evening. Can you spare a pot of tea with an energy boost?"

"Good evening, Zaq," Zheb called back. "Vee ver closing, yes, but for you—for you vee can make an exception. I vill brew a special pot."

The dwarf stopped his cleanup, leaving the rest to Joh, and jogged into the shop. Several minutes later, he returned carrying a pot and a stack of four cups.

"Here you go. Zis is a concentrated dragonroot tea viss

more sugar and ackernutcream zan you should likely have in an evening. You vant to be avake late tonight? Ziss vill do it."

"Thank you," Zaq said, taking the pot. His apprentices grabbed the cups, and Zaq gave the dwarf a handful of coins.

Downstairs, the group found Doodles happily gnawing on a branch of grimroot. Beside him, on the floor, were three pieces of trunk, each roughly the same size, and the beaver had even mostly smoothed out the tops and bottoms, leaving relatively cylindrical shapes.

"Good boy, Doodles!" Frank praised, walking over to pat the beaver.

The cat lounged on the table Zaq had designated for eating and relaxation. To be fair, the cat looked fairly relaxed, but still, no cats on the table.

"Get down. Get down. Get down," he scolded, carrying the teapot to the table and waving at the cat with his other arm. "The table is no place for cats."

The cat stood up, stretched, yawned, then moved to sit up straight on the corner of the table. Zaq put down the teapot and gently pushed the black fiend to the floor. After filling each of their cups, he laid out the plan.

"As you can see on the walls and the large slate board, I've been preparing for your return. I'm happy to explain any and all of it as we work. I've put out the existing distributor we have been using on that bench over there for reference."

Zaq watched as each of the apprentices walked up for a closer look at blueprints, schematics, parts and materials lists, and the existing distributor, which was currently lit up and humming. There was a lot of nodding and murmuring between them, bringing a smile to his face while he sipped the strong tea.

"I'll work to hollow out a space for the mana crystal in one of the log segments," Frank offered.

"That would be wonderful," Zaq approved. The lanky human had size as an asset, even if his muscles weren't overly developed. It was clear to anyone that while he was not a warrior or laborer, he was best suited for that task among everyone there.

"I see how the conduit should connect based on these diagrams here," Flek said, pointing at a portion of a schematic. "I'll clean it and prep it so we can attach it later."

"There are so many runes and all of these additional parts: gears, springs, antennae, and more," Wyndi said, reviewing the plans. "Would it be best if I started drawing the runes? Or collecting and preparing the additional parts?"

"The parts, if you would," Zaq answered. "The runes are important, and I'd like you all to have a chance at inscribing some of them. They are best done once all of the pieces are connected and in place. That way, the runes themselves become parts as we draw them, connecting to the other pieces."

"That makes sense," Wyndi nodded, lowering her goggles over her eyes. "I'll get to work then."

For the next few hours, they worked at their tasks and took up other small chores as needed. Zaq cycled through each of them, checking on their progress and making adjustments. In some cases, he took over a delicate portion he wanted to be sure was done just right.

By nine o'clock, the entire distributor had been assembled, and Frank moved the original, smaller version next to the new, larger one for comparison.

"Other than the runes, I think we accomplished a complete copy," Zaq said after walking around the table, inspecting both. "Yes, I think we can move on to the runes. Take the utmost care not to activate any of the runes early. In fact, do not connect any runes to the activation switch until the very end."

The runes proved to be even more of a chore, if for no other reason than that they were incredibly intricate, and a flawed rune meant carefully removing it without damaging any of the others nearby. The group had long since drained the teapot, but the energy from the concentrated tea and sugar still powered them.

Zaq had them each take turns drawing runes. It was difficult at times to hold himself back from brushing them aside and doing the work himself. However, they had earned the right to get this experience, and Zaq knew if his plans were solid, they could easily handle the job.

Hours passed as the delicate, arcane symbols were added, connected together, and connected to the various physical pieces of equipment. At well past midnight and closer to two in the morning, Zaq drew the final symbols connecting the rest of the work to the activation panel. He triple-checked that it was off before finalizing the connection, then dusted the entire machine with finalizing powder.

The runic weave covering the distributor flashed in a multitude of colors in three successive pulses, then settled into its final dormant state. Zaq took a step back, his eyes wet as he admired the creation.

"There we go. I can hardly believe we have it complete."

The three apprentices clapped and cheered, though with less enthusiasm than any of them expected they might have, given the late hour.

"I learned so much during the assembly," Wyndi said, clasping her hands with a large smile on her face. "Thank you for letting us do so much."

"Yeah, I never realized how complicated some of these machines can get," Flek added. "I'm still going to build my vehicle, but I suspect it may take a while based on what I learned tonight."

"I think my mom would be proud," Frank said, his face a

mix of joy and sadness. "She wanted a mage, but I think she'd be very happy with the artificer I'm becoming."

"There's only one thing left for this evening. Then we should all get some sleep before the field tests tomorrow," Zaq said, hovering his hand near the activation panel. "We turn it on!"

Zaq touched the panel and recited the activation command sequence clearly. Runes and gems lit up, gears turned, and antennae swiveled. A loud buzzing soon softened into a steady background hum. Each of the artificers pulled out their slates and rehomed them from the original distributor to the new one.

Chapter 30

Beta Users

Sleep eluded Zaq throughout most of the night. It wasn't just the concentrated tea and sugar he had consumed so late in the evening; it was exhilaration. Everything he had been working toward was finally coming together. Glancing at the clock, he found it was still only seven, and by the time he had returned home the night before, he had slept less than a handful of hours, but there was no point in staying in bed if he was awake.

"To think, I had spent so long convinced I could do it all myself. I just couldn't bear anyone stealing my ideas again. But, thanks to those kids, we actually have something working."

Zaq dressed in a basic brown work outfit after a quick shower, then hunted for something to eat in the kitchen. He toasted two slices of wheat bread in a pan with a generous amount of butter, then cracked two eggs into the greasy skillet along with four slices of bacon. He assembled everything into a sandwich, devouring it almost immediately.

After a quick clean-up, he pulled out his slate and dropped

a quick note to his team. *His team.* That had a nice sound to it. A smile crept across his face.

> Zaq: Meet me at the workshop once you are all up and awake. I need your help testing the new distributor today.

The pad stayed unchanged for several minutes before he gave up staring at it and left the house. He waved to his neighbor, Samantha, who was up early raking some leaves in her yard. She waved back and called after him.

"It looks like your cat is going to work with you."

He turned to see what she was talking about, only to see the black feline creature walking behind him, tail straight in the air. It looked up at him expectantly, but he rolled his eyes and turned back around to continue walking, calling out an annoyed response.

"It's not my cat."

He heard Samantha's laughter fading into the wind as he continued walking to the teashop.

Zaq didn't mind at all as he approached the covered patio, and the cat raced by him, down the alley stairs.

"I'd like a jug of dragonroot this morning, just the usual stuff, not the potent version from last night. Four cups as well. We'll bring them back up once we're finished. No time to chat this morning, the kids will be here soon, I hope."

"Zey are here. I believe so, anyvay," Zheb smiled and began filling a refillable jug that had the Mystic Leaf & Toadstool logo on it.

"Oh! I wonder if they even left," Zaq said, raising his eyebrows. "Funny. They didn't send a message on the slate."

"Zee bean pole did," Zheb said, handing him the jug. "Joh and I ver opening and saw him take his pet beaver avay. I'm not sure if I saw him come back yet."

"Thanks," Zaq said, trading the jug for some coins.

Downstairs, he discovered the beaver was, in fact, gone, but Frank had returned and was watching the humming distributor. The other two were sitting across from each other on the floor, sending messages back and forth with their slates. The cat was curled up next to Wyndi, who took time to scritch its head after each message she sent.

"Greetings and salutations," Zaq announced as he put the tea and cups on the relaxation station. "Did you stay here all night? Why didn't you answer my message this morning?"

Wyndi looked up at him with a quizzical expression on her face, still absently petting the cat.

"Your message wasn't a question. It was a request, and technically, we had already done what you asked. I didn't feel it needed an answer. If you were actually coming here to meet us, you would find us here whether we sent the message or not."

"Well, I suppose that's right," Zaq said, grinning at her practicality. "And I see you are already running some tests. Has everything worked as expected?"

"So far," Flek answered. "But we haven't done anything we haven't done before, so it's not really a great test case. How many tablets do we have? Do you have a test plan?"

"I do, indeed," Zaq replied, steepling his fingers. "I built several tablets while you were out collecting supplies. We have the four that each of us is using, plus twelve more. I think we should each practice making a tablet this morning. It would be good for you to see how it is done. Assuming this works as well as I think it will, we'll need a lot more."

"Oh! Can we replace the ones we've been using with the ones we each make?" Wyndi asked with a glint in her eye. "I think it would be divine if I could use a tablet I made myself. We can reset the originals we're using so others can use them."

"Oh yeah," Frank clapped. "I want to make my own."

"Me too," Flek said, hopping up from the ground and tossing his slate on a workbench.

"Very well. Very well," Zaq chuckled. "It would be good for you to feel some ownership over your own slate. You might even be able to make modifications to it over time. I'll make one here at this workbench, and you all can watch how it's done, then make your own."

Over the next hour, each apprentice made a tablet and wiped clean the original they had been using. Everyone registered their new slate with the large distributor and sent several test messages proving they all worked.

With sixteen tablets available for others, Zaq needed to decide who should participate in the testing. Or, more realistically, he had to figure out which sixteen people he could persuade to do it.

"Who do you think we can loop into the testing? My neighbor, Samantha, likely will, and of course, the dwarves upstairs. Alaquine and Glorya at the Inn Side Out are also likely suspects, and perhaps some of their waitstaff. Maybe that fellow at the mining company? Troshkin?"

"My father would likely help," Frank offered. "What about your parents, Wyndi?"

"As long as we can trust my dad not to take it apart," she grinned. "It would be good for him to see something I helped with. So, that would be two more."

"Alright, then. That leaves us still needing five?" Zaq mused.

"You mentioned the dwarves," Flek said. "What about customers in the teashop? There are often ten or more people on the patio. We'd only need to get five of them to agree."

"Wonderful idea," Zaq clapped. "That's an even better idea than you imagine. We don't have any ties to them. No biases. I think we should each take a stack of tablets and split up."

"Sure, but what do we tell them?" Wyndi asked.

"Right, right, this will all be new to them," Zaq nodded, stroking his short beard. "You'll have to show them how it works. After you have them register the tablet, send them a test message and have them send one to you."

"Sounds great!" Flek said, pumping his fist in the air. "I'll hit up the Inn Side Out. They know me pretty well, having spent several days there. Meet you back here soon!"

The goblin called out the last part as he ran up the stairs with a stack of tablets in his hands. The rest of the group just looked at each other and shrugged. They divvied up the list and went their separate ways. Zaq decided he would talk with Zheb and Joh, then Samantha, and finally Troshkin. Wyndi and Frank would get their parents and as many teashop patrons as they could.

Despite the teashop being the closest, there were quite a few customers, which was good for the apprentices but bad for the chances that the dwarves would have enough free time to talk. Instead, he walked his usual route toward home and then a bit farther to Samantha's house, where he knocked three times on the door.

"Zaq, is everything well?" she asked, looking him over.

"Quite well! Quite well, indeed," Zaq answered. "We're ready to test my industrial-quality distributor. I'm sure you remember my project. It's been stop-and-go for so many years. Testing day is here, and I'd love your assistance."

"You know I'm always here to help," Samantha assured him. "What do I need to do? How does it work? I know you mentioned it sends messages like so many of your inventions."

"Yes, yes, messages are the crux of it," Zaq nodded. "But

this is so much more than simple messages between you and a friend, like one might use a Mysti Message scroll. Let me show you."

He handed her a tablet and demonstrated how she could register herself using her name.

"Now watch. I'll send you a message."

> Zaq: Hello! This is a sample test message.

"There, you see. The words appeared right on your tablet."

"Well, yes, they did," Samantha agreed. "However, isn't that what happens with an emm-emm scroll?"

"Right you are, but look here, you can choose who to send a message to. Pick one person or a group. We can even see how many people have tablets now by looking at the list of users."

"Oh! I see. That is impressive. I'll just send one to you for now so I can try it out. Let me know if I'm doing it right."

> Samantha: Did I do it right?

> Zaq: You did!

"Oh! What is this?" Samantha exclaimed when she saw a small picture of a pumpkin appear on the slate.

"I wanted to demonstrate that it can send drawings as well. I was inspired by the pumpkin that I saw you recently put out as decoration for the festival."

"That is definitely lacking in the emm-emm scrolls. I'm guessing they won't be happy with you."

"Not my problem," Zaq shrugged. "I suggested variations on this idea numerous times, but they never wanted to research it. Their loss, my gain."

"Well, good luck to you then," Samantha smiled down at him. "I should just try sending messages and testing it out?"

"Yes, please," Zaq nodded again. "We need to exercise the system and look for any issues. I don't anticipate any, but it's new, so you never know."

"Thank you for including me in your test," Samantha said, partially closing the door. "I should get back to my baking, I wouldn't want to ruin what's in the oven."

"Fair enough. Fair enough. I need to hand out more of these. It's a busy day today."

Zaq visited Troshkin next, and he was happy to help with the testing. The dwarf even suggested they could use the tablets to communicate and work out a deal for more crystals. It may have been that he was just looking for more patronage, but it could also have been a sign he had faith in the system and saw that Zaq would need more materials.

Zheb and Joh were easy converts, just as he had suspected they would be.

"Zis is quite zee invention, Zaq," Zheb said after sending a couple of test messages. "Just sink, vee could allow customers to order via tablet!"

"Well, yes. Yes, you could," Zaq fumbled. "I hadn't even thought of that. Great idea."

Grinning to himself, Zaq ventured downstairs, where he found Flek with Wyndi, who was petting the cat again.

"Legs will be back soon," Wyndi informed him. "He just sent a message that he was leaving his father's place, fifteen or twenty min—wait a minute! That would be a great feature. What if each message displayed the time it was sent?"

"Splendid!" Zaq laughed with joy. "That's precisely the kind of thinking we need right now. We'll improve the system. Many improvements can be made right here on the distributor."

Only a few more minutes passed before Frank popped his head in and joined the rest of the team.

"Welcome back, Frank," Zaq said, waving him in. "With everyone here, I believe we can start testing the distributor more extensively. With twenty tablets connected, it should handle the load without issue. But let's be sure."

> Zaq: Hello, test users! Thank you for agreeing to help us. This message is being transmitted to everyone with a tablet.

The message popped up on each of the apprentices' slates, followed by several people declaring they received the message. Each one was sent to the entire server as they replied to everyone on the initial message.

Messages rolled in as the test opened the floodgates. Users realized they could send messages to everyone, and the replies were numerous. Soon, they began sending drawings and commenting on the drawings.

The sight was fabulous, even if it was a little overwhelming. Zaq was so absorbed in reading through the messages that he failed to notice the distributor's hum rising in pitch and intensity. The messages continued to flow, and the machine seemed possessed, finally making enough noise to draw everyone's attention.

The gears and antennae turned and spun faster than ever before. The deep blue mana crystal faded to a light blue, then clear. The hum turned into a mechanical scream, the gears spinning so fast the motion blurred. The cat hissed. Its hair stood on end, and it stared at the arcane artifact from the next bench over.

The whining, screaming hum finally broke with a crack of thunder, and the mana crystal flashed from clear to ebony black. Several bolts of residual mana flew from the device; most hit inanimate objects, but one struck the cat.

The cat let out a cry of torment, then made several hurking

noises. It leapt from the workbench it had been sitting on and wobble-ran toward Zaq. It was moving sporadically and spasming while continuing to make the odd hurking noise with each spasm. When the cat reached Zaq's feet, one more violent spasm shook the poor creature, and an enormous hairball landed on his boot.

In a move that surprised everyone, Zaq included, he momentarily forgot the arcane distributor and what had just happened to it, instead focusing on the cat at his feet.

"Oh, no. You poor girl. Let me make sure you weren't badly hurt."

Ignoring the wet clump of hair and who knows what else that covered his left boot, Zaq reached down and scooped the cat up into his arms. She seemed better now that the hairball had been expelled, but still looked wildly around the room from Zaq to the machine, and then back to Zaq. His fingers ran through the silky black fur, while his palm applied gentle pressure, and the cat nuzzled into the crook of his arm.

Chapter 31

Arboretum

"**W**org's breath!" Flek exclaimed. "What in the infinite hells just happened?"

"Clearly, it overloaded," Wyndi said, deep creases forming in her forehead. "I think the design accounted for messages from each user, but when they multiplied across all users, it was too much."

Legs nodded as he looked around, assessing the damage.

"I had thought something like—"

"Shut it!" Zaq snarled, tightening the hold he had on the cat when she startled at his outburst. "No one cares what you thought. None of it matters. This invention was clearly a waste of my time and all of yours. It's obvious, no matter how large a crystal or housing or conduit, it won't be enough. The entire idea was fundamentally flawed."

"Don't be so hasty," Wyndi said in a calm and measured voice. She did not like the way he had snapped at them and hoped to settle his anger. "Maybe we just missed—"

"No. We didn't miss anything. I'm done for. I'm going home. If I ever was an artificer, I'm no longer one of any use.

Find someone else to teach you. Stay or leave the workshop. It doesn't matter. You are dismissed from your obligations as my apprentices."

"But—" the words caught in Wyndi's throat as he abruptly turned and left the room to stalk up the stairs, carrying the cat while stroking her and murmuring something under his breath. This was so unlike the old gnome they had come to know. Wyndi felt she had failed him and herself.

All three apprentices stood silently watching Zaq leave. When he was gone, they each turned to look at each other with the same question in their eyes: Now what?

"It's not really all hopeless, is it?" Flek asked, looking to Legs, then to her in turn.

"Honestly?" Wyndi said, pausing longer than she should have while thinking on what to say. Failing to come up with anything she actually believed, she broke the uncomfortable silence. "I'm really not sure."

"I tried bringing up some concerns I had before," Legs said. "I didn't know this would happen. Obviously, I wouldn't have gone on that adventure for materials if I thought it would all fail. I thought maybe Flickerwhizzle knew how to deal with the potential of it overloading."

"I know, Legs," Wyndi shook her head and reached up to pat his arm. "I think we all had some concerns, but he seemed so sure this would work. And it was! That's the thing. It was working. But—but without addressing the cascading effect of so many users, he may be right. Maybe this is impossible."

"I don't think he's coming back to the workshop," Flek said softly. "At least not for a while. I want to clean up so the signs of this failure aren't all over the room."

"That's a good idea," Wyndi said, smiling at him and admiring how thoughtful he was. She wasn't entirely sure the Flek she first met would have made that same suggestion. "I'll help. Pitch in, Legs, we could use your height and strength for some of this, I'm sure."

"Of course," Legs chuckled. "I can't leave my team hanging."

Over the next hour, the three put away the loose parts and boxed up the dead distributor after making sure it wasn't going to have any more violent outbursts. Flek used some rags to clean up the remains of the hairball that had fallen off Zaq's boot. Wyndi gathered the mugs onto a tray for easier return upstairs. When she grabbed the jug of tea Zaq had brought down, she realized it was still mostly full.

The nice thing about the jugs from Mystic was their special enchantment to keep the tea warm for a long time. Wyndi saw no reason to waste perfectly good tea. Everyone was grateful for a warm mug of tea after their hard work.

"You know," Wyndi said, sipping her beverage. "The original distributor should still work. We should re-home our tablets to it. It had worked fine the entire time we were away. Not even the range had been an issue."

"Great idea," Flek said. "I'll set it up on a table. We might even want to bring Zaq a tablet in case he wants to reach us."

"Let's wait on that," Wyndi said. "I get the feeling he wants to be alone for a while. And I'm pretty sure the tablet will remind him of the failure."

"You're probably right," Legs nodded. "Good thinking."

"What about us?" Flek asked, and Wyndi felt his gaze linger on her for longer than she thought necessary. "The three of us, I mean. I don't want to give up on artificery. Despite what Zaq thinks, we could still learn a lot from him. I bet we could learn a lot from each other, too."

"We should definitely keep working together," Wyndi agreed, looking back at Flek, trying, yet again, to read the goblin's thoughts and intentions. "It seemed like he didn't mind if we used the workshop."

"That's a good idea," Legs added. "I'd like to keep working together. We have something else that needs our attention first, though."

"We do?" Wyndi asked, wrinkling her nose.

"Uh, yeah. Did all the excitement of building the artifact and the explosive failure make you forget?"

Wyndi let out an exasperated breath, but paused before pressing him further.

"Okay, yes, it must have. What are you talking about?"

"We agreed to plant the grimbark trees," Legs said flatly. "You struck the bargain; I'd thought you'd remember."

Wyndi slapped her forehead and realized she was still wearing her goggles over her eyes. She adjusted them so they sat up in the spot she had just smacked.

"That's right. I can't believe I let that slip my mind. We would be in big trouble with the forest walkers if we didn't follow through."

"Exactly," Legs said, smiling widely, showing off all his teeth. "So, anyway, I was thinking before we get wrapped up in things here in the workshop, we should do that. Who knows, once we're done, maybe Zaq will have calmed down and be ready to talk to us."

Now that Flek had the original distributor up and running again, they each registered their tablets to it before taking the remains of the tea upstairs.

"Ah! I vas hoping you vould come up," Zheb said when Wyndi returned the tray of used mugs. "I saw Zaq leave and vas looking very upset. And zee tablets he gave us, zey don't vork."

"Yeah," Wyndi said, sucking in a breath. "There was an incident with the experiment. Those tablets won't be working anymore. If you don't mind, if you could collect them from any customers that helped us test, that would be great."

"Sure," Zheb nodded. "I can do zat. If anyone comes by looking for Zaq, I vill get zeirs, too."

"Thank you," Wyndi smiled. "That would be a big help. We're going out for a while, but we'll be back later. Zaq may or may not be back soon. He took it pretty hard."

Legs had been thinking ahead about their bargain the whole time. Wyndi wasn't sure how she let it slip her mind, but Legs had even left some shovels and a pickaxe in the workshop when he returned Doodles to his father. All three of them carried a tool, and Wyndi had a pouch of seeds the forest walkers had provided her.

On the outskirts of the city, away from the road that ran along the river, Legs identified a nice plot of land. They each took several wooden stakes and created a perimeter around what they hoped would one day be a beautiful grimbark arboretum.

Legs used the pickaxe to loosen the soil, while Wyndi and Flek used shovels to dig homes for the grimbark seeds. The acorn-like nuts the forest walkers had provided didn't look like they would grow into the dense, sturdy trees they had seen in the grove. Then again, most nuts didn't look like they could produce any tree. Nature was fascinating sometimes.

Wyndi handed out the nuts to everyone, then dropped one in the nearest hole she had dug. The loose dirt was cool and claggy between her fingers. Autumn was not the ideal time for planting much, but she felt the grimbark trees would do fine, even if they didn't begin to sprout until spring. She swept a mound of dirt into the hole, covering the grimbark seed and patting it gently with her palms to pack the soil.

Repeating the process several more times, she eventually finished and wiped her hands against her thick canvas coveralls. Flek and Legs finished planting theirs, and all three looked around the clearing at the ten small mounds spaced far enough apart that they would one day make a beautiful grove.

"Good work," Wyndi said. "I think it will be very nice here once the trees grow."

"I can picture it now," Legs said. "Could be my father's trade as a woodsman, but I like the idea of creating this would-be forest. I think he'll be proud when I tell him about it."

"It's getting on in the day," Flek said, running his tongue over his fangs. "I don't suppose you'd all like to visit the Inn Side Out for some dinner?"

"I should really get these tools back to my father," Legs said as he gathered them into his arms. "You want to meet back at the workshop tomorrow morning? Maybe Zaq will have had a change of heart after a good night's sleep."

"Yes, let's meet at the workshop in the morning," Wyndi agreed, then turning to Flek, she set her jaw and clenched her fists before forcing herself to relax. "I'm free for dinner, Flek. If you don't mind it being just the two of us."

"Oh, right. Um, sure," Flek said, and Wyndi was sure she could see a faint mauve tint in his cheeks. "We could do that, yes. I'm still hungry, and—and company is good, yes."

"Wonderful, let's head there now," Wyndi said, letting out a breath.

The three of them headed back to the city proper until Legs reached the street he needed for his father's house. Wyndi and Flek finished the walk to the inn. The entire time, Wyndi kept her focus straight ahead.

"Oh, it's you two! Where's your tall friend?" Cal, the server, asked, still sporting a very full beard. "Do you have something in mind to order? Or would you like to hear the special?"

With so many questions at once, Wyndi wasn't sure which to answer or in what order. She finally landed on the first, then the last.

"Legs had to visit his father, so it's just the two of us. I think I'd like to hear about the special before making up my mind."

"Sure thing! Tonight's special is so rich and comforting. I nearly ate two plates before the dinner rush. Glorya made fresh pasta. She stirs a sauce made from heavy cream, butter, salty cheese, and garlic into each serving of pasta, then garnishes it with paper-thin shavings of cured ham. Alongside that, we have a salad with creamy, garlicy dressing and a sourdough loaf split open and toasted with garlic butter."

"Wow, that sounds amazing!" Flek announced. "I'm definitely having the special. How about you, Wyndi?"

Wyndi was torn. She had made progress in accepting she could eat more, but she was alone with Flek tonight, and that food sounded divine. It also sounded like it would go straight to her behind and thighs.

"I don't know. It sounds good, but I think it might be too much."

"Nonsense," Flek said. "If it sounds good, you should have it. We only live once. Besides, I'd feel bad if it sounded good to you and I ate it while you had something else."

"I guess you make a good point. It really does sound wonderful. I don't know how you can be so carefree with what you eat."

"Sounds like it will be two of the specials then," Cal said, grinning widely. "I just hope you two weren't planning on any kissing tonight with all that garlic."

Wyndi and Flek blushed profusely, looking at anything and

everything except each other or Cal, who just chuckled to himself and left for the kitchen.

When Wyndi finally managed to look at Flek, who had also settled enough to pay attention to her, she stumbled over her words.

"That's—well, that's just silly, isn't it? To think? Why would we be kissing? And after that garlic? A very good point there, right? And especially with all that food. You would never want to kiss someone who ate all that food."

She hadn't meant to say the last part, but her mind had been muddled, and the words were flowing as she tried to find the right ones to say about the preposterous idea of kissing. To her surprise, Flek just looked at her with a serious look on his face.

"Look, Wyndi. Cal was probably just being silly. But whether or not I would want to kiss someone would have nothing to do with what they ate. I already told you, I don't mind the extra you carry. I don't mind it on you, and I wouldn't mind it on anyone. You have to trust in yourself and be proud of who you are. And worg's breath! Eat whatever makes you happy."

"I'm sorry. You're right. I shouldn't get hung up on that. After everything my father drilled into me growing up, it's hard. But I like your way of thinking about it better."

"It is, isn't it?" Flek grinned.

Cal set down plates full of food in front of them, interrupting the moment.

"Here you go. I brought you some water as well. If you want anything else to drink or eat, just let me know."

"Thanks, Cal. This is good," Flek said, then looked at Wyndi with a glint in his eye. "Shall we?"

Wyndi didn't need any more of an invitation than that. She twirled the long flat pasta onto a fork, the thick sauce clinging to the noodles and flecks of ham caught up in the twists. The bite was pure heaven in her mouth—warm, creamy, and salty with just enough chew to make it last before swallowing.

The food was rich, and there was so much of it that they both took their time eating. Cal had been right about the garlic; it was everywhere and oh so good. When she was done eating, Wyndi looked at Flek.

"So, that was a lot of garlic. Incredibly tasty, though."

"Oh yes. A lot, but also not enough. I *love* garlic," Flek said with a dreamy look in his eye. "An interesting thing about garlic is that if you eat it, everyone thinks you stink, but if multiple people eat it, they don't think the others stink, or maybe they all just stink and can't tell. Either way, it kind of cancels out."

"So, Cal's silliness about the—you know. That wouldn't matter since we both ate the special."

"Right! That's what I mean. So, you think he was being silly, too? I mean, why would we—?"

Flek left the thought hanging there, half finished.

"Right, because you obviously wouldn't want to. Obviously."

"I wouldn't say that was obvious. I never said I didn't not think it was silly."

Wyndi squinted at Flek.

"Wait, what are you saying? Do you mean you didn't think it was silly? Are you saying you might be open to maybe—"

Flek reached out his hand and took hers.

"I'm not sure what I'm saying, to be honest. But I do think it might be worth exploring what we both might be thinking. I've still got my room here. Would you like to go there and talk some more? Maybe see if we can figure this out?"

"I'd like that, yes," Wyndi smiled, and he squeezed her hand.

Chapter 32

A Spider Web

Knock... *Knock. Knock. Knock... Knock. Knock.*

Despite the incessant banging at his front door, Zaq remained in his oversized armchair, where he had actually spent the majority of the night. His hair was disheveled, and his beard was scruffy from massaging it over and over while he ruminated about his failure. That cat lay curled in his lap. She also had not moved much over the course of the night.

"Zaq!" cried a muffled voice on the other side of the door. "Mr. Flickerwhizzle! We need to make sure you are well."

It was unsurprising to Zaq that those apprentices failed to give up when he dismissed them. Their determination was one of the reasons he had agreed to work with them in the first place. That trait was completely out of line in this case. He just wanted to be left alone. They would not be able to undo the failure.

Knock... Knock. Knock. Knock.

"We brought a jug of tea and some pastries!" called the

muffled voice. He was fairly certain it was Wyndi, but it was hard to be sure through the thick door.

They might not be able to undo the failure, but a pastry with some tea would actually be welcome. Zaq's stomach rumbled in agreement. He glanced at the bottle of barrel-aged rye whisky on the side table with not even a quarter left. His last glass was still half-full. He had barely eaten the night before and drank much more than he should have.

Zaq had slept it off, right there in the chair, and all that remained was that small amount of whisky, though the headache felt twice as large. He stroked the cat a few more times before coaxing her out of his lap. He had checked her thoroughly when he got home, and all signs indicated the blast of mana had spooked her more than doing any actual damage. The cat made an annoyed-sounding rebuke but hopped down to stare up at him from the floor.

"Coming! Just settle yourselves and stop knocking!"

Using the arm of the chair for support, Zaq launched himself up and out of the soft cushion, wobbled upon landing, but managed to steady himself. The alcohol had left his system, but he still had only just woken when they began pounding on the door. The belt cinched around his waist, securing the robe in place.

Zaq found three eager-looking faces staring back at him when he opened the door: two at eye level and one peeking down from overhead. He realized, despite closing up his robe, he must look a sight, and rapidly smoothed down his hair and beard with his hands.

"Tea, you say? And pastry? Very well, come in. Put it down in the dining room. I'll get some mugs."

Wyndi carried a bag that must have held the confections she had mentioned, and Frank carried a large jug sporting the familiar Mystic Leaf & Toadstool logo. They slipped past Zaq into the house and into the dining room, where he soon met them with the cups and a small pitcher of cream.

"I told you all yesterday that we were through. You have been dismissed and released from your contractual duties as my apprentices. You're welcome to use the workshop. I likely won't be back there for quite some time, if ever. But you don't need me, and I've got nothing else to offer."

Zaq poured himself a cup of tea, adding a dollop of cream and a spoonful of sugar before glancing down at the pastry Wyndi set before him. It appeared to be some type of deep-fried dough, but not like the fried cakes with frosting he had recently had. This was a lighter, leavened dough with swirls of cinnamon and gooey chunks of apple riddled through it. After it had been fried to a golden brown, Joh must have doused the pastries with sugar glaze because he could see the cracks and white flakes where the hardened shell had been broken.

"We know what you said," Wyndi said after a sip of tea. "We can't just give up. There has to be a way forward. And I'm sure you have loads to teach us. Beyond that, we were worried about you. Both you and your cat looked in pretty rough shape yesterday."

"The cat is doing fine, as am I," Zaq said, breaking off a piece of the dense pastry and popping it into his mouth. He chewed, the sweetness of the glaze enhancing the chunks of spiced apple. "We'll be even better once you've finished your tea and left my house."

"Flek and I talked quite a lot last night," Wyndi said, and Zaq noticed her cheeks flushed. "We discussed a lot of things, but spent some time talking through what was wrong."

"Yeah, I—*we're* pretty sure we know the core issue," Flek said with a furtive glance at Wyndi after catching himself. "The problems only really started to manifest when the full roster of users was sending replies to the entire population. The distributor couldn't handle the constant relaying as it worked to interleave the conversation."

"Right," Wyndi nodded. "When the messages were sent to smaller groups, it was fine. Even with multi-way replies, like we sent to each other, it didn't have issues. But the throughput issues compound at higher volumes of discussion participants."

"I've thought the same thing last night," Zaq shrugged. "That's the kind of thing I spent quite a lot of the evening thinking about, but it's no use. That may be the issue, but it's a significant issue. I don't think we can alter the distributor to handle that kind of load. We might be able to get twenty users to work with some improvements, but then it would just break at thirty or fifty or one hundred."

"Exactly," Frank agreed, flipping his hair back out of his face. "I've been trying to tell them that. The distributor is like a tired spider. Thankfully, it's not a real spider. I couldn't handle that."

"Right," Zaq nodded absently, then froze. "Wait. What? What are you talking about? It's not a spider, and it's not tired. It got overloaded."

"No, I mean it's like this, right?" Frank doubled down on his analogy. "It's like the people with tablets are at different spots on the spider's web. To facilitate communication, he has to run back and forth to all the people. When they send messages that go to everyone, it ends up being a lot of running. The spider gets tired. Obviously, the distributor isn't running anywhere, but it has to spend a lot of mana to basically do just that, shuttling the messages out to people and collecting the new ones, which then also get distributed."

"Be quiet a moment," Zaq said, holding up his hand.

"Wha—" Frank started.

"Shhhhh. Be quiet," Zaq hissed, and his eyes found an uninteresting spot on the ceiling, then lost focus.

"Yes!" Zaq exclaimed, standing up and pacing around the room. "That's exactly right, Frank. The distributor is a tired spider. But that's just it, isn't it?"

"Yes?" Frank asked, looking completely unsure despite the fact that Zaq was agreeing with him.

"We don't need the spider!" Zaq clapped, grinning ear to ear.

"But, Zaq," Wyndi said in a hushed voice. "You know, there is no actual spider. It was a metaphor. He was talking about the distributor. You know Legs. If there were a real spider involved, he'd have nothing to do with it."

"Don't be daft," Zaq said, waving a dismissive hand. "I know there is no spider. We don't need the distributor."

"But isn't that the whole point of it?" asked Flek. "The distributor distributes the messages. Without it, I'm pretty sure the messages wouldn't get, you know, *distributed*. Without the messages, you're basically left with a boring writing tablet."

"No, no, no," Zaq said, frustrated they weren't catching on to the solution. He didn't fully understand it himself, so it was no wonder he struggled to explain it. "You're missing the point Frank was making. He was right about the entire system."

"I was?" Frank asked, looking genuinely surprised.

"You were, my boy," Zaq nodded fervently. "The devices—the devices are the key. They do exactly what you said, or at least they could. They could develop a web between them. A network, if you will. It could grow as more tablets are added. Someday, we might even have a worldwide web. One that spans all of Aberterrene."

"How do you mean?" Wyndi asked. "How would we develop this web without a distributor?"

"That's the puzzle now, isn't it?" Zaq clapped again, clearly amused by where the conversation was going and the paths his ideas were taking. "But...I think it's a solvable puzzle. Unlike the puzzle we have been wrestling with."

"What can we do to help?" Flek asked, then hurriedly took several bites of his pastry.

"Let's finish our tea and pastries first." Zaq chuckled as he realized the goblin must have thought the group might abandon their morning treats. "It would be a shame to waste them. However, then, we should be off to the workshop once we're done. I'll catch up after I've had a chance to change. It's bad enough you're all seeing me in my robe, but I should put on a proper artificer outfit before leaving the house."

When Zaq arrived at the workshop, the apprentices had rounded up every slate they had handed out and had them arrayed on the workbenches.

"If the slates are the key, we thought it would help to have them here," Wyndi said, waving a hand toward them.

"A smart idea," Zaq nodded. "We'll need those and maybe more. That should be enough to do some tests and trials."

"Sorry, Mr. Flickerwhizzle," Frank said, clearing his throat. "In theory, what I said sparked this idea of yours, but I'm still not sure I even understand what this new idea is."

Zaq walked to the large slate board and picked up a piece of chalk.

"I've had time to think about it more, so maybe I can clarify. I assume you all know the basics of how a Mysti Message scroll works, correct? The patents have been on file for years now, and most artificers and would-be artificers have taken a look at the filings at some point or another."

All of the apprentices nodded and took turns looking at each other for confirmation. Zaq continued.

"When a pair of scrolls is created, a mana link forms between them that can span virtually any distance. It works because there are only two intertwined with each other. That won't work with our slates because we want more than two involved. That's why we had the distributor, like you see here."

Zaq tapped the board with the chalk as he finished the simple diagram. It was similar to one he had drawn for them before. He erased it all and began a new set of drawings.

"The idea I have now, thanks to you, Frank, is to come up with a way to link the tablets into a network. Mana connections won't work, but if we can connect them via another means, each tablet can be responsible for relaying anything it hears. If the message doesn't apply to the tablet, it would be passed on. If the message did apply, it would display on the tablet and then be relayed to the connected tablets. Each tablet doesn't need to be connected to every other tablet; it just needs at least one connection. The more it can form, the more robust and performant the network will be."

"Ah, I see what you mean then!" Flek cried. "It is like a spider web. Each node in the web doesn't connect to every other node directly. It only connects to a few, but the spider can easily reach any spot because the web has pathways throughout."

Zaq tapped excitedly on the slate with his chalk, spraying dust all over himself and the floor.

"Exactly right! You do see. The remaining problem is how to form the web. I've been thinking about it, and haven't landed on a solution yet. But that's what we're here for. That's what being an artificer is all about."

Chapter 33

The Ethereal Plane

The Zaq standing at the chalkboard was night and day different from the old gnome Wyndi had found that morning when they brought tea and pastries.

That morning, Wyndi had been shocked at the sight of him in a bathrobe, looking like he had just gotten out of bed—if he had even gone to bed in the first place. He and the house smelled of stale whisky, and the poor cat, who had been zapped the previous day, was dancing around his feet, trying to get his attention.

Zaq had seemed cognizant enough to realize he likely looked a sight and tried to smooth down his wild hair with his hands, but it hadn't done much good. He had perked up at the idea of tea and something to eat, so he was no longer drunk, despite the smell of alcohol.

The gnome before her now, standing excitedly at the large slate board, looked positively giddy compared to the man she found at his home that morning. Clearly, he thought he was on to something, and it was up to all of them to keep this mood going. The apprenticeships were back on! Maybe. Probably? Wyndi realized she should verify.

"Uh, sir? Zaq? Just to be clear, you are reinstating our apprenticeships? You'd like us to help?"

"Oh dear, oh dear, oh dear. Sprung sprockets! I forgot. I did release you, didn't I? Isn't that a quest on the brink of failure? I don't have any time for new contracts, and the original was clear and only enforceable until I released you."

"We never have had any betrayal or ill-will planned," Wyndi broached cautiously. "Would it help if we promised on our honor to stay true to the original agreement?"

"You haven't veered from the course yet," Zaq agreed. "Sometimes. Sometimes I think I just need to be more trusting and accept the help of others. Done. It's a deal. I believe you all will work with good intentions. Let's do this!"

"Excellent, now I can set my plan in motion," Flek said in a stage whisper.

Zaq shot him a look that nearly bored a hole right through the silly goblin's head.

"Kidding! I was just kidding! It was a joke!" Flek said, waving his hands and chortling at his bad idea of a joke.

"We all just want to help, sir," Legs said, settling a sense of calm over the group.

"Alright, alright," Zaq grinned, shaking his head in bemusement. "I believe you all. Like I said, I need to trust more. Back to it, then. As I said, I don't have a good idea yet. Do any of you?"

"I don't have an idea, as much as a question," Legs stated. "Why is it we can't make a web of mana connections? You said the scrolls work with a mana link. Why not set up a mana link between the tablets and multiple other tablets?"

"A good question, actually," Zaq said, writing and drawing on the slate. "The issue comes down to usefulness. In theory, that might work. The problem is, you would need to purposefully create each link, and it takes someone skilled in artificery. So, each time you wanted to connect to a new device, you would need to bring both devices to an artificer and have them create the link."

"That makes sense," Flek said. "I'm sure people wouldn't want to have to keep making new links like that. The web would never grow big enough."

"Exactly right," Zaq said. "We need a solution that can link the tablets without interference, ideally, without the users even knowing. The ideal solution would mean that tablet holders just need to be near each other, and a link would form, which would strengthen and expand the web."

Wyndi had been quiet the entire time, ingesting the conversation while letting her mind roam to possible solutions. Something about this idea of a web and spiders tickled her brain. She read something once that might be applicable, if she could just remember.

A light finally ignited, and she remembered the old book she had once read while helping her father with an interesting old device someone had brought in for repair.

"What if we used spiders? We've been talking about webs and spiders, but we haven't actually talked about using spiders. Could it really be that easy?"

"I'm sorry, dear," Zaq said, looking perplexed. "How would spiders help the situation? You realize that we can't physically connect the tablets? The connections would be broken in short order. That's why we don't just use a string. A spider web is even more fragile."

"Sorry, that's my fault," Wyndi blushed, her round cheeks turning bright pink. "I should have been clearer. I was remembering an old project my father worked on as a repairman. We had to consult some old texts in order to find the solution. The project, completely different from this one, used ethereal spiders. If we could convince an ethereal spider that it was in its best interest to bond with a tablet, then it could spin connections of ethereal webbing between any tablet it came near, expanding the web and connecting with its brethren."

"Oh yes! That's brilliant," Zaq beamed at her. "I recall now that I have seen ethereal spiders as integral to some artifacts. Or usually not the spiders themselves, but their webbing. We would, of course, be using their webbing, but by contracting with the spiders themselves, the network could expand into a web just like we want."

"But how do we contract with a spider?" Flek asked, scratching his beard. "Ethereal or not, they are still just spiders. Plus, maybe it's just me, but we're talking about a spider. Do we *really* want a spider living in or on our tablets?"

"It seems you may not know much about the spiders," Zaq chuckled. "They can be anywhere; in fact, there are probably one or two in this room with us. Or adjacent to this room? It depends on how you view the overlapping planar topography."

"What? Where?" Legs yelled, jumping up and brushing at himself.

"Calm down, Frank," Zaq said, waving his hands palm side down. "They've been around you your entire life. It's nothing new, and they don't interfere with you. Like I said, they aren't really *here*."

"What is the right way to describe it?" Wyndi mused. "I know what you mean. I learned all about the spiders. The ethereal plane overlaps completely with our plane. It's not like some of the other planes that might be above, or below, or somewhere off to the side of our plane. We can't naturally interact with anything in that plane and vice versa."

"Right you are," Zaq said. "However, there are spells and devices that can cross the barrier, and some inhabitants of the ethereal plane can naturally interact with ours in specific ways. The spiders are one such creature. They are also sapient and, in addition to their own language, can often communicate in several others."

"If we can't interact with the ethereal plane, or at least not without extra magic, how do we work with them on our tablet project? And can working with spiders ever be reasonable? Even if they are smart spiders? That might even make it worse." Legs shivered.

"My goggles have a mode for inspecting the ethereal plane," Zaq said nonchalantly, as if it were the most natural thing to have. Wyndi knew his goggles had to be loaded with features.

"That's amazing," Wyndi complimented aloud, despite the jealousy she held inside. "I wish mine could do that."

"Don't just wish!" Zaq smiled. "Upgrade them! If you aren't sure how, I'll show you how to add more features. If you are all going to be doing serious artificery, you need the right equipment. I likely even have some old goggles you could reference for different features. But first, I need to make a small device to create an audio bridge so we can converse with a spider if we find one."

The old gnome strode across the room to a box of miscellaneous parts and dug through them. He must have thought he had everything he needed for a device like that. Wyndi met eyes with Flek, and she raised her right eyebrow, jerking her head toward a box and asking an unspoken question. The goblin looked thoughtful for a moment, grinned mischievously, and nodded, already on his way to another of the parts bins with Wyndi following.

Legs seemed content to wait. In fact, he found a spot on the floor where he could lean his back against the wall. He didn't yet have any goggles, so he had nothing to upgrade. He would need to craft a pair, but that could take him several days. Wyndi heard him make an odd noise, and when she turned to look, he was patting his lap, trying to get the cat's attention. It worked, and the shadowy black cat cautiously approached, then settled into his cross-legged lap.

When she turned back to the box, Flek had already found the old pair of goggles she had thought she had seen while they built tablets the other day. Grabbing a multitude of different parts, Wyndi and Flek took everything to an open workbench and laid it out.

Zaq didn't seem to mind or care and was fully absorbed in building whatever device he thought might help him communicate. The old pair of goggles Flek had rescued from the parts bin was missing the straps, and two of what had to be at least a dozen lenses were cracked. Despite the defects, it provided more than enough information on how to add several upgraded features.

Both Wyndi and Flek removed their goggles and dove into the tedious process of upgrading them with new, exciting features. Wyndi increased the magnification levels on the distance and the microscopic lenses. She added several thermal and radiation visualizers, such as infrared and ultraviolet. After testing the new visualizers, she spied what parts Zaq was using for his acoustic bridge.

Flek pointed out how they could leverage one of the components to add visualization of the ethereal plane. They confirmed the mode worked by looking around the room for anything interesting or out of the ordinary. A breathtaking field of ethereal flowers, shimmering in a ghostly purple hue, filled half the workshop.

On the table with the original distributor that they had reconnected to their tablets, several spiders, similar to oversized tarantulas, were fixed on the pulsing mana crystal embedded in the grimbark.

"They work," she cheered. "And look over there, by the small distributor. We have many spiders visiting, hoping to get a taste of the mana crystal."

"What's that?" Zaq called, looking up from his project, which resembled a mechanical ear connected to an extended cone. "You found ethereal spiders?"

"We did," Flek said, pointing at the distributor. "There are several on that table, next to, or even on the distributor."

"That makes sense," Zaq nodded, already looking back down at his nearly completed project. "The spiders are drawn to concentrated sources of mana. Did you upgrade your goggles? Already? Well, color me impressed. I'm nearly finished here, and you'll be able to see them while we talk. What about Frank? He didn't work on goggles? Oh, he's with the cat. Thank you!"

The old gnome was definitely excited and in a good mood. He was speaking many more words than usual and sounded downright chipper. Looking over at Legs, Wyndi found he looked happy enough to be petting the cat. The other day, he had borrowed her goggles to make his tablet. She decided she would help him make a set of goggles once they had a solution for connecting the slates.

Zaq lowered his goggles and adjusted them, presumably to turn on the ethereal filters, and brought the audio bridge to the table holding the distributor. He flipped it on, and Wyndi saw several portions of the device that had previously looked like indents or holes now held glowing, ethereal parts connected to the bridge.

"Greetings and salutations," Zaq said, and the spiders stopped what they had been doing and turned to look at the device that had just spoken to them.

"Many hellos," one of the spiders said, stepping forward toward the device. The voice was light and airy like the sound of feathers dancing in the wind. "You see us. You speak to us. Welcome. Would you care to share in the mana radiation from the device?"

"We have no need of the radiation," Zaq answered. "Please, enjoy it. I would ask you to listen to a proposition if you would?"

"A proposition?" the spider asked. "A deal? A trade? What is this proposition?"

"First, allow me to introduce myself. I am Zaq, and these three here are my apprentices: Wyndi, Flek, and Frank."

"You are well met. I am Mackmyra. And the proposition?"

Chapter 34

Ethereal Web of Devices

Zaq retrieved two tablets and brought them over to the spiders. *Now, how best to explain the situation?* Nodding to himself, he moved to address Mackmyra.

"We are working on a project, and thanks to some insights from Frank, I was able to devise a possible solution, but it requires your cooperation. These tablets can be used to communicate. I know your kind need no such devices and have mental links with each other. However, for us, we need technical arcane assistance. We can easily connect two devices with threads of mana. If we try to add in more, it quickly becomes unmanageable."

"Threads of pure mana are ill-advised," Mackmyra whispered. "The price is high. The cost is wasteful."

"Exactly!" Zaq said, clapping his hands. "If you and your kind would agree to help in the ethereal plane, I believe I have a better solution. Any time two or more slates are near each other, you could spin a strand of ethereal web between the mana crystals."

"An efficient use of mana," the spider agreed. "The mana

flows through webbing. The webbing has low resistance. The information flows freely."

"You are picking up on exactly the point of it," Zaq practically giggled in his excitement. "And of course, since mana would manifest and travel the web in both the material and ethereal planes, you would all be welcome to enjoy a network rife with mana radiation."

"The plan is sound," Mackmyra said. "A contract is needed. Terms of service must be bound to tablet holders. The mana must remain strong."

"Ah, yes. I understand your dilemma," Zaq nodded. "If death or other extremely harmful topics are transmitted, the mana could become weakened. We also cannot allow people to interfere with the web themselves. Most would not have the means, but some could, and they must be bound against it."

"This one sees the truth," Mackmyra said, and several of the spiders nodded their heads. "Craft a contract worthy of the endeavor. We will spread the ideas, and a consensus will be reached."

"Wonderful! I will start work drafting the most complete and comprehensive set of terms and conditions for using the tablets on the network."

Zaq shut off the ethereal bridge and turned to the apprentices who had been quietly listening to the conversation.

"This is most wonderful news, don't you think?"

"It sounds amazing," Flek said. "If I understand correctly, these spiders will connect all of the tablets in a giant web or network. And the mana cost is low because it can transmit over the webbing, rather than needing to craft a thread of pure mana."

"But what about this contract you were talking about?" Frank asked. "I didn't understand that part. What are you drafting?"

"Ah, it's a nuance you see. Mana is susceptible to emotions and concepts," Zaq explained. "That is a good portion of how magic works. A lot of magic is about intent and channeling emotions. The spiders feed off mana and mana radiation. However, they don't want mana tainted with negativity. We must restrict the users from sending extremely negative content."

"I'm not sure if I love the idea of preventing people from saying what they want," Wyndi interjected. "That sounds like censorship."

"No, no. That's not the intent," Zaq assured her. "We won't stop them from saying anything; we just want to guide how they say it. This is a social network after all, with content shared among a large population, and now, with the deal I'm forging, the ethereal spiders as well."

"It sounds like a slippery slope," Wyndi said, sounding unconvinced. "But, now that you bring up content, it sounds like the mana requirements are going to be very low, even for a large number of users."

"Even better!" Zaq laughed. "The larger the number of users, the better it will be. Mana cost will shrink as the number of users increases and the ethereal network expands."

"If that's the case, do you think we can afford to send more advanced messages?" Wyndi asked. "With the tablets in our tests so far, we sent written messages and drawings. But could we send more?"

"More? What do you have in mind?" Zaq looked at her curiously. "What more would you put on a tablet than writing and drawings?"

"What if we allowed the user to capture sound and images from the environment?" Wyndi hypothesized. "We could record what is happening around them and transmit the recording. An audiovisual illusion could play out above the surface of the tablet."

"That's brilliant, Wyndi!" Flek cried. "Did you really come up with that right now?"

Zaq noticed the young gnome's cheeks blushing a vibrant pink. He wondered, not for the first time, if there might be something going on between those two.

"I didn't come up with all of it now, no," Wyndi admitted. "It's something I've been thinking about for a while, but had pushed aside. I didn't see how we could ever get it to work, considering how taxing text was. But now—now it might be possible."

"I believe it will be, yes," Zaq said. "It's a great idea, and I don't think it will require much extra work. We will need to incorporate some new runes into the tablets. I'll need to make sure the terms of service are strong enough to handle content of all kinds passing through the network."

"I'm pretty sure I saw some runes that could help with it when I was studying the rune book," Frank said. "I could work on the enhancements with Wyndi and Flek while you draft the terms."

"I understand the terms need to be strict," Wyndi said cautiously. "However, we need to be careful about restricting people too much. Can we just outlaw the most negative? No talking about, drawing, or creating audiovisual illusions of death, and, I don't know, dismemberment or other horrible violence? For most other things, whether it's negative or not, is very subjective."

"That's a good point," Zaq granted. "I agree. We shouldn't be too restrictive. I'll focus the terms on outlawing sending talk or images about death, torture, or deadly acts of violence."

"I can get behind that," Wyndi nodded. "That should

appease the spiders and still keep our freedom to communicate."

Zaq sat at a drafting table and laid out several pieces of parchment. Grabbing his most precise and fine-grained legal pen, he began writing practice versions of the terms, refining them until they were stronger. The cat had left Frank when he stood up to work with the other two and was sitting on the table next to Zaq. A low, rumbling purr vibrated the air as his hand firmly stroked her head. She pushed up into his palm, then settled down into a lump with all four paws tucked neatly under her.

From time to time, Zaq glanced at the trio of youngsters as they worked. It really had been silly of him to give up so easily after the catastrophic failure. He had been shaken, though, when the cat was struck, making it a true cat-astrophe. Chuckling to himself at his own wittiness, he turned back to the documents.

This new network of tablets had the potential to elevate his project to new levels. Zaq had always thought of the money he could make from his ultimate project, but now, he wasn't so sure. The network needed to be large, enormous even. Ideally, people all over the world would use his tablets, connecting everyone together. That meant getting them into as many hands as possible.

The larger the network, the more performant it would be. Zaq couldn't believe he was thinking this way, but he would worry about money later. For this to work, the most important thing was to spread the network as widely as possible. In any case, he was glad they had forced him to have the tea and pastry that morning, allowing him to confront the issues.

"I was just thinking of the tea and pastries we had this morning. I realize we've been working ever since. I'm feeling hungry. How about you three?"

"I could eat," Flek said immediately, before Zaq had even finished asking. "In fact, I'll go pick up something. Everyone okay with some sandwiches?"

"No, you stay here," Frank told the goblin. "You and Wyndi are making great progress. Those goggle upgrades are helping you a lot. I'll go get the food."

Frank left, and Zaq turned back to his writing but paused almost immediately to ask the remaining two apprentices a question.

"What should we call this? To make these terms of service strong and binding, we need a name for the whole system. Something to describe this intangible web of devices."

"What about the EtherNet?" Wyndi asked. "It's a network of ethereal strands of web that make a huge net."

"Perfect!" Zaq grinned and turned back to his contract notes.

Frank returned an hour later carrying a large bag of sandwiches and a jug.

"Food's here. I went a little farther than I needed to, so I could get these delicious sandwiches I had a couple of months ago. Braised pulled pork with pickled radish and carrots, fresh efreet peppers, and creamy dressing made with seven-chili sauce. Just like my grandma used to make, using a recipe from the southern lands."

"That sounds right up my alley," Flek said, licking his fangs. "What's in the jug?"

"Spiced hard apple cider. On my way back from the sandwich shop, I noticed a vendor setting up a stall. He was getting a jump on a good spot for the harvest festival. Even though he wasn't fully open, he sold me a jug."

"I hope those sandwiches aren't horribly spicy," Wyndi said. "I can handle some, but not the goblin-level spice that gets Flek excited."

"Oh no, we like our food to have a kick down south, but it's mild compared to most of what you'd find in a goblin clan. Milder than that campfire dinner Zaq sent with us that had me sweating."

"Campfire dinner, I sent?" Zaq asked, looking up from the terms of service documents. "I don't recall sending anything overly spicy."

"You didn't," Flek snickered. "I didn't tell the others at the time, but I enhanced your seasoning in that meal with some of my own spices."

"Flek!" Wyndi said, sounding mock-exasperated and giving him a soft, playful punch in the arm. "I found that really spicy, and poor Legs was soaked in perspiration."

"You all have to admit, it was good, wasn't it?" Flek grinned mischievously.

Wyndi and Legs both reluctantly nodded, and Legs began emptying the bag onto the recreation station. He grabbed several glasses and poured hard cider into each.

"Foods on, Zaq. Come and get it. Same goes for the rest of you."

Zaq put down his pen and straightened his parchments, putting a placeholder on the area he had been working on before climbing onto a stool at the rec table. Frank handed him a long, paper-wrapped sandwich. When he unwrapped the outer layer of paper, he found the sandwich wrapped again with another sheet of paper, folded tightly, and it had been sliced in half.

Picking up one half, he saw the long roll was stuffed with filling so much that the interior of the roll was heavily compressed. He peeled back the paper wrapping, leaving some to use as a handhold, and took a bite. The roll was fresh and soft, but had a solid chew to it. Fragrantly spiced juices squeezed from the pork while he chewed, mixing with the pickled vegetables and the creamy dressing. There was a definite kick, but nothing he couldn't handle. He was eating a fabulous sandwich.

"Strong pick, Frank," Zaq said after swallowing. "This is a superb bite."

"It is *really* good, isn't it?" Wyndi asked, her mouth still half-full. "But not overly spicy. You aren't too disappointed, are you, Flek?"

"Nah, this is good. Not everything can be as hot as back home. I've come to expect that, but this has a really nice flavor."

Zaq swallowed a large swig of the hard cider and smiled widely.

"Oh, that's a good one. I wondered if that vendor you mentioned was Forester's stall. That was him, wasn't it? A halfling fellow?"

"You're right, it was," Frank nodded. "You must know everyone around here."

"I wouldn't say that, but I do keep tabs on the folks making beverages worth drinking. Forester makes a delightful cider, as I'm sure you're finding out."

They all ate and drank until the sandwiches and most of the cider were gone.

"My terms of service are coming along, but still need some work," Zaq said. "How's your prototype coming?"

"I think we have it working," Wyndi said, hopping up from the table. "Would you like to see a demonstration? Come on, Flek. Let's show them. The spiders agreed to connect two of the tablets so we could do some testing, even though the terms aren't fully baked in."

Both Wyndi and Flek grabbed one of the two tablets they

had been working on. Flek ran upstairs and out of sight. Wyndi held her tablet so Zaq and Frank had a good view and made sure it was on and ready to receive.

A moment later, a small message appeared in the text area: "Incoming Illusion Matrix." Then a virtual cube outlined itself over the tablet, showing an image of the Mystic Leaf & Toadstool patio with Flek at a table, waving. His voice echoed from the tablet, "Be down in a moment!"

Shortly thereafter, Flek came bounding back into the room.

"Pretty nifty, isn't it?" he asked with a large grin plastered on his face.

"It worked perfectly. Great job," Wyndi told him, then turned to Zaq. "As you can see, we can now transmit these illusions to capture what's happening in the area of the other tablet. If you put on your goggles, you can see the ethereal web strand connecting these two tablets. I don't think this network will get overloaded. In fact, I'm not even sure if it can be."

"There are always limits," Zaq said, "However, I believe the limit on these will be so high, we likely won't run into it. Excellent work, both of you."

Ever curious, Zaq pulled down his goggles and activated the ethereal filter. A glowing strand connected the mana crystals embedded in each of the two tablets. Strands also led to the other tablets spread out on the workbenches, creating a dense lattice of connections.

Chapter 35

Just Need To Grab Something

Wyndi and Flek took turns taking breaks from upgrading the remaining tablets with the new illusion matrix feature. During each break, they let Legs borrow their goggles so he could gain experience adding the new runic recipe to power the feature.

"We're getting close to upgrading all twenty of our tablets," Wyndi told Zaq.

"Really? That's excellent," Zaq said, still focused on his writing. "I've almost finished this draft of the terms of service. I think they will suffice, but we should test out the new terms, your new illusion feature, and the general load."

"You thinking another test with our test user group?" Flek asked.

"That's exactly what I was thinking," Zaq said. "I don't believe we'll run into issues this time. But, I also didn't think we would this last time either."

"I don't think we'll get the same group exactly," Wyndi mused. "Some of our testers were customers at the shop upstairs. We should reuse as many of the same people as we can, but we can fill in with random other patrons."

"Yes, yes. Keeping as much the same as possible is ideal for a solid test. If you give me a few more minutes, I'll finish these terms, and we can fan out like last time. Before we leave, I'll need to add these terms to the activation sequence on the tablets. Instead of the activation calling home to register the user with the distributor, the activation will now bind the user to the terms of service as part of the activation process. Their identity in the EtherNet will be tied to them via the bond in the terms."

"It's almost like this new version is registering them with the universe itself," Wyndi added.

"That's not horribly far off," Zaq said. "Legally binding spell law is an interesting type of magic. It ties into deep magics much older than most other forms you come into contact with. Whether it is the universe, the gods, or ancient spirits, whatever is performing the binding works to enforce the contract at all costs."

"The activation will need to be modified for these terms," Wyndi said. "We'll prep each of the tablets so that they are ready to accept the terms and the runic seal as soon as you're done."

The three apprentices revisited each of the twenty tablets and opened and activated the runic sequence, modifying the runes and leaving a spot for the terms to be inscribed. The only thing the trio left for Zaq was the runic encoding of the terms of service into a singular rune pattern they could place in the open area.

Zaq finished the last clause in the terms and confirmed that the final version was acceptable to the spiders. He muttered several incantations, registering them with the universal binding spell laws and forging a runic mark. He shared the new rune with the others, and they each applied it to five tablets.

Each, in turn, re-registered their personal tablets, with the terms of service instead of the prototype distributor. After firing several test messages, they were satisfied that the new system would be much more robust and resilient than the previous versions.

Wyndi and Flek took their tablets upstairs to hit up the customers at the Mystic Leaf & Toadstool. They had decided they would work better as a team since they would be able to demonstrate how sending the new illusion-style messages worked. And of course, it meant they had some alone time together.

She had noticed Legs was clearly putting her and Flek in a position to be close to each other and work together. He really was a good friend, and despite his goofiness at times, he was socially aware of what happened around him.

Wyndi considered going out to her parents' place like she had during the last test, but decided against it.

"We can hit up the customers here first, then head to the Inn Side Out to revisit the folks you looped in on the first test."

"What about your parents?" Flek asked. "You had them in the first test, didn't you? Shouldn't we go see them? Or are you embarrassed to show me off?"

He flashed a wicked grin after his last remark, clearly not seriously thinking that.

"No, silly," Wyndi swatted at him. "The truth is, it was embarrassing to get the tablets from my father after the last test. I had to admit the test had failed, and I don't like failing in front of him."

To his credit, her father had offered to help repair the system, which is what he did after all, but he failed to understand that she couldn't just fix it. Fixing it would put it back the way it was, which would just fail again. Her father was never one to understand the concept of experimentation and invention. Still, he was happy with what he knew and enjoyed applying his knowledge of existing runes and machines.

While Wyndi had high hopes that this version of the network would work as they thought it would, she couldn't squish that nagging, *what if*, that lingered. Being confident that this test would work was one thing. Being confident enough to know she wouldn't have to look like a failure in front of her dad again was another. No, she would give a tablet to both her mother and father once the group had proven the network was sound in this next test.

"Maybe after we prove this works, we can take them some tablets and you can meet them."

"Deal!" Flek's grin turned into a smile, making her think that, while he hadn't been serious, he also hadn't been not serious.

Wyndi spied a wolfkin man who had been a part of the first test sitting at a table with a human woman who had not. Approaching the table, she cleared her throat.

"Yes?" the wolfkin asked, looking up at her as recognition lit his face. "Ah, it's you, with the tablets. That was quite a fun experiment, but it stopped working, so I brought it back here and left it with Zheb. Did he get it back to you? I didn't realize it was a limited-time trial."

"Technically, it wasn't," Wyndi's cheeks blushed as pink as her hair. "The test failed. *But* we learned from our mistakes and improved the tablets and how they communicate. We'd love for you to try again. Assuming it works, you're welcome to keep the tablet and continue using it."

"That sounds great," he said, then turned to his tea companion. "Christine, you should get in on this trial if they'll have you. The tablets let you send messages to anyone else who has one. You can even send to groups of people."

"Of course, she—Christine was it?—is welcome," Wyndi said, handing them each a tablet. "This time it works a bit differently. You'll notice the tablet is displaying a legal terms of service document. Please read it, and then agree by registering your name with the tablet."

"Ah, ha. So it's getting more official this time," the wolfkin grinned, exposing an array of sharp teeth. "I hope that means you got enough kinks out that you think it's worth the formality."

"We're pretty sure this version'll work," Flek said. "The terms are actually part of how it works. But you should see the new features, too."

"Oh, yes. You must see," Wyndi said, pulling out her tablet. "Watch as Flek and I send the new style of messages."

Wyndi and Flek both held their tablets up in front of their faces and activated the recording rune. They each waved, and Wyndi even blew Flek an imaginary kiss, then hit send. The messages showed up instantly on the opposite devices, and everyone was able to see the illusions form above the surface of the tablet.

A miniature gnome waved at the goblin and blew a kiss, and the goblin above Wyndi's tablet waved at her and flashed a grin, licking his tongue over his fangs. Wyndi felt her cheeks get hot and dismissed the illusion. That goblin was going to get a punch in the arm later.

"That is absolutely fantastic," the wolfkin said, then turned to focus on the terms. "I'm almost done here. It's pretty standard stuff, right? I figure a good skim is enough. And I just register with my name like last time?"

"Yes and no," Wyndi said. "The deep contract magic will bind to your core self regardless of what name you use. You can use your real name or feel free to provide a nickname for use on the EtherNet."

"Is that what it's called, then? Catchy," he said. "Alright, I'll agree to the terms like so, and I'll just use my first name, Jaxxon, on the EtherNet as you call it."

His companion, Christine, also finished reviewing the terms, but Wyndi noticed she had been more careful in reading them. There was nothing harmful in them. The opposite was true, in fact. They should even prevent harm, but she was glad to see the woman take care in what she agreed to.

"Thanks for this," Christine said, looking at both Wyndi and Flek in turn. "It looks like a lot of fun."

Several other customers at nearby tables had overheard and seen the demonstration. They all wanted to be included in the trial, so before they knew it, the apprentices had handed out all of their testing tablets. They spent the next several minutes helping people properly register and send a test message.

"I suppose we don't need to go to the inn," Flek said. "I hope Alaquine doesn't mind missing out on this trial. We can always give him a tablet later once we have more."

"You can still bring one to him if you want," Legs said as he rounded the corner. "Nice work handing all of yours out so quickly. I'm going to run this one out to my father's place, but you can have these three. Take them to the inn."

"Thanks, Legs," Wyndi said, taking the tablets. "We'll do that and meet you back at the workshop later."

At the Inn Side Out, Flek walked straight up to the bar, catching Alaquine's eye.

"Hey, Al. Up for another tablet trial?"

"Flek, good to see you. I'm not so sure. I told you when you picked the tablets up that it gave me a small mana shock. Nothing harmful, but surprising nonetheless. Or have you fixed that *feature*?" the elf grinned good-naturedly and quirked an eyebrow.

"It's fixed!" Flek exclaimed. Wyndi appreciated his confidence. "We actually re-worked how the entire system works. If you use the new version, you can be one of the first to join the new EtherNet."

Nice, Wyndi thought. He was already getting into sales and marketing mode with the new name.

"Let's have it then," the bartender said, holding out his hand. "I'll get Glorya and Jess over here. Cal is out today."

Wyndi and Flek demonstrated the new feature again. This time, Flek acted more appropriately, taking the scolding she'd given him during the walk to the inn to heart. Jess got very excited when she saw what it could do and immediately registered without even bothering to skim the terms. She then wandered off to play with the new toy, leaving Alaquine to shake his head and chuckle.

"I hope I don't regret having you give her one of those. I may have to set some new rules around tablet usage during her shift."

"I'm sure the novelty will wear off soon," Wyndi said, but she wasn't entirely sure she believed that. Part of her imagined that some people might end up using these tablets a lot.

After verifying everyone's tablet worked, Flek said, "Let's go up to my room. I need to grab something before we head back to the workshop."

"See you later," Alaquine waved, as the two made for the stairs. "Tell Zaq I said hello."

On the way up the stairs, Wyndi turned her head to Flek.

"What did you need to grab in your room? I thought we had everything we needed at the workshop for the tests."

"Oh, it's not for the tests. I'm going to grab you," he said, flashing a smirk showing all his fangs.

Wyndi squealed and ran away up the stairs, with Flek scrambling up after her.

Chapter 36

The EtherNet Project

The second round of testing went just as well as the team thought it would. They didn't even have to kick it off officially because the users were used to the tablets from the previous test, and the new illusion-style messages were intuitive. Messages began streaming in, often targeting the entire user base, but with no distributor to overload, the tablets continued to work without issue.

Zaq and Frank were in the workshop, but it wasn't clear what was taking Wyndi and Flek so long to return. It gave Zaq time to work one-on-one with the human, and they built him his own pair of goggles, complete with all the upgrades available. Once they both could see the ethereal spiders, Zaq turned on the ethereal bridge.

"Greetings and salutations," Zaq called to the spiders. "Is Mackmyra there?"

"I am here," a spider said, scuttling forward on the workbench. "Is there something wrong with the human?"

"What?" Zaq asked, turning to see what they might be

talking about. There, lying on the ground, was Frank, completely passed out.

"Oh dear," he fussed, bending to check on the young man. He gently shook Frank.

"Wh-what? Did you see?" Frank gasped. "Wyndi had said there were spiders, but I couldn't handle thinking about it. Just put it right out of my mind. But to see them—they're so big. I just can't. I don't think I can activate that mode anymore. I know they are there, and that's bad enough, but I can't look."

"Oh, come on," Zaq shook him. "They're friendly. They mean you no harm."

"I hope that's true, but I'll let you talk with them. I'll work on those update routines we were talking about."

Zaq simply shook his head with a wry smile. At least he would make progress on the plan they had hatched together. Frank would be working on a set of runes they could install on privileged tablets, capable of sending updates to all of the connected devices. This feature would allow them to add new capabilities to all of the deployed tablets.

Returning to Mackmyra, Zaq apologized.

"Forgive him. It seems you make him nervous. I wanted to check with you. Has there been any strain on the network of webbing?"

"The opposite," Mackmyra chittered. "It seems the more people use the tablets and send messages, the stronger the mana flow, strengthening the strands. The radiation into the ethereal plane is tremendous—more than we could have expected."

"That's wonderful to hear," Zaq clapped. "It's exactly what I had been hoping for."

"We do not foresee trouble," Mackmyra whispered. "We only ask that you continue crafting and distributing the devices. Our network will grow stronger."

"That's the plan!" Zaq quipped gleefully. "We're making

more today and handing them out at the harvest festival tomorrow. We'll give them to anyone who will take them and only ask for any donation they can spare."

Zaq shut down the bridge again and picked a workbench to sit and build more tablets. As he finished his second one, Wyndi and Flek came bounding down the stairs.

"Did you get lost handing out the tablets?"

The goblin looked at the young gnome, quirking an eyebrow, and then they both began giggling. Wyndi sobered up first and answered after a long delay.

"We, uh, just had some personal matters to attend to."

Zaq noticed Frank rolling his eyes and was now quite sure something was going on between the young gnome and the goblin. That was fine. He remembered some of his early romantic partners and the fun he had with them. The corners of his mouth curled up at the thought of one particular gnome —Victrola Cogwheeler.

Vicki had been his love interest in his early days at Mysti Messages. Her bright purple hair perfectly complemented her golden eyes, and her smile always brought out the cutest dimples in her lightly freckled cheeks. Zaq's long hours and hard work at the company were ultimately what lost her, but it had taken quite some time before he had realized. That's how wrapped up in his work he had been. He had eventually gotten over the loss, but still had moments like this where memories of her came back. Remembering her for all that she was never failed to bring out a smile.

He shook his head and returned his focus to the latecomers.

"Very well. Very well. I'm glad you're here now. We need to make as many devices as possible. I want to distribute them at the festival. I think we can ask for donations in exchange for a tablet. We can reinvest in making more and strengthening the EtherNet."

"I'll join in making some, too," Frank said, looking up from his notes. "I think I may have the upgrade runes nearly finished. Once I do, maybe you can review them while I switch to construction."

"I love that idea," Wyndi exclaimed. "There will be so many people out in the streets at the festival. It doesn't matter how many we make; I'm sure we'll run out fast."

"I was hoping to spend some time doing fun things at the festival with you," Flek said. "But we can hand out tablets first."

"Oh!" Wyndi gasped, her cheeks flushing. "I'd love that even more than handing out the slates. But, I'm sure there will be time for both."

Zaq reviewed Frank's upgrade runes, making minor adjustments and taking notes, then joined the apprentices in building tablets. They soon entered a pattern of efficiency. In the end, the tablets were not overly complex to build. Applying the runes took some care and precision, and the incantations to finalize them slowed them down. However, they devised a system that let them split the tasks, creating a small assembly line.

They worked late into the evening until their tiredness began manifesting as mistakes in the tablets. Zaq helped fix the various issues in the last batch and called it a night.

"Thank you, everyone. We have a lot of devices to give away tomorrow. Go get some sleep, and we can meet back here in the morning before the festival activities begin."

"I'll stay here, unless that's a problem," Frank said. "I've already got bedding under the workbench in the corner."

"Sleep well, Frank," Wyndi called from the stairs. She and Flek were already running up to the alley.

"Of course. That's fine," Zaq said. "I've definitely been known to crash in a workshop from time to time when I was younger. I need a soft bed these days, so I'll be heading home.

Are you sure you're going to do well on your own, considering your issues with the spiders?"

Frank looked around, then wiped the worried lines from his face.

"It really is fine as long as I don't see them. And, like you said, they aren't planning on hurting me. It's best not to talk more about it," he said with a shiver.

Zaq chuckled, then turned to leave. The cat seemed to appear out of nowhere and circled his legs, leaning in as she passed by and rubbing the length of her side against his shins. He reached out his arms, looking down at the cat, who got excited and reared up on her hind legs with her forearms outstretched, gazing at him with hopeful, yellow eyes.

Zaq lifted the cat into his arms and carried her back to his house. Along the way, she repeatedly nuzzled her head into the crook of his arm. Whether she was being affectionate or just seeking warmth from the chilly evening air, he wasn't sure, but he enjoyed it nonetheless.

The next morning, the streets were already filling up when Zaq returned to the workshop. Frank was up, and the new couple had returned. Presumably, they had spent the night at the inn. All three had wasted no time and were building several more tablets to add to the piles.

"Today's the big day!" Zaq beamed. "The festival is here, and there will be so many people in the streets, we'll be able to grow the network leaps and bounds. Don't worry if some people aren't interested. With a few demonstrations, I'm sure enough will want to grab one."

"Good morning, Zaq," all three said in unison.

"Grab an empty crate and load as many in as you can," Zaq

said. "I doubt we'll be able to load them all up, but we can always come back for a refill when we run low."

"Flek and I are going to work as a team," Wyndi explained. "The demonstrations and registration went much smoother when we could show off how they work."

"Teams sounds like a good idea. Can you put up with an old gnome of a partner?" Zaq asked, looking up at Frank.

"Of course," Frank smiled. "I bet I can learn a lot just by being near you. Plus, you know just about everyone in a twenty-block radius."

"I'm sure that's an exaggeration," Zaq said. "I do know quite a few people, but I doubt they know me well. I've always kept more to myself."

"Whatever the case, let's go," Frank said, as he piled tablets into a crate.

Zaq did likewise, and they left the workshop carrying boxes practically overflowing with devices. They emerged into the alley to find the streets absolutely packed with people. The cafe was standing room only on the patio, and a line of people waited snaking out of the door to the shop. There was no time for tea anyway, so Zaq took the lead and Frank followed.

A block down the street, the crowd formed a circle around a wind mage entertaining the onlookers with fun cantrips. She manipulated the wind, crafting vortices and swirling storms of multi-colored leaves that danced at her command. The people cheered every time the leaves threatened to lose cohesion, and then even louder when the mage kept the show going.

Leaves danced and formed animal shapes, funny faces, and monstrous beasts. At one point, the mage formed the leaves into a swirling tube shape, making a snake and chasing children who were running and screaming with delight.

Frank pulled out his tablet and recorded the leaves, then sent the recording out to everyone on the network. Zaq's tablet buzzed, and he pulled it out, showing anyone close the illusion of the dancing leaves that played out above the device.

"Send and receive messages just like these! Get one today with a donation of any amount for the EtherNet project."

Zaq and Frank were inundated with questions, and some people just thrust small pouches of coins at them, asking if they could have one. The concept was clearly a novelty, and the crowd seemed eager to try the new invention."

One by one, Zaq and Frank helped people accept the terms, register with the network, and craft their first message. In no time at all, their crates were half-empty, and the mage manipulating the leaves now had an array of devices trained on him.

Three streets over, in a wide courtyard, Zaq found a carving contest taking place. Just like with the wind mage, there was a crowd of onlookers watching the spectacle. Tables had been set out in rows with multiple stations set up at each one. Contestants could choose from a variety of fruits and vegetables to craft their carvings.

An elf had a collection of oversized apples and used a small knife to cut intricate designs in the fruit. He was a master with the tool, creating cuts of varied depths and scraping bits of peel away in the perfect spots. Each apple transformed into a detailed relief-sculptured face.

At another table, an orc worked on a single carving. She hollowed out an enormous pumpkin and carved an entire cityscape design. A glowing red crystal lit up the vegetable from the inside.

Altogether, a dozen contestants were working diligently on their food sculptures. Whoever was judging this contest would have a tough time choosing a winner.

Frank took his tablet to a table and set the record mode, then slowly walked from table to table, panning over the in-progress pieces of art. He panned up to catch the artist's face, then down to their creation. Once he finished the circuit, he crafted a message and sent it to Zaq, Wyndi, and Flek.

The tablet at Zaq's hip buzzed, and he made a show of pulling it from the holster and holding it out to view the illusionary message. This, of course, caught the attention of everyone near him, and he was peppered with questions about what it was and how it worked. Right in his element, he pitched the tablets just like he had with the previous crowd.

"Send and receive messages just like these! Get one today with a donation of any amount for the EtherNet project."

"Any amount, you say?" one young lizardkin woman asked. Her S's were drawn out even more than usual for her kind. "Are you serious? I could donate one copper? And still get one of those tablets?"

Zaq flashed her a winning smile and a wink.

"*Any* amount. We hope for more than a copper, but even a copper will do. In the end, it balances out. Those who can give more, do."

"It probably costs a lot to use it then," she accused, suspicion casting shadows on her face. "One of those subscription systems? I'd likely go into debt making frivolous illusions."

"I can see why you'd think so, but we've devised a system free of upkeep charges. Follow-up donations are always welcome if you enjoy the tablet, but certainly not necessary. We plan to apply for a grant if we can get enough users to justify it."

"You've got a deal then," she said, handing him a silver piece. So much for her only offering a copper.

Zaq realized this idea would have blown his mind even two weeks ago, but so much had changed in the last few days. Trusting in people's generosity was certainly a gamble. He honestly wondered how much an older version of himself would have donated for one of these devices.

As if the world was rewarding him for his faith in the donations of others, a halfling dressed in fine trousers, a crisp white tunic, and a vest with ornate needlework, approached.

"I'll have one of those if you still have one available. This should help your EtherNet foundation, I heard you talking about."

The man had a smooth face and a smile that forced large dimples in his cheeks. He held out a small pouch, which Zaq took, thanking him in return. The pouch was light, but clearly contained several coins. A handful of silver would balance out the single coin from the lizardkin.

Once the halfling had registered his device and left, Zaq dumped the contents of the pouch out so he could update his mental tally of the collection so far. His eyes just about leapt from their sockets when he found a platinum coin and three gold pieces. Whoever that halfling was, he had just subsidized a massive portion of the user base.

Chapter 37

A Harvest Festival Date

Messages of all kinds kept buzzing alerts on Wyndi and Flek's tablets. There were simple scribbled notes, still images, and audiovisual illusions. Some people chose to send messages out to the entire network, while a few people they knew were targeting them specifically. In either case, it was fun and exciting to see new content lighting up the devices.

Wyndi was having a good time watching Flek's face as he took in the multitude of sights and activities in the festival. He had told her that they only had a small celebration for the harvest festival in his warren. The event was celebrated worldwide, and any settlement on Aberterrene celebrated at least some form of the festival. But the celebrations could vary considerably and depended heavily on how much of a role farming played in the area.

"Look at that stall!" Flek yelled, pointing at a booth across the wide thoroughfare and licking his fangs. "We gotta go. Come on, I'll buy you a slice."

"Maybe we can just share one," Wyndi pleaded. She was

much more comfortable with herself now, and all of the attention and acceptance from Flek made things even better, but the festival held so much food and drink that moderation was still prudent.

"Fine, but don't complain if I end up eating more than my share," Flek flashed an infectious grin.

He ran ahead of her and stood in the short line. Seeing no reason to crowd the booth, Wyndi stood back, leaning against the side of a building to wait for him. The line moved quickly, and soon Flek was back with a thin slice of wood the stall was using as disposable plates.

The treat resting on top of the make-shift platter was enormous. The bakers running the stall had crafted layered pies. It wasn't entirely clear if they had been baked separately and then stacked, or stacked and then baked like some kind of giant pie. Wyndi had a suspicion they had been baked and then stacked. In either case, the slice of pie, if you could actually call it that, was layered with a whole slice of pecan pie, with a slice of pumpkin pie right on top of it, then topped with a slice of apple pie, and finally a slice of pear pie with cranberries. Why in the world were four pies needed to make this monstrosity?

Flek handed Wyndi a flimsy wooden spoon, and she sucked a small bit of drool back up into her mouth that she hadn't even realized had dribbled out. She took a spoonful, trying and failing to get some of each pie into a single bite. It didn't matter. The flavors all blended together so wonderfully, and each bite was a different combination.

Eventually, Wyndi slowed down and forced herself to stop. She didn't want a stomachache after all. Flek never slowed, and it didn't really surprise her when he scooped up the last bite. Before shoveling it into his mouth, he paused.

"Did you want the last bite?" he asked, with a sincere but hopeful look on his face.

She simply laughed, shaking her head, and the goblin stuffed his mouth full.

"I know the festival is fun, but we still have a lot of tablets to hand out," Wyndi said, scanning the crowd for the next best place to perform a demonstration of the devices.

"We will, don't worry," Flek said, forcing the last bite down. "I think I hear music from that direction. If there is a bard, we could capture it as an illusion."

"Great idea," Wyndi smiled and took his hand. "I'm pretty sure I hear it too, but I trust your ears over mine any day."

Wyndi let Flek lead her in the direction he had heard the music. Four blocks over, they found the source of the melody. A full band had set up with a gnoll lead singer, an orc on drums, a goblin with an accordion, and a troll playing a large bass. The band was in the center of an intersection of two primary roads through the city. A crowd surrounded them, filling the square, and they all danced in time to the music.

Wyndi waited for them to finish the song they had been playing when the two approached. Then, she gave Flek a gentle elbow.

"Let's both record the next song and see how it turns out. I'm curious what happens when a similar scene is recorded in the illusion array."

He nodded, and they both flipped their tablets into record mode as the next song started. The song was long, longer than she had expected, but the tablet didn't seem to have a problem recording for an extended period of time.

"You know what we need?" she asked Flek, but then answered before he had a chance. "We need to craft an update to send out that allows editing the illusions after recording. That was a long song, but I realize now that I might not want to send just one long message. If I could edit it into multiple shorter scenes, that would be nice."

"Great idea," Flek nodded. "We can send out that as a new feature using the update rune Frank made. For now, I'm just going to send this whole song. It was pretty good."

Wyndi decided he had a point and sent the full message, targeting the entire network population. She realized after sending it that the population had grown much larger. The EtherNet seemed to be doing fine, but maybe it wasn't a good idea to send messages to everyone.

"We should also—" they both started at the same time and then laughed.

"You go first," Wyndi said.

"I was just thinking we should come up with a way to filter who sees what, rather than letting people send to every single person on the network. Like some kind of maximum audience size."

"That's what I was thinking, too!" Wyndi cried. "But rather than limit how many people you can send to, what if we made it so you can just send it out with no particular list of recipients. People could subscribe to other people's updates or even just topics they would receive, no matter who sent the message."

"I like that," Flek nodded, then jotted a note on the tablet.

"What was that you wrote?" Wyndi asked, peering over.

"Just a note to myself about these ideas. I realized I can remember stuff if I send myself a message and don't look at it until later."

"That's actually pretty brilliant, you know?" Wyndi said in sincere admiration.

Right then, several nearby people got their attention, asking what they had in their hands that was making those illusionary lights and sounds. The two switched into vendor mode, pitched everyone on the idea of the slates, and requested donations in return.

"Have you ever wanted to send messages to more than one person at a time?" Wyndi asked the gathering crowd.

"Tired of the limitations and expense of Mysti Message scrolls?" Flek played off her.

"With an EtherNet tablet, you can send messages to single people, groups of people, or the whole network," Wyndi said, holding her tablet high above her head. Unfortunately, that didn't make it much more visible, considering how short she was, but the crowd got the idea.

"Thanks to a fantastic idea by my partner here, you can also send immersive audiovisual illusions," Flek said, building the hype up further.

"The best part is, during the initial rollout, you can get a tablet for a donation of any amount," Wyndi closed.

Everyone nearby who heard the pitch turned away from the music show and queued up to get a device, handing over pouches and handfuls of coins of various values in exchange. Many turned back to the band after receiving their tablet and registering with the network. Before long, new clips of the music performance were disseminated throughout the web of devices.

Once everyone in the area who wanted one had one, the duo left to explore the harvest festival, looking for other fun activities. Before long, they stumbled upon a contest featuring distilleries from around the city and beyond. While any whisky could be entered, the contest was designed to celebrate the rye whisky the city of Ryefeld was known for.

"Zaq would love this," Wyndi said, grabbing Flek's hand and dragging him over to join the crowd.

A judge was in the middle of explaining the contest, the prizes, and the availability of the whisky.

"And once the judging is complete, everyone is encouraged to try a sip and purchase a bottle from your favorite distillers.

There will be a ten percent discount available on whisky from the winner, subsidized by the contest, to encourage folks to buy from them."

Wyndi and Flek watched and recorded the judging, which consisted of the judges sampling each whisky and sharing their tasting notes with the crowd.

"Mirador Shore Distillery has entered a fine rye whisky. I appreciate notes of vanilla, black pepper, anise, and cloves on the nose. On the palette, I find the classic kick of rye spice, dried apricots, and a hint of caramel. The finish is warm with lingering spice."

Several more were sampled, and then they shared one that Wyndi thought sounded the best.

"Frey River Distillery has also entered a rye whisky. We do appreciate the rye entries. They're really keeping to the spirit of the contest. I appreciate notes of vanilla, oak, cinnamon, and a hint of mint. On the palette, I find more rye spice; this one kicks hard, then mellows, leaving candied spiced peaches and rich butterscotch. The finish is dry, with lingering spice notes."

"I don't care if that one wins or not, I bet Zaq would love it," Wyndi said, poking Flek to get his attention. "I'm going to get him a bottle to celebrate the success of the EtherNet project."

"That's a great idea," Flek nodded. "I'll pitch in."

Wyndi patiently waited, recording more clips of the judging, then sent messages to Zaq and Frank, sharing the event. Zaq sent a short text message back.

Zaq: I knew I took the wrong route through the festival. The whiskies you sent all sound amazing.

Wyndi: You might still get to try one of the best ones, trust me.

Zaq: What are you getting at?

Wyndi left his message unanswered and smirked at Flek. With the judging nearly through, they turned to face the contest. The lead judge grabbed everyone's attention.

"Thank you all for your patience. As you can imagine, judging these whiskies is hard work."

The crowd chuckled and clapped until the judge waved them down.

"After some deliberation, we landed on a unanimous decision. I am proud to announce that the winner of the Harvest Festival Rye Whisky Showdown is...Frey River Distillery."

Applause thundered throughout the square with whistles, hoots, and hollers adding to the noise. The judge let this continue for some time before waving his hands down to settle the crowd.

"You are all welcome to sample the whiskies just like the judges have. We encourage you to support these local distilleries and purchase a bottle or two. Remember, purchases at Frey River Distillery are discounted ten percent."

Wyndi joined the long line at the Frey River table and eventually purchased a bottle. Flek split the cost with her, and they stepped away from the crowd. With the bottle in hand, Wyndi posed next to a pile of hay bales covered in multicolored leaves. Flek recorded her holding the bottle out, turning it this way and that to show it off.

"This one's for you, Zaq," she said with a smile, looking directly into the blinking crystal on the tablet Flek held.

She had Flek send the message to Zaq, but asked him to copy the entire group so she and Legs could see the message and any replies Zaq might send.

> Zaq: That is incredibly generous of you! I
> can't wait to try it. This is the perfect gift.
> We'll meet back at the shop after our crates
> are empty. I'll share a round with all of you.

Peering into the crate, Wyndi saw they didn't have that many left. She and Flek took up a strategic post where they could capture the attention of anyone who had just finished purchasing some whisky. With small demos showcasing the messages streaming in from all the users on the network, they easily handed out the last of the tablets from their crate.

The donations varied significantly, but on average, people seemed willing to donate an amount that was at least high enough to cover the cost of the tablets. In many cases, they collected more, which helped to offset the cost for those who couldn't afford to donate much.

Chapter 38

Supply Run

The harvest festival would last several more days, yet they were already out of tablets. Zaq combined and counted all the donations collected the day before, finding they amounted to more than he might have expected if they had sold them. Perhaps it had been the joyous mood induced by the festival, but quite a few people had been very generous.

"I can't believe how much people donated yesterday," Zaq addressed the group after he finished recording in his ledger. "We have plenty to reinvest in crafting more tablets and spreading the network wider. We've exhausted my supplies on a number of crucial parts. I've made a list. We can split up and purchase what we need."

"Let's do this," Flek said, pumping his fist. "We can craft tablets all day and return to the festival tomorrow."

"You and Wyndi seem to make a good team," Zaq said, winking and handing Flek a pouch full of coins. "If you can stay on task, you two can purchase the items on this list."

"Frank, you're with me again, if you can put up with this old gnome."

The young man chuckled, a smile filling his face and twinkling in his eyes.

"Don't be silly, sir. You may be on the older side, but I'm glad to spend time with you, picking up those extra bits of knowledge you drop carelessly."

"You'll have to share some of that information with us," Wyndi said. "Don't hog it all for yourself. We're all supposed to be learning from Zaq."

"I can't help it if I'm the one around him," Frank deflected. "I'll swap with you. You can collect supplies with Flickerwhizzle, and I'll go with the goblin."

Wyndi looked at Flek, back to Frank, then blushed as an expression halfway between a grimace and a grin wrestled on her face.

"No, no. I'm sure I can learn more later. Just be sure to share what you pick up. We've got our list and the coin; we're heading out now. I doubt it will take longer than an hour, then we can start constructing."

Zaq and Frank left the workshop shortly after the couple ran up the stairs. The two items they needed the most were small mana crystals and brass gears. There were a few other items as well, but they shouldn't be that hard to find and should be available at most merchants.

"We've already begun developing a relationship with Troshkin at Ore-ange and Lapiz," Zaq said as they walked. "We should purchase the crystals there."

"Sounds like a good plan," Frank nodded. "A couple of streets over from their building is a gnomish-run company that does a lot of brasswork. I've not shopped there personally, but heard good things about their work."

"I like to support gnomish businesses when I can," Zaq

said. "Nothing against anyone else, but I feel I can trust gnomish-made clockwork pieces. It's in our blood."

"I've often wondered if you gnomes had gears, sprockets, and widgets running inside you," Frank joked.

"Some say the true form of Goroque Flamesplitter is a clockwork gnome—a full automaton, so maybe you aren't too far off the mark."

Religious texts usually showed the god of crafting and industry as a gnome. However, occasionally, he could be depicted as a gnome made of mithril, with hatches that opened on his front and back, revealing intricate clockwork systems of gears. He was rumored to have fathered the first gnomes, which is why many people assume the race is naturally gifted in artificery.

The streets were just as crowded today as they had been yesterday. Zaq hoped they wouldn't have trouble making their purchases. Some businesses closed completely during the festival, or if their business was related to the festivities, would often set up stalls in the vendor areas. Neither of the places they planned to go to should fall into that category, so there should be at least a skeleton crew managing the sales desks.

When Zaq arrived at his first stop, the only one in the reception area of Ore-ange & Lapiz was Troshkin. The place sounded a lot quieter as well, with only muffled noises coming from the back. There was very little work being performed.

"Hello, Zaq," Troshkin boomed, welcoming them immediately. "Too busy to enjoy the festival? I gave most of my staff leave to enjoy the celebration."

"I'm just glad you're open," Zaq said. "Frank and I are

collecting more supplies to build tablets. They have been quite a hit."

"Yes! Yes!" the dwarf said, bushy eyebrows twitching. "That device has been vondrous. So many messages come through. Of course, I find myself spending a bit too much time vith it, perhaps."

"It can definitely grab your attention for too long," Frank laughed.

"We spread them through the harvest festival yesterday, but today we need to build more," Zaq explained. "In order to build more, we need the small mana crystals like you've seen on your tablet. I'd like to purchase a full crate if possible."

"An entire crate of mana crystals that size?" Troshkin's eyes lit up. "That's a lot of tablets you expect to make."

"We need to grow the network," Zaq said. "Ideally, we can build a thick web here in Ryefeld before expanding out, but I know some at the festival likely come from other locales, so it may naturally spread beyond the city to an extent."

"There are a lot of traveling merchants attending the festival," the dwarf said, stroking his beard. "You should find a few villing to take a crate of your devices."

"But how would that work?" Frank asked Zaq. "We're only taking donations. Selling them through the trader seems to fly in the face of that."

"I'm sure we could find a solution with at least one trader," Zaq answered. "If someone won't work with us, I'm sure there will be another who would."

"In either case," Troshkin said, bringing the attention back to him. "Vee can sell you a crate of crystals. I'll be back shortly."

"We don't need all of the money from the donations, you know," Zaq continued, picking up where they had left off. "We can instruct the traders to take only donations, but they are welcome to either charge a delivery fee or take ten percent of the donations."

"That should work if we can find someone willing to take that deal," Frank agreed.

"I think the bigger problem will be making enough to send with the traders," Zaq mused. "I imagine we'll be able to give away any we make today to locals attending the festival."

"That's a good point," Frank said. "We'll worry about traders once we've had a chance to build up enough stock. Do you think we should arrange for deliveries of crystals?"

"Vee can do that," Troshkin said, having heard the last of Frank's question when he came through the door carrying a crate.

"Wonderful," Zaq clapped. "Having crystals brought by the shop would save a lot of time. Can we send you a message via your tablet with how many we need and when?"

"Vell vat do you know?" the dwarf laughed deeply with the rumble reverberating from his belly. "I hadn't even considered the efficiency of this device for business. I thought it only a toy based on the messages flowing through it."

"I'm fairly sure people are just excited about its novelty," Zaq said. "I only thought of using it to send a request because communicating with my apprentices was the first thing I did with it."

"But to answer your question," Troshkin said, "I can do that. Send vat you need with the tablet. I'll get it delivered to you."

"Frank, grab that crate, will you?" Zaq said, handing the dwarf a pouch of coins to pay for it.

Despite being near the shop Frank had mentioned, the two returned to the workshop first. The box of mana crystals was heavy, even for the human. Zaq sent Frank down to deposit the crate below while he ordered them tea. They had earned a break, after all, or at least he thought they had.

When Frank returned to the patio, he sat with Zaq and sipped a special tea blend Zheb had made for the harvest, full of baking spices and a pop of cranberries. Joh had made a fresh batch of cranberry orange muffins, and Zheb hadn't had to try hard to convince Zaq to purchase two of them.

"We still have a lot to do," Zaq said, after swallowing a bite of the tangy, sweet muffin. "But I thought we could spare a moment for a short break."

"Thanks," Frank said, smiling. "This muffin is delicious. Our break won't last long. I'll finish this in no time."

He was right, and before long, the two of them were back in the trade and commerce district. Frank led the way since he knew the location of the shop, but Zaq knew they were in the right place when he saw the moving assembly of gears on the sign adorning the building.

"Greetings and salutations!" cried the gnome behind the counter. He was apparently the only one working today. The shop was empty, and Zaq didn't even hear the muffled sounds of a small work crew like he had picked up at the mining company.

"And I return greetings and salutations to you," Zaq said in the traditional gnomish response. "I hope you can help us today. We need some brass gears and other small parts."

"That's one of the things we do best. I'm Pavolo Gearstamper," he introduced himself. "As you might guess from the name, gears have been in my family for quite some time."

"Wonderful. This is just the place, then," Zaq said, letting his eyes wander around the shop. He felt like a child in a candy shop when he realized he was surrounded by the most incredible selection of parts. Oh, the things he could make with all of these pieces.

"And how many gears and which sizes do you need?" Pavolo asked.

Zaq pulled out a scroll of parchment and unrolled it on the desk. He pointed at the drawings, complete with annotations of measurements and quantities.

"Can you fill this order?" he asked. "Do you have enough supply?"

The gnomish shopkeeper took the list and ran a finger down it as he read, nodding as he went.

"Yes. None of this should be a problem," Pavolo said. "I have it all in stock. This must be quite the project. Is the nature of it something you can share without breaking confidentiality agreements?"

"I can, yes," Zaq said, pulling out his tablet from the holster on his hip. "We are building a worldwide network of these devices. It's a communication device—look here."

Zaq brought up several messages, some simple text, and others much more elaborate with illusions.

"The tablet allows you to send messages privately to individuals or groups, but also lets you share your thoughts with the entire network."

"Er, Zaq," Frank pulled his attention. "Speaking of confidentiality. Shouldn't we file the EtherNet with AARI?"

"That is a good point," Zaq nodded. "After we purchase the parts here, you can take them back to the workshop. I'll head to the AARI office and file the paperwork. If nothing else, we can protect against others filing and taking the network private. I'd like to keep it open and available to as many people as possible."

Meanwhile, Pavolo had gathered all the parts on the list

into a large crate. Frank took it, while Zaq handed the gnome a pouch full of coins.

"We'll make sure to get you a tablet in our next batch. That way, we can hopefully order more parts from you as we need them. Do you make deliveries?"

"I would love to have one of these tablets," Pavolo said, his eyes shining with excitement. "But deliveries? Yes, we can do that. Send a courier with a letter like this list you showed me today, and I'll send a runner with your order."

Zaq looked at Frank, and they both laughed.

"It seems people still need time to get used to the Ether-Net," Zaq said. "I can send you a message just like the parchment, but it will show up on your tablet, once you have one. Complete with illustrations and annotations."

"Of course," Pavolo smacked his head. "Why send a person when you can transmit the message? Even as I was telling you I wanted one of these, I was still failing to grasp what I could do with it. To be honest, I just enjoy artificery artifacts no matter what they do."

"It's understandable," Zaq said, still chuckling lightly. "Thank you for the parts. We'll send someone over with a tablet for you later today or tomorrow."

Frank left for the workshop, carrying the box of gears and other small parts, while Zaq went the opposite direction to visit the AARI offices. He hoped they would be open, but there was a very real possibility they had closed for the festival.

Chapter 39

The Fate Quilter

Wyndi, her fellow apprentices, and Zaq had spent the entire day and well into the evening crafting tablets the day before. They had made so many, and it still seemed like it wasn't nearly enough. While they had worked, Zaq told them about filing the patent; he had included their names in the paperwork. They had forced themselves to take short breaks for food, but thankfully, with the festival in full swing, the many roving food carts were easily accessible. Even better, the food from the festival carts was tastier than the usual fare from mobile vendors.

The following morning, everyone arrived early at the workshop, except for Legs, who had evidently slept there again. It seemed he had come to terms with the idea that there were spiders in the workshop and was okay with it as long as he couldn't see them. Zaq brought two wagons he had procured from somewhere. They hauled boxes of the devices up to the alley, loading both carts full of tablets. Once they had the wagons full, Wyndi grabbed a handle with one hand and Flek's hand with her other.

"We'll see you later, good luck emptying your wagon!"

The couple had a plan they had discussed while lying on the bed the previous night. Wyndi had been looking at the server-wide messages and noticed excitement around the tablets was spreading. She thought that if they took their wagon to the busiest areas, there was bound to be at least a few people they had already provided with devices. These people, in theory, should help sell the idea to other folks in the crowd, since there would be more people to demonstrate how it worked and talk them up.

Wyndi eagerly pulled both Flek and the wagon through the crowded streets. They were surrounded by people, but what they needed was a large, open area. She pressed toward the heart of the city, where the royal castle stood, surrounded by the parliamentary buildings of the government.

Ryefeld was a constitutional monarchy, which, in practical terms, meant the royal family was almost always in good spirits, especially during festivals. King Wyland was especially fond of the harvest festival. He enjoyed being a man of the people and mingling with the populace. The prime minister and the rest of parliament were responsible for the hard work of actually running the government and the city. Meanwhile, the royal family was able to enjoy all the fun, carefree aspects of being a noble.

"See, I told you," Wyndi said gleefully as they approached the expansive courtyard. "King Wyland is out, and the crowd is thick. Even if there aren't tablet users in the group, we're sure to hand out quite a few."

"Maybe the king will take one," Flek suggested. "Imagine the donation he might give us."

"I wouldn't count on that, but the donations might still be substantial. A lot of well-to-do people gather when the king is making his rounds."

They had barely reached the edge of the crowd when a voice called out.

"Look over there! It's the gnome who was handing out the tablets. See, she even has that goblin with her."

Wyndi couldn't even see who had said it, but suddenly several people turned around to look at them. She felt somewhat self-conscious with all those eyes trained on her, but Flek was eating up the attention.

"This won't be hard at all," Flek grinned, grabbing a tablet and holding it above his head. "Perhaps you've heard of our EtherNet project? Who would like a tablet?"

Several people came forward at once, but thankfully settled into an orderly queue. One after another, people of all races made their way through the line and exchanged their pouches of coins for tablets.

Wyndi was so focused on the line of people that seemed like it wasn't going to end, she failed to notice the people who walked up behind her and Flek. The voice from right behind her made her jump and emit a small squeak.

"Happy harvest festival to both of you. What is it that has the crowd so excited?"

Wyndi and Flek both turned as one and looked up to see the face of King Wyland looking down at them. Wyndi fell into a bow and elbowed Flek until he joined her.

"That's enough of that. Stand please. This is a festival. Let's be merry and throw ceremonies aside. Tell us about these devices you are handing out."

"Yes, your majesty," Wyndi said, pulling herself up from her bow. She handed him a tablet and took out her own. Flek caught on quickly and pulled out his as well. "You see, it's a communication device. All the tablets are bound in a network, and you can send messages to anyone connected to the EtherNet."

"Watch!" Flek said, showing much less reverence. He clearly grew up in one of the rural areas that weren't governed by the city-states. "I can send simple text, drawings, or even elaborate messages like these."

At that, he held the tablet up and recorded the king and the surrounding crowd, then sent the message to Wyndi's tablet. The king watched as her device lit up and the illusion spun to life above the surface, showing him standing among a group of people.

"That is wonderous!" King Wyland announced. "We must have one. How much do you charge?"

"We're giving them away in exchange for donations. Whatever people think it is worth, or can afford to give."

"Preposterous. You are just giving them away? Who made these?" the king asked.

"We did. Well, and Legs, and it was Zaq's idea—but we helped come up with parts of it."

"We see," the king said. "Or rather, what you say resonates as truth, but we don't really understand. Elaborate on the others involved and why you are giving them away."

"As I said, it was Zaq's idea. That's Zaquocorin Flickerwhizzle. He took me, Legs—er Frank, and Flek here on as apprentices. We all helped come up with parts of the design and idea. As for why we're giving them away, it all comes down to the spiders."

"Right!" Flek said, jumping in. "The spiders were Wyndi's idea, but she might be too modest to tell you. We made a pact with the spiders in the ethereal realm. They are connecting their webs to all of the tablets, creating a vast network. The bigger the web gets, the stronger it becomes."

"We can already see the usefulness in a network spanning the world. Now, we most definitely need one. Simmons, give them the walking-around money we brought for the festival. You can send someone to retrieve more from the palace."

A tall, lizardkin man with draconic eye ridges and curled horns on his head stepped forward and handed Wyndi a sack. She knew it would be incredibly rude to peek in the sack, but even if the denominations on the coins were small, the heft of the bag suggested it was a large sum of money.

"Thank you," Wyndi said, reaching behind her blindly for a tablet, not taking her eyes off the king.

Flek saw her flailing arm, grabbed a tablet, and handed it to the king. He took it from the goblin with a nod, then Flek showed him the terms of service and how to register. The registration took a while because, not surprisingly, the king diligently read through the full terms and conditions.

"Very impressive set of terms you have here. We appreciate the environment you are attempting to create on this EtherNet."

"Zaq worked hard on those terms," Wyndi explained, making sure to give credit where it was due. "He said it was very important to the spiders that the mana be kept strong."

"Yes, he sounds like a wise gnome. We'd love to meet him. In fact, have him come by the palace tomorrow. We'll arrange something interesting. Simmons, get one of those tablets for yourself so we can communicate with each other."

Simmons nodded to the king and, since he was still near Wyndi, politely asked for a tablet.

"Of course," Wyndi said, grabbing a device and handing it to him.

"Thank you," he said. "That will be all."

That was evidently that. The king turned away, already tapping and experimenting with his new toy, and the lizardkin, Simmons, followed behind him.

Wyndi was sure there were other areas with good crowds where they could hand out tablets, but doubted they would be as interesting as meeting the king. Still, there were quite a few tablets in the wagon, so she and Flek made their way through the crowded streets looking for another opportunity.

They eventually came across a long line of people waiting their turn to speak with an old human woman sitting in a rocking chair with a quilt draped over her. Plenty of people milled around the area to give tablets to, but something about the woman intrigued Wyndi. If nothing else, she was curious about what everyone else found so interesting about her.

"Who's that?" Flek asked someone as he and Wyndi joined the line.

"You don't know of the Fate Quilter?" the young elven woman asked. "It's a good thing you got in line. She's very popular. Most people only get a basic reading when it's their turn. The lucky ones, though, get a square."

"Wait," Wyndi said, holding up a hand. "You're telling me the Fate Quilter is a real person? I thought she was just a legend."

"No, no," the elf giggled. She had glitter dust on her cheeks, making her pale green skin sparkle. "She is quite real, but most folks believe she is an avatar of Fate. When the Fate Quilter has a strong enough understanding of your fate, she captures it in a square that she adds to her quilt. The quilt has been growing for centuries, passed down from one quilter to the next when the time is right. Don't worry about cost either; she won't take any money. The Fate Quilter sees it as her fated role, but I've heard where ever she travels, the city leaders make sure she has all she needs."

"That sounds pretty interesting," Wyndi said. "Even a

simple reading could be fun. Would you like a tablet? Have you heard of the EtherNet project?"

Wyndi and Flek demonstrated the tablets to the elf and other people waiting in line around them. Soon, the line began to warp and lose its shape as people popped in and out of it to see the new devices. The quilter didn't seem to mind and continued to focus on each individual when they reached the front of the line.

Others in the area, who hadn't been interested in getting a reading, approached, asking about the tablets they saw everyone using. The pitch was becoming easier and easier as the network expanded and more people had tablets. Still, only about one in ten people actually took the tablets, offering what coin they felt comfortable donating. For many, they hadn't yet seen the benefits or didn't fully understand.

"It's incredible how strong the network is getting, even though we've barely handed out very many devices," Wyndi commented.

"Just think about when this spreads beyond the city," Flek said. "The ethereal webbing will connect everyone, everywhere. I can't wait until I have a chance to send some tablets back to Chubug. Being able to talk to my friends without traveling or waiting for letters will be great."

"In some ways, it's almost like we're shrinking the world," Wyndi said, a sense of awe in her voice.

"That's a slick way to look at it," Flek grinned.

They had been slowly making their way to the front of the line, and Wyndi waited patiently while the quilter spoke with the elf who had told her about what she was even in line for. The Fate Quilter gave her a simple reading, or at least Wyndi assumed as much, since she didn't add a new square to her quilt.

Wyndi could see that the quilt was large and emerged from

an old wooden chest, the lid of which was open. It looked like the quilt had folded over on itself several times inside the chest, and the end of it had been pulled out and draped over the quilter's lap.

The elf finished her discussion, smiled, and winked at Wyndi before leaving to join the surrounding festival crowd. Wyndi and Flek started to approach together, but the old woman held up a hand.

"One at a time, please. My visions are individual and easily confused, or they might even collapse if two or more approach."

Wyndi looked at Flek, but he simply made a shooing motion at her, and she stepped forward alone to speak with the quilter. They spoke in hushed tones that no one in the line could hear, not even Flek, who was not that far away.

"Oh my," the quilter said, "You are only the third one today. Welcome, my dear."

"The third what, ma'am?"

"The third with a strong enough fate to warrant a square, of course," the quilter laughed, causing the strands of gray hair that had escaped the bun on her head to dance.

"Really? I don't know how any of this works," Wyndi said. "It was only today I found out your quilt was real. What do I have to do?"

"Oh, you don't have to do anything," the woman assured her. "Just let me work and listen to the fate I see."

Time seemed to freeze as the world around them ground to a halt. Wyndi could move, but stood transfixed, watching the Fate Quilter work and listening to her premonition. She felt she understood what was being said, but at the same time, she felt it trying to escape her mind. Wyndi grabbed at the words and held on as she learned of her potential future.

Whatever spell had frozen time around them broke, and the sights and sounds of the world came rushing back in. The quilt now held a new square with an intricate design of shapes made from small pieces of fabric, forming a mosaic-style picture. Wyndi saw herself, Flek, and Legs in a workshop. The version of her in the quilt stood at a large slate board, while the other two watched.

Memories of the fate the quilter had described settled in her mind, but she knew some had been lost. What she did remember brought a smile to her face. The woman had spoken of her as head of the EtherNet project and the large team she would form with the help of her fellow apprentices, who would become fully fledged artificers. The Fate Quilter had foretold of a new age that would be sparked by the catalyst of the project, and how she would lead the effort, creating a lasting legacy for Zaq.

Chapter 40

Social Sorcery Foundation

In the workshop that evening, Zaq sat eating the rest of a simple meal he and Frank had picked up on the way back after distributing nearly all of their tablets. He still had a few left, but felt that was prudent in case anyone he knew closely turned up wanting one. Frank had pointed out a vendor selling hot sandwiches from her cart, not far from the Mystic Leaf & Toadstool. Figuring they would still be warm by the time they reached the workshop, Zaq bought one for each of them, and Frank bought two bottles of pumpkin ale from another nearby cart.

The warm sandwiches, made with rye bread, were layered with roasted cockatrice, mashed potatoes, cranberries, and stuffing. In the middle of the layering was a third slice of bread soaked in gravy.

"This extra moist maker in the middle of the sandwich takes it to another level," Frank said.

"I agree, the sandwich wouldn't be nearly as good without it," Zaq said, popping the last bite in his mouth before sipping on his bottle of ale.

He nearly choked when Wyndi and Flek came bounding down the stairs.

"We got rid of all our tablets, but that's not even close to the best news," Flek practically yelled, giddy with excitement.

"I got a quilt square from the Fate Quilter, which is amazing news, but still not the biggest," Wyndi said, catching her breath. "King Wyland would like to see you at the palace tomorrow."

"What? Why?" Zaq said, hopping up from his stool. "Is there a problem with the EtherNet? Does it break a law we weren't aware of?"

"The opposite!" Wyndi laughed. "He loves the idea. I told him it was your idea and that we helped you with it. I gave him a tablet. He thought it was amazing."

"I had no idea it would garner so much attention so early," Zaq mused, stroking his short beard. "This is big news. I'm glad it's set for tomorrow and not this evening. I'll need to pull out one of my old suits."

"You can," Flek said. "I'm not sure it matters. He had no problem with how Wyndi and I were dressed today."

"He may not have," Zaq agreed. "However, I would have a problem showing up in front of the king in a common outfit like this."

"He donated an enormous sum for his tablet," Wyndi continued. "He called it his walking-around money for the festival, but look at this."

She pulled out a sack of coins she had been guarding closely since their encounter with the noble. She grabbed fistfuls of coins from the bag. Most were copper and silver. The king likely knew vendors would appreciate not having to make change for larger denominations. However, there were also a large number of gold pieces and even a few platinum coins.

Zaq's eyes boggled at the wealth. Combined with what he

and Frank had gathered and the other donations Wyndi and Flek had, they would be able to ramp up production of the tablets to new heights.

"This is incredible," Zaq said. "I should be going home. I need a good night's sleep if I'm to meet with the king tomorrow. I don't know if I'll manage it, but I have to try. You three should come as well. I couldn't have done all of this without you. Whatever the king has to say, he should be saying it to all of us."

"We'll be there!" Flek announced for the group. "We can leave from your house when you're ready tomorrow. Just send us a message letting us know when."

Zaq didn't have many suits to choose from. Truth be told, despite having three, only one was, well, suitable. One of them was too snug, and another was so entirely outdated that he feared he might make a worse impression than if he had shown up in his standard workshop attire. That left a dark chocolate brown suit as the only viable option.

He chose a cream-colored tunic to wear with it and folded a pocket square out of a similar-colored handkerchief embroidered with gears made with gold thread. Eschewing his regular work boots, he opted for a pair of black loafers.

Looking in the mirror, he rubbed wax through his white beard and mustache, then styled it with a comb. After a moment of thought, he ran his waxy hands through the hair on his head and styled it as well, making a nice pompadour. When he was finished washing up, he went downstairs to leave the house. He had sent a message to the trio before getting dressed, expecting the timing would work out such that he would not have to wait long.

As it turned out, he had timed it well and had only been

standing outside for a few moments before he spied the kids walking up the street. They weren't dressed nearly as well as he was, but had still chosen some of their nicer-looking attire.

"Greetings and salutations!" Zaq called out as they approached.

"Good morning, Mr. Flickerwhizzle," Frank called. "You're looking quite dapper today. The king should be impressed."

"It's not too much, is it?" Zaq asked.

"Of course not," Wyndi assured him. "You look wonderful. I'm sure King Wyland will appreciate the attention to your appearance."

"Does everyone have their tablets?" he asked, looking them over and finding each of them wore a tablet holster on their belt, much like the one he had fashioned. Perhaps this would catch on and become the expected norm.

"Of course," Flek said, giving his a pat. "You never know who might be sending messages these days. Plus, if I'm ever bored, I now have what seems like a never-ending stream of interesting content to look at in the public messages."

"Let's be off then," Zaq said, leading the group down the busy street. The week-long festival was still in full swing, and even at this early hour, the streets were filling up.

An attendant at the castle entrance checked a scroll, then nodded.

"Yes, I see you are on the list of expected guests today. King Wyland has just finished with his last appointment. Follow me."

The catkin with orange and black striped fur led them down an expansive hallway decorated with statues and paintings. An ornate rug stretched the length of the hall, and Zaq felt sure they could have found the king just by following the carpet. Proper procedure, of course, meant following the norms and customs of the royal household, so he did, swiveling his head back and forth to take in the various works of art.

The throne was not nearly as impressive as Zaq expected, but somehow King Wyland commanded respect from his relaxed position on top of it. While the castle was old and had served to house generations of the royal family, the current king clearly preferred comfort over pageantry. The throne had comfy-looking cushions that the man relaxed into.

The catkin attendant cleared his throat.

"Your Royal Highness, King Wyland, I present to you Zaquocorin Flickerwhizzle and his apprentices."

"Well met," the king boomed, his voice echoing in the large room. "Thank you for visiting us today."

Zaq, Frank, Wyndi, and Flek, after an elbow from Wyndi, bowed, then rose.

"Thank you for calling on us," Zaq said. "Is there anything we can do for you? I understand from Wyndi that you have one of our tablets. Do you require instruction or assistance?"

The king chuckled, breaking the serious tone he had initially set with his formality.

"No, no. We find it incredibly intuitive to use. Good work! We called you here because as soon as Wyndi and Flek explained the nature of this device and the EtherNet you created, we knew this would change not just this city, but the world. The social sorcery at play here is impressive."

"I appreciate your vision, Your Highness," Zaq said. "I'd like to hope that's the case, but it's too early to tell."

"It's not too early if we set things up properly and provide the resources necessary."

"Excuse me, sir?" Zaq cleared his throat. "How do you mean?"

"We have gathered parliamentary approval to establish the Social Sorcery Foundation for the continued development of the EtherNet project. Funding has been established to support the work in perpetuity."

"That is most generous, Your Highness," Zaq replied.

"It's not generosity that motivates us. It is clear to us that this will change the course of fate. Besides, we did not do much. Parliament had to do the heavy lifting. That's the great perk about being king. We get the fun job of telling wonderful citizens like you the good news."

"There is just one thing," Zaq hedged, looking from the king to his apprentices and back again. "I'm grateful I've been able to finish what had been the project of my dreams, but I'm just an old retired gnome. I'm not the best choice to operate such an enterprise. However, I have a recommendation."

"Let's hear it then," King Wyland said, still smiling warmly.

"My apprentices have shown great aptitude, and their ideas helped shape the EtherNet. Of particular note is Wyndi, or rather, Ailawyndi Crinklepot. As their mentor, I hereby declare them full artificers. I believe Wyndi has what it takes to lead this new Social Sorcery Foundation. As a side note, I like the name. It's quite catchy."

Wyndi let out a small squeak when he said her name.

"But Zaq, you aren't too old. You have many years ahead of you, and we all have so much more to learn."

"I may have many years ahead of me, but I want to enjoy them. I'd like to relax, do some gardening, and cook delicious food. I'm content now, knowing that what I've built will have a good home. As for your learning, I'll let you in on a secret. Call it a final lesson."

"What would that be?" Wyndi asked.

"Yeah, I want to know the secret, too," Flek chimed in.

"A true artificer, one skilled in the craft and with the right mindset, knows they are never done learning. You can learn from each other, from books, and from me on occasion. Don't think that just because I'm handing over the reins of this operation that I won't want to come by and tinker from time to time."

Wyndi and the other two apprenticeship graduates chuckled.

"Of course, you're welcome and encouraged to come by the workshop any time you want," she said. "I'm sure there will always be some endeavor that could benefit from your experience."

"Well, then," King Wyland said, pulling all of their attention back to him. "We can tell the faith you have in Wyndi and the others is strong. We trust in your judgement. We will have parliament officially appoint Ailawyndi Crinklepot as the head of the foundation."

The king gave a slight, almost imperceptible nod to the catkin, who stepped forward.

"Thank you all for coming, and congratulations. Please, follow me out."

With the audience clearly over, Zaq and the others bowed, then turned to follow the attendant out of the castle. Once they were far enough away from the palace, Zaq addressed the group.

"That was certainly unexpected. This foundation is an excellent idea, and I just know you are going to lead it well. Thank you for accepting it, Wyndi. I know I put you on the spot there."

"It wasn't a complete surprise," she admitted, giving Flek a wink. "I just hadn't expected it so soon. I never told you about what the Fate Quilter's square showed me."

"Well, you'll have to tell me now," Zaq said. "Why don't we all experience the harvest festival together today? You can tell me your story, and we can see what other fun activities, food, and drink we can find."

They spent the rest of the day doing just that. Wyndi filled him in on what the quilter had shared with her. Flek refused to say anything about the reading the old woman had provided him. It had been a simple reading, but he claimed that if he told, it might not come true. No one pressed him, and instead, they enjoyed all the entertainment the festival had to offer.

By the end of the day, Zaq bid the trio farewell and walked home. When he approached his house, he whistled, and the black cat came running from the shadows, circling his legs and rubbing against him. He opened the door to his home, allowing the cat to follow him in, and then went to his study, where he poured a glass of his best rye whisky.

Zaq sat in his favorite chair, letting the cushions envelop him. With a pat on his lap, the cat leapt up, letting out a soft meow. She circled twice, dancing on his lap before settling down into a lump across his legs. He sipped his whisky with one hand, stroking his other through the cat's fur. A low rumbling purr vibrated through his fingers.

"I suppose you need a name to make this arrangement more official. I think I'll call you Vicki."

About the Author

Alex Peachy lives in the Pacific Northwest, and to stave off the cold and lack of sun, he writes cozy fantasy novels full of warmth, whimsy, and magic. The stories Alex creates explore identity, community, and personal growth themes. He shares his home with his wife, son, and their three adorable cats. His favorite cat considers Alex her human and often demands to be held. You can find him writing and sipping on a glass of good whisky in the evenings. Alex encourages you to take the time to slow down and relax. Grab a cozy book from Alex or another of your favorite authors and escape into a world of magic and adventure.

You can find Alex on the internet in a number of places:
AlexPeachy.com (Sign up for the newsletter)
tiktok.com/@inlightsyrup
instagram.com/in_light_syrup
bsky.app/profile/inlightsyrup.com
facebook.com/AuthorAlexPeachey

Join the discussion about Distilled Magic:
www.reddit.com/r/DistilledMagic
discord.gg/C8pbQPrFsa

If you enjoyed this book, please consider writing a review. Reviews are extremely important to indie authors like Alex.

Aberterrene Series
Distilled Magic
Social Sorcery